TIES

&

LIES

black
TIES
&
white
LIES

KAT SINGLETON

Entangled Publishing, LLC
644 Shrewsbury Commons Ave., STE 181
Shrewsbury, PA 17361
rights@entangledpublishing.com

Amara is an imprint of Entangled Publishing, LLC.

Visit our website at www.entangledpublishing.com.

Edited by Victoria Ellis of Cruel Ink Editing & Design
Cover design by LJ Anderson
Cover images by Larysa Marchenko/GettyImages,
liya_s1104/Depositphotos
Edge design by LJ Anderson
Interior design by Britt Marczak
Interior image by Shanina/GettyImages

ISBN 978-1-64937-927-6

Manufactured in the United States of America

First Edition July 2025

10 9 8 7 6 5 4 3 2 1

ALSO BY KAT SINGLETON

BLACK TIE BILLIONAIRES

Black Ties and White Lies
Pretty Rings and Broken Things
Bright Lights and Summer Nights

PEMBROKE HILLS

In Good Company

SUTTEN MOUNTAIN

Rewrite Our Story
Tempt Our Fate
Chase Our Forever

For all my besties who are just looking for the simple things in life—a hot billionaire to spoil you with gifts and orgasms. Beck is for you.

Black Ties & White Lies is a sexy and swoon-y contemporary, stand-alone romance. However, there may be some elements that might not be suitable to all readers including a headstrong, I-saw-her-first billionaire hero, a very grey line between boss and employee relationship, secret inappropriate thoughts about your brother's girlfriend, and sex on the page... *lots* of pages. Readers who may be sensitive to these topics, please take note.

Playlist

Mastermind - Taylor Swift

Satellite - Harry Styles

You Are In Love - Taylor Swift

About You - The 1975

Souvenir - Selena Gomez

Wildest Dreams (Taylor's Version) - Taylor Swift

Falling Like the Stars - James Arthur

What Have I Done - Dermot Kennedy

Happiest Year - Jaymes Young

What a Man Gotta Do - Jonas Brothers

Stay - Gracie Abrams

wRoNg (feat. Kehlani) - ZAYN

Want You Back - 5 Seconds of Summer

Dirty Thoughts - Chloe Adams

All for You - Dean Lewis

1

Margo

"Margo, Margo, Margo."

A familiar voice startles me from my computer screen. Spinning in my office chair I find my best friend, Emma, hunched over the wall of my cubicle. Her painted red lips form a teasing grin.

Pulling the pen I was chewing on out of my mouth, I narrow my eyes at her suspiciously. "What?"

She licks her teeth, flicking the head of the Nash Pierce bobblehead she bought me ages ago. "Who did you piss off this time?"

My stomach drops, and I don't even know what she's talking about. "Are you still drunk?" I accuse, thinking about the wine we consumed last night. We downed two bottles of cheap pinot grigio with our roommate and best friend, Winnie. Split between the three of us, there's no way she's still tipsy, but it's the best I could come up with.

She scoffs, her face scrunching in annoyance. "Obviously not. I was refilling my coffee in the lounge when *Darla* asked if I'd seen you."

I stifle an eye roll. Darla knew I'd be at one of two places. I'm always either at my desk or huddled in front of the coffee maker trying to get the nectar of the gods to keep me awake.

Darla knew *exactly* where to find me.

She just didn't want to.

You accidentally put water in the coffee bean receptacle instead of the carafe and suddenly the office receptionist hates you. It's not like I meant to break it. It's not my fault it wasn't made clear on the machine what went where. I was just *trying* to help.

"I haven't heard from her," I comment, my eyes flicking to Darla's desk. She's not there, but her phone lights up with an incoming call. Darla rarely leaves her desk. It isn't a good sign that she's nowhere in sight. The sky could be falling, and I'm not sure Darla would leave her perch.

Emma rounds the wall of my cubicle, planting her ass on my desk like she's done a million times before, even though I've asked her not to just as many times.

"I'm working." Reaching out, I smack her black stiletto, forcing her foot off the armrest of my chair.

She laughs, playfully digging her heel into my thigh. "Well, Darla, that *amazing woman*, told me the boss wants to see you."

"I thought Marty was out for meetings all day today?"

Emma bites her lip, shaking her head at me. "No, like the *boss*, boss. The head honcho. Bossman. I think it's somebody new."

She opens her mouth to say something else, but I cut her off. "That can't be right."

"Margo!" Darla barks from the doors of our conference room. I almost jump out of my chair from the shrill tone of her voice.

Emma's eyes are wide as saucers as she looks from Darla back to me. "Seriously, Mar, what did you do?"

I slide my feet into my discarded heels underneath my desk. Standing up, I wipe my hands down the front of my skirt. I hate that my palms are already clammy from nerves. "I didn't do anything," I hiss, apparently forgetting how to walk in heels as I almost face-plant before I'm even out of the security of my cubicle.

She annoyingly clicks her tongue, giving me a look that tells me she doesn't believe me. "Obviously, I knew we had people higher up than Marty, they're just never *here*. I wonder what could be so *serious*..."

"You aren't helping."

There's no time for me to go back and forth with my best friend since college any longer. Darla has her arms crossed over her chest in a way that tells me if I don't haul ass across this office and meet her at the door in the next thirty seconds, she's going to make me regret it.

I come to a stop in front of the five-foot woman who scares me way more than I'd care to admit. She frowns, her jowls pronounced as she glares at me.

Despite the dirty look, I smile sweetly at her, knowing my mama told me to always kill them with kindness. "Good morning, Darla," I say, my voice sickeningly sweet.

Her frown lines get deeper. "I don't even want to know what you did to warrant his visit today," she clips.

Your guess is as good as mine, Darla.

"Who?" I try to look into the conference room behind her, but the door is shut.

Weird. That door is never closed.

"Why don't you find out for yourself?" Grabbing the handle,

she opens the door. Her body partially blocks the doorway, making me squeeze past her to be able to get in.

Whoever this *he* is, doesn't grant me the luxury of showing me his face. He stands in front of the floor-to-ceiling windows, his hands in the pockets of the perfectly tailored suit that molds to his body effortlessly. I haven't even seen the guy's face but everything about him screams wealth. Even having only seen him from behind, I can tell that he exudes confidence. It's in his stance—the way he carries his shoulders, his feet slightly apart as he stares out the window. Everything about his posture screams *business*. I'm just terrified why *his* business is *my* business.

When they said boss, they really meant it. *Oh boy.*

What have I done?

Even the sound of the door shutting behind me doesn't elicit movement from him. It gives me time to look him up and down from the back. If I wasn't already terrified that I was in trouble for something I don't even remember doing, I'd take a moment to appreciate the view.

I mean *damn*. I didn't know that suit pants could fit an ass so perfectly.

I risk another step into the conference room. Looking around, I confirm it's just me and the mystery man with a nice ass in the empty space.

Shaking my head, I attempt to stop thinking of the way he fills the navy suit out flawlessly. From what I've been told, he's my boss. The thoughts running through my head are *anything* but work appropriate.

"Uh, hello?" I ask cautiously. My feet awkwardly stop on the other side of the large table from him. I don't know what to do. If I'm about to be fired, do I sit down first or just keep standing and get it over with?

I wonder if they'll give me a box to put my stuff in.

His back stiffens. Slowly, he turns around.

When I finally catch a glimpse of his face, I almost keel over in shock.

Because the man standing in front of me—my apparent boss—is also my ex-boyfriend's *very* attractive older brother.

2

Margo

"It's been a while, Margo," Beck drawls, his scowl making me squirm. I forgot how sexy his voice was, especially with my name on his lips.

"Beck..." I say in disbelief. My ex-boyfriend, Carter, had told me that his brother was successful. But then, the whole Sinclair family was wealthy. I'd been so swept up in Carter I hadn't really paid too much attention to it. Quite frankly, I tried to forget Beckham ever existed. But now, with Carter out of the picture, and Beckham "Beck" Sinclair standing in front of me, it's hard not to be hit in the face with just how successful he is.

The shiny cufflink he fiddles with probably costs more than my rent. The suit, probably more expensive than the fuel-efficient car I share with Emma. When I met Beck, he hadn't looked like this. It'd been during a weekend trip to one of their many vacation homes in the Hamptons. He was dressed incredibly casual compared to the way he stands in front of me right now.

Beck smiles but the gesture doesn't make me feel any more comfortable. In fact, it has quite the opposite effect. I almost wish Darla had followed me in; maybe it'd alleviate some of the tension radiating between us. My insides are jumbled, and I feel completely disarmed by the way he's looking at me.

He stares at me with unwavering attention. Reaching out, he points to the incredibly oversized table in front of us. "Have a seat, Margo." His tone leaves no room for discussion. Like a child, I follow his command immediately. I pull out the large leather office chair from in front of me, wincing as one of the wheels squeaks loudly as I attempt to pull it out.

Unlike me, he takes his seat with grace. I, on the other hand, had to struggle with the stuck wheel and embarrassed myself with loud grunts as I tried to get the chair far enough away from the table to take a seat.

His blond eyebrows stay raised as he stares at me with what looks like amusement. Eventually, I manage to plop my ass in the chair. My cheeks are on fire, making any attempt to mask the embarrassment futile. There's no way he doesn't see the red hue of my face as I comb through any potential reason for his arrival.

I scoot the chair up to the table, finding the nerve to look him in the eye as I fold my hands in my lap. "*You're* the boss? What are you doing here?"

Beck drinks me in, his eyes raking over me slowly.

I'm right here, Violet.

The words catapult into my mind, flinging me back to last summer. It was a little over a year ago, only weeks before I found out that Carter had been cheating on me during the entirety of our relationship. It was something Beck had said to me late one night when he caught me doing something I shouldn't have. At the time, I hadn't said anything about him having my name wrong. At the time, I hated that I didn't quite hate the way it sounded coming from his lips. The way it rolled off his tongue did funny things to me.

I stare back at him, the moment we had during the summer combined with how stunningly handsome he is now only makes this encounter more awkward.

"Beck?" I ask, unsure. My voice shakes, betraying me. One deep stare from him and I'm at a loss for words.

His fingers steeple underneath his chin, his shiny watch catching a beam of light. "You've been ignoring my calls."

I pick at my cuticles underneath the table, a nervous habit my mom has chastised me about for years. No matter how hard I try not to, it's no use fighting the urge. I'm disarmed under his deep, indigo gaze.

"I didn't have anything to say to you—or Carter," I snap. It's crazy that Beck and Carter are brothers. They're complete opposites. Carter is tall, but the tone to his muscles wasn't super defined like Beck's. He preferred running over lifting weights. Most of all, he preferred to golf eighteen holes with his elitist friends. *Or* fuck anyone that wasn't his actual girlfriend. He was probably getting a decent workout judging by the amount of people he was screwing a week that *were not me.*

Did Beck know Carter wasn't faithful?

It doesn't matter. Carter and I are done. I thought by never seeing Carter again I'd never see his brother, either. I certainly never expected to have to call him *boss.*

Carter is tall, but Beck is taller. Where Carter has muscles from his rigid diet and obsession with cardio, Beck has more defined muscles everywhere. Underneath the sleeves of his tailored suit there are biceps that I'd dreamt to sketch one day. During that weekend with his family, I caught a glimpse of what he hides underneath his button-up shirt. His abs are the wet dream of any artist. Painter, sketch artist, sculptor—*anyone* would love to be front and center with his six-pack. *Or is it an eight?*

He clears his throat. When I pull my gaze from the delicious veins of his hands, I find him smirking at me. "Are you done?" He's blunt, even if there is a tinge of amusement laced in his voice. I've been alone in this conference room with him only for a few moments, and the tension between us could already be cut with a knife.

"Done with what?"

"Eye fucking me."

I almost fall out of my chair at the boldness of his words.

"I wasn't—"

A corner of his full lip twitches. "You totally were, Violet. Don't pretend like you weren't."

My jaw snaps open and shut. Why is he using that name again? Why do I still love it? I have no freaking clue how to respond to him.

Again, he's my new *boss*. Or at least I think he is. That's what Emma called him. Darla seemed to be under the same impression. I need to know how long he's been in charge.

And why is he here?

Most importantly, why is he staring at me like he wants to have his way with me?

"My name's not Violet."

He runs his thumb over his plump bottom lip. "I know."

Shaking my head, I wonder if maybe I had more wine last night than I remember. Am I dreaming? This entire scenario can't be real.

"I'm sorry," I begin, taking a deep breath. "I'm just wondering why you're here? I'm a little confused about what's happening..."

Sighing, he pushes the chair far enough from the table that he can cross one leg over the other. His ankle rests on the opposite knee, his perfectly shined shoes catching the light from the windows.

"You were ignoring my calls," he explains, seemingly annoyed that he's having to repeat himself.

"Yes. We just talked about this. I didn't want to talk about your brother."

"No, we didn't talk about this. We *started* the conversation, but then you decided instead of listening, you were going to undress me with those large eyes of yours." A loud vibrating sound halts his words. His straight eyebrows pull in as he reaches into a pocket inside his suit jacket. His eyes quickly scan the name on the screen before he silences the call. Tossing his phone onto the black wood table, he focuses on me once again. "If you'd been listening the first time, and not eye fucking me, you'd know I was telling you that me calling you had absolutely nothing to do with brother dearest."

I bite my tongue, wanting to ask why he's referencing Carter with such disgust. There's clearly more to his feelings toward his brother than I'm aware of. Carter never seemed like the biggest fan of Beck, but he didn't speak like he totally hated him. I can't say the same from the tone of Beck's voice just now.

"It didn't?"

"Fuck no," he spits. For a moment, there's an angry fire in his eyes. I've always been told I'm too curious for my own good, and I feel it in this moment. Everything in me is yearning to ask why he looks so angry when speaking of Carter, but I keep my lips sealed. I'm far more interested in why he's here. "You're better off without him. I'd never try and convince you otherwise."

"I didn't know that. I figured you were calling for him. I blocked his number after he called forty-six times in one night."

"Pathetic," he growls under his breath.

He straightens, both feet on the ground once again. Beck leans over the table, getting as close as possible to me. "Well, you ignoring me caused me to have to resort to other options."

"Like what?"

He shows off his large wingspan as he widens his arms, gesturing to the dingy room around us. He looks out of place here, the fading paint on the walls and the fraying, stained carpet not fit for someone as regal looking as him. "Like buying this company."

He did what? Surely I'm not understanding this correctly.

"What does buying this company have to do with me ignoring your calls?"

"Stop asking questions before you've even thought about it," he fires back. "Isn't it obvious? I bought the company so you had no choice but to talk to me. I am your boss now, after all."

Excuse my French, but *what the actual fuck?* People don't buy companies just to talk to someone. They call, or show up at their house, or I don't know...send a fucking email. Not buy companies.

"No you didn't."

Beck shakes his head at me. The movement shakes one of his perfectly gelled locks of hair out of place. One strand rebels and hangs in front of his eyes until he finally pushes it out of the way. "I can assure you, Margo, I most certainly did."

3

Beck

She looks entirely out of place in this dark, crummy office space. Margo Moretti shines too bright to be working at 8-bit Security. Her usual black hair looks dull underneath the terrible lighting of the room. Even her eyes, the light green a color I'd never seen before until I first met her, don't hold the same vibrancy that I know them to have.

"Stop messing with me, Beck. That's ridiculous."

I shrug, wondering how a woman as beautiful as her ever fell for my brother. "You're probably right. It is ridiculous. It doesn't change the fact it's what I did. I needed to talk to you."

"What could we possibly have to talk about if it's not about Carter?"

I wish she'd stop saying his name. He doesn't deserve it. He never deserved it, but I'm not sure anyone really would deserve to have their name fall from her lips. I only had the pleasure of getting to know Margo over the span of a weekend—and it was more observing her than speaking with her—but it was enough time to realize she lives her life like it's her world—and we're all just living in it. She was polite just enough to my parents but didn't fold underneath my father's pestering questions about what her family did for a living. Margo smiled and joked enough for me to know that every reaction from her was genuine, but still had to be earned. She spent time with Carter, proving that she's a loyal girlfriend who enjoyed his presence, but was never clingy. The moral of the story was, I don't know how someone like Margo ended up dating someone like my brother. By the end of what I have planned, I'm hoping to have the answer.

I clasp and unclasp the Rolex on my wrist. Not daring to look away from her. I don't think I could if I wanted to. There's a long pause between us. She squirms in her chair, clearly anxious as she waits for whatever I have to say. Finally, I ease her tension, or maybe I add to it, by speaking up. "You're getting promoted."

Her plump, puffy lips separate. There isn't a hint of makeup on her mouth, yet her lips are the perfect shade of red without going overboard. I fucking despise that my brother knows exactly how her lips taste. "Promoted? Why?" she asks, bewildered.

My fingers tap on the table, my eyes flicking to my vibrating phone next to my hand. She looks down as well. "You can get that if you need to."

It's rang a handful of times since she joined me in the room. I've ignored every single call, something that is out of character for me. I'm usually on the phone more than not, but right now, I want to give her my full attention, even if she's taking precious moments of my time by asking dumb questions.

I flip my phone over, putting the screen face down for the time being. "It can wait," I lie. I'm supposed to be joining a meeting via a phone call in five minutes, but I already know it's one I'll be missing. I refuse to talk to anyone else before I have the chance to finish this conversation.

Margo runs her fingers through her hair but eventually grows bored with the action and tosses the long locks over her shoulder. "Look," she begins, her voice tight. "I don't know if this is some sick, twisted joke of yours to get payback on me for breaking up with your brother, but I want no part of it."

My thumb glosses over my bottom lip again as I inspect every one of her movements. I'm puzzled by what Carter has told her that has her thinking I'd ever go to these lengths to get back at one of his ex-girlfriends. Especially knowing that he was unfaithful to said girlfriend over the entirety of their three-year relationship. My brother and I aren't close. I've never meddled with his love life, and I never had the desire to—well, until he met her. We don't have the kind of relationship where either one of us give a damn about what the other is doing.

The sound of my exhale of annoyance echoes around the otherwise silent room. Leaning forward, I look Margo dead in the eye. Whatever she sees on my face finally makes her stop fidgeting. "I don't know how many times I need to say this to get it through your head, but listen closely, Margo, because I despise repeating myself."

"I'm listening," she whispers. I bask in having her full attention.

"My brother has absolutely nothing to do with the reason I'm here. No part of me thinks you should get back with him. Quite frankly, I'd find it rather pitiful for you to go back to him, considering he wet his cock with half of the NYU population while you were together. So, let's make it clear from here on out. My motives for being here, for buying this company, have nothing to do with the punk I have to call blood. You got it?"

Her fingers have turned white from gripping the armrests of her seat so tightly. When she pulls her hands from the chair,

I wonder if there'll be half-moon indents from her nails on the stained leather. Margo is silent, apparently stunned by my words because she doesn't strike me as someone who's often rendered speechless.

"Words, Margo. I need words to know you understand."

"I'm trying to understand," she finally gets out, her eyes still pinned on me. She watches me closely, her eyes slightly narrowing. I can almost see the gears in her brain working overtime as she tries to decipher my intentions for being here. I fight the urge to tell her it's no use. I still don't understand what compelled me to take the lengths I did to get to this moment. But for this to work, for me to get what I want, I need her to have some semblance of understanding.

"Let me explain further," I begin. My shoulders find the back of the chair once again as I lean backward. "I'm now the proud owner of this shithole. I had to fight numerous investors for them to back me with this purchase, but in the end, they couldn't tell me no. I have the money to fund it with or without them. This company was low on the list of startups I'd care to invest in, but I needed to speak with you, so here we are."

Margo laughs manically, disbelief in her doe-eyed stare. "Normal people don't buy companies to talk with their brother's ex-girlfriends."

I scoff, shaking my head. "It's insulting that you think I'm normal. I'm far from normal, Margo. I'll go to great lengths to get what I want."

"And what you want is to have a conversation with me?"

My lips press into a thin line. "Not exactly." *What I want is* you. *At least for the time being.*

Margo falls into her chair with a loud sigh. "You're probably the vaguest person I know."

My lip twitches. "I'm not vague on purpose. You keep interrupting me with questions, not letting me get to the point."

"Say no more. I'll keep my mouth shut until you make this make sense." Being dramatic, she holds her thumb and index finger in front of her lips, miming zipping her lips and throwing the key over her shoulder.

She looks childish, her cheeks puffed out with her lips sealed shut. There's a mischievous gleam in her eyes, making me question if this is a good idea or not.

"Like I said earlier, you're getting promoted."

She opens her mouth like she's going to argue, making me raise my eyebrows. Her eyes roll as her mouth snaps shut. I can tell it's taking everything in her not to interject with what is no doubt another one of her questions. I silently hold eye contact a few seconds longer, waiting to see if she'll manage to keep her mouth closed or not.

Apparently she can. *Good girl.*

"Your days of doing graphic design for this place are over. Starting Monday, you'll be my new assistant."

Fire erupts in her eyes. "No way. I didn't graduate with an art degree to become your little errand girl."

"Stop being dramatic. You didn't graduate top of your class at one of the best art programs in the country to do graphic design *here*." Reaching to the middle of the table, I grab one of the pens that sit in a plastic cup. I hold it up, turning it in my hands. "Your art is better than this, Margo. This logo is terrible, and I know it isn't because of you." I keep inspecting the pen as I let the words marinate between us. I squint. "Has no one told Marty this face looks like a cock with balls?"

She chokes on her laugh, her eyes wide as she tries to bring air into her lungs. Eventually, she gains composure. Her fingers come up to wipe at the smudged mascara underneath her eyes, the tears from her laughter making black splotches underneath her eyes. "I think Marty almost fired me when I told him I thought the addition of the smiley face with a nose looked a little...*phallic*."

I smirk. "A little? The eyes look like two rounded balls with a small cock in the middle." Each time I say *cock*, I swear her cheeks get slightly more red.

Margo attempts to move a stray lock of hair from her face, but the piece is too short to stay behind her ear. She huffs, blowing her bangs away from her face in defeat. "The logo is terrible, I get it. I didn't have a choice. Marty threatened me if I didn't create it the way he envisioned it. So I did it, because I've got to pay my bills." She looks me up and down, her eyes halting at the watch on my wrist. "Not all of us were born with money."

I bite my tongue. Now isn't the time for us to get into an argument about money—*my* money. "Do you want to spend the rest of your life doing graphic design for an almost unlivable wage?"

"At least it's some form of art," she fires back. "Being your assistant wouldn't allow me to have any kind of creativity."

"False. I'll make sure you have time for your art."

"And what is my *art,* Beck? I doubt you know."

"You like to draw, Violet. You done with your questions now?"

4

Margo

So many words fly through my head, none of them managing to leave my mouth. It doesn't happen often, but he's rendered me speechless.

Beck's smile is almost predatory. He knows his answer has taken me by surprise. I'm backed into a corner, unsure how to get myself out of it. I hadn't expected him to remember my favorite creative outlet. Especially since Carter always told people I painted, even though he'd never seen me with a paintbrush the entire duration of our relationship. I just assumed that's what Beck would've thought I did, too.

"Tell me what it means to be your assistant." I try to fold my arms across my midsection in a defensive position, but all it does is make the wire of my bra dig into my rib cage even further. My hands slide into my lap instead, my eyes still watching Beck carefully.

"Does it matter? You start Monday."

"I haven't even agreed to it yet."

"It'd be silly for you not to say yes. It's a significant pay bump, and you'll be out of this place." His finger loops in the air, bringing attention to the lackluster conference room we're in.

"I'm terrible at making coffee," I argue. "Ask Darla."

"There's more to it than that..." For a fraction of a second, Beck looks nervous. The look is erased almost as quickly as it first showed up. But as fast as it was, I still saw it.

"What is it?"

His cheeks hollow out, making his sharp cheekbones even more prominent. "I need you to not only become my assistant but also my fiancée."

The chair underneath me groans loudly as I lean forward, looking at him in shock. "What did you just say?"

"I'm in a bit of a"—he picks at a non-existent piece of lint on his sleeve—"*predicament*," he finally finishes. "One I need your help with."

"You need *me*?"

"I've made a mistake." He keeps his voice level, but there's the smallest bit of vulnerability in his eyes when he looks at me. "Recently, a gossip site ran an article on me that features numerous photos with me and multiple different women in the last month. Like, a good number of them..."

My eyebrows raise. Carter had mentioned Beck never did relationships. He meant it as a dig at his brother. Looking back, it seems Beck doesn't make any fake promises. At least he's upfront about not wanting to commit to women, *very* unlike his brother. Carter will make the promise and just fuck it to shreds behind your back.

"And that involves me how?"

"My board is upset. They say it reflects poorly on the company."

"Why? You're allowed to have a personal life."

He blinks, a slight grin on his lips. "It doesn't quite work like that, Violet."

I cross one leg over the other. "I'm still trying to figure out how I play into this."

His fingers tap against the table, catching my attention. They're long, slightly thicker around the knuckles. *I wonder how they'd feel inside me.* Blinking quickly, I shake my head. *Where the fuck did that come from?*

He's completely unaware that my mind is only half listening, the other half wondering how many he could fit inside me and still feel pleasurable. Beck continues to talk as I try to rid my brain of the dirty thoughts of my new boss, AKA him. "I was told I need to maintain a stable relationship for at least a year, or they feared investors would become uneasy. No one wants to invest in a company whose face is plastered all over magazines being penned a playboy billionaire."

I bite back a smile. "It's kind of catchy."

He does nothing to hide his grunt of disapproval. "I've never tried to hide the fact that I can't stand most people. The thought of tolerating someone for a year makes my skin crawl. That is, a year with anyone except...*you.*"

My ass almost flies out of the chair. *Surely* I heard him wrong. I want to make some kind of witty remark, but the unreadable look on his face has me snapping my mouth shut. I hold back the comment, stunned by how he brazenly stares back at me.

"People wouldn't believe it if we told them we all of a sudden started dating. But...they'd believe it if we went from working closely together with you as my assistant and it developed into more."

"Now it's starting to make sense..."

"I bought this company because I needed a reason for us to be brought back together—hence the reason I now own 8-bit Security. You work closely with me as my assistant and in a month or so we'll tell people we've fallen in love."

"That seems quick."

When he smiles at me, I understand why so many women fall at his feet. It's magnetic, bright but predatory. Enough to make my core clench because never did I expect it aimed at *me*. "When you know, you know."

And then Beck Fucking Sinclair winks at me, and I swear to god in the moment, I'd do anything he asked me to. His hotness is a shock to my system, something I'm nowhere near equipped to deal with.

"The whole idea seems highly unnecessary. Don't you own the company your board sits on or whatever? Tell them to go fuck themselves."

He actually laughs at my comment. A loud, throaty laugh that for some reason feeds my soul. I'd do anything to hear it again.

I made broody Beck Sinclair laugh. I want to do it over and over until his stomach hurts from laughter.

Beck shakes his head at me, his eyes lingering on my returned smile. His attention to my lips has me absent-mindedly licking them. "While I've thought about doing that a million times, it's not something I can quite commit to. You see, I don't hold all the power when it comes to my company. No matter how much I want to. I've got to clean it up or I'll lose important investors. It's not a risk I'm willing to take."

"What if I'm not willing to agree?"

His teeth dig into his lip as he bites back a smile. He attempts to wipe the smile from his face by running his hand over his mouth, but it doesn't do much. When his hand falls back to his armrest, he still grins at me. "I can be very persuasive, Margo Moretti."

Is Beckham Sinclair flirting with me?

Am I into it?

No. I *can't* be into it. I dated—*loved*—his brother for years.

Bad, Margo.

But god, with that grin on his face, it might feel *so* good to be *so* bad.

I'm silent, still wondering in the back of my mind if this is some sort of joke. Am I on some sort of reality TV show where they play an epic prank? That's totally something Emma would sign me up for as a cruel joke.

My eyes scan the office for any hints of hidden cameras.

"So, I become your assistant, then your fiancée, and then have to go back to normal with my tail between my legs when you end our engagement after the year is over? Have everyone think you grew tired of me? No thank you, Beck. It's a no from me."

"We could tell people you ended it. Whatever you want to say to them, I'll do it." The hurried way he gets out his words has me stopping to wonder why he seems so invested in getting me to agree to his ludicrous plan.

I'm quiet long enough, my foot tapping against the carpet as I think through his words, when he feels the need to fill the silence with more of an explanation. "I'll get you an interview with Camden Hunter."

My foot stops immediately. "How?"

"We went to boarding school together. He's one of my best friends."

I snort. "I'm shocked you have friends. You don't seem like the kind of person to form attachments."

His eyebrows pinch together on his perfectly wrinkle-free forehead. "I form attachments just fine. I'm just picky about who I choose to form them with. Am I to assume your answer is that you don't want an interview with him?"

"You assume correctly. I don't want to be hired by Camden—owner of one of the most elite art galleries in New York—just because you know him. I don't want my dream job handed to me."

There he goes, making my heart flutter just from the sound of his laugh. It's deep and rumbly, a sound that is felt from my head to my toes. "It's cute you think I have that kind of power with Camden. He's charming but ruthless. It wouldn't matter if I begged him on my knees to hire you. While he'd find it hilarious, he'd never feature someone's art he didn't love. I'll get you the interview to show him your work, your ideas, but it'd be up to you and your talent to solidify the partnership."

Why is the thought of Beck on his knees making me feel hot and bothered? Do we have AC in here? It's *got* to be the lack of airflow and not the mental picture.

My eyes narrow to pinpricks as I mull over his offer. The picture he paints doesn't seem so bad. I'd pretty much sell my soul or *any* non-vital organ to even be in the same room as Camden Hunter. The son of two of the most world-renowned artists, it was only natural that the moment he opened his own gallery, it'd be the talk of the city. While Camden isn't known to be an artist himself, he's got the best eye there is. If he even *looked* at any of my drawings, I could die happy.

"I can't believe you know Camden Hunter," I comment, my voice full of wonder.

He runs his thumb over his lip, a gesture I'm learning he does often. "I can't believe you hero worship him. I knew him when he had acne and braces."

My mind tries to picture the not only brilliantly talented at spotting art, but a work of art himself Camden, with braces and acne. "I refuse to picture him like that."

Beck shrugs dismissively. "I'll deny I said this, but he could still get any girl he wanted back then—braces and all."

My nose scrunches. "That's more like it."

Beck's large hand rests on the table. For some reason, I keep focusing on his fingers. I've never wanted to draw the veins on the back of a hand so bad. They're so freaking sexy, and I don't understand why. I itch to run my finger over them, to trace them all the way up his arm, even getting the luxury of feeling the skin that's hidden underneath his suit.

"So, what do you think?" His dark, strikingly blue eyes focus on me. "Are you open to hearing more about my offer?"

5

Beck

I've never cared to know what people are thinking. Other people's opinions on things have never really interested me. Until I laid eyes on the fiercely stubborn woman sitting across from me.

The moment she stuck her tiny little hand in mine at our summer house, the countless rings on her fingers scratching against my palms as we shook hands, I wanted to know what she thought of me. I was curious to know what she thought of her boyfriend's older brother. She'd barely told me her name and I had countless questions I wanted to ask her. I've never wanted to know every detail about another human being until I met her.

Then I saw her draw in her sketchbook and the only thing I wanted to know more than how she viewed me was what she was drawing in that little book of hers.

We'd barely spoken the rest of the weekend. I tried to avoid her when possible.

Except one night that weekend. The night that is forever burned in my mind.

Just as badly, I wanted to know what she was thinking when she met me. I'm desperate to know what's going through her head.

Margo clears her throat, breaking me from my memories and bringing my attention back to her.

Has she already made up her mind to say no? I'd use every one of my breaths to get her to change her mind.

Is she considering it? I'll make sure it's worth her while.

Has she made the decision to say yes? I'll give her anything she wants and more.

Unfortunately for me, Margo doesn't let on to what direction her head is going in—at least not yet. "I need more details on how this is going to work before I agree to anything."

"Done." My answer is immediate. Standing up, I walk around the table until I'm standing right next to her. Reaching up, I undo the button of my suit jacket and let it fall open. I slide my hands into my pockets and sit on the edge of the table. If I scooted over an inch, her knee would brush up against my leg. I'm tempted to do it just to feel some sort of connection between the two of us. "What else do you want to know?"

"What does being your assistant mean? And what happens to your other one? Do you fire them?"

I scoff. "No. Polly still keeps her position, except she's going to stay more grounded in New York. You'll be based in New York with me, but you'll also travel with me when needed."

It appears she just realized that to do this, she'd have to uproot her entire life and move across the country from California to New York. "I'm supposed to move?"

"We can't be engaged and live on opposite ends of the country."

Her bottom lip juts out in a frown. "My friends are here, not in New York. We all moved out here together. I can't leave them."

I bite back the urge to remind her that she also moved out here for Carter.

"I'll fly them out there. Or fly you here. You choose. I've got a jet with staff always on standby. We'll figure that out easily."

"You have a jet? With people on standby?"

"Yes. It's waiting on a tarmac right now. I try to avoid California as much as I can. I much prefer the Northeast."

She laughs. "Yeah, you totally have the New Yorker vibe. Rich, full of themselves, and grumpy."

I ignore her comment. She probably thinks they're supposed to be insults, but those adjectives don't have power over me. I know who I am. She isn't wrong with her assessment.

New York and I fit together perfectly.

"What other reasons do you have to convince yourself this won't work?"

Margo rubs her lips together, her eyes seeming to focus on the small amount of air between our bodies. It wouldn't take much for us to be touching, just a slight movement from either of us and our bodies would connect. "Well, there's the obvious reason that it's totally fake. How do we expect people to believe us? My friends will know it isn't real…"

"We'll have to convince them it is. For this to work, we need everyone—including friends and family—to think that we're madly in love with one another. My board can't know that I'm deceiving them or it'll make things even worse."

It already bothers the hell out of the people on my board that I have the control I do of my own company—one that *I* created. When I sold it years ago at twenty-five, they expected me to take the money and give someone else the position of CEO. I hadn't created Sintech Cyber Security just to sell it and disappear. The only reason I sold it and created a board of directors was because I had visions of what I wanted Sintech to become. Now, every single relevant social media platform uses the company I created for data security. As much as it sucked to admit, I couldn't do it alone. To expand, I had to relinquish some control. But not all. If the board believed I settled down, that my "playboy" ways were behind me, they'd get off my back. The focus would come off me and my personal life and go back to where it *should* be—on the company. On how we're keeping consumer's data secure as social media becomes more prevalent in the average consumer's life each day.

Margo sits back in her chair. Her thighs clench together so tightly, I'm wondering the reason behind it. "What's your family going to say about us, Beck? Won't they be upset that you're engaged to your brother's ex?"

Scoffing, I shake my head. "They adored you. Both my mom and dad were upset when they heard what Carter did to you. They'd love to see you again and won't care if it's because you're now with me."

I'm amazing at reading people and studying their body language to know exactly what's going on in their heads. My ability to read someone even though I hardly tolerate them ends with Margo. I can't determine the look on her face. It looks apprehensive, but by the way she rolls her lips together, I'm wondering if I'm breaking her down and slowly convincing her.

"I'm not trying to upset Carter."

My jaw clenches. I abruptly flip her chair around, her back now to the conference table. Her eyes are wide as saucers as she stares up at me in shock. Crowding her space, I lower my body until we're eye to eye. "Say his name again, and I'll bend you right over this table and fuck you until the only name you can say is mine. You'll be so full of me you won't even remember who you were thinking about before."

Her chest heaves up and down, her breasts brushing up against the lapels of my jacket. "I'm not trying to upset... *him*," she corrects. Her voice comes out forced, like it's taking everything in her to try to keep her tone level.

That makes two of us.

The leather armrests groan underneath my tight grip on them. My back is tense, and I know I should pull away. If someone were to open this door, they'd find Margo and I in a questionable position. Nothing inappropriate has happened between us here, but the words that just left my mouth were far from appropriate.

"I shouldn't have said that." My words are a complete contradiction to what I'm feeling. I want to kiss her lips and lick them until my brother's name never comes from them again.

"Beck," she breathes. Her tongue peeks out to lick her Cupid's bow. I have to rip myself away from her before I do something to ruin this plan I have for us before she even agrees to it.

"That was inappropriate. I apologize, Margo." My features mask into a look of indifference. I have to get my shit together. No one gets to me, and I need to remember to keep it that way. Even when it comes to her. "Let's just agree we don't need to say his name, okay? He's moved on. I'm fairly certain he has a new girlfriend he's no doubt already cheated on. He won't care."

For a moment, Margo looks sad. It hadn't ever occurred to me she may still have some lingering feelings toward my dickwad brother. That'll have to change. I make no move to comfort her. I stay firmly in place standing above her, a respectable few feet between us before I do something that'll have HR breathing down my neck.

"If we do this, we need rules, or terms, or I don't know the fancy word I'm supposed to use, but we need *something*. For me to even consider it, I need to know we're on the *exact* same page."

"Tell me your terms, Margo."

6

Margo

On the outside, I hope I at least appear put together. With Beck no longer in my personal space, the spicy scent of his expensive cologne overtaking my senses, I'm attempting, yet horribly failing, to think straight. I'm at least *attempting* to appear normal. On the inside, I'm freaking the fuck out.

The only thing in my mind is a constant replay of Beck's words. The mental image of me bent over this table, wondering what it'd feel like to have him take me from behind. These are *absolutely* thoughts I shouldn't be having—especially about my new boss who is also my ex's hotter older brother. I'm apparently about to partake in a fake fiancée charade with him; plus, I'm now having dirty thoughts about the two of us and this table. It all equates to a *terrible* idea.

"I don't want to be embarrassed again, Beck," I say, my voice lowered as I try my best to keep it steady. The last thing I need is for my voice to give away the effect his words have on me. "Everyone looked at me like I was pitiful when it came out that Car—"

I almost slip up and say the forbidden name, but quickly correct myself—"*your brother* had cheated on me for years. If people are going to think we're engaged, you can't be seen with other women. I refuse to ever be embarrassed like that again—even if it's fake between us."

There's not a hint of deceit in his eyes when he says, "I wouldn't do that to you, Margo. No one will be seen with me but you."

My stomach unexplainably flutters from his words. It's *tragic*. Carter messed me up so much that I think it's romantic when my possible, soon-to-be, fake fiancé promises not to be seen with another when we're fake engaged.

Men. They really can do a number on you and not even give a shit that they did so.

"I know that you have uh...*needs*," I start, fumbling with my words. I've now committed to this train wreck of a topic though, so I keep trekking even though I feel my cheeks begin to flush. Without even meaning to, my eyes flick down to the crotch of his suit pants, furthering the redness coating my cheeks. "So, I understand that you'll have to have those *met* with someone, but if we do this, I just don't want that to be public. I don't want anyone else to know of you, ya know, getting those needs met. I promise to do the same for any of my, you know...needs." I never thought the word *needs* could cause me to blush in embarrassment, yet here I am, red as a tomato.

Beck's nostrils flare. The angry look in his eyes has my gaze darting away from him in fear. Suddenly, two strong fingers are grabbing me by the chin and forcing my head to look up. His fingertips dig into my cheeks as his face hardens in anger. "Let another man even think about taking care of you when you're my fiancée and they're as good as dead." His voice is seething. I have no idea where all of that anger came from, but it does something to my insides.

My lips part and close again as I think of what to say to him in response. He keeps a strong grip on my jaw, his eyes narrowed as he watches my reaction carefully.

"Margo," Beck says through clenched teeth. There's a muscle in his jaw ticking away. Our closeness is the only reason I'm able to see it. I wonder if it always feathers like that, or if it only does when he's filled with rage.

I'll have to find out.

"Tell me you understand," he demands, his voice tense.

"Understand what?" I ask, my brain feeling like mush. Being this close to him has me at a loss for words. It's the scent of him, feeling the heat radiating off his body, really it's the overwhelming presence he exudes.

Ever so lightly, his thumb brushes over my cheekbone before he rips his hand away. His arms cross his chest in a defensive position. The movement has the fabric around his biceps bunching, the tailored suit almost *too* tailored to his bulging biceps. "If you agree to this, there will be no one else in your life, Margo. For the year, or however long it takes to get the point across, you're mine."

I'm still half wondering if I'm having some sort of bad reaction to the wine we had last night. Or maybe I'm having some sort of fever dream? There has to be an explanation for what's happening right now. This can't be real life. Beckham Sinclair can't be asking me to be his fake fiancée. He can't really be forcing me into being exclusive—even if fake—with him. I'm living in an alternate reality. Hearing Beck say "you're mine" wasn't real…

But it was. It is. This is all very, very real.

This is every woman's dream, and I'm just waiting to find out what the catch is.

I straighten my body in the chair, crossing one leg over the other. "If I agree to that then you have to agree to it, too. It's not fair for you to expect me to not be with anyone else if you're going to be with other women."

His indigo eyes flash, but I can't pinpoint with *what*. I want to say it's desire, but the idea is absurd. Beck can easily get any woman he wants. There's no way he's looking at me with that kind of desire. "Just you, Margo. No one but you."

My heart pounds erratically in my chest. He isn't even as close as he'd been a few minutes ago, but I still feel his presence everywhere. I'm losing a grip on the situation, and I need to regain it before my heart does something stupid like wanting him. "I have another rule," I rush out, rising to my feet because it feels odd to be sitting down looking up at him.

Even standing in heels, I have to bend my neck to look up at him, and he's not even standing to his full height as he rests up against the conference table. "Enlighten me," he clips.

I point between us. "Nothing can happen between us. Lines can't get blurred. No kissing *or* anything else," I add as an afterthought.

His laugh takes me by surprise, making me jump. "Oh, Margo. We'll have to convince many people that the two of us are engaged. We'll most certainly have to kiss. As for the *anything else*"—he says it sarcastically, like the words are in quotations—"I can assure you that we won't be fucking unless you beg for it."

I don't know how Beck manages to make the word "*fucking*" so hot, but every time he says it, I find myself clenching my thighs tighter and tighter.

My eyes narrow. "I can promise you that won't be happening, so we're good there. It's a maybe to the kissing."

His smirk feels like a challenge. "I'm not worried about it. Sooner rather than later, we'll be kissing. And trust me, you won't want to do it just for show."

I snort. "You're so full of yourself. That won't happen." Even as I say the words, lacing conviction into every syllable, I find my gaze resting on his full lips. Without ever kissing him, I'm confident that kissing Beck Sinclair will feel like sleeping with him. His kiss would be sinful. It would do things to me no man has been able to achieve. I know all of this without ever being touched by him.

It's the reason nothing can happen between us.

He clicks his tongue. "Never say never, Violet."

"Never," I respond immediately, drawing out the word to get the point across.

Beck crosses one leather shoe over the other, his feet now crossed at the ankles. "Now you're making this a game. It's making me far more interested in kissing you."

I snap my fingers, cutting whatever the hell is happening between us right now short. "Back to the agreement, Beck."

He runs a finger down the wood top of the conference table. Bringing the finger to his face, his lip upturns at the small amount of dust that coats his fingertip. "Is there anything else holding you back from saying yes?"

"Just about everything," I retort.

Beck sighs, clueing me in that he's annoyed with my reluctance. Or is it anger? Maybe it's a bit of both. He raises his wrist, the movement pulling the sleeve of his suit back to show off his watch. He checks the time on it, his eyes widening slightly in alarm. "Look, Margo, I've missed one meeting and I'm about to miss another in the time we've been in here. What's it going to take for you to say yes?"

Rubbing my lips together, I think about how I want to answer his question. If I'm being honest with myself, I'm far more eager to say yes than I thought I'd be. It may be because I'm entirely curious to see what it'd be like to be Beck's fiancée, even fake. Deep down, maybe I'm bitter enough about what Carter did to me to want to say yes just to make him jealous. Although, he'd have to give a shit about me to be jealous, and I don't know even if me showing up to a family function as Beck's fiancée would get any kind of emotion out of him.

The main things holding me back are leaving my friends and thinking of the aftermath of what happens when Beck and I end the fake engagement. To agree to his proposition, I'd have to trust him when he says we can handle it however I see fit.

"I'm really not a man that likes to wait."

My mind is muddled with all of the reasons I *should* be saying no to him. First and foremost, I'm still hurt by what his brother did. Moving all the way across the country with somebody else, even if fake, probably wouldn't be my best idea.

But I *love* New York.

My heart belongs there. I came out to California because it's where Emma and I got job offers. I've told myself I didn't move here because it's also where Carter took a job, but if I'm honest with myself, I wanted a job here because of him. Winnie followed along because it's Winnie. She can go anywhere—live anywhere—with all the money her family has.

I've always wondered what would've happened if I'd stayed in New York. I don't regret moving out to California, but I'm not meant for the West Coast. Now I have my chance to move back there, but not only move back, to have the chance to show my art to Camden Hunter. It's a once-in-a-lifetime opportunity. I just have to pretend to be Beck's fiancée for a year to do it.

"If I agree, we're doing it on my terms, Beck. I'm sure new rules will come along, and I need to know you'll agree to them even if our charade has already begun."

He thinks my words through for a minute. I can tell it's killing him, to agree to relinquish some of the control he so desperately needs. He tucks his hands into his pockets while his gaze focuses on me. "Agreed."

"So then it's settled," I say, wondering if I'll come to regret this decision.

Rubbing his hands together, he stands to his full height. It only takes him two steps to close the distance between us. Looking down at me, his face is masked to all business once again. He reaches into the hidden pocket of his suit, pulling out a business card. The card is stuck between his pointer and middle fingers as he holds it out between us.

I look at it, confused. If he's about to be my fake fiancé, why am I getting a business card? It seems a little formal in my opinion.

"We'll be in touch," he demands, pushing the card up against my chest. He leaves me no choice but to take it.

And without any other parting words, no thank you or even a goodbye, Beck leaves me all alone in the conference room.

All I can manage to think is *what did I just agree to?*

7

Beck

It's been two days since I met with Margo, and two days of staring at my phone waiting for her call.

She's supposed to start this coming Monday, and it's already Friday morning. I figured she'd at least want to know more details on what the next few days will look like.

I've come to the conclusion she must've misplaced my card. I purposefully make it difficult for anyone to find a way to contact me—not wanting my phone to be overloaded with calls or messages. The poor girl must be struggling to get ahold of me.

A long sigh escapes my lips as I finish up another virtual meeting. The last couple days have been filled with call after call in an effort to integrate the company Margo worked at into my own. I didn't expect quite so much extra work when I bought it, but that's mainly because we found ways it can actually be useful. There are specific proprietary algorithms 8-bit owns that Sintech should be able to use to improve some of our social platform data encryption. It'll take some overhaul of 8-bit to make it best serve us, starting with getting rid of that god-awful logo, but the acquisition hasn't been a *complete* waste.

Stretching in my chair, I take in the view from the penthouse suite of the hotel I'm staying at until Sunday morning. My moment of peace is quickly broken when the vibration of my phone rattles against the desk. Eagerly, I grab for it, expecting to see an unknown number on the screen—Margo's. Instead, I see my assistant's name glaring at me. Frowning, I answer it. "Yes?" I clip, not bothering with a greeting.

"Good morning," Polly says, her tone cheery like usual. The woman is old enough to be my mother, in fact she's older than my own mom, yet it doesn't seem as if the world has hardened her over the years. I on the other hand, can feel my sanity slip away with each useless meeting. I don't know how Polly has put up with me for years, but deep down, I'm grateful for it. She's a wonderful assistant, always doing her job no matter what I ask. I'm just pissy this morning because Margo hasn't contacted me yet.

"Hi," I answer, trying to soften the gruffness in my tone slightly.

For the next fifteen minutes, Polly and I iron details we've been needing to work through. The entire time, my mind travels elsewhere. I can't stop thinking about Margo, even when discussing important topics at hand. Eventually, we get to a good stopping point. Polly is efficient. Even from New York, she's able to keep a reign on things so that even when I'm out of the office, I can count on things running smoothly.

Before she hangs up, I get an idea. Standing up, I take the phone off speaker and hold it to my ear. My shoes click against the marble floor of the penthouse suite as I rush to my room. "Polly?"

"Yes, Mr. Sinclair?"

I grab the jacket off its hanger, the suit freshly steamed thanks to the hotel staff. I press the phone between my cheek and my shoulder as I slip my arms into the sleeves. "Clear my schedule for the rest of the day. Something's come up."

"What?" she asks, not hiding her shock.

Walking to my nightstand, I set my phone on it, putting the phone on speaker again. "Something's come up today, Polly," I explain, grabbing my silver cufflinks and working them through their slots. "Please reschedule any calls I had on the books. Or assign them to Brian; he can inform me of anything that needs my input or approval. If any of the meetings can be turned into an email, do that. It may be hard to reach me for most of the day."

Polly has worked with me long enough to know not to ask any further questions. She sighs, bold enough to let me know she's displeased with my abrupt change before saying, "I'll get it done, Mr. Sinclair."

"Thank you," I say before hanging up.

Once I'm ready, I race to the elevator.

There's somewhere I need to be. Someone I need to see.

. . .

Stepping into the lobby of 8-bit Security, I find the lone security guard paying closer attention to the game on his phone than who is walking in the building. My loud footsteps break him from whatever app he's playing. At the sight of me, he almost jumps out of his chair, then presses a hand to his chest while his shoulders move up and down with a deep breath.

"We weren't expecting you today, Mr. Sinclair," he exclaims, rushed. Now standing close to him, I find crumbs of whatever breakfast he had still stuck in his large mustache. A paper towel with a grease stain sits next to his wireless mouse, more crumbs scattered around it from whatever pastry he just ate. He fumbles with his keyboard, muttering under his breath for an excruciatingly long minute.

My patience wearing thin, I lean over the desk. "Look"—my eyes scan over his uniform until I find a name tag—"Barry, you and I both know that I have the highest security clearance there is here. I don't think we need to bother with printing me a guest pass, do we?"

Barry coughs, looking up at me, his eyes full of panic. "Uh, sir, is this a test?" he squeaks. "I'm not supposed to let anyone in without a pass." He looks back at his computer, typing a few more things. He reaches up and smacks the side of his computer tower. His eyes get large when he realizes I just watched him smack his computer.

Swallowing, I look at him. "Barry," I say tightly. "I own this fucking company. I'm going to go on up and not bother with getting cleared. You got it?"

He looks unsure as he nods. I don't give the guy much room to argue.

People give me odd looks as I step through the glass doors of the office. Darlene, or at least I *believe* it was Darlene, jumps from her seat when she sees me approaching the sea of cubicles. "Mr. Sinclair, we weren't expecting you today."

I barely spare her a second glance. "I wasn't aware I needed to announce each time I was going to stop by."

She follows closely behind me as I weave in and out of the cubicles, my eyes scanning over everyone working at their desks.

"You don't, sir, I just would've made sure—"

Turning abruptly, I stop in front of her. Her mouth hangs open as she looks up at me. Even when trying to smile up at me, her mouth still turns down in a frown. "I don't need you to follow me, Darlene. I'll take it from here." I dismiss her with a simple flick of my wrist.

At first, she doesn't get the hint. It takes me making a shooing motion in the air for her to turn around, her shoulders tight as she makes her way back to her desk.

No longer having to deal with Darlene, I scan the large office space, my eyes searching for one person and one person only.

There she is.

Margo's back is to me. Her long hair falls all the way down her back, the tendrils tamed stick straight. She's engaged in conversation with somebody, her hip propped against a desk. The woman listening to her is engrossed with whatever she is saying. I stop, watching Margo for a few moments before either one of them notice that the office has gone quiet, all of them with their apprehensive eyes on me.

I get it. When the boss shows up, everyone loses their damn minds. It's like they forget to work. Or maybe they're just never great at working at all. Hopefully, for the sake of business, it's the former. Lucky for them, I don't plan on staying long. As long as Margo cooperates.

Which could go one or two ways with her.

Margo talks animatedly with her hands. Upon closer inspection, she grasps something. The bobblehead in her hand swings around in the air. At one point, her coworker has to step slightly to the left to avoid being smacked in the head with the item.

My lip twitches in amusement. It doesn't take long for my feet to eat the distance between us. I come to a stop at Margo's back. Her coworker notices me right away. She freezes, her hand stuck in the short blonde strands of her hair.

"Margo," the coworker hisses, hastily finishing her task of clipping her hair back.

"I'm not done talking!" Margo chides, angrily setting the bobblehead on the cubicle shelf.

Is that Nash Pierce?

The blonde smiles playfully, raising her eyebrows. "Mar, I'd advise you to stop this conversation until we get home. Someone is standing behind you, and he looks pretty pissed." The blonde—maybe also a roommate—doesn't hide the amusement in her voice.

Margo spins on her heels immediately, her puffy lips parting when her eyes land on me. When she looks me up and down, I can't help but wonder if she likes what she sees.

"*Beck*?" she gasps. Her green eyes are wide as they travel over my features. It's like she's trying to figure out if I'm actually here or just a figment of her imagination.

"*This* is Beck?" The girl attempts to whisper, but it comes out more as a yell. "You didn't tell me our new boss looked like *that*!"

Margo aims a dirty look in the girl's direction. "Shut up, Emma. He's not that special to look at."

Someone busts out laughing from a few cubicles away. They quickly try to hide the laughter with a cough, but it's too late. Margo gives them a dirty look, muttering something incoherent under her breath.

"Stop lying to yourself," the coworker—Emma—mumbles. "That's the best-looking man I've ever seen." She bites into an apple I just now notice she's holding. She chews on it loudly, not shy about looking me up and down.

"I think I hate you," Margo snaps, shoving what must be her friend from the cubicle space. Her friend fights her by digging her heels into the ground. Margo is smaller than Emma, but still manages to move her a few feet.

I reach out to tap the bobblehead she'd been swinging around minutes before. As the head bobbles up and down, I look at her with a bored expression. "Working hard?" I ask sarcastically.

She scoffs, looking over her shoulder at her computer screen. "Emma and I were going over a new design before you walked in."

"Is that so?"

"Yep," she answers confidently.

Emma smacks her palm to her forehead, groaning dramatically.

My eyes flick to the computer monitor, to the flashing login screen, the evidence clear as day that Margo hasn't even logged in for the morning, let alone looked over a design.

"You're not even logged in, Mar." Emma grabs Margo by the shoulders, turning her until she's face to face with the proof of her lie.

"Oh..." I can only see her profile, but her wince is obvious.

Margo tucks her hand into the back pocket of her jeans as she spins to face me again. "What are you doing here?"

"I'm just going to go get to work," Emma mumbles. Her fingers wiggle with a goodbye as she rushes to her own desk.

"You've been ignoring me," I state, pinning her with a scowl. This is the second time the woman has had the nerve to disregard me. It's something that won't happen again.

"To ignore someone, they first have to call."

"I gave you my business card. Something I rarely hand out, might I add. You not calling is as good as ignoring me." I let my eyes roam over her workspace. For someone who's worked here for some time, her space is pretty boring. It's not like I can talk. The only things on the walls of my office are my framed diplomas. But that's the way I like things—clean and simple.

Margo doesn't strike me as the clean and simple type. She seems wild and chaotic, someone who likes things unhinged and messy. I imagined her desk being unkept, her artwork hung with mismatched thumbtacks. The only signs anyone works at the desk are the coffee mugs that are haphazardly placed.

She shrugs. "I figured if you wanted to talk, you'd call."

I fight the urge to roll my eyes at her. She gets under my skin more than I care to admit. It shouldn't bother me she didn't call me, yet I've lost sleep wondering why my phone hasn't rung with her voice on the other line.

Taking a deep breath, I point to the purse she has sitting underneath her desk. "Grab your things. We're leaving."

Her arms cross her chest as she tries to make herself look tough. It doesn't work. If anything, she looks annoyingly adorable with the pose, her eyebrows pinched together in what's supposed to look like a mean expression. "I have to work."

One of my eyebrows raises. "You work for me now, remember, Miss Moretti?"

"I'm well aware," she spits back.

I smile, taking a step closer to her. We're still a healthy distance apart. Noticing all of the eyes that are focused on us, I lower my voice as I speak next to her ear. "As my new assistant, you have places to be."

"It's not Monday yet," she aggravatingly points out.

My eyes turn into slits as I drink in the smug look on her face. "I changed my mind. You're needed today. Right now."

"I'm working."

"Yes. For me. Now, I'm not a patient man, Margo. You have five minutes to grab your stuff and meet me in the lobby. Don't make me wait."

She wipes her face clean of the smug smile. Instead, her face screws together in anger. "What happens if I make you wait?"

The smile she gets is lethal. "I don't think you want to find out."

I leave before I do something in front of all these people I shouldn't. On my way out the doors, the annoying secretary stands up, almost tripping over her hideous shoes as she chases after me. "When can we be expecting you again, Mr. Sinclair?"

If it were up to me—never.

"Darlene," I begin, gritting my teeth. A minute has already ticked by. Margo better hurry, or she's going to get more than she bargained for if she makes us late.

"It's Darla, sir," she corrects. Her voice is nasally. I wonder how anyone can stand listening to her speak for any length of time.

I don't give a fuck what her name is. I just want her to leave me alone.

"Darla. You're going to have to hire a new graphic designer. Margo's been promoted."

She's left no time to argue or ask questions. My palms slam into the glass door as I make my way back to the lobby. Barry smiles nervously at me as I stop to stand off in a corner.

I glance at my watch.

She has three more minutes before she's late.

8

Margo

'm late by *over* five minutes.

In my defense, it's not really my fault. Emma takes four of those minutes by trying to get me to explain where I'm going with Beck. She doesn't believe me when I answer truthfully. I have no freaking clue what Beck has planned for the day, what his motives are for showing up on my last day of work at 8-bit. But damn, I might be a little excited to find out.

When I finally convince her that I'll give her updates the moment I know what's happening, it takes another four minutes for me to grab my things and check my appearance in the compact I keep in my handbag.

The last minute is spent rushing out. Darla attempts to fire questions at me on my way out, but all I do is give her a smile. "I'm going to miss you, Darla," I lie. Wrapping my arms around her, I give her one tight squeeze. I won't miss her in the slightest, but part of me will miss this place. Even though I hated what I did here, it was my first real job. I got to start with Emma, and it's a bit bittersweet to leave it behind.

Who knows, maybe I'll be back whenever this thing with

Beck ends. But I hope to never be back again.

Beck looks pissed when I step into the large lobby. He's got his phone pressed to his ear, clearly engaged in a conversation with someone else. The call seems civil. The look in his eyes is anything but.

I'm in trouble. The deep set of his brows tells me as much.

Why does the thought excite me a little?

He doesn't say a word when I come to a halt in front of him. He continues to speak with whoever is on the other line. Beck acknowledges my presence by tilting his head toward the exit. Words aren't needed for me to catch on to what he wants.

His long legs make their way toward the exit. Beck doesn't even look over his shoulder to see if I follow. He doesn't have to. I'm too intrigued by why he showed up on my last day of work, leaving no room for arguing that I needed to leave with him.

Even though it's obvious he's upset by me being late, he holds the door open for me. Before I leave, I turn and give Barry my sweetest smile. "Goodbye, Barry! I'll miss you." I blow him a kiss, loving how Barry eats the attention up by pretending to catch the kiss and tuck it in his pocket.

When I turn back to leave, I find Beck has ended his call. His eyes are locked on me like magnets. I wish I knew what the look on his face meant. The anger is wiped away for the moment, but I can't quite put my finger on what's replaced it.

As soon as my feet hit the sidewalk, he's letting the door close behind him and guiding me toward a waiting black SUV. A guy dressed in a suit waits in front of the rear passenger door. As soon as we near the vehicle, he's plastering on a smile and pulling the door open.

My feet skid to a stop. I anxiously look over my shoulder, wondering if getting into this car is a good idea. I guess Beck is my boss—and soon-to-be fake fiancé—so I should trust him. But a part of me feels a bit apprehensive. It's probably the fact that the two of them are dressed like they're about to go to a formal event and I'm dressed in a pair of fraying Levi's.

I look between the guy holding the car door open and Beck. "I didn't get the memo to come wearing a gown. My apologies."

The man tries to hide a smile. His cheek twitches as he fights with all his might to keep a straight face.

Beck doesn't look quite as amused. He's now climbed into the back of the car, his arm outstretched like he's waiting to help me get into the car. My body feels tingly as he looks over my outfit. "I'm going to have to have a chat with HR on dress code," he clips, his eyes focusing on the large hole at my knee. My tan skin peeks out from the space.

I look down, taking in all the different holes in the pants. I shrug, completely unbothered by his comment. "Oh, it totally goes against the dress code. Darla wrote me a pink slip the moment I stepped into work this morning."

It's Beck's turn to fight a smile. He's much better at it than his driver, however. I mutter my thanks to him as I slide into the backseat of the SUV, completely ignoring Beck's outstretched hand. He doesn't say anything as it falls to his side. "So, you're breaking the rules right after you've been promoted?"

Beck's driver, I still need to get his name, softly shuts the door after me before he rounds the car and gets in.

I shake my head. "I've always followed the rules. But today being my last day and all, I figured I might as well wear something comfortable. If it were up to me, all companies would have casual Fridays."

"Noted." His eyes snap to my side. "Buckle your seat belt."

I bite my tongue, wanting to tell him that even if he's going to be my boss, he doesn't have to always tell me what to do.

He must disapprove of my silence. In one swift motion, he's reaching across the space, grabbing the seat belt and buckling me in.

"I'm not a child. I can do it myself."

Beck pins me with a glare. His face is dangerously close to mine. So close that his hot breath tickles my cheeks. His smell surrounds me. For a fraction of a second, his gaze focuses on my lips. He rips his sight away from my parted lips, his stormy eyes looking into mine. "Too late."

I tear my eyes from his, too caught up in the moment with him for my own good. I should be angry with him for catapulting into my life and changing everything so quickly, but I'm also thrilled at the possibilities of what's in store.

"Where are we going?" I question, looking out the window as the driver pulls the car away from the curb.

"Before we do anything, I need you to sign this." Beck pulls a packet from a briefcase and plops it between us.

I pick it up, my eyes roaming over a bunch of legal jargon that goes over my head.

"It's an NDA, Margo," he explains, watching me closely. "You're expected to sign it before we go through with this."

I frown, trying to understand what everything means. Flipping from one page to the next, I find highlighted sections where I'm supposed to sign my name. Watching reruns of *Law and Order SVU* hasn't given me enough knowledge of law terminology to even begin to understand a thing. I look at Beck with skepticism written on my face. "I don't understand any of this." I wave the packet around in the air between us. "How do I know that I'm not signing away my first-born child to you?"

The driver spits out a laugh. I smirk, happy I got the calm and collected guy to finally break.

"Glad you find her hilarious, Ezra." Beck gives the driver—Ezra, apparently—a dirty look through the rearview mirror. Ezra, however, only makes eye contact with Beck for a fleeting moment before he pins his eyes ahead of him, suddenly very focused on the road. "Sorry, sir." He coughs. "It *was* kind of funny."

I beam, looking at Beck with a satisfied look. "I like him already."

"Thank you, Miss Moretti," Ezra comments, his eyes still focused on the road ahead.

Beck sighs dismissively at the both of us. He looks at the packet I still hold between us. "I can assure you I'm not having you sign away anything. All of my staff sign NDAs. It's standard protocol. Your *best friend,* Ezra, signed one as well."

"Sure did. Hopefully, I didn't sign away my first-born child," he says sarcastically. "My future wife may not be happy to know that."

Beck snorts, slightly leaning forward to get Ezra's attention. "You don't even have a girlfriend," he responds dryly.

Ezra's eyebrows raise to his hairline. "That you know of, sir." He winks at me through the mirror.

The gesture manages to further annoy Beck. Angrily, he snatches the packet from my hand and places it on the leather seat between us. His fingers trace over some of the sentences as he begins to explain what everything means. My eyes travel over the words he reads out loud, so far confident that I'm not signing some kind of shady deal.

Once he makes it through three pages of the packet, he looks up at me through his thick eyelashes. "Need me to keep going or do you trust me enough to know that I'm a civilized human being that wouldn't trap you into anything crooked?"

"I don't know if *trust* is the correct term when it comes to you."

Beck makes a face, making it seem like my response actually

offended him. "Fine," he bites, slipping his phone from his suit pocket. "I'll call my lawyer to review it with you then, if that's what it'll take."

His fingers are quick at typing something on his phone. Taking myself by surprise, I reach across the bench seat, placing my hand on his forearm. "Wait," I say. Even the way the suit feels underneath my palm tells me it's expensive. It's soft, a light gray that looks great up against his pale skin tone.

Beck looks at where my hand rests on his arm. I pull it away, meeting his eyes. "Don't call your lawyer. I'll sign it."

His eyes bore into mine. I try not to squirm in my seat. Half of me loves having his undivided attention like this. The other part of me wants him to look anywhere but me. I can't handle having him watch me like he's leaving so much unsaid. "But you don't trust me." It doesn't take a rocket scientist to hear the disdain in his voice.

Rolling my eyes, I reach for the handbag at my feet. I rifle through it, searching for a pen.

"What are you doing?" Beck finally asks.

I pull random things out of the bag, wondering why I can't find a single pen in here. Typically, this bag is like the one from *Mary Poppins*, full of unexpected treasures. Today, it's full of random things except the one thing I need—a pen. "I'm looking for a pen," I grumble, pulling out my makeup bag and moving it out of the way.

"Don't bother," Beck responds. He opens his briefcase and holds up a pen. "Use this."

Snatching the pen from him, it feels heavier in my hand than I was expecting. Even this man's pens feel expensive.

I set the packet in my lap, using my legs as a makeshift table as I sign on each dotted line.

9

Margo

"Are you going to tell me where we're going yet?" I prod, hoping he'll finally answer my question.

"We're going to your apartment."

"We're what?" I shriek.

"We're going to your apartment," he repeats, slower this time, like I didn't understand him the first time he said it. I understood him perfectly. I'm just in shock he knows where I live.

A sound of annoyance falls from my lips. "Not possible. You don't know where I live."

Ezra makes a sound from the front seat. The noise has Beck tossing him a threatening look immediately. "I know exactly where you live, Margo," he declares, his voice level.

"I don't believe you."

He shakes his head at me. His pointer finger digs into his temple as he looks out the window, his eyes focused on the passing cars. "It's cute you think I don't know everything there is to know about you."

Impossible. "You know nothing about me." For starters, we barely uttered a few sentences to one another at his family's vacation home.

Words weren't really needed.

I shake the thought away as quickly as it came to be. The last thing I need on my mind is that memory. One thing I can count on is the fact I doubt Carter said much to Beck about me. I'm reminded of the fact that even though they're brothers, Beck and Carter aren't close. The last thing I imagine is the two of them sitting down and talking about me.

He looks from the window to me, a cocky smirk on his lips. "You forget I own the company you work at. Any knowledge they had on you, I now have right here"—he taps his temple—"and that includes your address."

I let out a defeated sigh, slumping down in my seat and crossing my arms over my chest. "That's creepy, you know."

"It's using the resources I have at my disposal."

My phone vibrates. Giving Beck a dirty look, I unlock it and check the group chat with my roommates. My eyes track over the lengthy conversation they had in the time since Beck stole me from work.

Emma

> Winnie. You'll never believe who showed up to whisk our very own Cinderella from work for the day.

Winnie

> Beckham Sinclair???
>
> Oh my god. He showed up?
>
> Don't leave me on read. I need DETAILS!!

Emma

> Sorry. Darla just yelled at me for being on my phone.
>
> YES!!!! He graced us with his beautiful presence. NO ONE TOLD ME HE WAS THAT HOT.

Winnie

> Why isn't Margo responding? Margo…we need details. Like right now.

Emma

> She might be having hot car sex with her new boss. I would if my boss looked like that.
>
> Well. I guess technically he is my boss. Too bad I didn't get offered that assistant position. I'd assist him right to the bedroom.

Winnie

> Emma!! He's your boss.

Emma

> I'm pissed I didn't know how hot he was. Margo didn't mention that.

Winnie

> I'm in a dumb group with girls from high school who send every picture of him posted on the internet. They all still hold out hope he'll give them an ounce of attention.

Margo

> He's not that good-looking.

I smirk, my eyes bouncing to Beck who is also looking down at his phone. If he only knew the text I just fired off to my best friends. He'd probably say something cocky about how my reaction to his every move says otherwise.

Emma

> Shut up. Were you banging?

Margo

> No. He's taking me to our apartment.

Emma

> WHEN I'M NOT THERE?! What the hell, Margo. I could give him a tour of my bedroom.

I laugh, catching the attention of both Beck and Ezra. I mask my reaction immediately. I don't want to risk Beck reaching across the car and stealing the phone from my hands. It seems like something he'd do. I look back at my phone. Emma will lose her mind when I have to pretend that Beck and I have become fake engaged.

Winnie

> Why is he taking you there?

Margo

> I guess I'll find out.

I ignore the rest of the messages for now, despite feeling my phone vibrate countless times. Ezra turns onto a familiar street, cluing me in that Beck wasn't lying. He knows where I live and that's where we're going. "Care to tell me why we're going to my place?"

This actually does make him smile, except the smile is anything but friendly. It's devilish, making my stomach sink as I wonder the meaning behind it.

"We're getting you all packed. We fly back to New York tomorrow."

I swear this man is trying to send me into a tailspin. "I don't think I heard you correctly. We can't leave tomorrow."

"And why's that?"

"Because I have friends here. I need to pack. I need more time to move across the country."

There's a speck of humor in his eyes as he leans deeper into the hand that holds his head. "You would've had that if you called me. Sorry, but duty calls. I need to return to New York tomorrow. I'd much have preferred tonight, but I'm being generous and giving you the evening. But that's as far as my generosity goes. You'll be leaving with me tomorrow since you're supposed to be in the office with me Monday morning."

I anxiously pick at my cuticles. I normally take a week to pack for a long weekend. How the hell am I supposed to pack for uprooting my life and moving halfway across the country in one night?

My mind reels as a thought pops into my head. "If you had my address, then you had my number."

He shows off his perfectly straight white teeth when he grins. "This seemed way more efficient."

My argument stays in my throat as Ezra pulls up to the apartment complex. Beck must've really done his research, because we even pull up to the correct building. Ezra puts the SUV in park as Beck and I have a silent stare-off. I refuse to look away from him. I may have signed away the next year of my life to him, but he doesn't just get to tell me at the last minute to pack all my things and move away tomorrow.

"I'm not leaving tomorrow."

"How else do you plan to get to New York by Monday morning?"

He's got a point. But I refuse to let him win this one. He's steamrolled into my life suddenly and taken control of everything. I want some of that control back, even if it's in the form of determining when I move to New York and begin this charade I'm going to take part in.

"I'll get a flight on my own," I answer confidently. It'll probably drain my entire bank account to do so, but I'm prepared to do it just to win this battle with him.

He grunts in disgust. "I'm not allowing you to fly coach." He says *coach* the way someone talks about bed bugs or lice. Like it's the most disgusting thing on the planet. I, for one, have found some coach flights quite delightful. A bag of pretzels *and* a cookie? That's pure luxury.

"Your entitlement is showing," I snap as Ezra gets out of the car. He clearly doesn't want to have to listen to Beck and I battle it out. *I wouldn't either if I were him.*

Beck clenches his jaw, something I'm learning he does a lot. It seems he's in a constant state of anger when he's with me. I'm not trying to push his buttons. I just don't want him to think he can show up at my job on my last day and then have the audacity to pack my things and force me to get on a jet with him tomorrow.

Unbuckling his seatbelt, he slides across the leather, moving the briefcase that acted as a barrier between us. He crowds me with his body, even as I try to scoot away from him. My back presses into the door. I have nowhere to go. I don't even have anywhere to look but into his dark, stormy, indigo eyes.

He presses his palm into the window by my head. Our thighs press against one another, no other parts of our bodies touching. "I'm not letting the woman who is about to be my fiancée fly coach when I own a private jet."

"Plenty of people fly it every day."

He grinds his teeth, fire in his eyes. "Plenty of people aren't you."

Fuck.

No.

The way Beck looks at me right now makes me want to agree to anything he says. There's concern, but also determination. I know without a shadow of a doubt that this is a battle I won't win. It doesn't matter anyway. Right now what I want to battle is my heart, because it liked him saying "plenty of people aren't you" *a little* too much.

"Go pack, Margo."

This close to him, I marvel at how his porcelain skin doesn't have a trace of any facial hair. I wonder if he freshly shaved this morning, or perhaps it doesn't show well because he has blond hair. In my head, I'm already creating a mental list of the things I need to pack and what I'll leave behind for my friends. But I don't want him to know that. Pushing his buttons, getting him riled up and seeing that muscle in his jaw tick is much more fun.

"No."

He smacks the glass next to my head, making me jump. Tearing himself away from me, he tosses his door open like it's the thing that's pissed him off. I don't have time to even gather my thoughts before he's ripping my car door open. His large hands catch me underneath my armpits, saving me from falling flat on my ass in front of both him and Ezra.

Even after I gain my footing Beck leaves one of his hands on me. It trails down a few inches until he's holding me by the bicep. I try to yank it free, but his fingers keep their firm grasp.

"Let go," I demand.

Instead of listening to me, he tightens his fingers, pulling me in the direction of my apartment building. "After you," he growls, completely calm and collected no matter how many times I try to pull my arm from him.

Finally, I yank hard enough to get my arm free. But looking at him from the corner of my eye, noting the smug look on his face, I wonder if he let go because he didn't want to deal with me fussing a second longer.

"You're not coming with me."

"I wasn't planning on it, but then you started acting like a child, so now I'll be coming in and helping you pack so you'll be ready to catch a flight. *Tomorrow*."

His tone makes it obvious there's no reason for me to argue, but it doesn't stop me from trying one last time.

"You can't make me," I bite.

He bites his lip, quirking an eyebrow at me. "Margo, I can promise that you're coming with me tomorrow one way or another. If it means I have to throw you over my shoulder to get you to New York, then I'll do it. Even if you're kicking and screaming."

The two of us stare at one another, our chests heaving as we both refuse to back down. Finally, I break eye contact, my eyes searching for Ezra. I'm hoping that I've made a quick friend in him and that he'll back me up, but I'm out of luck. He's got his phone to his ear with a wide smile as he talks to somebody on the other line.

Letting out a loud groan, I stomp toward my apartment. I don't have to turn around to know Beck is hot on my heels. His angry stare is like a brand on my neck, scorching and making me more annoyed with each step closer to my front door.

"I'm tired of you bossing me around," I mumble, reaching into my pocket for my keys.

"Get used to it," he clips.

10

Beck

Margo isn't shy about making her feelings known about the unexpected departure tomorrow. I've been sitting on the edge of her bed, taking in the mess that is her room, as she loudly packs her bags. She can't do anything without adding some theatrics to it.

Her bathroom door slaps the wall as she flings it open, a large toiletry bag in her hand.

Even when she tosses the bag in her open suitcase, it's thrown harder than necessary. She walks to her closet, flicking through the clothes on the hangers. The hangers make loud scraping noises on the rod as she looks through them, occasionally pulling clothes off the hanger and tossing them onto the bed.

"You know packing all of this isn't necessary," I note, picking up a sweater that seems to have seen better days. I hold it by the collar, noting the fraying threads scattered throughout the worn knitting.

Margo turns around, giving me a dirty look. I'd never tell her this, but the look is far more endearing than it is intimidating. "I need clothes to wear."

I pull at one of the loose threads of the sweater. "We'll go shopping in New York. You can't wear this to work."

Her eyes narrow. "I don't have money to buy anything at any of those fancy stores in New York."

Throwing the old sweater on the bed, I take a deep breath. My fingers pinch the bridge of my nose as I think about what I want to say without offending her. I have to tread lightly. I know Margo enough to know she'll put up a fight if I tell her I'll buy the clothes for her, even though I have more money than I know what to do with. I'm not going to allow her to show up to work in clothes that are obviously old, the fabric now more itchy than it is comfortable. "I'll buy the clothes, Margo. I have accounts with multiple stores where you'll find what you need. Just please make it better than...*that*." I point toward the discarded sweater.

"I'm not your little project to take pity on and dress up all nicely to impress whoever you want me to impress."

My phone has already rung countless times during the twenty minutes I've sat here as she's deciding what to pack. My patience is wearing very thin. Her comment is just about sending me over the edge of what I can handle. I don't see the point in her taking the time to pack some of these things when she'll never wear them because I'll just buy her all new stuff. It seems pointless. Standing up, I close the distance until I'm backing her into her tiny closet. She attempts to run away from me until her back is hitting her clothes. I stare down my nose at her, impressed by the defiant look in her eyes. "You're not, and never will be, my little project. I didn't mean it that way and you know that. You'd just rather argue than allow me to do *one* thing for you."

She opens her mouth to do what I'm learning she does best— argue—but I put my palm over her lips before she can do so. "So, here's what's going to happen. You're going to pack the things you *need*. The things I can't buy you when we get to Manhattan. Sentimental shit or whatever. You can leave whatever you want here, to give to your friends or keep for whenever you visit. Truthfully, I don't give a fuck what you do with it. And then we're going to leave here. We have a few places we need to be today; you can tell your friends you'll have a goodbye dinner with them or fuck, even breakfast with them tomorrow, and then we're getting on the jet tomorrow afternoon. Understood?"

I feel her angry sigh against my palm. Her breath is hot against my skin. My mind can't help but wonder what her breath would feel like up against far more intimate parts of me. My cock stirs in my suit pants at the idea. I remove my palm from her lips. "And for the record, you could wear a paper bag and impress anyone."

Margo places her small hands on my chest and pushes against me with an angry groan. I smile, letting her push me a few feet away from her even though I was having fun unnerving her a little with my close proximity. She may think she's playing it cool, but I could feel the warmth from the rush of blood in her cheeks. I felt every sharp intake of breath against my palm and could see the curious desire in her eyes.

Shocking me, instead of arguing, Margo turns around and begins to rifle through her closet once again. Bored of just sitting on her bed and looking at work emails, I walk around her small room, itching to find out more about her just by what's in here.

I'm busy looking at a bunch of Polaroid pictures she has taped to a floor-length mirror when she speaks up from behind me. "Just *for the record*"—she mocks the tone I just used—"I'm going to spend so much of your money on new clothes."

"Wouldn't expect anything else." I smile, reaching to grab a picture of Margo with a huge slice of pizza next to her face.

The giant thin slice with large, round pepperonis is instantly recognizable as a New York-style pizza. The sweatshirt she wears with large NYU letters on the front also clues me in to the fact that this must be from her college days. I pull it away from the mirror, and there's a ripping sound as the tape comes off the glass.

Holding the picture in front of me, I let my eyes roam over her face. She looks so happy, completely carefree. Her hair seems to be a few inches shorter than it is now. It must be from her early college days. It'd been about the same length it is now when I first met her in the Hamptons. She stares right at the camera, her mouth slightly open like she was laughing at whatever the person behind the camera was saying.

Various sounds come from behind me as Margo continues to pack while I look around her room. I neatly stick the picture back to the mirror, moving on to look at the next thing. My feet come to a stop in front of what must be her art space. It's tiny. A small wooden chair sits in front of a desk barely large enough to fit a sketchbook and a holder of drawing utensils.

I slide my finger underneath the cover of her sketchbook, itching to know what she's spent countless hours drawing on the pages within. I've got it raised a few inches, the beginnings of a sketched hand appearing when it snaps shut.

"Those aren't for you to look at." Her voice is quiet, her breath quick with what might be nerves.

"Why not?" I push, my voice low. My mind flashes with a memory. To a hot summer night when the moon was high in the sky and questionable decisions were made. "I seem to vividly remember a time when you let me look at every single page of your sketchbook. At what you'd drawn. *Who* you'd drawn…"

The air around us becomes electrified. Her pouty lips open as she stares at me in shock. Neither one of us had ever acknowledged that summer night—until now. "That was different."

Her gaze travels from mine to where her fingers splay across the cover of her sketchbook. I pull mine from beneath the cover and first page. My fingertip slides across the cover until it meets her finger. Lifting my hand, I put my hand over hers. The size of our hands is a stark difference. Mine dwarfs hers. I link my fingers through the empty space between hers, letting mine hook around until they rest against her palm. I lift our joined hands, removing them from the cover.

"I don't see how," I utter, still keeping her hand in mine as I place them on the edge of the desk. "If anything, I feel like now I'm even more entitled to know what you've been drawing. Tell me, is it still me you draw in there, Violet?"

She snatches her hand from mine, the moment gone between us. "I have no idea what you're talking about," she snaps, stealing the sketchbook from the desk and stuffing deep into her suitcase.

Lies lies lies. She knows *exactly* what I'm talking about.

My lip twitches. "If you say so."

One of these days we're going to talk about what happened that night. But I'll let her warm up to me more. I'm not typically a patient man, but for her, I can be. It'll be well worth the wait once we finally acknowledge it.

11

Margo

Beck wasted no time getting us to New York. He essentially gave me one night and the morning to say goodbye to my friends and get my things packed before he showed up at my apartment early this afternoon, hurrying me to get ready so we could catch our flight.

I argued. If he owned the jet, couldn't he technically be late?

I've never felt truly poor. My family did what they could to get by. My parents lived paycheck to paycheck to make things work, but we were loved and we were taken care of. I didn't want for much of anything growing up. Sure, I wanted the three-level Barbie Dreamhouse and only got it a year after it first released and it was on clearance, but all the things I truly needed, and even most of what I wanted, I had. I was a happy kid growing up, even if my family didn't have a ton of money.

The first few months after college could arguably be the time when I felt the most poor. I was living off Ramen and off-brand snacks that were on sale because they were about to expire. In the moment, it felt like the New York way to live.

At least it was *my* version of the New York college kid way to live.

Standing in the foyer of Beck's penthouse high-rise apartment, it's just now occurring to me how incredibly rich he is. My first clue should've been that he lived in Manhattan. One month's rent for a teeny-tiny studio here is almost triple what we paid to live in a three-bedroom in LA. My second clue should've been the fact that Beck had to swipe a keycard in front of a sensor when we stepped into the elevator before he pressed a glowing button with a *PH* on it.

Of course he lives in a penthouse. And of course it's the most gorgeous space I've ever seen.

"Are you just going to stand there and gawk?" Beck's footsteps echo off the black marble flooring. He stops at a lavish gold entryway table, putting his wallet and keycard into a ceramic bowl.

My feet stay planted on the fancy carpet of the elevator. It dings three times before the doors close in on me. With a yelp, I squeeze between the closing doors, almost dropping my purse in the commotion.

Beck smirks from the middle of the room. His fingers wrap around the handle of my suitcase, his eyes watching me closely.

"Thanks for the help," I say sarcastically.

"I thought you could manage on your own." Turning around, he walks past a large staircase. He turns his head slightly to speak over his shoulder. "Come on, let's leave the gallery."

I laugh, shaking my head as I step next to the staircase. The side is all glass, the stairs white with gold metal accents. It's very modern and expensive looking. "I've never heard the word *gallery* used in that context."

Beck walks past an enormous dining table, his hand still perched on the handle of my suitcase as he wheels my cheap-looking suitcase next to a grand table. My old duffle bag almost slides off the top of the suitcase with his jerky movements. I gawk in awe at the table that sits next to my things. It looks to be made out of some kind of black stone that probably has some kind of fancy name. It looks incredibly heavy. I wonder how many people it took to get it up here. "Gallery..." I repeat, testing the word on my tongue. It feels odd to use it to describe a location in a home.

"Yeah, that there is the *gallery*. And right now, we're standing in what's called a *dining room*," he says condescendingly.

I stick my tongue out at him. "I gathered, *asshole*."

Stopping, he lets go of my suitcase and walks toward the most luxurious kitchen I've ever seen. Beck runs his finger over the dark countertop. "This right here is called a *kitchen*." He draws out the syllables of the word, explaining it to me like I'm a toddler.

I ignore him. If he wants to be a dick, I'm not going to engage. Instead of spewing the various insults running through my head, I take in the space that's going to be my home for at least the next year.

There's no way Beck had anything to do with decorating the space. It looks *too* nice. Even with the dark color scheme, it's inviting. It doesn't feel too cold or unwelcoming. The kitchen is what catches my eye. Cabinets take up the entire wall, the dark wood of them have a slight sheen to the material. The wall of cabinets and counter space meet floor-to-ceiling windows on one side. On the other, it meets a wall that houses two ovens, a little nook with a fancy-looking coffee machine, and then the biggest refrigerator I've ever seen.

My feet take me into the space. I slide my hand over the cold countertop of the expansive island, right in the middle of all of it. My fingers trace over the delicate fissures in the dark stone, stopping at a sink that seems large enough for me to fit in—if I wanted. The cabinets, the faucet, all the details of the kitchen are a shiny brass color, fueling the modern look of the kitchen. The color palette works well together. Although I'm sure Beck had nothing to do with it, whoever did design it did a wonderful job.

"Have you ever cooked anything in here?" I stop admiring the kitchen and instead look to Beck, deciding to admire him instead.

He is my future fake fiancé after all.

Beck holds my gaze. He leans up against the lip of the countertop. His hands leave his pockets. One smoothes down the fabric of his tie while the other pulls at the knot around his neck. I watch in fascination as he loosens the tie around his neck until he pulls it off completely. "There's a lot you don't know about me, Margo Moretti, beginning with the fact that I actually enjoy cooking when I have the time."

My lips part in shock. I'm trying to picture Beck in this kitchen cooking, but I can't quite produce the image in my head. It seems too messy, too casual for someone who seems to be in a suit and tie ninety percent of the time. "*You cook?*"

Beck folds the tie nicely and sets it next to him on the counter. "Why does that shock you so much?"

I inch my way to his refrigerator, pulling the large doors open to inspect what he's got inside. I was expecting a bunch of take-out containers, or maybe nothing in there at all, but it surprises me how well-stocked it is with fresh ingredients. Looking over my shoulder, I find Beck watching me with a smug look on his face.

I close the doors, turning to face him once again. "I don't know. I just expected you to be the kind of guy who had a private chef cook for him all the time. It's hard to imagine you cooking. Wouldn't that ruin your suit and all?"

He laughs softly, pulling his body from the countertop and closing the distance between us. I hate how my pulse spikes as he gets closer. The problem with Beck is that he's easily the most attractive man I've ever laid eyes on. His personality could use some work, but even with his harsh demeanor, he's got this magnetism to him that draws me in. I could choose to fight it, or I could let it pull me in. I'm not sure which one would be worse in the end, but I need to keep my hormones *and* feelings in check with this deal.

I've already had my heart broken by one Sinclair brother, I'm sure as hell not letting the other anywhere near my freshly mended one.

Beck's hands press into the matte black refrigerator over my head. He doesn't touch me, but his presence is so looming—dominating—that it actually feels like he's touching me everywhere. "I do have a private chef that cooks most of my meals. But it isn't because I don't enjoy cooking or know how to, it's more for convenience."

His breath tickles my skin. My tennis shoes do nothing to give me any kind of height, so with him this close, it brings attention to just how vastly different our heights are. I'm only a few inches over five feet on a good day. He's got to be at least a foot taller than me, but I'm a terrible judge of that. I know Carter used to brag that he was six feet tall, and Beck definitely has a few inches on him.

He leans in closer, our foreheads almost touching. I want to know what cologne he wears. He smells like bergamot mixed with something else, something sweet—maybe jasmine. Whatever it is, I can't get enough. I want to bury my face against wherever he sprays it in the morning, to inhale the scent until it's forever imprinted in my mind.

"You're quiet for once," he observes. I don't tell him the reason I'm quiet is because I'm imagining pressing my face to his neck just to lose myself in his scent. His intoxicating indigo eyes roam my face. He doesn't bother to hide the fact he's staring right at my lips.

Does Beckham Sinclair want to kiss me?

Do I want to kiss him?

Our conversation from a few days ago rings in my mind. He told me we'd be kissing sooner rather than later. I scoffed at the idea, but with him looking at me like this, I can't help but wonder what'd happen if we did.

I press my shoulders into the cold metal doors of the fridge, trying to escape him, even if I know it's no use. "I just couldn't picture you cooking. Do you wear an apron to keep yourself all nice and clean?"

Beck removes his hands from over my head, but his feet stay planted in the same place. Keeping eye contact with me, he deftly undoes the top button of his button-up. I expect him to stop there, but he doesn't. Once the top one is undone, he pops the button from the next hole as well. After three buttons are undone, I can see the splatter of his blond chest hair.

"What are you doing?" I whisper, half-panicked as I watch him all too closely. Even as my gaze is focused solely on his fingers as they continue to undo each button, I feel Beck's gaze watching me intently.

"I'm starving. And sorry to disappoint, I have no apron. Can't get this shirt dirty. So I'll just have to…" He leaves the rest of what he was going to say up to the imagination as he quickly untucks his shirt and undoes the last button.

And holy hell, seeing Beck stand in his kitchen with an undone button-up and his abs on display might be the hottest thing I've ever seen.

I don't know where to look first. There's the fire in Beck's eyes. I swear they burn so brightly with desire that it makes my body feel hot all over. There's also the ripple of muscles in front of me. I'd barely have to lift my hand and I'd be reminded of what his abs feel like underneath my touch.

When Beck rolls his lips together as he stares at my own mouth, I'm lost in the lust of the moment.

I want to feel him underneath my touch more than I've ever wanted anything.

I'm about to act on impulse when he makes the decision for me. He leans in, letting his nose brush against my jawline.

Holy fuck. My breath is mixing with Beck's breath.

Are we going to kiss? To fuck? God, I want it so bad even after telling him days ago that we could never cross the line.

Right now, I want to say screw the line and have Beck screw *me*.

"Margo," he breathes, his hand coming to rest next to my head. I have to steady myself by doing the only logical option, placing my hands against his hard abdomen. As soon as my skin connects with his, I feel his muscles clench underneath my fingertips.

I didn't know someone could feel so hard and warm and intoxicating.

Maybe he's right. I'm tempted to beg him to fuck me.

"Yes?" I pant.

Beck leans in even closer, lining his lips right next to my ear. A featherlight kiss is pressed against my cheekbone before he speaks. "I need in the fridge."

It takes a moment for my brain to process his words, but as soon as it does, it feels like cold water has been thrown on me.

And then I get the hell away from him.

12

Beck

*R*egret.

It lingers all around me as I watch Margo dart across the kitchen.

There's the regret of allowing myself to almost kiss her, to discover what she tastes like.

And then the regret of knowing she would've let me kiss her and I didn't.

Her words from that dingy conference room still ring in my head. I don't know if she wants it. I don't want her backing out of the deal before it's barely even begun. So I stopped myself, even when every fiber of my being wanted to lift her onto the countertop and have my way with her.

"Margo." I sigh, missing the warmth of her hands against me a little too much. Now, with my shirt open, it feels too cold without her touch.

She doesn't bother to look at me. I can't say I blame her. For a few seconds, she allowed herself to be vulnerable and gave me a glimpse of the lust in her eyes. Instead of waving a white flag and fueling the simmering fire between us, I threw a bucket of cold water on us and doused the flames. She's embarrassed. I don't have to look at her face to know it.

"Look," I begin.

Her spine straightens as she grabs the handle of her suitcase. She talks to the windows, not my face, when she speaks up. "Could you point me to where I'll be sleeping?" she asks. She tries hard to mask the shakiness in her words, but I catch it.

My palms run down my pants. I take a step toward her. "Sure. Let me walk you there and grab your bags."

When she looks over her shoulder, the embarrassment is masked with anger. "No. Just tell me where I'm sleeping, and I'll find it."

I clear my throat, pointing toward the lofted upstairs. It wasn't my intention to piss her off. Or maybe it was. Fuck, I really don't know when it comes to her. "No." When I reach her, I pry her fingers from the handle. She aims a dirty look my way but I don't pay it any attention.

"I'll do it," she hisses. "Just tell me where I'm sleeping."

Ignoring her, I head toward the staircase. As soon as I reach the bottom step, I lift her bags and begin to take the stairs two at a time. When I make it to the top, I look down to find her staring up at me from the bottom. Her hands are on her hips in an annoyed position, her lips pursed.

"You can come up here and choose which room you want, or I can choose for you. Make me wait too long and I'll choose the worst one."

Whatever she mutters under her breath, I don't catch it. Even though she's clearly annoyed, she does come up the stairs. Stopping in front of me, her eyes roam over the landing. Through the glass banister, you can see down to the lower floor. There's a sitting area up here. I couldn't begin to remember the last time someone actually sat there, but it looks nice.

She yanks her suitcase from my grasp, almost falling backward from the exertion. Looking me in the eye with an angry gleam in her own, she blows hair from her face. "This has to be one of the most expensive penthouses in Manhattan"—she rolls her eyes—"even the worst room here is a luxury compared to what us *common* people are used to."

Done with the conversation, or probably more likely done with *me*, Margo rolls her suitcase down the corridor, leaving me watching behind her.

She's not wrong, none of the rooms are bad. Whichever one she chooses, she'll be comfortable.

But none of them are the same room I sleep in. And for some reason I can't put my finger on, I'm a little bitter that we'll be sleeping on two different floors.

It seems too far.

Before I can think too deeply about what the hell she's doing to me, I leave her to pick out a room. I head back downstairs, leaving my shirt hanging open as I look through the refrigerator to find something to eat.

Nothing says *I'm sorry I almost kissed you* like a homemade meal.

I just have to decide if I'm sorry for almost kissing her, or if I'm sorry about not kissing her.

• • •

It takes me an hour to make a roasted chicken and vegetables. I plate it over a bed of rice and a special sauce that has impressed every person I've ever made it for.

Too bad Margo doesn't make another appearance.

After cooking for an hour, I figured she'd make her way

downstairs. She said she had brunch with her friends, and she ate on the plane, but she has to be hungry. I figured she'd at least want something small to eat. Apparently, she wants to avoid me more than I'd expected because after waiting at the table for forty minutes, I come to terms with the fact she isn't coming back down.

The nice thing would be to drop something off by her door, to apologize for whatever happened earlier. But I'm not nice. It's never been an adjective someone's used to describe me. So, I eat without her. I package up the leftovers and leave them in the fridge.

And then I work late into the night. I stay up much later than I intended, my mind too muddled with the thought of her sleeping upstairs to sleep peacefully.

13

Margo

No matter how much I want to, I can't avoid Beck forever.
Although, I do feel like I could stay cooped up in this
room forever and be satisfied if I had food. I almost thought
about choosing the smallest room up here just to prove a point to
Beck, but after thinking it through further, I realized he probably
didn't care what room I chose. Choosing the smallest one would
only end up biting me in the ass. He'd still have what I'm sure
is the best room downstairs, making no difference to him what
room I was in. After coming to the realization, I chose the largest
one up here.

It feels more like a room at a luxurious hotel than a guest
bedroom. I'm not complaining. The queen bed is larger than the
full one I was used to sleeping on. I don't know what the mattress
is made of, but it felt like sleeping on a cloud.

I should've slept perfectly.

I didn't.

Instead, I dreamed of the desire in Beck's stupid gorgeous but
cunning eyes. I dreamt about what his lips would feel like against
mine. I even thought of all the dirty things that could happen

on all the surfaces of his kitchen. As the sun peeks through the floor-to-ceiling windows of my bedroom, I turn into the mattress and groan. Where I should feel chipper and ready to experience New York again, all I feel is exhaustion and partially wound up.

My phone vibrates on the nightstand. Sighing, I push myself off the bed to grab it. The moment I swipe to answer, I can hear the familiar sound of my best friends arguing.

"Ask her if she boned Beckham." I'd know Emma's voice anywhere.

I also would recognize Winnie's sigh of disapproval anywhere. Emma and I constantly get it from her. "Emma!" Winnie scolds. "He's her boss. They can't sleep together."

"Shut up, they totally can and she totally should. Seeing that man in person, I'd honestly disown her as a friend if she didn't let him give her the ride of her life."

Smiling, I shake my head at both of them. It hasn't even been a day since I've seen the two people I'm closest with in the world and I already miss them terribly. "Good morning," I say.

It catches both of their attention, their arguing halting immediately. "Margie!" Winnie says excitedly, using a nickname she gave me the first time she ever smoked weed.

"Hi Win," I respond. I sit up in bed, pulling my knees to my chest and putting the phone on speaker.

"Did you hear everything we just said?" Winnie asks cautiously.

"You know she did," Emma pipes up. "I meant every word I said, Mar. You better be riding him like a pony the next time we see you. I want to hear all about how big his dick is."

I snort, fixing my tangled hair into a bun on the top of my head. "I'm his assistant, Em. Not his sex toy. There will be no riding his dick. Sorry to disappoint."

I don't have to be with Emma to know she's dramatically jutting her lip out in a puppy dog face. She's been using the face on us since we all met in college. It doesn't work like it used to, especially since I can't see her right now. "You're no fun," she drawls. "I'm having a dry spell and wanted to live vicariously through you."

There's silence, and then a gasp is heard from the other line. "Winnie!" Emma shrieks.

"What's going on?" I question.

"Winnie, you need to explain this text right now," Emma demands. There's rustling, a loud crack, and then the line goes dead.

I stare at my screen confused. "Hello?" No one answers. When I attempt to call Winnie again, it goes straight to voicemail. I try Emma's number, but it only rings before a voice comes over the line telling me that Emma's voicemail box is full.

"I'd like to think of myself as more of a stallion than a pony."

I yelp, almost jumping off the bed from learning I'm not alone.

"What the hell, Beck!" I shriek, throwing a pillow at him. He leans in the open doorway, completely unfazed by the feather pillow that hit him right in the abs.

Speaking of abs, I'm hit with the memory of seeing them on full display last night. I actually got to touch them, feel them tighten underneath my touch. It was hot as hell.

"I should be the one saying what the hell. Your friends referenced me as a pony." He takes a few steps into the room, leaving the door to the hallway open behind him.

It's only now that I'm struck with the realization that Beck is dressed casually. At least casual when it comes to Beck's standards.

He wears a pair of dark navy blue chinos, and a white-collared shirt with a sweater slipped over it. It's not the most casual thing a man could wear, but for Beck, it's basically like wearing a pair of baggy sweatpants and an old T-shirt.

"What are you doing here?" I ask, changing the subject. He stands in the entryway of my room dressed like he's about to go to Sunday brunch. Which I guess he might be. It actually is Sunday.

His eyes look over the space, almost like it's his first time seeing the room. Maybe it is. He made it seem like his room was downstairs. It's possible he never comes up here if there isn't any need to. When I'd taken a peek around upstairs last night, I found two other rooms, both smaller than the one I chose, and then an office space that had floor-to-ceiling bookshelves on two of the walls.

"You slept long enough. We have plans, and since you weren't going to wake up on your own, I had to become the alarm clock." He steps over my suitcase that I left on the ground, clothes spewing out in all directions as I'd angrily looked for a comfortable pair of pajamas last night. "Except, it turns out you didn't need an alarm clock. Your friends woke you up enough with references to my cock. Or excuse me, you *riding* my cock."

I fall back into fluffy pillows with a mortifying groan. One day I might actually kill Emma for that big mouth of hers. Even from the other side of the country her antics are getting me in trouble. Closing my eyes, I pull one of the pillows over my face. Maybe if I close my eyes hard enough and mutter some kind of prayer to the god of embarrassment or whatever, I'll be able to disappear into the mattress and never look Beck in the eye again.

"Oh, don't be shy," he muses, his voice a little closer than it'd been before. "It wasn't the worst thing to imagine."

I groan again, shaking my head erratically underneath the pillow. I'm going to blast every single one of Emma's embarrassing stories all over the internet. Even better, I'm going to paint a very detailed picture of the time she threw up all over the nice couple in front of us in Cabo. We'd all been entirely too hungover to go on an excursion, but we rallied and went anyway. At least, we attempted to rally. Emma ended up blowing chunks all over the twelve-passenger van—and its passengers—fifteen minutes into the ride.

I'm dreaming up all the other embarrassing stories I have on Emma to get back at her when I feel two warm hands over the top of mine. It makes me jolt. *What is he doing?*

"Margo," he says, his voice steady. He pulls on my fingers, trying to unlatch them from my tight grip on the pillow. I dig my fingertips into the pillow with all my might, clutching it so hard to my face that I can barely breathe.

"No," I snap, holding onto the pillow for dear life. I should've just looked Beck in the eye and told him there was no way I'd ever ride him. I could've made a disgusted face and cracked some kind of joke to make things way less awkward.

"Why are you hiding?" He grunts, pulling on the edge of the pillowcase to slide it from my grasp.

I clutch it like a lifeline. "Because I'm busy planning the demise of my best friend. Leave me to it." Unfortunately, Beck is relentless and much stronger than me. He pulls the pillow from my clutches with one easy tug.

I squeeze my eyes shut, feeling Beck's presence looming over me.

"Open your eyes," he demands. I feel the mattress dip slightly underneath my body. The asshole is making things worse by taking a seat and not disappearing.

"Go away." My arm reaches out in an attempt to push him off the bed. I squeeze my eyes so tightly that I have to feel around for him. My fingers brush up against what I think is his thigh. I'm feeling around when I feel his large hand on top of mine.

"Woah there, Violet." A low rumble of laughter comes from his chest. He gently guides my hand from what I think was the tip of him. Which would be wild because holy fuck if that was the tip of his dick, that thing is huge.

He's right. Definitely less pony and more stallion.

The realization of what he's packing between his thighs has my eyes popping open. He stares at me with a cocky smirk. My cheeks burn so hot with embarrassment that I do the only logical thing a hot-blooded woman can do when her ex's older, way hotter brother, who is her boss and about to be her fake fiancé, is looking at her like that. I shove him off the bed, throwing my entire body into the effort.

Maybe now he'll take the hint.

Except I throw too much of my body into it. Instead of Beck getting thrown off the bed while I stare at him triumphantly from the cozy mattress, the two of us both tumble to the ground.

Luckily, or somewhat unluckily depending on how you look at it, I end up landing directly on top of Beck. We hit the ground with a loud *thud*, despite the cushy rug underneath our bodies. My cheek presses into his hard chest. His hands gently press into my hips with just enough pressure to make sure I'm steady.

My hair creates a shield around me as I stare down at him, mortified.

He only fuels the embarrassment as he carefully pushes me off him, my butt connecting with the floor. Beck stands up gracefully, straightening out his outfit. He looks down at me.

His face is serious except for the slight raise of his eyebrows in amusement. "Trying to jump my bones?"

"Ew, no." Although judging by what I just felt, jumping his bones would probably be a great—maybe slightly painful—time.

Except it's Beck. This is Beckham Sinclair we're talking about. Why can't I stop thinking about his dick? Why am I wondering if it'd even fit inside me?

"The heated look in your eyes says otherwise," he states matter-of-factly.

I push myself off the ground, grunting at him in annoyance as I stand up.

Beck smirks, tilting his head in my direction. "Your perky nipples *especially* say otherwise."

Eyes widening, I look down at the evidence of the dirty thoughts I was just having of him.

"Traitors," I mutter, quickly folding my arms across my chest and pinning him with a bored look. "I have no idea what you're talking about." I lie through my teeth.

His returned smile lets me know he doesn't believe a damn word I'm saying. Instead of doing what I expect and further pointing out that clearly my nipples get annoyingly excited around him, he drops it.

Just as quickly as he swept into my room, he's heading back toward the exit. Stopping in the doorway, he taps the doorframe with his knuckle two times. His face almost looks pained as he looks over his shoulder. "Get ready. Fast."

"Why?"

"We have appointments to go shopping. I'll be waiting downstairs."

He doesn't leave any room for argument, or questions. He flies out of the room like his ass is on fire.

Two things I've learned in the last few minutes.

One, I think the impenetrable Beck just had a reaction to seeing my nipples hard after feeling him—and I liked it.

And two, apparently rich people need appointments to go shopping.

14

Beck

"Beck." Margo clutches onto my arm with caution in her tone. "I don't think I can go in there."

Her fingers dig into the fabric of my sweater as the two of us stand in front of the looming building. She looks at it like she's about to go to a haunted house or some kind of terrible doctor's appointment and not one of the best places to shop on Fifth Avenue—Bergdorf Goodman.

I pull our bodies out of the way of a zooming bicyclist before the two of us get taken out by a Lance Armstrong wannabe. I bite my tongue, resisting the urge to call out the asshole for riding on the sidewalk instead of on the road.

"It's just a store," I remind her, trying to pull her in the direction of the building. We're already five minutes late for the private personal shopping session I booked for her. Being late is not something I normally tolerate and somehow with her, I keep finding myself being tardy. It annoys me, but that frustration might be left over from our little encounter this morning. She barely brushed up against my cock, and I was hard as a rock.

She gives me a dirty look. "It's not just a store, this is the store for rich people—people with class. I don't belong in there."

I quirk an eyebrow. "Is this you saying you don't have class?"

Margo pulls her arm from mine, rolling her eyes at me. "I have class, just not *Saks* or *Bergdorf* kind of class. That's for people who grew up in boarding schools and whose families have summer and winter vacation homes." She looks over at me, a smile tugging at my lips. "People like *you*."

She's not wrong. I did all of my schooling before college at a boarding school. My family has a house in the Hamptons, in Vail and various other properties around the world. I grew up trailing my mother through the aisles of Bergdorf Goodman, wishing to be anywhere but there.

My hand runs over my chin, the slight scruff of facial hair scratching my palm. "Odd. I didn't know there were qualifications to step foot inside." We both focus on the large stone building. There are multiple floors to the store, each one housing a different department. And this is only the women's building. Across the street from us is the men's.

Margo takes a hesitant step back, causing my attention to move from the building to her. She rakes her hands down her body, seeming to point out her outfit. "The qualifications are that I look like I'm going shopping at Target." She pulls at the bottom of her oversized sweatshirt, the garment long enough to travel all the way down to her mid-thigh. The sweatshirt and leggings combination is paired with a pair of white sneakers. The shoes seem to at least be new, the white a stark contrast to the dirty sidewalk beneath her feet.

"Well, I told you we had a private shopping session with an associate."

"I thought that meant I wouldn't really be seeing anyone. Hence the word *private*. Now I'm going to have to walk into a store with a bunch of women who will probably think I'm some kind of fixer upper project for you or something like that."

She has a point, but it doesn't really matter. Yeah, Margo will probably get some weird looks, but deep down all of those people are most likely miserable inside and would've judged even if she came dressed accordingly. That's just what people at this level do. "Why does it matter what anyone else thinks?" I prod.

"It doesn't." She sighs, pushing her hair off her shoulders so it falls down her back. "But it should matter to *you*. These are your people. Shouldn't you be embarrassed or something to be seen with someone dressed like a *commoner*?" She says "commoner" sarcastically, her spunk returning despite her discomfort with her clothing of choice.

Turning so my back faces the building and I'm face-to-face with her, I pull on one string of the hoodie. "Something you need to learn real quick if you're going to survive here is that everyone else's opinion of you is bullshit. You can't give a damn what they think or you'll be miserable—*just* like them. It's why they'll stare at you a little too long. Why they'll turn their noses up at you and gossip to their uppity friends. They want to make you feel miserable because that's how they feel."

Her eyes soften slightly. She seems to be regaining her confidence, becoming unapologetically herself by the second.

"In reality, every single person in there that looks at you like you don't belong is just pissed because it takes them thousands in clothes, fancy makeup, hair stylists and cosmetic surgeons to look even half as beautiful as you do in a sweatshirt with a minimal amount of makeup on."

Taking a step backward, I grab her hand and pull us toward the building. We're no doubt close to ten minutes late at this point. If I were anyone else, they probably would've canceled my appointment and moved on to the next person for the day. The stylists make their money based on commission. Waiting around for customers is not the way they earn their paychecks.

My fingers grip hers until we reach the elevators. I press the button and immediately two doors pop open. I pull her inside, finally letting go as the doors close.

I turn to look at her, finding her already watching me carefully. Her eyes jump all over my face. Her lips part and close repeatedly, like she wants to say something but isn't.

"What?" I question, just now remembering to press the floor we need.

"Nothing," she mumbles as the elevator begins to rise.

"The look on your face makes it seem like it isn't nothing but rather *something* running through your mind."

Her eyes find the floor as she pretends to be really interested in her white shoes. "It's just that Beckham Sinclair, the *billionaire bachelor*"—she teases—"the guy who dates models, actresses and heiresses, called me beautiful." Her voice sounds whimsical, like she doesn't believe it happened, which can't be the case.

Margo is the kind of beautiful that doesn't go unnoticed. There's no way she doesn't realize it.

"I fail in comparison to your usual type," she continues. It's mildly irritating how she speaks of herself.

The elevator dings as the door opens. She takes a step forward, even though she has no idea where to go. Before she steps out of my reach, I grab her elbow, pulling her closer to me. The loose fabric of her sweatshirt sleeve bunches underneath my grip. Margo looks up at me, confusion in her eyes. I lean down, holding eye contact as I take a deep breath in.

"You could never fail in comparison to anyone, Margo."

15

Margo

His vibrant eyes bore into mine as he looks down at me. The air around us feels electrified. Or maybe it's the warm flush all over my body making it seem that way. When Beck's eyes flick to my lips, I know without a shadow of a doubt that I'd let him kiss me if he wanted to, no matter how angry I was with him after last night.

"Mr. Sinclair?" A voice comes from behind me.

Beck stares at my pursed lips for a few moments longer before he looks over my shoulder. The desire in his eyes burns out as quickly as it came. His features fix into business as usual. The moment dissipates into thin air.

Disappointment erupts in my chest.

"That's me," he answers, stepping around my body. Even though he no longer watches me, he does keep the moment somewhat alive by sliding his hand down my back until it rests at the small of my waist. His hand softly nudges me forward. My feet step forward on their own accord, my mind too busy wondering if I imagined Beck wanting to kiss me or not.

The woman waiting smiles wide at us. "Great." She pins her eyes on me, no hint of judgment in the way she looks at me, despite my lack of preparedness for shopping somewhere so posh. "And who do we have here?" Her tone is sweet, not condescending at all. I like her already. I love her style even more.

Beck removes his hand from my waist the same moment I take a step forward and hold my hand out to the woman. "I'm Margo," I answer.

Her hand is cold as she places it in mine and we shake hands. "Margo..."

"Just Margo." She's probably used to women who won't respond unless you call them ma'am or by their last name. I don't need that kind of formality. It seems weird and unnecessary.

She nods before hooking a thumb over her shoulder. "Well *just* Margo, I'm Quincy."

It doesn't shock me at all that she has a cool name like Quincy. It fits her incredibly well. "Let's get you back in the room and see what you think," she continues, taking a few steps back.

I look at Beck with a questioning stare. His only answer is to hold his arm out in front of him. "After you."

I have no idea what having a fancy shopping assistant entails, but I'm thrilled to find out. I'm already taking everything in as she leads us down a hallway with peach doors and tile floor that is a shade lighter in color.

Stopping in front of one of the doors she grabs the handle. I expect to find a tiny room behind her with a few outfits hanging up. What I see when she opens the door blows my expectations out of the water. "Welcome to our VIP suite," Quincy says, stepping into a room that can only be described as luxurious.

My eyes bounce around, not knowing what to take in first. There are a few different spaces in the large room, meant for multiple people to take advantage of the VIP suite at once. At the moment, the only people in the room are us. She walks to the very back, stopping at the largest staged dressing area in the lounge.

I stare at our reflections in a mirror that reaches from floor to ceiling. It has parts that come off the side, giving you the ability to try on an outfit and inspect it with a panoramic view. A velvet couch sits against another wall, the seat large enough to fit three or four bodies. Expensive looking pillows sit on each end of it. Beck takes a seat in the middle, looking somewhat out of place next to the glitzy, shimmery fabric of the pillows. A circular coffee table sits in front of it, expensive magazines stacked neatly on top. A few shoe boxes are laid out next to the magazines, the lids still on.

Quincy stops in front of a shiny clothing rack, running her hand over the various items hanging on it. "Mr. Sinclair here filled out a form on your outfit preferences, so I went ahead and picked out options according to what he filled out along with current style trends. I can always pull more after you try some outfits on. Sound good?"

I nod, too busy staring at Beck to use words to answer her. For some reason, I'm hooked on the fact Beck took the time last night to fill out the survey. I doubt he has any idea what my usual style is, but it's really the thought that counts.

"You did?" I ask, my voice tight, butterflies taking flight in my stomach.

Beck waves at the air dismissively. He pulls out his phone and looks down at the screen, not bothering to answer my question. He doesn't have to. The sentiment still matters either way, even if he doesn't want to bring any attention to it.

All three of us are silent for a few beats. Eventually, Quincy claps her hands together before pulling a few pieces off the clothing rack. "Let's try some things on!"

I risk one more glance at Beck, but he's too interested in his phone to pay me any attention. Quincy hands over an outfit, an encouraging smile on her face. She points to a large door to the left of the couch Beck sits on. "If you want to change in there and once you have it on, we can talk about the fit and what you like and don't like about it."

"Got it." I take a step into the room and shut the door. Even the dressing room is way more extravagant than necessary. There's another large mirror in the space, a velvet rose gold chair and an end table with business cards and bottles of water. I hook the hangers over a hook on the wall, taking in what Quincy picked out for me to try on first. A small blush creeps up my neck when I notice the set of lingerie hanging from another hook on the wall. I pull at the tag on the bra, shocked to find the bra is my exact size. I'll have to remember to thank Quincy for the thought. My old sports bra and brief cut underwear probably weren't the best choices of undergarments for the day. In my defense, when Beck told me we had a personal shopping appointment, I thought someone would just walk through the store with me and help me choose outfits. I didn't think about someone else picking them out for me and having to try them on.

The bra and thong of choice by Quincy will pair better with trying things on than my choices this morning. My only problem is if I put the lingerie on, especially the thong, I feel like I've got to take it home. Shrugging, I pull the tags off the nude lace fabric. Quincy does this all the time. It must be the thing to do here.

It doesn't take me long to strip out of my leggings and sweatshirt. Once my bra and underwear are off as well, I fold them neatly and stuff them into the very bottom of my purse. Next, I hook my arms through the bra and fasten it on my back, marveling at the way it fits my breasts perfectly. It's extremely comfortable, but still manages to give them a good lift. I step through each side of the thong, pulling it up my hips and arranging each side above my hip bones. Despite the high cut of the fabric, it's extremely comfortable. The thin fabric makes it so there are no panty lines.

I take a step closer to the clothes hanging on the wall, inspecting the outfit Quincy had picked out for me. The gray sweater dress looks incredibly comfortable but also chic enough to wear to work.

Now that it's October, the fall chill is in the air here in New York, something I'm thrilled about. I never loved that California didn't have four seasons. I love seeing leaves change on the trees in Central Park, the air smelling different when summer rolls into fall. Even though it annoys most people, there's something special about bundling up in the frigid cold of January here. I love wrapping an enormous scarf around my neck and attempting to cover every inch of my bare skin. It's then exciting when the bite of winter disappears and flowers begin to bloom. I hadn't realized how much I craved experiencing every season until I was left with really only having one in California.

I gently remove the sweater dress from the hanger, marveling at the buttery soft feel of the fabric. It slips onto my body effortlessly, embracing me in a luxurious fabric I'd wear every day of my life if I could.

Stepping in front of the mirror inside the room, I take in my appearance. Not only am I in love with the feel of the dress on my body, I'm obsessed with the way it fits me. I run my hands over the fabric, smoothing it out. It stops at my mid-thigh. A pair of sheer black tights would make it appropriate to wear to the office as Beck's assistant, but I could easily dress it down by not wearing tights and instead wearing a pair of thigh-high boots. I grab the black leather jacket off the hook and shrug it on, loving the way the outfit transforms with the addition of the leather jacket.

As if she's a mind reader, there's a knock on the door followed by Quincy's voice. "I've got a pair of boots for you to try on. Mr. Sinclair took a guess on the shoe size."

Opening the door, I find her holding up exactly what I envisioned pairing the dress with if I was dressing it down. I grab them, thanking her and shutting the door again. Taking a seat, I slip each one on. I pull them all the way up my leg until there's only a small amount of skin showing between the top of the boot and the bottom of my dress. There are laces on the back of the boots that fall to mid-calf.

The boots are a perfect fit. I have no idea how Beck knew the things he did, but by the first outfit and the way it fits, he didn't do badly at all when he filled out the information for the appointment.

Instead of looking in the mirror in the small room, I open the door and step into the larger area where both Beck and Quincy wait. Quincy stands next to the mirror, beaming as I take a step onto the platform and do a small twirl.

"That looks stunning," she notes, making eye contact through the mirror. "What do you think? Do you love it or did I miss the mark?"

I stick a leg out, taking in the complete outfit in the mirror. "You didn't miss the mark at all. I love the look of it. Totally my style. And everything fits perfectly."

Quincy looks in Beck's direction. "Well, I had some help." I follow her gaze to Beck. I hate the twinge of disappointment when I find him paying close attention to his phone.

I watch him for a few seconds longer, willing him to look at me. For some inexplicable reason, I want him to look me up and down. I want him to look at the small amount of thigh showing and have him wonder what it'd feel like underneath his touch. I want to observe his every reaction as he takes in the way the dress clings to my back, showing off my curves in a way that leaves little to the imagination.

All the willpower in the world doesn't get him to look at me. Eventually, I turn around and return Quincy's smile despite the feeling of disappointment I feel in my stomach.

"I'm in love," I confirm, spinning all the way around on the platform and letting out a small giggle.

"Perfect," Quincy notes, returning to the rack full of clothes. "Let's see what else I can get you to fall in love with."

16

Beck

Margo's beauty is as equally captivating as it is frustrating. As Quincy fusses over one of the many outfits she's tried on, I continue to pretend to focus on my phone. Sitting in this dressing room as Margo plays dress up is the last thing I should be doing right now. I've got a never-ending to-do list thanks to my impromptu urge to drop everything and fly to California to finally convince Margo to hear me out and agree to my offer. After coming home last night and using today to get her situated instead of working, there's a list a mile long of shit I need to get done.

I could've easily sent Margo to do this alone. At first, that'd been exactly the plan. I was going to have Ezra drop me off at the office before he dropped her off on Fifth Avenue to buy whatever she wanted. Last minute I frustratingly changed the plan, deciding to come with her as opposed to getting work done.

"I don't think I've disliked a single thing you picked out," Margo tells Quincy. From the corner of my eye, I see her turn to look at herself from all angles in the mirror.

"I'm happy to hear that. I need to do another sweep to bring in some more options for you. Any requests while I go look?"

Margo stops spinning. I can feel her watching me from the mirror, but I fight the urge to look up and meet her eyes. I'm still dwelling on the moment from earlier and the stark realization that I wanted to ravish the mouth of my little brother's ex-girlfriend.

If Quincy hadn't shown up, I would've done it. I wouldn't have been able to stop myself. Margo's mouth looked so kissable. I wanted to turn her lips a different color with the assault of my mouth against hers. I wanted to witness the tan skin around her mouth turn pink from the crash of our lips. I wanted it so badly that I was going to take it without any thought of the repercussions or thoughts on the so-called terms she'd laid out.

The jury's still out if Quincy showing up was a blessing or a curse. But one thing's for sure, the thought of Margo stripping her clothing behind the door to my left has distracted me way more than I care to admit. It's taken everything in me to not demand Quincy leave so I could follow Margo into the room, shut the door and finish what we started in the elevator.

The memory of my heart pounding against my chest when I'd come to the realization I wanted to kiss the woman who was my assistant and my soon-to-be fake fiancée has me devoting my time to answering emails on my phone. It's the only thing keeping myself in check.

Apparently, I've missed bits and pieces of a conversation between Margo and Quincy. When I get out of my head, I find Quincy standing at the door to the VIP suite. The look on my face must look confused enough that she feels the need to explain. "I'm going to go pick out a few more casual"—she winks at Margo—"outfits. As well as a few more pieces that can be dressed up and down."

I give a quick nod, my pulse thumping at the idea of being left alone in here with the woman who's taking up way too much of my headspace.

By the time I look away from Quincy, Margo has stepped back into the private dressing room.

I sigh, running a hand down my face as I do everything in my power to keep myself planted on this couch. My intentions weren't entirely pure when I decided to offer Margo the fake fiancée agreement. But I hadn't had the intention of allowing myself to kiss her quite yet. The thought alone makes everything more complicated than what it's supposed to be. It doesn't change the fact that I ache to do it, consequences be damned.

The fact is that after watching Margo watch me in eager anticipation, her heavy breaths confirming she wants to kiss me as badly as I want to kiss her, I can't think of anything else.

My phone vibrates, a fortunate distraction, as my eyes watch the door she stands behind. My pulse runs rampant at the thought of her undressing behind the door. I can't help but mentally picture what she hides underneath her clothes. I want to study every inch of her bare skin, paying close enough attention to every inch the same way she does before she sketches someone.

An aggravated growl involuntarily falls from my lips as my cock hardens in my pants.

Get it the hell together.

The truth is, no other woman has captivated me the way she does. I don't know if it's the knowledge that she and I are going to pretend to be in love that has me losing grip on the situation or if it's something else entirely.

I'm having a battle of willpower with myself when Margo speaks up from behind the closed door. "Uh, Beck?" she asks, her voice hesitant.

I look up from my phone to the door. "Yes?"

"I think I need your help."

"What is it?"

"My zipper. It's stuck and I can't get it."

"I'm sure you can figure it out," I say harshly.

She lets out a groan. "I can barely reach. I don't think I can get out of this on my own."

My eyes rush to the door to the suite. Maybe Quincy will return any minute and come to Margo's rescue. Except deep down, I know better. When she left, she made it seem like she may take some time. She even left the menu for the cafe on another floor for us to call in food if we needed.

Quincy wasn't coming back any time in the immediate future. Which is bad for Margo, who needs help, but terrible for me because the knowledge of knowing we're alone for the time being is catastrophic.

"Try a little harder," I demand. It's a last-ditch effort to keep a leash on myself.

Margo's aggravated moan only fuels the growing erection in my pants. "I've tried, Beck," she whines. "I can't get it, and it feels too tight, and I just need your help before I accidentally rip a piece of fabric that probably costs more than my entire wardrobe, okay?"

"Fine," I bark, a little too harshly. It's not Margo's fault that I'm suddenly desperate for her. Maybe it isn't so sudden and it actually is her fault. She's just completely unaware of the matter.

A string of curses falls from my lips as I open the door and find her facing me. There's panic in her eyes as her hands bend behind her back, fussing with what I'm assuming is the stuck zipper.

I take a step in, shutting the door behind me. My eyes roam over her body, unable to look anywhere else than the short, figure-hugging dress draped over her body.

"A little help here?" Margo turns so her back faces me. She watches me through the mirror, her fingers still clasping the zipper.

"I thought the point of today was to find you work attire. You can't wear this into the office."

Her hair gets in the way of the zipper as she shakes her head at me. She takes a step backward, her arms falling to her sides. Her spine straightens as I sweep her long hair to the side. I barely brush over her bare skin and it's enough to have me clenching my jaw.

"I wasn't planning on wearing this to work," she whispers.

I ignore her, my knuckles skimming her back as my fingers grab onto the zipper. She only managed to lower it an inch or two from the top of the dress before extra fabric got stuck in the teeth. I give the zipper a tug, pulling her body slightly closer to me with the force.

Her ass brushes against my front, making me suck in a breath. I was already holding on by a loose thread. I'm seconds away from losing it and ripping this pathetic excuse of a dress down the middle and crashing my lips against hers. It'd be the best kind of mistake to kiss her until both our heads are spinning.

"I really wasn't," she continues. I yank again on the zipper, trying to get the small amount of silk stuck in it out. It doesn't work. Her little yelp about does me in.

"If you say so," I speak through clenched teeth. I'm aggravated with myself because I've never been someone who loses control easily. It's hard for me to give it up, and here I am unable to control myself in her presence.

I'm mostly pissed off that I'm not already kissing her by now.

I look up from trying to get the zipper undone, finding her watching me closely. Her cheeks have a perfect flush to them. Her deep inhales and exhales confirm that she feels the same things I'm feeling.

"Stop looking at me like that," I snap, looking back at the zipper. I pull on it again, but it won't budge. However she managed to get the fabric caught, it's going to be harder than I was expecting to get her out of it. If she hadn't put something on that was so perfectly molded to her body, we'd easily be able to slip it over her head and get it off that way.

"How am I looking at you?" She takes a tiny step backward, pressing herself against me even more, even though it isn't necessary.

"You're looking at me like you want to be—*need* to be—kissed," I declare. The hand not holding the zipper slides slightly down her waist, gripping the fabric at her hip.

"And what if I do?"

My fingertips dig into her hip, bringing her body flush against mine. "Don't say things you don't mean," I warn, leaning in so my lips flutter against the tender skin of her neck.

"I'd never." Her small hips grind against me, snapping whatever resolve I had left.

17

Margo

Beck forcefully grabs me by the hips, spinning me to face him before I can do it myself. The sudden movement gives me no choice but to grab his forearms to steady myself. He guides our bodies across the small room, pressing my body against the mirror. It's cold against the exposed flesh, but it makes no difference to me. I'd stand in the coldest of places to have Beck looking at me like he wants to devour every inch of me.

His hands move from my waist to my neck. He isn't gentle as he pulls my face closer to him. There's a slight pain in my jaw where he grips me so tight, as if he's afraid if he were to let go that the moment would end.

My mouth parts with the brush of a thumb across my lips. He runs it across over and over, making my knees weak in anticipation of kissing him. "Violet," he rasps, eyes focused on his thumb.

"Why do you call me that? It isn't my name."

He pulls at my bottom lip. "It is to me."

"Why?" I grab at his sweater, attempting to pull him closer so he'll just kiss me already.

His penetrating indigo gaze finally moves from my lips. He makes eye contact with me briefly before he grabs a lock of my hair.

"Your hair," he explains, holding it between us. "You had purple streaks in it that summer. They were the perfect shade of violet. It's the first thing I ever thought when my brother brought you home."

"What was the second?"

"That I fucking hated the way my brother knew how you tasted when I didn't."

"Maybe it's time you find out." My breath comes in spurts, my heart threatening to beat right out of my chest.

"About fucking time."

Whatever answer I could give is taken away by the press of his lips against mine. I'd much rather this response anyway. Beck cups my face in his palms, his thumbs pressing into my cheeks as he kisses me with expertise.

First kisses are usually awkward and without rhythm. That isn't the case with Beck. There's the excitement of kissing for the first time but also familiarity with the pace. Our bodies knowing exactly how to kiss without ever having done it with each other before.

His tongue fights against the seam of my lips, determined to get inside. I open willingly, savoring every last second of the kiss. It's wild to witness Beck come unhinged like this, to feel him lose himself in kissing me. It's much more than a kiss, it's as if he's marking me. His body is hard against mine, forcing me even deeper against the mirror. The glass is cold, his body warm. The soft curves of my body press into the hard slopes and planes of his. If I didn't grip his sweater so tightly, I'd melt into a puddle at his feet. Even if I didn't hold onto the fabric like my life depended on it, the tight hold as he cups my face might be enough to keep me on my feet.

"Margo" he mutters, his voice strained as he bites my bottom lip between his teeth. "Fuck," he groans out, searing his lips to mine, tongue swiping against them. "If your lips taste this delectable, I can only imagine how phenomenal other parts of you taste."

My thighs clench together at his words. I'd do anything to have him taste me anywhere and everywhere he desired. "If your tongue is that good in my mouth, I can only imagine how good it is at other things."

I feel his growl against my lips as he traps my mouth with his again. His palms drop from my face, inching up the bare skin of my thighs instead. I hate that I wasted time ever kissing anyone else. None of them knew how to kiss the way he does. He does it with haste, but such expertise, that I could get lost in doing it forever.

His fingers play with the hem of the dangerously small minidress. He slides them underneath the fabric, reaching up to palm my ass. The fabric now bunches against my waist. If the zipper wasn't still stuck, we'd easily be able to get it off and I could feel his mouth press against other parts of me.

"Violet," he says, breaking the kiss, his fingers still kneading my ass.

"Hm?" I answer, my body in a trance from kissing him. Later on, I'll dwell on the nickname, obsessing over the fact he gave me one in the first place. I've never loved a nickname as much as the one he's penned for me. Furthermore, the meaning behind it will be stuck in my mind for weeks to come.

"There's not a chance in hell you're ever wearing this in public." Goosebumps appear all over my skin from the heat of his gaze as they travel over my body.

I open my mouth to respond when a knock from outside the door has both of us jumping.

"I'm back with a few items for you to test. I'll need to go to another floor to find some more casual options," Quincy says, completely unaware of the state she's found Beck and I in.

Beck smirks, leaning into place kisses against my neck. He licks and then bites softly as I do everything in my power not to moan.

"Okay," I answer, my tone unusually breathy.

"Where did Mr. Sinclair go?" The sound of hangers scraping against the rod fills the silence.

I have to bite my lip when Beck teases me by running his fingertips over the inside of my thigh. I give him a look, begging him to stop before Quincy catches us like this.

My panic only seems to fuel him further. I didn't expect to see this commanding yet playful side of him as he shakes his head, not hiding his sly smirk.

"He uh," I moan when his lips kiss the top of my breast. The silk corset top of the mini dress pushes my boobs almost all the way to my chin, the delicate flesh almost billowing over the top of the fabric. "Had to step out and take a call," I lie. The scrape of his teeth against the tender skin has heat pooling between my legs. The thong Quincy left in here must be soaked from the unexpected encounter with him.

Quincy clicks her tongue. "Odd. I didn't see him out there."

A blond eyebrow quirks as Beck calls me out for lying. I don't know what else he expects from me. Quincy doesn't need to know that he has me all hot and bothered in the expensive dress she picked out for me.

"Yeah, *odd*," I respond. Beck mocks me by mouthing my words back, leaning in to kiss me once again.

"I'll be back in a few," Quincy answers, as she must finally get all the new items she's brought in hung up.

"Sounds good," I chirp, letting out a sigh of relief a few moments later when it's silent on the side of the door.

Beck takes a step back, heat still in his blue eyes. "Maybe it's time we figure out how to get that dress off you."

All I can do is turn around, moving my hair to give him access once again.

When I meet his eyes in the mirror all over again, it feels so much more different, and complicated.

I haven't even started as his assistant and we've already broken the terms I've laid out.

18

Beck

Ezra gives me an unreadable look as he finishes loading the last of Margo's things into the trunk of our city car. All of the bags almost didn't fit, they wouldn't have if some of the items purchased today were actually in stock instead of being delivered at a later date.

Margo and I drifted from one store to the next, establishing an entirely new wardrobe for her. She stands next to me, anxiously messing with the sleeve of her sweatshirt she insisted on wearing out of the store despite the tens of thousands of dollars of new clothes I just bought her.

"I'll never be able to repay you for this," she says softly, looking at the pile of bags and boxes in the back with regret.

I angle my body toward hers, my fingers twitching at my sides to reach out and touch her. In fact, ever since I got to taste and touch her in that dressing room, I haven't been able to think of anything else. Which is unfortunate, because I can't be intimate with her in public. Not yet. Ezra no doubt has questions about Margo's sudden appearance in my life, but it wouldn't be preferable even if he were to see us pretend to be anything but boss and assistant for a little longer. For us to keep up the charade, people must first believe us to have had some sort of professional relationship before announcing to everyone that things turned serious.

"I'd be livid if you ever tried to repay me for it," I reply. She chews on her bottom lip, clearly not getting any reprieve from my words.

"It just feels weird for you to buy me all of that. Some of that stuff was so expensive."

I shake my head at her. "The price doesn't matter. I've got enough money to go around, trust me."

She tucks her hands into the large pocket on the front of her sweatshirt. "Well, I tried choosing the less expensive things, but it's hard when most items don't have their price even listed. What's the point of that, anyway?"

I watch Ezra close the trunk. He nods at me, cueing me that we're good to go. He steps around us and opens the rear passenger door even though neither one of us steps to get in. "Most people shopping there don't necessarily care about the price," I offer. It feels weird coming out of my mouth. She does have a bit of a point.

I turn to slide into the backseat of the car, but she stops me by grabbing my sleeve. My head turns, watching her curiously wondering what she wants to add. Taking a deep breath, she watches Ezra get into the car before she focuses on me once again. "I just wanted to say thank you. Really, *truly*," she emphasizes. "No one has ever done that much for me, and I know it's because you have to be seen with me at work and don't want to be embarrassed by my clothes, but it still means a lot. I would've been fine just getting clothes at Target or wherever."

My lip twitches in amusement. "Yeah, but are Target dressing rooms so...*fun*?"

Her eyes get wide. The slight chill in the air isn't what's causing the tinge of pink spreading over her cheeks.

I leave her with a smile, hoping she's replaying our kiss in her head like I've been doing all morning. My body glides over the leather seat as I climb in the back of the city car. It takes a few moments before Margo follows suit, a dazed look still on her face.

She's silent the entirety of the car ride. Not that I had time to talk with her much, anyway. My phone rang with constant calls, people needing me nonstop.

Margo looks confused when Ezra pulls up to a large building, the top of the sky-rise building appearing to kiss the clouds all the way from the bottom.

"Where are we?" she asks, looking through the window.

I tap her thigh with my knuckles moments after Ezra opens the door. "We're looking at your new office, Violet. Scoot. I'll give you a tour of the place."

Her eyes go wide in horror as she looks down at her body. "You didn't tell me we were going into work!" she hisses, pulling on her baggy sweatshirt. "I would've worn one of the countless new outfits if I knew someone would see me."

The panic in her voice is quite obvious—and totally adorable. I give her leg another shove. "Go, Margo, it's fine."

She shakes her head furiously, looking at Ezra with an apologetic look. "I'm not going in there looking like this," she demands. Her body settles deeper into the seat. The tantrum reminds me of a toddler, but she does it way cuter.

"Margo," I warn, sliding into her space and getting her body to move an inch just by pressing my thigh against hers. "You can get out of the car or I can make you. I can't get out on my side without risking a crazy New York driver ramming into me, so I cannot get out until you do. *Sooo*, get out."

Her fingernails attempt to dig into the leather to keep herself planted.

"I can't have the first time all of my coworkers see me be in an old NYU sweatshirt."

Ezra and I share a look of humor. I shrug. "Why? Are you scared they'll think you're a tourist?"

She scoffs. "I bought this on campus when I attended there, thank you very much."

I push my hips into her harder, making her body move a few more inches until she's basically hanging off the side of the seat. People walking by give us curious looks, but none of them stop to say anything. The fact that some people have even noticed us is shocking enough in a city so busy.

"No one is going to see you," I reassure her.

"You don't know that," she argues.

I tilt my head back and forth, pressing my lips into a thin line. "Actually, I do. I've made it an unspoken company policy that no one is supposed to come into work on Sundays or holidays. Work-life balance and all."

My words seem to take her off guard. Her head swings my way in shock. "You did?" This disbelief in her voice should offend me.

I nod, nudging her until she finally obeys and climbs out of the car. At the last minute, she almost trips over the curb. Ezra and I both reach out to catch her at the same time.

Once she's steady on her feet, I finish climbing out of the car, Ezra closing the door behind me. "Typically the only person ever there on the weekends is me. I promise you."

Her teeth dig into her lip like she has something else to say, but at least for the time being, she keeps it to herself.

No longer putting up a fight, she tilts her head up to look at the building towering over us. "You own this?"

I chuckle, laying my hand on her mid-back to guide her toward the entrance. "No, we rent the top seven floors."

We leave Ezra back at the car as we walk to the revolving door entrance of the building. Stepping inside, I give Tom a friendly smile as he sits at his desk, looking to be enjoying a calm Sunday here. On a weekday, this floor would be packed full of people coming and going. We share the building with some very well-known companies and law firms. This floor is usually full of people going about their business during and after normal working hours. I've learned over the years that Sunday is the safest day to come into work if I want to be around the least amount of people possible. I'll still share the elevator with the occasional person or small group, but it's nothing like the typical work days where it takes ten minutes just to catch an elevator.

Any other day I'd walk right past Tom, scanning my badge as I walked through the metal detector, but today I bring Margo and I to a stop in front of it.

"Good afternoon, Tom." We share a familiar smile. It's hard not to return his smile. We've developed an unlikely friendship, even though he's old enough to be my father. You'd never know his age because his jokes and spunk remind me more of an eighteen-year-old frat guy. Plus, not being a prick to him like some of the other people who pass through these doors every morning gets me some VIP perks. For example, sometimes he gestures for me to take the employee stairs so I can climb to the second or third floor and catch an elevator that way instead of waiting in line in the lobby.

Tom gives me a knowing smile before he pins his attention whole-heartedly on Margo. I don't blame him. Even in an old college sweatshirt, her beauty captures anyone's attention. "Mornin' Mr. Sinclair." His voice is gravelly. My guess is from his fondness of getting home from work and smoking a cigar. I've given him a few rare cigars over the years, grateful for his familiar smile even when I come into work a brooding dick because some new investor has pissed me off or someone thinks they can take advantage of me.

He gives Margo a wink. "And who is this nice young lady you've brought in this morning?"

Margo beams at him, no doubt making Tom's bad heart beat faster than it's supposed to. "I'm Margo," she answers, reaching across the desk to shake his hand. "Margo Moretti," she finishes.

Tom looks a little shocked that she's holding her hand out to him, giving him her full attention. He's used to the pricks and uptight women who work here. None of them spare him a second glance, let alone take the time to shake his hand.

He takes it, his calloused hand enveloping hers. "I'm Tom. Tom Banks." She stares at him in wonder. If it were anyone but Tom, I'd feel a tad jealous at the huge smile Margo aims in his direction. I do know that Tom has been married for thirty years, and the only thing he loves more than this job are his wife, children, and herd of grandchildren.

Margo laughs. The sound thaws my black frozen heart a little. It wouldn't take much for me to get used to the sound. "Tom Banks? Like Tom Hanks but with a *B*."

He smiles at her triumphantly, eating up the fact that she finds him funny. "Sure is. Except I'm much more handsome."

"Well, obviously," she responds, propping her elbows on the counter of his desk.

I clear my throat, moving an inch closer to her. "Miss Moretti is my new assistant. Could you add her to the system for me and get her a badge? Most mornings she should be coming into work with me, but on occasion she'll be coming in alone, and she'll need the clearance so she doesn't have to get a visitor pass."

"Sure thing." He's quick at printing off a piece of paper, clipping it onto a clipboard and handing it to Margo. "If you could just fill out all of this information for me. Do you have a driver's license?"

"I do actually," she answers, pulling out her license and handing it to him. Margo gets busy filling out the form as Tom works at getting her license scanned in. Most people here don't have a license. I keep mine updated for when I travel, but I rarely ever drive. Most of the time Ezra drives or I'll walk if it's close enough.

Tom finishes up and places her license in front of her. He gives me a questioning glance. "If you don't mind me asking, what happened to Polly, Mr. Sinclair?"

"You wondering if you'll no longer be getting your homemade sourdough every Monday morning?" I tease.

Tom looks a little embarrassed as he shakes his head at me. "She's always been kind to me. I just wanted to check in on her."

I stop giving him shit. While I'm sure he does enjoy the homemade bread from Polly, I know I do, his intentions do seem pure in asking her status.

Margo hands the clipboard back to him as I take a breath before speaking. "Polly is still my executive assistant, but as she ages, I don't want to make her travel with me like she used to. She'll be handling my affairs here while Margo will be traveling with me and assisting me in other ways. Like getting my coffee."

She narrows her eyes at me, trying to get a read on if I'm serious or not. I'm still deciding what tasks I'm going to have her do when we're not traveling.

"Glad to hear it," Tom mutters and focuses on his computer screen as he fills Margo's information into the computer.

"We'll see if Mr. Sinclair here will trust me getting his coffee or not."

I lift my eyebrows. "And why's that?"

She shrugs, a taunting smile forming on her lips. "I'm known to be a bit clumsy and absent-minded. I would hate to mess up or even spill your fancy coffee order."

"Hot Americano, no cream with two sugars," I deadpan.

"I pegged you for an oat milk in the coffee kind of guy," she teases.

My tongue clicks. "Says the girl who betrayed New York and moved to the West Coast. Tell me, Margo, what's your order?" I hold a finger in the air, stopping her from answering me. "No, wait, let me guess. An iced lavender oat milk latte."

She bites her lip, a small frown appearing on her perfect lips.

I smirk, grabbing the badge Tom just made Margo and holding it in the air between us. "Am I right?"

Rolling her eyes, she plucks the card from my grip. "It's a generic coffee order," she gripes.

Margo mutters a quick goodbye to Tom before she steps away, clearly annoyed with how I got her coffee order correct. I've got a stellar memory. It's annoyingly perfect. I have the inability to forget almost anything. Therefore, I remember her order from her trip to the Hamptons to meet my family.

Tom beams, watching Margo stop in the middle of the lobby. She pulls out her phone, giving herself some kind of distraction. "She seems like one that'll give you a run for your money, Mr. Sinclair," he notes.

I look away from Margo to look at him. I nod my head. "You're probably right, Tom."

He whistles. "I like her already."

Me too. The problem is, it's maybe a little too much.

19

Margo

"I can't believe this is the view you have from your office." I marvel at the city below us. "You can see everything. It's stunning."

My nose presses to the cold glass as I can't get enough of the breathtaking view below me. I've always been in love with New York. My heart belonged here the moment I first visited for a college tour. One of the saddest days of my life was when I packed up my things and moved to LA. I was meant to be in the hustle and bustle of the city. But at the time, I thought I'd made the right choice.

"The view from here is spectacular," he agrees, his voice coming from behind me. I hear him take a step in my direction, but I don't turn around to face him. I'm too busy looking at the only place I ever want to call home.

It's funny how things worked out. Never could I have imagined that the reason I returned to New York would be because of Beckham Sinclair.

I feel his presence next to me without even looking over. Even from the time we met in the Hamptons, I've always been oddly aware of him. It was like we knew, or at least understood, each other—and with barely ever speaking. I think back to the night he found me drawing on the beach, using only the moonlight to fuel my sketches.

We hadn't even exchanged many words that evening. I could smell the alcohol on his breath as he leaned over my shoulder, inspecting what I'd been sketching. Somehow under the glint of the moonlight and his smell engulfing me, I hadn't been embarrassed about what he'd found—*who* he'd found.

His shoulder brushes against mine. "What are you thinking about?"

I longingly look at the city for a few more moments. I'll do anything to stay here, to find a way to get Winnie and Emma to move back here and make this our home all over again. LA was kind of like a sellout. And now that I'm back, I'll do whatever it takes to stay here. To be one of the many calling New York home. Part of me aches to know the stories of the people below. When I was in college and had days where I wasn't busy, I loved to sit in bustling coffee shops and at outdoor cafes and just sketch the people around me. Sometimes I'd create a whole life for them in my head. Instead of drawing them sipping coffee in a booth, I'd draw them somewhere exotic, somewhere mundane, different scenarios for different people depending on the story I felt was right for them.

"Margo?" Beck's knuckle brushes over my cheek.

When my eyes find his, I can't hide the sadness in them. "I never want to leave here again," I admit. It's weird how a city you didn't grow up in, one you only spent a few years living in, can feel like home.

His eyebrows furrow. "Then don't," he offers hoarsely, letting his knuckle brush ever so slightly over my bottom lip before he stuffs his hand into his pocket.

Breaking eye contact, I look around at his giant private office. I'm interested to see him here at work, doing his thing. Does he spend a lot of time in here or is he more hands-on? Are most of his minutes spent in meetings in the lavish conference room we walked by on our way in? I have so many questions. So many things I want to find out.

I take a deep breath in, inhaling the scent of him. "It's not that easy. What if things don't work out? What if I can't find a job here after, you know, our...deal? God, it'd be a shame to move back to California after being back."

"Why?"

"Because being back is just a reminder of how much I belong here."

"You don't have to go back if you don't want to. Even after all this is said and done, you deserve to be wherever makes you happy."

I study him for a few moments. It's still surreal that all of this is happening. Not only am I now working for *the* Beckham Sinclair, but soon I'll be his fiancée. Everyone but the two of us will think that he's fallen for me, and I him. It wouldn't be so bad to pretend forever with him, but there'd always be the hope that it could be more.

It's why I can't kiss him ever again. At least not like we did last time. A show for others is acceptable, but when it's just us two, I can't handle kissing him and knowing it's all fake. One big lie.

"That's the thing," I begin, holding his eyes. "I want to do anything possible to stay. I want that interview with Camden. I want to show him my art and prove myself. I want it more than anything else. That's why I don't want to jeopardize this deal we have by kissing you again."

He nods slowly, not giving me any inkling of his feelings on the matter. "What does kissing me have to do with Camden, exactly?" If I didn't know any better, I'd say there was a hint of jealousy in his tone.

"It's just that when you kissed me today, lines got blurred in my head. It didn't feel fake. It didn't feel like it was for show to clean up your image and for me to get the job I've always wanted. It felt real even when I knew it wasn't, and I don't need that right now."

Beck clears his throat like he's about to speak, but I beat him to the punch. "Look, it's embarrassing to admit this, but your brother really screwed me up. I just don't know if I can handle knowing when it is and isn't for show."

His hand clenches at his side, the veins on the top of it becoming more defined. "You and I were both there earlier this morning, Margo. That wasn't for show, and I'm offended if that's what you've made it out to be."

Beck towers over me as he brings himself toe to toe with me. His indigo irises darken with anger, a storm forming in them. I don't know how to respond to him, or what his answer even means. Is this him admitting that it's real? He's already fucked with my head so much, and my first official work day isn't even until tomorrow.

The look in his eyes makes me wonder if we've both messed with each other's heads. Maybe the fake gig won't work as well as we once thought.

"Tell me not to kiss you again and I won't. But don't make that moment less than what it was. I've thought about it all god damn day. It wasn't a fucking show, and you know damn well it wasn't."

He leaves me all alone in his office, but he doesn't go far.

Flicking on the lights of a conference room, he sits down and spends the next hour on a phone call.

Maybe him ignoring me as I take in this office space is him punishing me. Or maybe he knows that I could stare out the window of his office all day if I could, the sight having to be one of the best in the city.

Either way, neither of us speak for the duration of our time out and about. In fact, we don't even speak when we make it back to the penthouse.

20

Beck

I probably could've handled our conversation at the office better. The issue was, I'd been offended she dismissed the kiss so easily. That she thought so low of me. How could she think I'd kiss her in private for the sake of anyone else? Sure, if people thought we were engaged and we were at an event or something I'd give her a chaste kiss to make this arrangement more believable.

But this morning, in that dressing room, the only person I kissed her for was myself. I thought about kissing her in bed into the early morning the night before and I thought about it the entire morning while shopping before it happened.

I kissed her because the thought of not kissing her made me feel empty inside.

I should've known better. She wasn't ready. She'd said as much when she laid out her terms when agreeing to becoming my assistant and then fiancée. I'd just been too blinded by my primal want for her, and by the way she basically dared me to kiss her, there was no stopping myself.

By the time I actually cared to apologize to her for how I

acted, it was too late. I could tell she was upset with me. I'm smart enough to know when a woman wants nothing to do with me, and those were the vibes I got the entire ride home.

She smiled and fawned over Ezra as he helped her bring bags and boxes of clothing up, but any time I attempted to help it resulted in a dirty look.

Ezra ate it up like candy, clearly aware that something was going on between Margo and me.

It was four hours ago when we piled Margo's new items in her room, and she all but slammed the door in my face.

I spent two of those hours in the private gym and sauna, trying to work out some of the pent-up frustration. I'm still in disbelief that she tried to diminish our kiss into nothing. I'm even more enraged that her trust issues stem from the man whose picture appears on my phone.

Angrily grabbing my phone from the kitchen counter, I swipe to answer. "What do you want?" My tone isn't friendly, although it never is when it comes to him.

He laughs, but there's no actual humor to it. "Sup, big bro?" Blaring music muffles his voice. Wherever he is, whatever he's doing, it isn't quiet.

"Why are you calling me?" I clip, grimacing at his use of the words *sup* and *bro*.

"I got a fun tidbit of information today," he taunts. I know he wants me to ask what, but I don't. I'm not going to fall into whatever trap he's attempting to lay.

"And I give a shit why?"

The oven timer beeps behind me. I walk to it, opening it up and taking a peek at the teriyaki salmon I have in there.

Carter chuckles on the other line. "Because, Beckham, it has to do with you and a certain ex-girlfriend of mine."

Fuck.

I knew he'd learn of Margo working for me, and eventually becoming my fiancée, but I must admit, I didn't think it'd be so soon.

"I repeat. I give a shit why?"

"I think it's me who should give a shit. Why are you out with Margo? You know I'm still in love with her."

I scoff, grabbing a spatula and turning the green beans that are cooking in the pan. "Didn't you cheat on her throughout the entirety of your relationship?"

"I was immature," he counters, slightly slurring his words. The realization doesn't shock me. Carter has always been someone who likes to hit the bottle a little too hard. "I was stupid for what I did to her, but I want her back."

Like fuck, I want to say out loud but I bite my tongue. Carter can't know about the little agreement Margo and I have. Not now, not ever. Even if Margo didn't hate him, there's still no way I'd ever allow my brother to hurt her again. He's stupid and pathetic, too busy thinking with his cock all the time to realize he's got a good thing when he has it.

I won't let him make that same mistake again. Not if I have any say in the matter.

"She's working for me as an assistant." I change the subject, divulging only a little.

"She'll be mine again, Beckham. Just wanted to remind you of that."

I stop, holding the phone to my ear as I think his words over. The last thing I need to do is get in a pissing match over Margo with my brother. I have to choose my words carefully, not wanting him to know how much the thought of Margo ever getting back with his sorry ass makes my blood boil. Even seeing her with him at our family home in the Hamptons, knowing he was unfaithful to her, upset me more than it ever should. Now I'm even more invested in her, more than I'm willing to let him or anyone else know, and it'll be over my dead body that my brother ever gets her back.

"Beck?"

"I don't know why you think I care, but she's only working for me, Carter. Who you are dating, or want to date, means nothing to me. Do what you want." I press end on the phone call, hating the way that sentence felt coming from my mouth. I have to tread carefully when it comes to him. The last thing I want is for my brother to come in and try to convince Margo to get back with him. She seemed adamant that she'd never get back with him, but she was also honest in the fact that he really hurt her. When people have the power to hurt you, they have a hold on you that makes you do unexplainable things. Things you never saw yourself doing.

Taking a deep breath, I pinch the bridge of my nose between my fingers. I hadn't expected Carter to be so open about wanting Margo back, but then again, Carter has always wanted what he couldn't have. Once he finally gets what he wants, he grows tired of it. I'm not sure how one could ever grow tired of Margo, but he did.

I've told Mom I think he was too spoiled as a child. It's clear as day now with how he wants Margo back in his life at the mere mention that she's working for me. My parents were good to me. I was loved and encouraged, but they were still much harder on me than they were on Carter. I appreciate the difference between us. I had to work for things I wanted. Carter had it all handed to him. One thing he won't be handed is the chance to have Margo again—I'll make damn sure of that.

The smell of burnt garlic fills the kitchen. "Shit," I curse, turning around to move the burning vegetables in the pan. I think I've got it before the green beans are completely done for. I douse them in a bit more oil before shaking the pan to disperse the liquid. Turning the temperature down on the gas range, I walk toward one of the ovens built into the wall. Opening it, I take a look at the salmon and find it crisped to perfection. I shield my hand in an oven mitt and pull the salmon out. Now that the heat for the vegetables is turned down, I do what I should've done a while ago—find Margo.

I take the stairs two at a time, coming to a stop at the end of the hall in front of her door. She has it closed, music sounding from the other side. Now that I stand in front of it, I wonder if this isn't such a great idea. She's more than likely still angry with me, and deep down I'm still frustrated with her as well. Showing emotion makes my skin crawl and I've seemed to already let my guard down enough with her for one day.

Before I can think better of it, I bang my knuckles against her door three times. Nothing happens. I shift on the balls of my feet, knocking three more times, but louder this time. I'm about to knock a third time, annoyed by the fact she's ignoring me, when the door swings open, a freshly showered Margo on the other end.

She gives no indication of her mood when she pins me with her green eyes. "Hi," she says, her tone even.

I scratch my neck. "I...uh." Words seem to fail me as my eyes roam over her body. She wears a pair of drawstring pajama pants, a bow neatly tied right underneath her belly button. The pants look good, but it's what she wears as a top that's making my pulse spike. She wears some kind of cross between a tank top and a bra. It stops right over her belly button, the thin fabric molding to her body. Straps thinner than my pinky hold the top up, and it's obvious she wears no bra underneath by the outline of her nipples pushing through the fabric.

"You…" Her lips twitch as she fights a smile. Her arms cross her body, allowing me the time to gather my words now that I'm not staring at the outlines of her nipples and imagining how they'd feel in my mouth.

"I have a truce," I offer, placing my hands in the pocket of my lounge pants.

"And what's that?"

"I made dinner."

"Is that code for you had a chef make it or you made it yourself?"

"What did I tell you? I enjoy cooking and for it to be a proper truce, I made it myself. Slaved away in the kitchen and everything to say I'm sorry for being a dick earlier."

She stares at me, probably deciding if she wants to accept my apology or not. I'll leave her no other option. I won't go back downstairs unless she's going back down there with me. Both of us acted childish earlier and I don't want to go into her first day at the office tomorrow with her upset at me.

"You were kind of a dick earlier," she finally offers, losing the battle with fighting a smile.

"Yeah well, it's part of my charm."

Her eyes narrow. "Apology accepted." She acts like she's about to step out into the hallway before she changes course last minute. The door begins to shut right in my face. Before she can fully shut it, I slap my hand against the wood, wrapping my fingers around the edge so she can't shut it.

"What do you think you're doing?" My grip tightens as she attempts to close it. She'd actually close it on my fingers if I allowed her to.

"I can accept your apology and not want to eat with you." There's not a hint of fear in her eyes. In fact, I think it's the opposite. She looks thrilled as she tries to push the door all the way shut.

If it's a game she wants to play, then it's a game she's going to get.

"I'm amending our terms to this agreement."

"Considering we've already broken our terms, I don't know what good that does us," she fires back.

"Don't care. Starting now part of the job—the offer—is that if we're both home, we're eating dinner together."

Margo shakes her head. "That wasn't part of the agreement and you can't just add things to better fit what you want."

I smile, catching her off guard and forcing the door open. "I'm your boss, remember. I can do whatever the fuck I want." I take a step closer until I'm crowding her space. "And right now, what I want is your ass downstairs seated at the dinner table."

"I'm off the clock. Right now, you're just Beck. You're not *Mr. Sinclair* until tomorrow. I don't have to listen to you." She means to say "Mr. Sinclair" mockingly, but it has the opposite effect. Her sweet tone only fuels my growing erection.

"I've already cooked you one dinner you didn't come down to eat. It isn't happening again."

"You can't make me."

An idea pops into my head. Grinning ear to ear, I pin her with a wide smile. "Oh Violet, yes I can."

21

Margo

The ground is swept from underneath my feet, completely catching me off guard.

"Beckham!" I scream, smacking his back with all my might. "Put me down right now."

His footsteps don't falter one beat. He continues down the hallway, undeterred by my slaps and attempts to wriggle free from his grasp.

"Smack my ass again, Margo, and I'll bend you over my knee and return the favor."

"You wouldn't even dream of it," I seethe, kicking my legs back and forth. The movements only make him grip me even harder as he brings us down the stairs.

His laugh is sinister. "That's where you're very wrong. Nothing would make me happier than to dream of making that tight little ass of yours red, other than actually doing it, of course."

If I wasn't mad at him for earlier today and then for taking me down here against my will, I might be totally turned on by the comment. Let's be honest, my clit throbs at the mental picture of his handprint on my ass. I'd gladly accept the sting of his palm against my sensitive skin if it meant he'd be playing with other parts of me as well.

What? No. I clench my thighs together, attempting to get my clit and mind on the same page that we're currently pissed at Beck.

"Wow. Did me talking dirty to you really get you to shut up? I'll have to try it more often."

His actions are a complete contrast to his words as he gently sets me on one of the chairs at the kitchen island. He smirks at me, laying a hand on the armrests on either side of me. Whatever has gotten into him, it's shifted the balance between us. I hadn't expected him to be so brash, to talk so dirty to me. If anything, I thought reminding him of the terms we set going into this fake fiancée situation would deter him from me.

The way he leans in until his lips are barely brushing over mine shows it's the complete opposite.

"Tell me, Margo, is your pussy wet at the idea of me spanking you? Fuck, it'd hurt at first, but I promise I'd make you feel good after."

I'm stunned. I'm completely at a loss for words. I expected our conversation after this kiss and the conversation at the office to make things awkward. Beck had other plans, like taking an axe to all the reasons us hooking up is a terrible idea and appealing to the part of me that wants him so fiercely that I'd say fuck the terms if it meant he made good on his word and did all the things he's threatening.

He clicks his tongue as he pulls my bottom lip out from between my teeth. I hadn't realized I'd been doing it, but it was all in an effort to stifle a moan at him saying *pussy* and *spanking* in the same sentence. They sounded filthy but hot as fuck coming from his mouth.

"Don't worry, I'm just as turned on—maybe even more—by

the thought of how wet you are underneath those pajama pants of yours. If my words can make you that wet, I'd have the best time figuring out what certain parts of my body can do to you."

My sexual history is filled with one vanilla encounter after the other. I already know just by the dirty mouth on Beck that sex with him would be anything but.

My palms reach out to grab the soft fabric of his T-shirt. In a last second decision, I have to figure out if I want to pull him to me and kiss the hell out of him and force him to make good on every one of his promises, or if I want to shove him away and force the space I desperately need from him to get my shit together.

I choose the latter, pushing at him with all my might. "Stop," I plead, my voice completely unconvincing. The only reason I'm able to get him away is because he lets me push our bodies apart.

He stands, his toned arms no longer caging me in. When he walks to the other side of the counter, grabbing plates from a cabinet, I'm able to take a solid, deep breath for the first time since the moment he showed up at my bedroom door.

"Did you hit your head or something since we were at the office?"

His back is to me as he plates whatever he's made. Whatever it is, it smells delicious. My stomach growls, eagerly wanting whatever food he's prepared. "Not that I recall," he deadpans. "Why?"

I wiggle in the chair, trying to find a position that's comfortable and makes me feel my throbbing clit a little less. Even the smallest brush of fabric against the swollen part has me almost panting with need. His words have had such an effect on me. He's right, if I can pretty much get off by just that filthy mouth of his, I know other parts of him could make me see stars.

"Because you seem to have forgotten our earlier conversation. The one where I said that we probably shouldn't, you know, kiss and stuff since you know, we're pretending to like each other and all."

He looks over his shoulder. "I thought I made it clear this afternoon that I wasn't pretending."

My mouth snaps shut. I have no idea what's happening anymore. I went from kind of wondering if Beck was into me to him full-blown admitting that he's attracted to me.

Silverware clatters as he reaches into a drawer to his left. He's silent as he places a plate in front of me. The dish looks like it came from a fancy restaurant, not made by him in the comfort of his own home. There's what looks to be perfectly cooked salmon with some kind of glaze drizzled over it paired with green beans that look to be the perfect amount of charred and seasoned. I can smell the garlic, my stomach growling in anticipation.

Beck places another plate next to me, properly putting silverware next to both our plates. I should thank him but I'm too busy working through the sudden shift between us in my head.

He doesn't take a seat next to me. Instead, he steps out of the kitchen and disappears for a few moments. When he returns, he carries a bottle of white wine in one hand and two glasses in his other.

Without words, he sets the glasses down in front of him. He works with expertise to open the bottle of wine, his forearm muscles rippling the entire time. He doesn't ask me if I want any, pouring two hefty glasses and pushing them across the counter so one sits in front of my plate and the other in front of his.

"I probably shouldn't drink this much wine before my first day," I admit, trying to break the tension in the room. It doesn't help much. I'm still throbbing between my legs, and it doesn't seem in his nature to relent in whatever crusade he's begun.

Beck stabs the salmon with his fork, pulling off a perfect flaky bite. He places it in his mouth, chewing and swallowing before speaking. "I know the boss." He shrugs. "Something tells me he won't care if you start the day with a wine headache." He takes a big bite of the green beans. "Plus, that boss has a new assistant who will be grabbing him coffee to start the day. Nothing cures a wine headache like a cup of *normal* coffee."

The way he emphasizes "normal" is clearly a jab at my coffee order. Rolling my eyes at him, I hold my fork in the air and point it at him. "Don't knock my order until you try it."

"I'll be sticking with my usual." He takes another bite of his food, almost halfway through his piece of salmon when I haven't even taken my first bite.

I spear some salmon onto my fork, brushing the piece through the sauce he has on top before popping it into my mouth. A moan falls from my throat immediately, my eyes rolling back in my head with how delicious it is.

"I never imagined the first time I made you moan that I wouldn't even be touching you."

"This is delicious." I shovel a large bite into my mouth, opening wide to fit salmon and green beans at the same time.

"My roasted chicken was delicious as well, but you didn't seem to want anything to do with it last night."

It takes a moment for me to finish chewing before I swallow. I wash the bite down with the wine, the sweetness of it pairing deliciously with the dish. Part of me wants to ask Beck how much the bottle of wine costs, but I decide against it. It's probably better I don't know. It's too delicious and I don't want to crush my dreams by knowing this glass of wine costs a pretty penny.

"One, I didn't know you'd made food. And two, I just needed some space from you. You've only got yourself to blame for that."

He raises his eyebrows, his wine glass perched in front of his lips. "Tell me why I should blame myself for you not getting to enjoy my roasted chicken?"

"Because you're the one who has been all over the place. You come to my office all business as you offer to hire me as an assistant and then ask me to be your fake fiancée."

"I distinctly remember how red you turned when we decided you'd never mutter Carter's name again," he interrupts.

That same blush creeps up my cheeks as I remember how abrupt his words had been in the conference room. "Okay well maybe not *all* business. But then last night, right there"—I point to the refrigerator—"it felt like you wanted to kiss me. But then you made me feel..." I sigh, not knowing what word to use. "I don't know, silly, I guess? When you told me I was in the way I just felt silly. It made me feel like I'd misread the situation or something. So yeah, I didn't want your roasted chicken."

"You didn't misread the situation. I stopped because I remembered how you'd been the one to tell me we couldn't kiss."

"What a gentleman," I quip. "Did that same sentiment not last until today?"

His laugh is low and rumbly, sending shivers down my spine. "Oh, Margo, I'm no gentleman. I kissed you today because you basically begged me to. I only have so much restraint. You may have once told me that you didn't want us to kiss, but you asked me in that dressing room. Who am I to say no?"

We both focus on clearing our plates. I'm quite shocked by how tasty the food is. When Beck had told me he cooked, I didn't think it would be this good. Is there anything this man can't do?

With my plate now clean, I wrap my fingers around the stem of my wine glass and take a large sip. I take a deep breath, knowing I need to bite the bullet and start a conversation I've been dreading all day.

22

Beck

She doesn't have to say a word for me to know exactly what she wants to talk about. I've been expecting her to want to talk more about our conversation at the office. In fact, I've been eager to discuss the terrible terms she set for herself and this agreement.

I've always been someone who gets what they want. And what I want is Margo Moretti.

One taste of her was not enough. My appetite for her only grows stronger, nowhere near satiated by the brief encounter in the dressing room. There's so much more I want to do with her—to her—and it all begins with her accepting the mutual attraction between us.

"Say whatever you'd like to say, Margo," I clip. My hands cross in my lap as I wait for her to yet again piss me off and downplay the chemistry between us.

Margo shifts in her chair, crossing and uncrossing her legs nervously. She'd be terrible in the boardroom by the way every emotion can be seen on her face. Her eyes look to the city skyline behind me, like it can give her some magical answer.

"I'm going to be honest here, I hadn't expected things between us to get so heated. Especially *so* fast. For there to be so much…tension."

My finger runs up and down the stem of my wine glass as I process her words. Cocking my head, I process every emotion on her face. "You didn't?" My tone comes off a bit incredulous as I remember that night at the beach. There's no way she didn't expect tension.

The slight narrowing of her eyes at me tells me her mind is replaying the same exact memory as mine. She lets out an aggravated sigh. "No, I didn't, Beck. You're *you* and I'm *me*. Yes, I was going to be your assistant and yes we were going to pretend to be engaged, but I expected it to end there."

"No one's to blame for that but you. I thought I made my attraction to you pretty clear when I laid out my offer."

She gulps down half of her glass of wine, and I'd given her a pretty generous pour. "You're literally known to be this womanizing playboy billionaire, I thought that was just how you talk to women in general."

"I find that often, with the women you're referring to, there isn't much need for conversation."

A small amount of white wine falls from her lips, landing on her thin tank top and creating a small wet stain. "Do you always just say what comes to your mind?" She wipes at the dribble of wine still left on her chin.

I shrug before taking a sip of my own. "Occasionally. Typically, the things running through my head are much worse."

"I don't even want to know."

"Going back to your earlier statement, yes, I've never been one to beat around the bush with women. I haven't had to. I came to you with an offer that benefited the both of us. It's an added bonus that there's clearly a mutual attraction between us. I don't see the point in fighting or denying it."

"Easy for you to say. You're known for being cold and calculating, some people also speculate if you even have a heart."

"Have you been reading articles about me, Margo?"

Her eyes roll. "It's just an observation. People think you don't form attachments outside of your company."

"Well people don't really know me. I prefer to keep it that way. I can form attachments just fine, I'm just picky about doing it. I don't particularly see anything wrong with that. Shouldn't we all be that way?"

"Okay, noted. Either way, I can't say the same for myself. I know myself. After being hurt by Ca—my last boyfriend—I don't want to go mistaking lust for something else. I like to feel wanted, I want to feel wanted, and I'm flattered someone like you could ever want me. However, I also know how easily it would be for me to misinterpret the relationship."

I have to think carefully about what to say. A large part of me wants to point out that not all men are pieces of shit like my brother, but on the other hand, a large number of men are *exactly* like my brother. There's definitely a line of women who could say harsh things about me if they wanted to. Not because I cheated, I've never been in an established relationship for that to happen, but many have faulted me for taking what I want from them and leaving them. I've always been upfront. I'd never care about them the way they desired. But in the end, if I didn't give them what they wanted—a relationship—then I was the bad guy. No matter how many warnings I gave.

"Are you just going to sit and brood and not tell me what you're thinking?"

"You know, I find myself being more upfront with you more than anyone else," I point out, meaning every word.

"I don't believe you."

I hold her eye contact, running my thumb over my lip. "Then I guess I need to do a better job of proving that to you then, don't I?"

She looks stunned, clearly not expecting that to be my answer. I use her silence to my advantage. Leaning forward, I grab one of the legs of her barstool and drag it closer to me. Her hands find the armrests to help steady herself. I pull her closer until our knees bump against one another. "Here's the deal, Margo. I'm attracted to you. I planned on going forward with our deal either way, but I'm going to be honest when I say the fact that there's clearly chemistry between us is an added bonus. We both have needs, and since we agreed those needs won't be taken care of by other people, it's only logical we can use each other instead. But I'd never force myself on you, and I'm not going to beg for you to admit what I know is happening between us. So, if you say you don't want to kiss me again or do far more fun things, then that's your decision." I give her one last tug, pulling her body so it sits between my knees. The inside of my thighs press against the outside of hers, her knees dangerously close to my cock.

"But the moment you realize that it's useless to fight the tension between us, I will have you spread open on every fucking surface of this penthouse. I'll prove to you just how much you deserve to be worshiped. You'll find out very quickly how exquisite it'd be if not everything in this agreement was fake."

Her tongue peeks out to eagerly wet her lips, a dead giveaway of how my words affect her. She wants that same thing I do. In fact, I bet her pussy is soaked right now as she envisions herself wet and needy for me in various spots of this home. Fuck, I'm hard just imagining it. I'd love to have her bent over this island, have her screaming in pleasure as I prove to her how much of a tragedy it'd be for us to deny the attraction between us.

I reach across the small space between us, running my thumb over the spot she just coated on her lip. There's nothing more I want at the moment than to lean in and taste her again. I want to taste, test, tease her, find out how long it'd take for her to moan in ecstasy against my lips.

I have so many plans for her. So much I want to do, but I'm not doing any of it until she's done living in denial.

"I'll play by your rules. I'm not going to kiss you again. I'm not going to do anything until you're on your knees begging for it, and even then, I might deny you the way you're denying yourself right now. But know that one day you won't be able to deny this any longer. Your pussy will be so swollen and soaked for me that you'll be desperate for me to worship that little cunt of yours the way it deserves. I might give in at the moment, but I shouldn't. I should make you wait the way you've made me wait just because you feel like downplaying the chemistry between us instead of recognizing it for what it is. Whatever happens, when I finally bury my cock inside you, which we both know will happen, I'm going to take out my frustration on you and you're going to eagerly—greedily—love every moment of it."

If I pushed hard enough, I think I could change everything and have that moment be right now by the hungry look in her eyes. Her breaths are quick, her nipples hard underneath the fabric. She's horny, completely turned on by my words.

"Unless," I say under my breath, staring at her lips.

"Unless?"

"Unless right here and now you tell me you want it. If you tell me to fuck the terms right now, I'll do everything I've mentioned and more. I'll make you feel so good you won't remember every other pathetic man you've been with before who thought they knew how to satisfy a woman. I'll make you come and come again until you're exhausted for your first day tomorrow. I'm giving you this one opportunity where I'll forget how damn angry you've made me by saying that this is fake. Take it, and you'll be coming in two minutes, mark my words. Leave it, and you're going to have to beg when you finally admit to yourself how bad you want it."

"I can't."

I click my tongue, shaking my head in disappointment. "What a shame. I was so fucking ready to bury my face in that sweet pussy of yours."

I get up, grabbing both our plates and putting them in the sink for the house cleaners to take care of tomorrow.

My cock fights my briefs, wanting to do everything I just said to Margo. I ignore it, no matter how much it pains me. I'm angry she's fighting this, but it doesn't change things for me. Every single one of my words is true.

I'm going to have Margo, but not until she's a good little girl begging on her knees for me.

23

Margo

A hand plays with the waistband of my PJ pants. I lean into it, trying to turn my body to give the hand more access as I wake up from a deep slumber.

"God, you're so wet for me," a recognizable voice says from behind me. I grind my hips against Beck's obvious erection.

"Touch me," I plead, trying to line my core up with his fingers. It's no use, he taunts me, softly running his fingers over the sensitive flesh right above where I want him most. My hips rock back and forth as I desperately seek the friction I need.

"You'll have to beg for it," Beck's deep gravelly voice says against my ear. He bites at the spot behind my ear, sending shivers all the way down my body.

"Beck," I moan, rocking back and forth so much, frustrated that I don't feel his fingers against the throbbing spot between my thighs. "Beck, please."

Cold air hits my entire body, making my eyes fly open. I look around me, realizing that I was dreaming—and the person in my wet dream is staring back at me with a triumphant look on his face.

Beck looks delicious this morning, standing in front of me in a black tuxedo that is tailored perfectly to his body. He wears a black shirt underneath, and he's paired it with a black tie. All of the black matches the darkness in his eyes.

His smile is so fucking dangerous as he clutches the comforter in his hands, pulling it completely off the bed. "Having a wet dream about me?"

I look down in horror at the pillow between my legs. I think I was gyrating against it, thinking it was Beck and not an inanimate object. *What in the actual hell.*

"No," I snap, trying to grab the sheet at my feet and pull it over my body. Beck is too quick for me, snatching it and pulling it as well. "Don't be so full of yourself." Looking down, I find my sleep tank bunched to the side, my boob close to spilling out the armhole. I try to discreetly fix it, all while he stares down at me with a storm of desire in his eyes.

"Mhm," he says. "Beck," he mimics, his normal deep tone a few octaves higher than normal. "Beck, please." His moans are dramatic and nowhere near what I sound like, but god I'm so freaking wound tight that even him mocking me turns me on.

I bury my face in my hands, dying of embarrassment. I need to lock my door if he's going to keep showing up in here unannounced and finding me in mortifying situations. "I *never* said any of that," I lie, willing time to go back ten minutes and for him to never have witnessed me having a wet dream about him.

At least, I think that's a wet dream. I've never had one about anyone. I'm pretty dang sure if he hadn't woken me up, it would've gone a lot further too.

"What are you even doing here in the first place?" I accuse, looking at him from across the bed. He stands at the foot of it, both my sheets and comforters in his grasp as his eyes take their time looking me all over.

"I'm waking my assistant up. We're already late. I have a meeting in twenty minutes."

Screeching, I look down at my phone. I set an alarm. In fact, I set *seven* alarms to make sure I got up before the sun today to get ready for my first day of work. I look at the screen, trying to tap it until it lights up. No matter what I do, it doesn't light up.

Shit. I must've forgotten to charge my phone last night when I ran up here after another strange and intoxicating moment with Beck.

I was too horny to think straight, apparently—which resulted in me forgetting to plug my phone in.

"Fuckity fucking fuck fuck!" I mutter, flying out of the bed toward the massive walk-in closet. It's huge for a master bedroom, let alone a guest bedroom. I'm not complaining, especially after the brand-new wardrobe Beck got me.

Hangers and clothes fly in every direction as I try to find something to wear. Normally, I'd lay out whatever outfit I wanted to wear out the night before. This is the one time I didn't do it because I returned to my room with my head in such a mess.

Finally, I find a blazer that'll go perfectly with a pair of high-waisted pants Quincy picked out just for me. Both of them scream business, and if I want people in the office to take me seriously from the very beginning, this is the perfect way to start.

Aside from the fact that I might make both myself *and* the boss late for the day.

"Haven't heard that one before."

"Why didn't you wake me sooner?" I yell, pulling my tank top off and throwing it on the floor. I've made a mess of the closet in the minute I've been in here, but I don't have time to clean up. I'll do it tonight when we get home.

"I tried." Beck's voice is closer this time. I look over my shoulder, finding him filling the closet entrance.

"A little privacy here?" I yelp, covering my boobs with my hands.

Beck sighs, turning around and leaving the space he just filled. "I knocked countless times. You weren't waking up, so I had to barge in."

Weird. I don't normally sleep that hard.

I strip from my PJ pants and slide each foot into the pant legs and bring them up my thighs, fastening the button above my hips. I'm looking for a blouse to pair underneath the blazer when Beck returns. He squeezes his eyes shut, a lace bra hanging off his pointer finger between us. "Put this on," he demands. "No one in the office gets to see those perfect pink nipples besides me."

"So you did see!" I snatch the bra from his grip. It doesn't take me long to hook it at my back and get it righted on my body.

One eye pops open slightly, looking to see if I'm dressed or not. Apparently he deems me dressed well enough even though I'm only in my bra and pants. He opens both hands and gives me his familiar Beck smirk. "I didn't see anything on purpose. You should've told me you were naked in here."

"*Sure*, you didn't mean to."

"I have no reason to lie about that, Margo. Either way, no man is seeing those in the office. There are a bunch of horny men I work with, and the last thing I'll be able to do is work if I'm imagining all of my coworkers fucking my fiancée."

I slide a white blouse over my head, holding my left hand out between us. "Future fiancée," I correct, pointing to my bare ring finger. "I have no ring."

He bites his lip as I push both arms through the sleeves of my blazer. I'm having to get ready faster than I imagined I'd have to for my first day, but at least the new wardrobe gave me plenty of amazing options to quickly choose from.

Now, what torture device of a shoe do I want to wear for the day?

My eyes scan over the shoe shelf, taking in the numerous pairs of red-bottomed shoes I now apparently own.

Even Winnie, with her rich as fuck parents, only has one pair of Louboutin shoes. And those were a twenty-first birthday gift.

"We'll have to fix the ring problem then, won't we?" he fires back. If he's trying to call me on a bluff, it won't work.

"That's all on you, Beck. You do the proposing. I want a big, fat diamond on this hand. People wouldn't expect anything less."

He runs a hand through his perfectly styled blond hair. I remember how it looked last night, the tendrils still wet after he showered and not bothered to gel it after doing whatever he'd done for the majority of the late afternoon. I liked that Beck, but this clean-shaven boss look totally does it for me as well.

"You're the one that keeps pointing out that this is fake. Is a proposal necessary if it's *just for show*?" The way he says just for show makes me wonder how much I wounded his ego by my insistence on keeping things platonic between us. Well, as platonic as two people who want to jump the hell out of each other's bones can be.

I slide a pair of nude brown heels off the shelf, sliding my foot in each one. The shoes give me a few extra inches, allowing me to look Beck in the eye a little better than before. My hand runs down his black tie, smoothing it out even though it wasn't necessary at all. I play with the silver clip on it. "The sentiment behind the proposal might be fake"—I begin, risking looking up at him—"but we could still pretend."

The tension lingering between us is so thick. Part of me wants to find out if his words were true. If I wanted to kiss him, would he let me? Or would I have to beg for it like he threatened? It'd be so easy to find out. It'd feel so good, but I think better of it.

No matter how badly I want to sleep with Beckham Sinclair—which is past the point of bad and encroaching on desperation—I know better. He's the older brother of the man who broke my heart. The much better, hotter, richer version of Carter. I know how easily I'd give my heart over to Beck, and it's not something I'm willing to do.

Fucking him would probably change my life. Eventually I'd mistake lust for love, and I'd be back in the terrible cycle of heartbreak I've been trying to avoid after Carter.

I attempt to step around Beck but he grabs me by the elbow, pulling me against his body. "Ezra is going to drop me off at the office for my meeting and then will return for you. Get ready." He looks me up and down. I look put together from the neck down, but I definitely have to get makeup on my face and do my hair before anyone in that place can see me. "Make an impression when you show up, Margo. You are the future Mrs. Sinclair after all."

Beckham Sinclair plays fucking dirty. He leans in, grabbing both of my cheeks and eyeing me with a look that doesn't seem as simple as lust. Not at all.

And that's your problem, Margo, I tell myself. *You'll mistake want for something far deeper when it isn't.* It's a dangerous flaw to have when your heart isn't as whole as it used to be.

He lays a soft kiss on my forehead before stepping away and leaving the closet.

I'm left watching him, wondering why I just want to allow myself to sleep with him already.

I'm scared he's right. It'll happen eventually, and the dark glint in his eyes tells me he'll make me beg for it. Beckham Sinclair doesn't like his ego bruised, and I've done that by denying him. The best part of it all—or maybe the worst—is I'm extremely turned on by the thought of him making me beg.

24

Margo

To: MargoMoretti@SintechCyberSecurity.com
From: BeckhamSinclair@SintechCyberSecurity.com

Just got to the office. I'm about to walk into a meeting. When I leave, I expect coffee waiting for me. Absolutely no hint of lavender or anything else they do on the West Coast.

Don't be late.
Beck

 I drop the hot curling iron into the sink, reading his email three more times to make sure I read it right. Is that really my job now? Am I getting this dressed up to get him coffee? Sighing, I start typing a response, feeling brave with him not right in front of me.

To: BeckhamSinclair@SintechCyberSecurity.com
From: MargoMoretti@SintechCyberSecurity.com

So I've gone from designing penis pens to grabbing coffee? Not sure if that's an upgrade or not.

Your glorified coffee runner,
Margo

Happy with myself, I smile, placing my phone on the counter and picking up my curling iron once again. I've already completed putting a small amount of makeup on. I probably had way too much fun with all of the new products I got while shopping. It made putting makeup on a lot more entertaining than I usually find it. Some of the products I had no idea what to do with, or what order to use them in. Do I use cream blush after foundation but before bronzer? Does eyebrow gel go before the pencil? These are questions I'll have to ask Emma and Winnie the next time we talk. Luckily, my dark, thick eyebrows don't exactly *need* any product on them, so I swiped some gel on them and called it good. I'm positive my friends will jump at the opportunity to show me how to use the new products, both of them far more into makeup than I've ever been.

I'm finishing up curling the long tendrils of my dark hair when my phone pings. Triple checking I've turned the iron off, I place it on the hot pad for my hair tools and check the new alert. I'm biting back a smile reading Beck's response.

To: MargoMoretti@SintechCyberSecurity.com
From: BeckhamSinclair@SintechCyberSecurity.com

You'd rather do anything than design those hideous pens ever again. You know it. I know it. Let's not pretend that was enjoyable in the slightest.

I would've grabbed coffee with my assistant this morning, but she was too busy having a wet dream about me. Tell me, was I licking that little cunt of yours or was I fucking it?

The object of your wet dreams,
Beck

Blush isn't even needed for the color I feel heating my cheeks. I picture him sitting in a room full of board members or investors, whatever fancy meeting he has today, typing out such filthy thoughts. It shouldn't make me feel so hot, but it does. Beck may be holding true to his promise by not making any physical advances toward me, but he doesn't appear to be relenting with his words. Which could be a problem, because the dirty words rolling off his tongue feel just as good as his tongue against mine.

To: BeckhamSinclair@SintechCyberSecurity.com
From: MargoMoretti@SintechCyberSecurity.com

I'm not answering your question because the dream didn't involve you at all. You should be working.

Your assistant who'd never dream of having a wet dream about her boss,
Margo

P.S. Can you say things like that in a company email? Seems like a potential HR problem.

My eyes travel over the still unopened boxes of makeup I have from the trip yesterday. I look for the perfect lipstick, wanting something that'll pop on my lips but not seem like too much for a first day. Red might scream *I want to fuck the boss* a little *too* much.

I settle on a shade that's a perfect mix between pink and nude. It glides effortlessly onto my lips, moisturizing them to perfection. The last thing I do before leaving the bathroom is spray a few spritzes of my new Baccarat 540 perfume and call it good. Grabbing my new Prada handbag from the desk in my guest room, I deem myself ready to head into work.

As I climb down the stairs to the main level, I wonder if I'll have to contact Ezra or how I'll go about getting to the office. If worse comes to worse, I can take a taxi to work. I faintly remember the cross-streets of the building.

I'm not left worrying about what to do next for long. I find Ezra sitting at the huge dining table, a magazine in one hand, a disposable coffee cup in the other.

"Good morning, Miss Moretti," he says cheerfully, looking up from the magazine.

I give him a warm smile. "You really can call me Margo. I won't tell the boss."

This makes me chuckle. "If you insist." He grabs the magazine and tucks it under his arm. As he reaches to grab his coffee, I catch a glimpse of the front cover.

"Is that Beck?"

Ezra and I look closely at the magazine in his grasp. I find a scowling Beck looking straight into the camera. There's a large headline with the name of the magazine, *Corporation Insider*.

"He argued about doing it," Ezra notes, my eyes reading over the headline. Apparently he was being featured for being one of the youngest to sell a company for the price he did while still maintaining a prominent spot on the board and keeping a majority of control.

"That doesn't shock me one bit." Ezra hands me the magazine, allowing me a better look at it. Opening it up, I flip through the pages until I find a full-page spread about Beck and his business. He looks angry in all of the photos. But at least this article is one ran with his permission, unlike the one that led us to our current situation.

"I didn't know all of this about him," I mutter, eyes taking in every word on the pages. I loved Carter for years, but he didn't hide his entitlement. Sometimes it was a turnoff for me, but for the most part I knew he was entitled going into dating him so it wasn't a deal breaker for me. Him fucking half my college graduating class was the issue. I kind of assumed that Beck was the same way, that his rich family history is what led to him starting his own company and in return selling it for an ungodly amount of money.

Ezra whistles, low and under his breath. "Mr. Sinclair isn't exactly the sharing type."

If the article is correct, which I assume it is since he willingly did it, Beck didn't use any of his family's money to fund his start-up. In fact, he talks about working odd jobs around campus just to earn funds for the company. He eventually talked some fraternity friends into investing in his vision before building the company from the ground up. Knowing this information unnerves me for some reason. I imagined Beck having the same entitlement and silver spoon that his brother did. Carter has never worked a job that didn't pay him above six figures. A nice modest livable wage was *beneath* him. His words, not mine.

The article doesn't go into any detail on why Beck didn't just have his father invest in the company. I've met his dad, and he seemed like a good guy—especially for someone so rich. He treated me kindly and didn't talk down to me; not even when he was fishing for questions on who my family were and where I came from. It never felt like he thought any less of me with his line of questioning, it just seemed he genuinely wanted to get to know me.

"Interesting." I hand the magazine back to him, remembering the title of the article so I can search it online later tonight. Now I'm wondering what else I don't know about Beck.

I push all my questions about who he is to the back of my

mind. Plastering on a smile, I tilt my head toward the gallery, as Beck would call it. "I'm ready to head in whenever you are."

Ezra doesn't say anything. Like Beck, he seems to be a man of few words. I follow him into the elevator, my mind reeling with questions about Beck. I always imagined his dad was a big reason why he had the company, but I've learned that's not the case. There's got to be so much more I don't know about him, but I'm dying to find out.

My mind is lost the entire ride to the building. Even my phone ringing multiple times in my purse doesn't pull me from my thoughts. The only thing that finally breaks me free is Ezra putting the car in park and turning around to look at me.

"Beck said you'd need to stop here first." I look out the window, finding a coffee shop with a navy blue awning.

I shake my head, grabbing my purse from the seat next to me. "Off I go to get him caffeine so he isn't grumpier than his typical Beck grump self."

This makes Ezra belt with laughter. He claps his palm against the steering wheel before opening the door and loping around the car. My door opens, a grin still wide on his face. "I think you'll be good for him, Margo," he states plainly.

I step out, careful not to twist my ankle in the process by the height of my heels. "You're only saying that because I'm getting his caffeine for the day."

The returning look from Ezra is one that I can't quite read, but I don't have the time either. He's shutting the door and heading back to the driver's side before I can say anything else. "See you later!" he yells, hopping into the car.

I join the line of fellow New Yorkers all waiting for a coffee. It feels refreshing, to be back in the hustle and bustle of the city. In LA, people act like they don't give a shit about you but stare at you and judge you. In New York, people act like they don't give a shit about you because they truly don't. Everyone in line is so preoccupied with their own lives, they don't have time to judge mine.

The woman in front of me looks like she is leaving a spin class, or maybe I'd peg her more as the hot yoga type. Whatever it is, she holds her head high as she stands in a mass of people who all wear business attire.

My phone vibrates again. Knowing I have a few minutes before it's my turn to order, I pull it out. Excitement runs through my veins when I see the notification is another email from Beck. I'm liking the thrill of wondering what he'll respond back with a little too much for someone who shoved him away yesterday when he so clearly wanted more. *More* meaning me pinned underneath him as he did every single dirty thing he promised he'd do to me.

To: MargoMoretti@SintechCyberSecurity.com
From: BeckhamSinclair@SintechCyberSecurity.com

My meeting is over, yet I have no assistant here and no coffee.

These are both problems.
Beck

To: MargoMoretti@SintechCyberSecurity.com
From: BeckhamSinclair@SintechCyberSecurity.com

When I told you to dress to impress, I still meant you needed to show up to work.

My patience is wearing thin.
Beck

The second email comes in less than a minute after the first.

I begin to type a response back to him, but I realize it's probably better to make him wait. He can sit and stew in his conference room a bit longer, wondering where both his assistant and his coffee are. I'm determined to do a good job at being his assistant, wanting to earn the large paycheck I'll now be receiving, but I can't help but toy with him a little. He makes it too easy. It's too fun to make him actually show emotions.

When I get to the counter, I order both Beck and I coffee. I bite back a smile when I add a little extra to his. Not a lot, but just a tiny little something extra to spice up his boring coffee order.

The baristas are quick. In no time, I have my coffee and I'm ready to head into work. I delicately balance the drink carrier between my hands as I walk down the street. Beck hadn't been wrong when he mentioned how close the coffee shop was to the office. That was probably the reason that so many people in business suits waited in line. I bet a lot of them work in the same office as me, or one of the towering buildings next to it.

Tom gives me a huge smile as I walk toward his desk on my way to the elevators. I walk up to the counter of his desk and gently set the coffees on the lip, careful that I don't spill anything. Reaching into my purse, I grab a small pastry bag from inside. I set it on the tall counter in front of me, sliding it across to him.

"I thought you might be hungry," I explain, as Tom's eyes light with excitement. "It's no homemade bread or anything."

"It's perfect, Miss Moretti." He opens the bag with enthusiasm, pulling the scone out and admiring it.

"How'd you know the bacon cheddar was my favorite?"

I shrug. "It was a wild guess."

"You were already on my good side, but I appreciate you thinking of me this morning, Miss Moretti."

My hand waves dismissively before grabbing my coffee again. "Catch you later?" I ask, taking a few steps back.

"Don't let Mr. Sinclair be too hard on you," he responds.

"I'd never." I turn and walk to the elevators, waiting with a fairly large group of people to go up.

My phone alerts with another message from my bag, but I don't risk freeing one of my hands to reach and grab it. The last thing I want to do is spill the coffee floors away from the person it's intended for.

People file out of the elevator as we climb higher and higher, stopping frequently to let people off. Eventually, we make it to the floor I need.

My stomach rolls a little with nerves as I take a step off the elevator. What do I do if Beck is currently in a meeting? Do I just stand awkwardly? Wait in his office? He hadn't really filled me in on what to do once I got here other than give him his coffee, of course.

I'm busy worrying about what to do when I see him lift his arm in the air from a seat in one of the conference rooms. The crystal clear glass lets me see through as he pushes his large rolling chair away from the table and gestures for me to come in.

I awkwardly smile, not looking forward to making my entrance in front of the table of what's got to be at least ten men and one woman.

"There you are." Beckham hastily gets up from the chair, opening the glass door for me and ushering me inside. He leans in next to my ear. "About fucking time," he growls, low enough for no one else to hear. He plucks his coffee from the tray, holding it in his hand as he faces the group of people all watching us carefully.

"Everyone, I'd like for you to meet my new assistant, Margo Moretti." He looks over at me, his eyes blazing a hot trail down my body. Heat prickles up my spine as I think back to him watching me dress this morning, on the tension in the small closet space. His lip upturns slightly in an appreciative manner. Hopefully that means he likes what he sees.

I plaster on my best smile. "Nice to meet all of you." I'm praying that Beck doesn't go through every single one of the people sitting at the tables and introduce themselves. There's no way I'll remember their names if so many are being told to me at once.

"These are some board members and investors. We'll do introductions another time though. Let me show you to your office."

He walks to his seat at the table, grabbing a legal pad from the table as well as a cup of coffee identical to the one I just gave him.

I wave goodbye to them as he guides me back through the door we came through.

"I see you have coffee," I say through a tight-lipped smile.

Although there's humor in his eyes, it doesn't reach his mouth. He's all business in this boardroom, that cocky smirk of his I've seen more and more throughout the duration of our first weekend together not making an appearance.

He brings it to his perfect full lips, ones that I've felt strong and sure against my own. His throat bobs up and down as he takes a large gulp. "Ah," he says, finishing the drink before tossing it in the trash next to him. "My assistant was late. I couldn't go into the meeting without anything, so Ezra and I stopped earlier."

I gasp, following him through the rows of people working at

desks. "That traitor." Now I understand the apologetic look on Ezra's face as he dropped me off at the shop. I should've known they'd already been once just by the cup of coffee he'd been drinking from.

We weave through the people, Beck occasionally stopping and introducing me to various associates before moving on. Unlike my previous job, there's not a cubicle here in sight. It's far more open, allowing people to have conversations and not feel isolated.

I'm expecting my workspace to be in the throng of people on the floor, but he takes us to the very back of the line of personal offices, where he showed me his own office yesterday.

He stops in front of his office, giving me a casual smirk.

I take a sip of my coffee, narrowing my eyes at him. "Why are you looking at me like that?"

He doesn't say anything, he just opens the door and points me inside. "It's no longer my office," he declares as I walk past him. "It's now yours."

25

Beck

Margo watches me with a confused stare. Her eyes pop from the office to me. "We were here yesterday and you said this was *your* office."

I gently nudge her into the room, letting the door shut behind me. "It *was* my office, but now it's yours."

"Why the sudden change?"

"Simple. This one has the best view. I don't appreciate it the way you do." I could've watched her stare at the city below her all day yesterday if she'd let me. It's probably what I would've done if we hadn't gotten into the fight. When I stomped off angry, setting up camp in the conference room as she stayed in here looking out the windows, I contacted the building staff and asked them to do some rearranging. The corner office does give the best view of the city. If you stand along the glass windows in the far corner, it feels like you're floating in the sky.

"Beck," she whispers, staring at me with too much emotion. It makes my chest feel heavy and tight. It constricts longingly as her eyes gloss over. "You didn't have to."

I take a cautious step toward her, testing the space between us. Both of us hold our coffees, the drink like a barrier in our hands from me getting any closer to her. "I know I didn't have to. It doesn't change the fact I wanted to."

Her lips pop open as her eyes search my face. For once, I don't know what she finds in my features. I've always been good at putting on a mask of indifference. In fact, it wasn't really a mask. It's my personality. I just typically don't care about others—until her. I wouldn't have been able to keep this office knowing that she could've appreciated it so much more.

"What about you?" The ice shakes in her cup as her hand drops to the side.

I shrug, turning my head to look at the connecting door between the offices. "I'm not far, just through that door. My new office is what was supposed to be yours."

"I thought I was going to get a cubicle or maybe a desk next to yours," she jokes, setting her drink down.

"We don't have cubicles here. I believe in a more collaborative workspace."

"I noticed. Why do I get a private office then?"

"Because the only person you need to collaborate with is *me*." I walk to the door that connects our two offices. My new one used to be Polly's but I moved her to a different floor to oversee one of our new projects we just took on. She has the largest room on that floor, a slight upgrade from the one that was intended to be Margo's before the plan changed yesterday.

I open it, pointing to my new office. It's only slightly smaller than this one, but it doesn't have the corner view that allows the view of Manhattan she fell in love with.

"See, we can now easily collaborate."

Margo rolls her eyes at me, turning to take in her new space.

"I can't believe this is mine. Does an assistant need this much? If I'm just your coffee girl then I hate to break it to you Beck, but I don't think I need any kind of office, no matter how much I love what I'm seeing here."

"You're going to be in charge of much more than just grabbing me coffee," I tell her. And then I take a seat across from her at her desk, and we go over her tasks while here at Sintech.

26

Margo

To: MargoMoretti@SintechCyberSecurity.com
From: BeckhamSinclair@SintechCyberSecurity.com

Stop looking at me like that. It's been an agonizing week since the dressing room, and your lips are all I've thought about since. Bite them again when looking at me with those doe eyes and I'll forget all about making you beg.

Aren't rules in place to be broken?
Beck

To: BeckhamSinclair@SintechCyberSecurity.com
From: MargoMoretti@SintechCyberSecurity.com

You need to stop looking at me like that. I'm trying to do my job and take notes. Pay attention.

You pay me to work. Let me do my job.

Your assistant,
Margo

To: MargoMoretti@SintechCyberSecurity.com
From: BeckhamSinclair@SintechCyberSecurity.com

It's hard to pay attention when one of my most trusted advisors keeps stealing glances your way. If he looks at you again, I'm going to make a scene and show him that if you're going to be anyone's, you're going to be mine.

Careful leading him on, Violet. I'm a very jealous man.
Beck

To: MargoMoretti@SintechCyberSecurity.com
From: BeckhamSinclair@SintechCyberSecurity.com

Ezra will be picking you up tonight without me. I've got a meeting. I'll still be home for dinner.

You should be waiting for me when I get home.
Beck

To: MargoMoretti@SintechCyberSecurity.com
From: BeckhamSinclair@SintechCyberSecurity.com

You looked too peaceful sleeping when I stopped by to wake you up. Ezra will pick you up whenever you're ready for work. Grab yourself (and me) a coffee on your way in.

I wish we stayed up late last night for reasons other than work.
Beck

To: BeckhamSinclair@SintechCyberSecurity.com
From: MargoMoretti@SintechCyberSecurity.com

I'm attaching the documents you asked for. I've also left a few comments for changes that I think may work better.
Margo

To: MargoMoretti@SintechCyberSecurity.com
From: BeckhamSinclair@SintechCyberSecurity.com

If I didn't know how talented of an artist you were, I'd beg you to stay at Sintech forever. I've accepted your comments and sent them to the marketing team.

You continue to amaze me.
Beck

To: BeckhamSinclair@SintechCyberSecurity.com
From: MargoMoretti@SintechCyberSecurity.com

Winnie, Emma and I are doing matching costumes for Halloween this weekend. Would you want to join?

I think you'd look good in leather.

To: MargoMoretti@SintechCyberSecurity.com
From: BeckhamSinclair@SintechCyberSecurity.com

I can't think of anything I'd rather do less than a coordinating costume.

Can't wait to see you in leather.
Beck

To: MargoMoretti@SintechCyberSecurity.com
From: BeckhamSinclair@SintechCyberSecurity.com

I'm second-guessing implementing casual Fridays per your request. I've never been turned on by a pair of jeans. I can't think straight with you in jeans. It's been almost a month since you turned me down.

Are you ready to beg yet?
Beck

To: BeckhamSinclair@SintechCyberSecurity.com
From: MargoMoretti@SintechCyberSecurity.com

If you take away casual Fridays I quit. Morale seems to be much higher since people get to dress comfortably on Fridays.

You're welcome for the suggestion.
Margo

PS... you bought the jeans. I'm glad you love them.

To: MargoMoretti@SintechCyberSecurity.com
From: BeckhamSinclair@SintechCyberSecurity.com

Don't mistake my words. I'd love to rip the jeans from your body. I actually despise the jeans. They remind me how much I fucking want you.

Why aren't you mine yet?
Beck

I jump when a loud tinging sound breaks me from the journey through my favorited emails in my inbox. It started off innocent. At first, I learned of the feature and favorited an email Beck sent me just so I'd remember to complete the task. But then he kept sending me emails that sent my pulse into overdrive, and in a few weeks' time I had a nice little collection of emails between the two of us that had me questioning why I just don't give into him already.

It's getting harder and harder to resist Beck. We live together, work together, and basically do everything together. I'm not complaining about it. I actually love it more than I probably should. But because of all the time spent together, I'm getting to know Beck for who he is.

And he's nothing like his younger brother. They couldn't be more opposite if they tried.

Which makes my excuses for why Beck and I can't give into the sexual tension for us weaker and weaker.

I'm getting attached to him no matter what, even if we haven't kissed again after that day in the dressing room over a month ago. Things haven't been completely innocent with us either. Looks have lingered at home and here at work. We both have come up with excuses to spend more and more time together. The only time we spend apart is if he has meetings that I'm not needed for or when we both go to separate beds at night.

I'm wondering how much longer I can last. His advances continue. Beck isn't shy about making it clear what he wants— me. At least for the next year. And I'm running out of reasons to deny him.

A flashing notification at the top corner of my desktop computer has pulled me from my imagination of all the *fun* Beck and I could have if I wasn't so set in my ways.

I open the email, noticing it's from Beck. My eyes flick to the glass window in front of me. From it, I can clearly see out into the conference room where he sits through a presentation from one of his heads of development. Except when I look at him, he isn't watching the presentation on the screen. He's staring right at me.

I instantly look away like I'd been caught reaching into the cookie jar. Metaphorically, I guess you *could* call it me reaching into the cookie jar when I know I'm not supposed to. The cookie jar in this instance is just Beck's dirty, teasing emails.

My eyes track over his email, trying not to show too much of a reaction knowing he still might be watching me.

To: MargoMoretti@SintechCyberSecurity.com
From: BeckhamSinclair@SintechCyberSecurity.com

Should I be jealous? You've been staring at your computer monitor with a smile on your face for thirty minutes now. Now you're crossing your legs. What are you looking at, Violet?

Focus on me.
Beck

My cheeks twitch as I fight a smile. An idea pops into my head. One that has no business being there, but one I can't resist. My focus stays pinned on the keyboard in front of me as I type out a response.

To: BeckhamSinclair@SintechCyberSecurity.com
From: MargoMoretti@SintechCyberSecurity.com

Make me.

I'm busy feeling proud of myself, addicted to the thrill of the cat-and-mouse game Beck and I have going on when my office door is slammed—loudly. Looking up, I find an angry-eyed Beck staring at me.

"Miss Moretti." He keeps his voice steady despite the deep, gravelly tone to it.

"Yes, Mr. Sinclair?"

Beck looks over his shoulder, out the glass windows that everyone can see into it. It isn't hard to miss the curious eyes that are pretending not to watch the both of us in here. It's like being in a fishbowl. With the dangerous glint in Beck's eyes right now, I'm not sure I'm thankful that all my coworkers can see in right now, or if I hate that they can.

"Do you think it's cute to send emails that get my blood pumping damn well knowing I can't act on it?"

I sit back in my chair, crossing one leg over the other as I look up and down his towering form. There's an angry set to his shoulders. His jaw is clenched so tight I'm wondering if he's grinding his teeth down in the process. "I'm afraid I don't know what you're talking about."

I run the top of my pen over my lip, knowing exactly where I'm drawing his attention with the movement.

"Maybe I should bend you over this desk right now and punish you for punishing me."

I stick the pen between my teeth, smiling around it at him. "In front of all your employees?" My tongue clicks. "Something tells me HR would think that's a *very* bad idea."

His nostrils flare as he watches me closely. He takes his time answering me. It's like he can read my mind, knowing that his silence—mixed with his menacing stare—is enough to make me squirm.

My stomach drops when he runs his thumb over his bottom lip before it turns up in a sinister smile. "God, it'll be so good when I finally have you on your knees. Maybe I'll punish you just as much as you've punished me."

Before I can respond, he straightens his back. He takes a step closer, his eyes flicking to my computer screen. I hastily try to close out of the tabs that show me re-reading all of our old messages. The smile that had my skin prickling with intense need has disappeared, the mask he uses for work back into place.

"Tell me, how do you feel about Colorado?"

My eyebrows pinch together on my forehead in confusion. "Excuse me?"

He runs a finger down the edge of my desk. His touch dangerously close to my exposed knee.

"We've got a business trip to go on. Tomorrow."

"Tomorrow?"

His knuckles tap against my desk. "*Tomorrow*," he confirms.

And then he leaves me alone in my office, wondering how the hell I'll survive traveling with him without finally giving in.

27

Beck

"Beck, I think we should pull off at the next exit."

I grunt, my eyes focused on the road in front of us. The windshield wipers swipe in rapid succession, but even with their rampant pace, they're still not very helpful. With the thick snow flurries pouring from the sky, it's hard to really see anything on the road.

"We'll be out of the snow soon," I answer, trying to calm her nerves. She seems nervous as hell sitting next to me. In hindsight, I maybe should've accepted the invite to stay at the residence of the man who just agreed to invest enough into the company to streamline a development that's been in the works for two years now.

I was too prideful to accept. I hated the way his son stared at Margo. He watched her like he wanted her. The last thing I was going to do was stay in that house with all of them to ride out a snowstorm. Not with the knowledge of how bad his annoying, golden-retriever-acting son looked at Margo like he was just waiting to sink his claws into her. I know the look of desire when it comes to her well. It's because I've been wearing the same look for a while now.

I shouldn't have brought Margo in the first place. Granted, part of the reason she thinks she was hired was to travel with me. But the moment I saw the son's eyes light up when Margo stepped from behind me at the beginning of the meeting, I regretted ever bringing her.

"If this radar is correct, it's supposed to snow for at least the next twelve hours. And that's as far as it'll let me see."

"Those things are never right."

"Oh, so you're a meteorologist now?"

"And you are?" I accuse, throwing her insult back at her. I'm not a fucking meteorologist, although it seems like a good gig because they're wrong half the time and still get to keep their job.

"All I'm saying is that I'm not trying to die in a snowstorm. So if you want to keep driving to try and make it to your little airport, fine be my guest. I think it's dumb considering there's no way they're flying in this, but you can give it a try. I, on the other hand, would love for you to drop me off at the next exit so I can ride out the snowstorm in the warmth and not fear for my life."

"I'm not leaving you alone in an unfamiliar place."

"And driving recklessly in the middle of a blizzard is a better option?"

If I wasn't white-knuckling the steering wheel, I'd look over at her and give her a dirty look. She might have a valid point, but I'm still under the impression that sooner or later we have to make it through the worst of the snow. It came on pretty sudden, the small flurries easy to see through at first before it started dumping snow.

"Beck." She raises her voice at me. I can feel her gaze hot on my cheeks.

"What?"

"I think there's a town close called Sutten Mountain. Pull over at the next exit. There's got to be somewhere for us to stay."

"No. We're almost out of it."

She groans, her hands flying into the air in frustration. "We are *not* almost out of it. I want to get out of the car and stay somewhere! We should be passing an exit any minute. We're getting off there."

"Last I checked, I'm the one driving."

I have to squint to see through the snow. Maybe she is right. I thought that the snow would lighten up if we just kept driving, but the visibility is becoming worse and worse. Even with the all-wheel drive of the SUV, I can feel the tires slip every now and then on slick patches.

"Oh look," Margo says sarcastically. From the corner of my eye I can see her holding her phone up to her face as she reads something on it. "Apparently they've shut the interstate down three miles ahead due to the storm. *Weird*. It's as if we're in an actual fucking dangerous snowstorm!"

"Watch your tone," I warn, hating that I was wrong in this scenario.

"*Watch your tone,*" she mocks. "God, you're so stubborn and frustrating. Can you just admit that you were wrong and pull off?"

"*I'm* frustrating?" I laugh maniacally, leaning forward in the seat to try and see better through the gusts of wind blowing snow all over the road. "You've frustrated me from the *moment* I met you. So before you call me stubborn, look at yourself, sweetheart."

"*Sweetheart?*" she says in disgust. "Don't talk down to me, asshole."

I take a deep breath, looking for any indication of the exit she apparently thinks is close. "I'm not talking down to you."

A sarcastic laugh fills the tense space between us. "Just because you're mad that you're wrong and I'm right doesn't mean you have an excuse to be a dick."

My teeth grind together as I keep my mouth shut. There are so many things I'd like to bring up to her, like the fact that *she's* been the one who's been hard-headed from the moment I kissed her. She may be frustrated with me for the moment, but I've been frustrated for over a month now. I say none of this, knowing that we aren't seeing eye to eye right now to begin with.

"You're sure the interstate is closed up ahead?"

"Would you like to check yourself?" she seethes. I brave a look at her out of the corner of my eye. She shakes her phone at me, some sort of app pulled up that appears to have traffic updates on it.

"Give it to me," I instruct, pulling one hand off the wheel to hold it in front of her.

"No freaking way!" she yells. "Put both hands on the wheel now. Are you *crazy?*"

My fingers wiggle as an aggravated sigh falls from my mouth. "Give me the fucking phone so I can check where I need to get off."

"I told you, it's the next exit."

"Do you see an exit anywhere?" I point out, growing more frustrated with her by the second.

"Put both hands on the wheel and I'll look again," she demands.

I growl, hurriedly reaching out to try to pluck the phone from her hands. It doesn't work. She screams, the sound causing me to jump. She immediately reaches across the space between us, grabbing the steering wheel.

"Hands off," I scold, trying to push her hands away so I can do my job and get her somewhere safely.

"Oh, so *now* you're worried about safety?"

I try to pull her hand off the wheel, but her little fingers are wrapped around it so tightly it's proving harder than I expected.

In my efforts to try and get her grip off the steering wheel, I miss the sign for the exit. Everything happens in one big blur. I'm trying to turn the wheel toward the exit ramp that's coming into light before us. Unfortunately, Margo sees it at the same time. She jerks at the wheel, trying to point it out. The mixture of our movements together causes the wheel to go too far right. In slow motion, the tires skid down the unused exit ramp, wet snow coating the surface. One moment we're perfectly lined up on the road, the next the sudden movements of the wheel have us skidding off the side of the road and down a small embankment.

My arm reaches out to Margo immediately, crossing her chest to try and shield her from any impact. Her scream ricochets off the SUV walls, sending my heart into disarray in pure panic that she's hurt.

Somehow we get lucky, and the car comes to an almost immediate stop, the tires getting stuck in the thick mud and snow mixture on the side of the road.

The impact is so soft that not even the airbags deploy.

I look at her immediately, scanning her face and body for any indications that she'd been hurt. "Are you okay?" I rush, reaching out to rub my fingers down her cheek to make sure she's okay.

"Don't touch me," she angrily answers, pushing my hand off her. "I'm *fine*."

I'd be upset with the tone she uses with me if I wasn't so fucking relieved that I hadn't been responsible for her getting hurt.

"Well, that's one way to make sure we stop," I say, knowing I sound like the dick she's accusing me of being.

"Really? That's what you're saying right now?"

"Was there something else I'm supposed to be saying?" I pull out my phone to attempt to call for help. Ezra is waiting at the private airport for us. He might be able to do something. Or l can at least try to call a tow truck.

"Yeah, how about *I'm sorry I almost killed you, Margo?*"

I shoot her a look. "You're the one who was grabbing the wheel! Do you have a death wish?"

She lets out an aggravated sigh. "The only reason I grabbed the wheel is because you took a hand off it! I was just trying to keep us safe."

I roll my eyes at her. "I don't think it's *ever* a safe choice for the passenger to grab the steering wheel. Did you take driver's education classes?"

"You're being an asshole right now."

"Oh, I'm sorry. Should I be thankful for your assistance in getting us stuck in the middle of fucking nowhere?" I wave my phone between us. "With no fucking service."

Her lips form a little *O* as my words register with her. She looks down at her phone to confirm my statement for herself.

We have no service.

I reach up, pinching the bridge of my nose with my thumb and index finger as my eyes squeeze shut. I take a calming breath, trying to think about what our options are.

Essentially, we're fucked. We have no service. It's getting dark outside. Snow falls down in thick, wet clusters that make it hard to see anything. Add in the wind and the bitter cold and it's a fucking nightmare outside.

Plus, there's the fun fact that the only sign of civilization is the small hint of light in the distance.

"We could maybe wait for someone to drive by?" Margo offers.

I keep my eyes shut, biting my tongue before I bite out a response that I may regret.

With a deep breath, I attempt to see if pressing on the gas pedal does anything. Maybe if I can press it hard enough, we can get unstuck. My efforts prove futile. We don't move an inch.

"Stay in the heat," I command. I angrily pull at the door handle, shoving the door open. I get hit in the face immediately with the blistering cold. Even pulling the collar of my coat to try and shield my face doesn't do enough to fight the bitterness of the wind.

The headlights of the SUV blink, illuminating the night. Bending down in front of the vehicle, I look at both front wheels.

"Fuck," I mutter, noting both wheels a fourth of the way dug into mud. I don't think there's any way to get out without a tow.

Perfect.

I stomp back to the car, relishing in the warmth once I take a seat in the driver's seat and pull the door shut.

"How sure are you that there's a town near?"

She picks at her cuticles, something I've noticed she does when she's nervous. If I weren't so pissed at myself for putting us in the situation, I'd reach over and try to calm her nerves. I don't know what to do in this situation, so I'm going to stay on my side of the SUV and stew in my anger. "I mean, it was an exit where I *think* it said something about a town called Sutten Mountain or something like that. Surely there are businesses? I think…"

"You *think?*"

"Yes Beck, I think. It made it seem like there is, but I don't want to say I'm totally confident in that."

With an angry sigh, I figure out what to do. I turn to face her. "You stay in the car. Keep it locked and keep it on. I'll be back."

Her mouth flies open, fear in her eyes. "You're going out in *that?*" Her eyes look out the front windshield, where the visibility has declined even more—something I didn't know was possible.

"I don't have much choice. I need to find us help."

She chews on her lip for a few seconds. "I'll go with you. Maybe we can find somewhere to stay for the night."

"You're not going out in these conditions." My tone is harsh, but I don't care to soften it. I might lose my god damn mind if I have to watch her trudge through the bitter cold and snow because I was too fucking jealous to stay at the nice, warm place we were offered earlier.

"Staying in the car waiting for a serial killer isn't that great of an option either," she spits out. Her arms cross over her chest defensively. The stare she pins on me is probably supposed to scare me. It doesn't.

"Something tells me even serial killers aren't out in weather like this."

Her eyebrows lift to her hairline as she leans slightly closer to me. "Oh, so now you're admitting how terrible the conditions are?"

My eyes roll. "The conditions are shitty out there. You aren't going out in it."

She defiantly stares back at me, zipping her thin coat all the way up to her chin. "If you're going out there, so am I."

"Not a fucking chance."

"You're not my boss."

Despite how pissed off I am, my lips twitch with humor. "*Actually*, I am. So it's settled. You'll stay here."

I open my door once again, hoping that my abrupt ending to the conversation will deter her from her stupid idea to follow me to what I hope is a town.

The car shuts off. I turn to figure out what the fuck she's up to when her passenger door opens. She steps out, holding her arms close to her body in an attempt to keep warm. She dangles the keys in the air, her hair blowing all over the place from the wind.

"We've got to lock it since we'll be gone."

"Get back in the car, Margo!" I yell into the whistling wind.

She fucking ignores me. The lights blink twice, indicating that she's locked the car before she starts walking down the side of the road in the direction of the lights.

My dress shoes slip in the snow as I rush toward her. "Margo," I hiss, catching up to her.

She ignores me, her eyes trained on the lights ahead of her.

"Stop ignoring me," I demand.

Snow hits the both of us in the face. We might as well fucking freeze out in this storm. And it's completely unnecessary for her to freeze right along with me. She should've stayed in the car.

"Then stop trying to tell me what to do," she yells against the wind.

"Now's not the time for you to be fucking stubborn," I seethe. Her shoulders have already begun to shake from the cold. With the way the wind beats down on both of us, it should be only minutes before her lips turn blue.

She continues her trek down the road. I don't think the pair of fuzzy boots on her feet are much better footwear for the snow than my dress shoes. I'd let her know of that fact if she wasn't so hellbent on ignoring me.

With a loud groan of anger—at myself and at her—I rip my coat off and eat the distance between us. Without warning, I shove the coat over her shoulders, trying to pull it up and around her ears so at least she'll be a little more warm.

"What are you doing?"

Without the coat, the wind cuts right through my suit jacket and thin button-up. I try to hide how fucking cold it is. It doesn't matter. I'd strip completely fucking naked in this storm if it meant she'd be even slightly warmer.

"If you're not going to listen, then I'm at least going to try and keep you from freezing to death."

"What about you?"

"Should've thought about that before you insisted on following me." Stuffing my hands in my pockets in an attempt to keep them warm, I head down the road, knowing she'll follow closely behind me.

As the lights get closer and closer, I can't help but become even more pissed off with myself for the decisions I've made today.

28

Margo

The Uggs on my feet are sopping wet as we step through the doors of the small inn. I feel like a wet dog, every inch of my clothing cold and sticking to my body as we make our way to the person waiting for us at the front desk.

The old woman sitting behind the counter gives us a warm smile, tucking the book she was reading into her lap. She pulls off a pair of hot pink readers. "Oh dear," she says with a worried expression, taking in both of our disheveled appearances. "Did you get stuck in the storm?"

We give each other a look, the two of us still hot inside from our fight. Beck's lips press into a thin line as he looks back at her. "You could say that," he says, his voice low.

"It's a lot of snow for November," the woman muses, nowhere near deterred by the growly tone of Beck's voice.

Beck grunts, tapping his fingers against the counter. He looks at me briefly from the corner of his eye. I bite back a snarky comment about the numerous warnings I gave him about the snowstorm. I warned him they'd shut down the roads and overpasses if it got too bad. It's not my fault we're in this situation.

"Are you needing a room for the night?" She straightens the glasses on her nose, warmth in her eyes despite Beck's continued grumpiness.

"We'll need two rooms. The two most expensive ones you have."

The woman clicks her tongue. "I'm sorry sir, because of the snow we only have one room…" She looks between us, uneasiness finally starting to seep over her features.

"Fine," he snaps. I want to chastise him for the tone of his voice with her. It isn't her fault he decided he was a weather expert. *Stupid, stubborn man.*

He aims a dirty look in my direction. For a split second, I wonder if he can read my thoughts. He looks away from me, pinning his angry stare on the nice woman. "As long as it has two beds, we'll take whatever you've got."

She turns around, taking a set of keys off a nail behind her. "We have our honeymoon suite left. The people who reserved it for their honeymoon didn't make it because their flight got cancelled." She jingles the keys in front of her. "Lucky for you," she adds, her tone chipper once again.

Dread settles in my stomach. Beck must be coming to the same realization as me. The honeymoon suite doesn't strike me as a room that has two beds.

He clears his throat, taking the keys from her hand. "The honeymoon suite has two beds?"

She shakes her head. "No, dear, only one. It's rather large though if you're waiting for marriage or you know"—she looks between us awkwardly—"need some space between you and your girlfriend."

I cough, choking on my spit in embarrassment. It might be a slight tinge of amusement too because *oh my god* is Beckham Sinclair blushing?

"Are there any other inns or hotels around that would possibly have something with two rooms? Nothing against this place, but my *assistant* here and I need two beds."

"I'm afraid not. There's a few in the heart of Sutten, but I don't think there's any transportation that could get you there."

I lay my hand on his bicep, taking in the frigid fabric of his button-up. The starched, freezing cold fabric seems almost frozen to his body. "It's fine." I try to keep my voice calm. "We'll figure it out."

His nostrils flare as he stares me down. I'd give anything to know what's going on in his head. He'd been so angry with me earlier, the two of us bickering more than an old married couple. Now he doesn't look as angry, but there's another emotion I just can't get a read on. He shoves the keys into his pocket and then pulls out his wallet. He lets out a resigned sigh. "We'll take it."

I bite back the urge to tell him he shouldn't sound so put out with the thought of sharing a bed with me. He's told me various times all the ways he wants to fuck me, so clearly he doesn't find me disgusting. I'd gladly share a bed with him if it meant my toes would thaw and I could get out of these freezing clothes.

Speaking of, I lean over the counter and smile softly at her. "Is there any chance you have a gift shop here or anything where we can buy new clothes? I'm desperate for something warm and not completely saturated in freezing cold water."

She finishes writing something in a small little journal of hers, running Beck's credit card and handing it back to him. "We sure do, hon. Let me take you to it. This inn is run by my husband and I. He's out making sure the snow doesn't make us lose any power. I can get you taken care of in the shop as well."

The woman slowly walks toward a small opening with a wooden sign above it identifying it as their gift shop. As soon as we step in, there are various animals carved out of wood covering an entire shelf. She catches me looking at them. "My husband carves those," she says proudly, picking up a carved moose the size of my finger and turning it in her hand.

"They're stunning," I tell her. I can't imagine the steadiness it takes in a hand to get the details so perfect using a knife. I'm more than impressed by the craftsmanship.

She hums a response, ushering us deeper into the store that's no bigger than my own room at Beck's place. Her hand reaches out to point to two racks of clothes. "I'm afraid these are the only options we have." She looks at Beck, starting at his head and looking all the way down to his feet. "Although I'm unsure if these will quite fit you," she says apologetically.

He takes a step forward, beginning to rifle through the rack. "I'm sure I can find something." He pulls a hoodie off the rack, looking inside at the tag. Apparently meeting his standards, he hands it over to me. "Take this."

"I'll leave you two to look. Come to the counter at the front when you're done and I'll get you all rung up."

I politely smile as she turns around. "Thank you."

Beck shakes the hoodie, gesturing for me to take it.

"Beck, this thing is like three sizes too big for me."

He continues to look through the clothing, not bothering to look at me. "It's the warmest fabric they have. Your lips are blue from being so cold, so forgive me if I don't give a flying fuck how big it is on you as long as it keeps you warm."

My mouth snaps shut as his response takes me off guard. His words alone send warmth down my body. My silence has him looking over his shoulder for a brief moment. "No arguments from you? I'm shocked. It's seemed to be your mission to argue over *every damn thing* today."

I scoff, hugging the sweatshirt to my chest. I stick my hands inside the fabric, loving how soft and warm the fleece inside feels against my cold hands. "I wouldn't call it arguing if I was pointing out the fact that we shouldn't have been out on the roads with an impending snowstorm and all."

He pulls a set of plaid pajamas from the rack, checking the tag for the size. A grunt leaves his chest. I fight the grin that wants to make an appearance at fancy Beck donning a pair of red and black plaid pajamas, a giant bear on a pocket on the chest that reads *I'm beary tired*. It's something that belongs on a child's pajama set, not one made for a grown man.

"There's nothing else in my size," he groans.

I lift the sweatshirt. "There's no way this wouldn't fit you." Taking a step toward one of the racks, I try to find one of the cheesy pajama sets in my size. They don't look as warm as the hoodie in my hand, but still far better than the frozen outfit I currently wear.

Beck suddenly turns to me, eating up all the distance between us until our mingling breaths warm the other. "Do you not listen? I'm not taking the warmest thing for myself because you need it. Now find a pair of pants that'll fit you and let's go find some other things we'll need for the night."

He leaves me standing there watching his retreating form, my jaw almost hanging to the floor. No matter how much he's pissed me off today, that primal, nurturing side of Beck I just witnessed has me feeling a range of mixed emotions.

Following his instructions, I look through the options, not finding much. Eventually, I find a pair of long johns I'm almost certain are supposed to be worn as underwear when you go skiing, but it's the best I can find given the circumstances.

When I find Beck, he's piling various toiletry items in his

arms. A box of toothbrushes almost falls to the floor as he shoves two phone chargers into the pile.

"Need help?" I offer, taking a step closer to him. My voice comes out odd, my mind—and ladybits—still reeling at the authoritative yet gentle tone of his voice a few moments ago.

"I've got it," he growls.

"Okay," I mutter under my breath. I leave him to it, deciding to search for some sort of food to snack on. It's seemed like ages since we ate. Maybe Beck's mood will improve if he's fed, his anger could be because he's hangry. At least I hope that's the case. A night snowed in with him when he's this testy doesn't sound like my ideal way to ride out a snowstorm.

I stand in front of the meager selection of food they have. The options could be better, but I guess it could also be worse. They *do* have red licorice, which happens to be my weakness, so that's a win in my book. A pile similar to Beck's begins to build in my arms, except mine with food instead of toiletries. I add a few different bags of beef jerky, apparently made by someone local, as well as a few bags of potato chips. I walk by a small refrigerator grabbing a few water bottles for the room.

My food choices aren't likely up to Beck's standards, with all the fancy meals he's cooked or had prepared by his chef, but it's the best I can find given our circumstances.

The two of us meet back up in front of the inn owner. I drop all of the items on the counter, looking up at her. "I'm sorry, I think I missed your name earlier. I was too cold to think straight."

This warrants another growl from Beck. I ignore him, waiting for her to answer.

She types a code for each item into the register. "My name is Carmen and my husband is Leroy if you happen to run into him at all."

"Thank you for fitting us in. I don't know what we would've done if you'd been full. We spun out on the road and we'll need a tow to get anywhere else."

"I'm sorry to hear that," she sympathizes. "Leroy can help you tomorrow, weather—and roads—permitting."

Carmen moves on from ringing up the food items and moves to the things Beck had laid out nicely on the counter. To be honest, half of the things he grabbed are things I definitely would have forgotten to grab if it weren't for him. No matter how mad I am with his stubborn ass, I can appreciate his Type A personality thinking of things I wouldn't have.

Finally, she gets to the clothes, a few pairs of socks I hadn't grabbed going into a paper bag last. Another thing Beck thought of that I appreciate. My toes have never been so cold in my life.

Carmen finishes getting us checked out and then offers to walk us to our room. I agree to it at the same time Beck says he'll find it. Carmen ignores his answer, opting to lead us up a staircase and down a few hallways before we stop in front of a large wooden door. HONEYMOON SUITE is etched into the wood, two bears kissing underneath it also carved permanently.

She smiles bashfully, watching the both of us take it in. "Housekeeping had it set up for the newlywed couple so don't mind the extra additions in the room, they come with the suite so enjoy them." Carmen winks at us and then leaves both of us standing in front of it.

With an angry groan, Beck reaches into his pocket and sticks the key through the hole. He barely gets a look inside when I swear I hear him mumble, "I'm fucked."

29

Beck

"Well this is nice," Margo pipes up from behind me. I ignore her, biting back an insult about the room. This isn't nice. This will be pure torture. Being respectful of Margo's wishes has been testing every inch of restraint I've ever had. Now the anger sizzling between us and the knowledge that her warm body will be sleeping inches away from mine has my thoughts muddled with the lust. The large bed with rose petals scattered all over it doesn't help the situation.

I'm mostly pissed at myself for not listening to her the first time she warned me about the snowstorm. I wanted to get to our final destination, to focus on work and be riddled with meetings where I wasn't drowning in her presence.

A man can only hold back so much, and I've learned that keeping Margo by my side constantly wasn't my best idea. It could've been until she put the stupid rule between us that we couldn't kiss or touch or do anything behind the scenes because my prick of a brother didn't treat her the way she deserved to be treated.

I haven't been restraining myself around her because I'm a

good man either. If she had given me any other excuse other than the one she gave, I would've already found a way through her defenses. The walls she put up between us would be obliterated and we'd already have given in to the clear attraction between the two of us.

Margo says a few things but the words don't register with me. I half-hoped there'd be a couch or something for me to sleep on in here. I'm not granted that luxury.

"I really don't understand why you're the one acting all pissed off," she blurts, finally catching my attention. "If anyone should be pissed, it's me. You've been a dick to me when I was the one who warned you of the snow to begin with."

I drop the bags from the gift shop on the table. I don't give her any kind of response, knowing it's better if I keep my mouth shut. Instead of saying something I'll regret, I take angry steps to the bathroom. I immediately reach for the shower, turning the water to its hottest setting. It heats up quickly despite the cold weather outside, steam begins to build quickly in the room.

"Beck!" Margo stops in the opening of the bathroom, fire in her eyes once again. I get why she's pissed at me. I've been a dick to her, but I'm still too riled up to apologize.

The sight of her still tinted blue lips, the soaking wet clumps of her hair that were once frozen, make me hate myself. If I had just listened to her about the snow, we wouldn't be in this situation. We'd be warm in a luxury hotel, bickering about something completely mundane.

"Get in," I demand, angling my head to the shower.

Her mouth pops open. "You ignore me and then think you can just boss me around?" She shakes her head in frustration, disappearing back into the room. "Not going to happen, Beck. You don't control me."

I follow hot on her heels. "Last time I checked, I'm your boss."

An aggravated sound falls from deep in her chest. "I'm off the clock."

I grab her elbow, turning her to face me before she sits down on the large king-sized bed.

My teeth grind against one another, threatening to break underneath the pressure. "Get. In. The. Shower."

Her eyes flick to where I hold her. She shivers underneath my grip, just another nail in the coffin of the regrets I have for the day.

"No."

"Yes."

She attempts to rip her arm free, but I stop her, applying more pressure.

"Why the hell do you want me in the shower anyway? Is this your way of getting me naked?"

I roll my eyes at her preposterous reasoning. "If this was an attempt to get you naked, Violet, you'd already be naked and greedily taking my cock on that bed behind you."

This stops whatever witty remark she was going to fire back at me. Her mouth snaps shut. Even with her silence, her anger is palpable by the defiant set of her shoulders and the look in her eye.

"Why does it matter if I take a shower or not?"

My fingers twitch against her wet sleeve. "Because your teeth are chattering and your body is trembling from the cold and if I have to watch you suffer for another minute because of the decisions I've made, I might lose my god damn mind."

For a split second, I think she's going to listen to me. My words appear to take her so off guard that she might actually do as she's told. *It was a nice thought while it lasted.* Defiance sparks in her eyes moments later, her arms crossing her chest. "I'm fine."

I sigh, running a hand down my face. There's no way she's fine. I'm fucking freezing and my clothing is thicker than hers. My coat provides her with a bit more of a layer, but it still isn't enough. She has to be cold, and her refusing to do something to warm up just to spite me is childish. I'm not in the fucking mood to deal with it.

"Just remember I tried to do this the nice way," I growl.

Lines appear between her eyebrows. "What do you—"

Her words stop the moment I heave her over my shoulder. All of the water on her makes her heavier than normal, but she's still light in comparison to other people.

She kicks her legs up and down as I step into the bathroom. "What the fuck, Beck!" she screams, hitting my back repeatedly. "You can't just pick me up like a fucking caveman whenever you don't get your way."

Still carrying her, I step into the shower and let the steaming hot water cascade over both our clothed bodies. Her body slides down my front as I drop her, an angry look on her face when she looks up at me.

Water runs down both of our faces, steam billowing around our bodies. "You can't just fucking freeze to death because you're trying to prove a point to me," I fire back.

Reaching between us, I yank on the zipper of the coat I loaned her. It falls to the ground, totally forgotten as I do the same thing with the thin coat she packed for herself.

Her hand smacks mine. "You're not taking my clothes off."

"You take them off, or I will, but keeping the frozen clothes on you does nothing to warm you up."

She takes a step to the shower door, trying to retreat. I hook an arm around her middle, pulling her hard against my body. "For the love of god, Margo, stop fucking fighting."

Her body is tense against mine. Layers of clothing separate our bodies from touching, yet I swear I can feel the heat of her skin against my fingertips. I hold her against me until I finally feel her body relax.

She takes a step away from me, turning around and moving the wet hair from her face.

"Fine. You win. But *only* because I'm cold."

I let out a sigh of relief, waiting for her lips to turn back to their natural red color that drives me fucking wild. She stares at the ground, stripping one layer after the other until she's wearing a lingerie set that's way too fucking sexy for her to wear on a business trip.

"What the fuck is this?" I seethe, my eyes zeroing in on her hard nipples fighting against the black lace appliqués of the bra.

She steps deeper into the stream of the water, letting out a small moan as she's engulfed in the heat.

This might actually be the worst fucking idea I've ever had. I'd only been thinking about getting heat back to her body but I hadn't imagined what it'd be like being confined with her in a shower, especially after I've found what she was hiding underneath all those god damn layers.

"Margo," I growl.

Her eyes pop open, looking down at her body. She has to know how fucking sexy she looks right now. "This"—she begins, running her hands through her hair as the water flows through the long strands—"is a little something you bought me."

I pinch the bridge of my nose, turning so my back faces her. Now that she isn't shivering, my mind is becoming more clear.

The primal need for her is returning. I'm no longer thinking about the cold from earlier, and instead I'm thinking about all the delectable ways I could warm her up.

My fingers angrily work at the buttons of my suit jacket. The custom suit cost thousands of dollars and is probably ruined by the snow and mud it is now covered in. It doesn't matter. Right now what matters is getting the hell away from her and the tiny scraps of clothing that are covering the parts of hers I've spent far too long fantasizing about.

The shower door crashes against the wall loudly as I swing it open. I'm lucky it didn't break. It doesn't stop me from slamming it shut behind me in frustration. I run out of the bathroom as fast as my legs will take me, needing space from her.

Fuck this business trip.

Fuck the snowstorm.

And fuck how badly I want to bury myself inside her and fuck all the anger right out of her.

I rip my tie from my body, throwing it to my feet. I'm angrily shoving my pants down my thighs when I hear her voice from right behind me.

She must be a fucking ninja, because I didn't hear her turn off the shower or leave the bathroom. I must've been too busy lingering in the anger of being stuck in this situation to hear her at all.

"Why are you so mad at me?" she asks from my back.

I work at the buttons of my shirt, not daring to face her. I don't know if she's covered her body more or not, but my restraint is paper thin right now. If I see her in that set of lingerie again, I might just lose control and rip it from that perfect fucking body of hers.

"I'm done talking." My words are short, leaving nothing up

for interruption. I truly don't want to talk right now. I'd much rather put our mouths to better use, but I can't exactly say that out loud. Or I could, but it wouldn't do anything but prove to me that deep down she wants me, but she won't let it happen.

"Well, I'm not," she snaps, looping around me to stand in front of me. At least she's wrapped a white towel around her body, shielding her flawless body from my view.

I catch her looking me up and down. I intended to be fully dressed in the god-awful pajama set I found in the gift shop by the time she stepped out of the shower, but yet again, she couldn't just fucking listen to me.

My shirt hangs open, giving her a view of the muscles I work hard to maintain. Her eyes catch on my navy blue boxers, further fueling the hard-on I had by seeing her in lingerie.

"Do you ever do as you're told?" I sigh, putting my hands on my hips.

She hugs the fabric of her towel closer to her. "Sometimes. Tell me why you're mad at me, and I may actually listen to you."

"You don't want to know why I'm mad."

"You don't get to tell me what I do or don't want."

"If you ask me again, I'm going to tell you, and I promise you don't really want to know."

"Tell me why you're mad."

There's no hint of reservation in her eyes, only pure defiance. There are so many things I'd do to her to wipe the smug look from her face.

I pull my arms from the sleeves of the dress shirt, throwing it onto the bed next to us. "I'm livid because I'm stuck in this fucking hotel room with you, and the only thing on my mind is how bad I want you. I'm fucking desperate to kiss you, taste you, fuck you. I want to spend the entire night finding new ways to keep that perfect body of yours warm. You want to know why I'm pissed? Because I know deep down you want all of those things too, you're just too stubborn—too god damn afraid—to let it happen. And for once in my god damn life, I want something— need something—I can't fucking have. So there you have it. I'm livid because I want to fucking make you mine, and you won't let me because my brother was a dick to you and you're not over it."

She stares at me wide-eyed, blinking over and over. My chest heaves up and down. My throat is hoarse from shouting the words at her, needing to get them off my chest. There's no going back now. She knows how I feel. I've told her how badly I fucking need her, and now I need to prepare myself for whatever excuse she's going to give why we can't just give in.

Except she doesn't do it. In fact, it isn't what she says…it's what she does.

The towel drops to the ground.

The lingerie is long gone.

Margo is naked in front of me. Her fingers play with her nipples when she looks me in the eye. "Is this the point where I beg?"

30

Margo

I'm completely and utterly fucked. Metaphorically.

Physically? I hope to be by the end of all this.

Beck's tongue peeks out to wet his lips, and I applaud myself for how long I've fought the undeniable chemistry between us.

I gave denying him a good try. I stuck to my guns for longer than I expected to. But at the end of the day, I'm tired of having wet dreams about my boss. My future fake fiancé. My ex's older brother. I'm ready for him to make good on every dirty threat he's ever made.

I'm ready for Beckham Sinclair to fuck me. I want to know what it feels like for him to bury himself inside me. I'm desperate to feel all of him, to know nothing but him filling me as deep as I can take him.

His thumb runs over the spot he just licked. I half expected him to fly across the room and have me bent over already once he saw me naked. At the very least, I expected him to kiss me.

The growing erection in his boxers is proof of how badly he wants me, he's just not acting on it yet.

A low growl erupts from deep in his chest. "I meant every fucking word when I told you you'd have to beg for me to fuck you."

"Tell me how to beg and I'll do it," I answer immediately.

He smirks in appreciation, running his palm over his cock. "Oh I will, don't worry about that." He takes a step closer to me.

Out of habit, I cover the intimate parts of me with my hands. It's not that I don't want this. I had time to think about it in the shower. I stripped out of my clothes in there and left fully knowing what I wanted. It's what I've wanted from his first threat in my old office.

His hand is warm against the tender skin at my back as he pulls my body against his. "Don't cover yourself in front of me," he demands. "I've waited far too long to see every bare inch of you for you to shield it from me."

I swallow, arching my back to look up at him. "I want you Beck," I admit, all anger at him dissipating by the lust in his eyes. "You're right, I've wanted you from the beginning of this agreement. I'm just scared that with you, it'll be different."

His fingertips are punishing as he digs them into the skin at my hips. "It better fucking be," he growls, pulling my body into his and crashing his lips against mine.

God, I forgot how good he kissed. Even the stroke of his tongue against mine has my body hot with need. You'd never know the two of us were on the brink of hypothermia an hour ago. Heat now envelops the space around us. His knuckles brush up against the side of my ribcage as his hand travels up my body.

Just as he's circling the darker skin of my nipple, he pulls his hands away. His grin is cocky as he bites his lip.

"Lay down on the bed."

I freeze, confused by the demand. "What happened to me begging?"

He lifts me by the hips, once again carrying me like I weigh nothing. He throws me down on the bed, my body bouncing against the soft mattress filled with rose petals.

Beck fits his body between my legs, looking at me like a man who's been starved. Maybe I *have* been starving him. It's been fun—and hot as hell—teasing him for this long. It's morbid of me to admit, but I liked the cat-and-mouse game we've been playing.

Something tells me everything he's about to do to me will be much more fun.

He crawls onto the bed himself, his body looming over mine. He kisses around my nipple, licking and sucking the tender skin around my peaked bud but not putting his mouth on the part of my breast that wants him most.

Teasing me, and enjoying it by the mischief in his eyes, he repeats the same movements on my other breast. My back arches when he starts to kiss down my stomach, his fingertips light as they also rake down my body.

His hot palms hit the inside of my thighs, pushing them open so he can get a perfect view of the wetness between my legs.

"Trust me, Violet, I always keep good on my promises. I'm going to make you beg so hard for me to fuck you. But first…"

His finger brushes against my swollen clit. "First?" I moan.

"First, be a good girl and keep your legs spread open for me. I need a fucking taste of you."

He seals his mouth against me, and I learn somehow he's even better at licking my pussy than he is at kissing me.

My fingertips fist the comforter, needing something to hold onto as he ravishes me. He proves that he *had* been starved. I deprived him of what he wanted—me—and he's going to make me regret ever making him wait.

I loathe myself for ever denying myself of the feel of his tongue working against me.

"This pretty little pussy of yours is dripping wet with need for me." He sticks a finger in, followed by another. He spreads them, stretching me in the most delicious of ways.

"You're so tight." He twists his fingers in an effort to stretch me.

"Will you fit?" I moan as his thumb brushes over my clit.

His breath is hot on my inner thigh. "Don't worry, baby, I'll make sure you're ready to take all of me."

His tongue working in perfect rhythm with his fingers is all the promise I need. It feels too good, I don't care how bad it'll hurt to feel all of him inside me. I'm desperate for it, wanting to feel him fill every last inch of me.

I reach up to play with my nipple, adding to the sensations running over my body with his actions combined with mine. An orgasm begins in my body. "Beck," I moan, "I'm so close."

Instead of my words pushing him to work harder, it does the opposite. He pulls away, smirking at me. This smirk is way hotter, seeing the proof of my arousal coating his perfect lips.

"You can't come yet, baby," he says, a hint of apology in his voice. "You've made me wait so long for this, and I meant it when you'd have to beg first."

I groan, so fucking close to an orgasm, but not close enough.

I should've known he wouldn't let me off so easily. I've tortured him for over a month, I should've expected him to make me work for it.

Frustrated, I lean up on my elbows, looking at him between my legs. "I gave you the chance to have me beg."

He shrugs, standing up, he sticks his hand in his boxers and frees his cock. My mouth opens at the sight of it. It's massive. He runs his thumb over a bead of pre-cum, working it down his length.

"I told you, I had to taste you first."

"And now that you have?"

"Now it's time for you to beg, Violet."

31

Beck

She slides off the bed. I fight the urge to grab her and say to hell with the begging. I want to taste her orgasm on my lips, feel her pulsating against my tongue before I ever bury my cock in her.

The problem is, I'm a proud man. When I told her she'd have to beg for it, I meant it in the moment. I'm not someone to go back on my words, so instead of licking and lapping at her, I take a seat on the edge of the bed. I flick my eyes to the open space between a TV console and the bed.

"Go over there and get on your knees."

She looks at the open space cautiously, her fingers absentmindedly drifting to her pussy and running through the wetness I created.

I click my tongue, running my hand down my shaft. "Not so fast. You're not allowed to touch yourself right now."

She works her lip between her teeth. I expect her to argue. For once, she doesn't. Like a good girl, she walks to the space in front of me, tenderly falling to her knees. Her eyes are wide as she watches me carefully.

"That's more like it," I praise, stroking myself. Every fantasy I've had about the woman in front of me fails in comparison to the view of her in this moment.

Margo sits back, placing her perfect bare ass on her heels. "What do you want me to do next?"

I lean back, one arm resting on the comforter to hold my weight while the other continues to stroke up and down my hard length. I've never been a patient man, but I could practice all the patience in the world if I had the view in front of me.

Her hand skirts over her bare skin, her fingers flicking her pink, hardened nipple.

"Hands on your thighs," I demand. The aggravated groan that passes her lips only fuels my desire to draw this out for a bit longer, to really make her pay for denying me for so long.

"I want you to apologize," I begin.

"What do I need to apologize for?" She wiggles, trying to get some kind of friction.

"For making us wait this long when we both knew this would happen eventually."

"What would happen eventually?"

"Us fucking, Margo. I'd given you the chance when you first moved to New York with me. I'd been ready to fulfill every fantasy, every desire you ever had, and you denied me."

Standing up, I walk toward her. I can't keep my hands off her for long. Now that she's given me the chance to touch her, to prove to her who she belongs to, I can't stop. I circle her, one hand still stroking up and down my cock like I have all the time in the world.

"I'm used to getting whatever I want, whenever I want it. Instead of you letting me make your pussy weep for me, you made me wait. You denied me. Worse, you blamed it on my fucking little brother that never ever deserved you. I was furious. Apologize. Tell me how sorry you are for denying the both of us, and then maybe you'll deserve my cock."

I move a lock of hair from her face, tucking it behind her ear. She leans into my palm, brushing her cheek against my skin.

"I'm sorry."

I run my finger over her bottom lip, pulling it down. "Sorry for what?"

"I'm sorry for making you wait." Her body quivers as I press my thumb into her mouth. She wraps her lips around my digit, allowing me to press deeply into her throat. I sigh in approval, pulling my thumb out and brushing it over her chin. "It was hard," she adds.

"You didn't just make *me* wait, baby. You made *us* wait. It was agonizing. Pure torture."

She's so fucking beautiful that it hurts. Seeing her on her knees, willingly doing what I ask of her, is excruciatingly sexy. The hottest fucking thing I've ever seen. I've already forgiven her for making me wait. The sight of her willing to beg is enough to wipe the slate completely clean. But she doesn't need to know that. For the time being, I'll enjoy the show, knowing very soon it'll lead to me burying my cock in her and never leaving.

My fingers brush over her cheek. "I know it was hard, baby. That sweet little cunt of yours wanted me, even when you were insistent on depriving me of it, you couldn't quite shake me. I haunted you even in your dreams."

"No you didn't."

My fingertips press hard into her jaw, jerking her head to look up at me. "You want to repeat that?"

She smiles. *Fucking Margo Moretti.* Even when she's on her knees begging for me to fuck her, she finds a way to be defiant.

"You didn't." She stares at me, not a hint of remorse in her green eyes.

"You're going to regret saying that." Letting go of her jaw, I back up a few steps, reclaiming my seat on the edge of the bed.

Margo runs her lips together, attempting to hide her satisfied smile. I want to wipe the sassy smile from her face by shoving my cock through her lips.

So that's how it's going to be. My cock grows even harder. I love seeing her on her knees but having her push back a little is hot as fuck. I'll make her more than pay for it.

"Open your legs."

A small crease forms on her forehead.

"Slide your knees open," I instruct. "Give me a view of that puffy pussy."

She does exactly as I say. Opening her thighs up so her wet and needy cunt comes into view again. I lick my lips, still tasting her on my lips. Now that I've had one taste of her, it'll never be enough. I want to taste her every single day, feel her come against my tongue, writhing in pleasure, every morning before I leave my bed.

"Now what?" she asks quietly. Her voice isn't as confident as it was a few moments ago. Maybe now that she's spread open in front of me, she's lost some of that sass. Or maybe she's tired of me making her wait. She should've thought of that before she let me kiss her and told me I couldn't do it again.

"Play with yourself."

"You just told me I couldn't."

My hand pauses. "I changed my mind. Now do as you're told and play with yourself."

Her cheeks flush, the tender skin already slightly pink from the sting of the wind earlier.

I raise my eyebrows at her, tucking my cock back into my boxers for a moment. I lean forward, watching her expectantly.

For a few moments, neither one of us moves as she watches me, completely unsure. Finally, her hand snakes up her thigh and slides against the wetness. My mind is taken back to the morning I walked into her room and found her moaning my name in her sleep. No matter how many times she wants to deny it, I know she was getting off to a dream of me. She'd been writhing against one of her pillows in a way that had made my cock raise to attention.

Her pointer finger rubs up and down against her slit.

"I want you to get yourself off as you think of me. This time, you won't have any choice but to admit that it's me that has your pussy so wet and needy. You lied when you said you weren't fantasizing about me in your dreams, now I'm not going to give you any other option but to come apart in front of me, my name falling from your lips in pure pleasure."

She circles her clit. Every nerve in my body wants to spring off the bed and touch her for myself, but I resist the temptation. I need to see her do this, to admit that I drive her fucking wild, even when I'm not touching her. It's the same thing she's done to me. Her small little hand has never touched my cock, and I've fantasized about her way too much for it to be healthy.

"Why don't you come here and do it?" She taunts me by rocking back and forth against her hand, her finger slipping inside her.

I smile, leaning forward. "Is that you begging?"

"Please come fuck me Beck," she pants, her finger picking up pace inside her. Her other hand begins to get in on the action, rubbing one of her nipples between her thumb and pointer finger. "I'm sorry I've made you wait."

"Good girl," I say. "That's a good start."

Her eyes are hooded as she watches me. "I'm close," she admits, rocking back and forth even faster. She grinds against her own hand, trying to get the friction she wants but it must not be enough yet.

I watch her closely, my fingers twitching to take the spot of hers. Her hair falls down her shoulders, brushing up against her perfect peaked nipples as her hips sway in a perfect rhythm.

I can't wait to fuck her. I'm going to mar the perfect olive skin of her body, leaving my mark by bites and sucks. I'm going to pound into her so hard that she'll feel me for days. I'll make her knees weak from taking me over and over again.

My hips lift off the bed just enough for me to slide my boxers down my thighs. I let them fall to the ground, my cock springing up eagerly.

Her breaths pick up, a moan falling from her lips. She's about to come. But I'm not ready for her to finish yet.

"Now beg for me to let you come."

Her fingers don't stop, and she doesn't give any indication she's going to do as she's told. She rocks back and forth against her hand, so close to an orgasm that she refuses to relent.

"Margo," I warn. "Stop or you're not going to be getting anything from me tonight. That little finger of yours better do a damn good job at getting you off for the night if you don't listen to me right fucking now. Because that's all you're going to get if you don't do as you're told."

She throws her head back with a groan, but her finger stops pushing inside her. She slides it out, rubbing the wetness against the inside of her thigh.

"I want you to beg for me to let you come," I repeat.

"Even if I'm the one doing it?"

"Yes."

"That doesn't seem fair."

"What isn't fair is how long you pretended that this wasn't inevitable."

"I need to come," she pants, her fingers inching closer to the spot she wants me most. "I told you I'm sorry for making you wait. I don't know what I was thinking. Now *please*, Beck, I need to make myself come or I need you to do it."

"Let me watch you make yourself come apart, baby. As long as you fucking moan my name while doing it."

This time she coaxes two fingers inside her, moaning as she pushes them as deep as they will go.

"Imagine that's me fucking you, Margo."

Her eyes flutter closed as my hand finds my cock once again. If I weren't so determined to fuck her all night until she can't walk tomorrow, then I'd finish just by watching her come. "I'm stroking my cock, imagining what it'll be like to feel your pussy greedily take me."

"Oh god," she moans, her body shuddering with pleasure.

I shake my head. "No, I told you I wanted you to moan *my* name when you come. God isn't the one making you dripping wet all over your hand."

"Beck…" The hand that cups her breast trembles as she kneads at the tender skin.

"I've thought about all the different ways I'll slide into you."

"Tell me how," she pants. She presses her fingers against her clit, rubbing in circles as her hips move side to side.

I smirk, matching her pace and stroking my cock at a faster pace. "Every meal we've had together at that kitchen counter or at the dining table, I've imagined myself propping you on the table and making you the meal instead. I've thought about all the places I'd lick and taste before I'd pull you to the edge and rail into you."

"Beck," she gasps. Her moans send tingles down my spine. Why does she have to be so fucking sexy without even trying?

"At the office, I've imagined bending you over my desk and burying myself inside you from behind. I've envisioned marking that perfect ass of yours with my hand every time you've stood up to me in front of *my* employees. I've imagined in *vivid* detail what the red print will look like as I shove into you from behind, making you pay for questioning me in front of the people I employ."

Her head falls backward with a loud groan. I have to slow down my own hand before I come just at the sight of her.

"I'm close," she pants, bouncing up and down on the ground. Her fingers work at pressing her clit. Her free hand pulls at her nipple. I can tell the moment she's pushed over the edge when her mouth parts and a loud moan escapes her lips. "Beck," she breathes.

"That's it," I praise. "Say my name as you come, baby. Remember who's making you feel like this. Remember who told you you could come like a good girl after torturing me for so long."

I watch in awe as she comes back from the orgasm. *Fuck*, I can't wait to feel her ride the waves of her release against my cock, my mouth, my fingers. I'll take any god damn body part of mine.

Finally, her eyes flutter open. She takes in me rubbing my cock, her tongue peeking out as she stares at it greedily.

"You're looking at my cock like you can't wait to taste it, Violet."

She licks her lips dramatically, knowing exactly what she's doing to me as I rub myself up and down. "I can't wait," she answers.

"You want me to shove my cock down your throat? To punish that mouth of yours for even saying this would never happen between us?"

She nods enthusiastically, staring at me hungrily.

"Use your words. Tell me how bad you want it."

"I want to fucking taste you, Beck. I want to be the one who drives you wild, to feel you harden in my mouth. I want to test how far I can take you, even though I don't know how far it'll be with..." Her eyes widen as she looks up and down my length.

"Show me how bad you want it. Crawl to me and fucking beg for it."

32

Margo

I f I didn't see the serious look on his face, I'd think he was kidding. Never in my life have I had to beg like this for someone to fuck me, and I especially haven't had to crawl to them to prove how badly I need them.

But Beck isn't like anyone else. He knows it and he wants to make sure I know it. It's my punishment for ever even attempting to deny the connection between us.

I should probably look into why it turns me on so much. If any other man told me to crawl to them, I'd tell them to go to hell and demand they crawl to *me*.

Any man but Beck.

For Beck, I lean forward, my palms connecting with the scratchy shag carpet. My knees already have been rubbed raw from getting on them to beg. Or maybe it was from the way they slid across the carpet as I chased my own release. Either way, I'd gladly crawl across the room toward him if I knew what the end goal was.

His hand moves up and down his thick length, his thumb running over the tip before he repeats the movement all over again. I've never been one who really enjoyed giving a blow job, but I'm eager with anticipation at the thought of running my mouth over him, even though I'm terrified how I'll even fit him in with how thick and long he is.

"Crawl to me, Margo."

I do as he says, slowly closing the distance between us.

"You're so fucking sexy," he mutters, looking at me like I'm the sexiest thing he's ever laid eyes on.

I'd be embarrassed doing this with anyone else, but it's all different with him. Even on my knees crawling to him, I feel sexier than ever before. I come to a stop between his spread legs. My hands tentatively reach up and run over his hard thighs. There's so much muscle, I could take my time studying every single one, committing them to memory so I could go back and draw them with immaculate precision.

"Only you could make me do that," I tell him, taking my time running my hands up his legs. The hard floor bites into my knees, but I barely feel the discomfort. Even though I just came, I'm ready to do it again. This time with him touching me. It doesn't even matter to me what part of him is doing it, as long as *he's* the one doing it this time.

He grabs me by my hair, yanking on it to pull me toward him. My knees hover over the ground for a moment as he pulls my face close to his. "You've got that fucking right." His fingers rub tenderly at the sore spots of my hair. "And don't you dare ever forget that."

His words make the spot between my legs ache with need, but the look in his eyes is what makes my clit absolutely throb. There's so much possession in his gaze, like he'd burn the world down if I ever even thought of getting on my knees for any other man. Right here, right now, I wouldn't dream of doing anything with any other man but the one sitting in front of me.

I stare into his eyes, wondering what the hell is happening here. I expected us to angrily fuck each other and get it out of our systems, but the fire in his eyes, the desire I'm sure he sees in mine, makes it clear that this won't be a one-time thing. My pussy clenches at the thought—of the possibilities.

I wanted to do so much with Beckham Sinclair. Right now, I want to make him unravel by my mouth on his length. I glance down at it, running my tongue over my lip.

"If you keep staring at my cock like that, I'm going to have to shove it down your throat and see how deep you can take it."

My lips part as I lean down to get closer. "Try me," I whisper.

"Do you think you deserve my cock after making me wait so long to have you?"

"I'll make it up to you."

He swallows, his defined Adam's apple bobbing up and down. His fingers flutter softly down the side of my face. The normal sharp look in his features softens, the desire still shining brightly through them. "Just tell me if it's too much, Violet."

His words are all I need, fueling my desire to make him come undone in my mouth. I look away from his gaze, focusing on his massive erection. The top of it glistens, precum leaking from the tip.

"Are you just going to stare?" he asks, his voice gravelly.

I reach up, curling my fingers around it. He's thick, my fingertips nowhere near touching as I rub up and down his length once. His cock jerks in my hand, his head falling backward in pleasure.

"Fuck," he growls. I watch him in fascination, observing what happens if I squeeze a little tighter as I move my hand a bit faster.

His teeth clench as I take my time committing the feel of his heavy cock in my grip. My fingertips run over the thick veins that cascade down the shaft. I lean in, my mouth hovering over his tip. I sigh, determined to fit as much of him as possible in my mouth.

Opening wide, I press my tongue against my teeth as I begin to take him. My lips stretch around him as I push as much of him in my mouth as I can take. Air hisses through his teeth as I push myself a little farther, the tip of his cock hitting the back of my throat.

Beck's fingers tangle in my hair once again as he softly sets a rhythm. I try to open my throat, allowing even more of him inside me. Even as I take as much as I can, my eyes misting from the pressure I feel at the back of my throat, there's still so much of him left I can't take. I stroke up and down at the base of him, my fingers working in sync with my mouth.

"God damn." Beck groans, applying more pressure to my scalp as he shoves himself even deeper down my throat. I almost gag, but I fight it, trying to take as much of him as physically possible. The sounds he makes, the way his stomach muscles tighten each time I take him as deep as possible, sends shivers down my spine. Everything about this is hot as fuck.

"That's it, baby," he breathes. "Open that throat for me. Fuck, you're doing so good." His fingers tighten in my hair. "I'm going to go faster now, Margo. Just tell me if it gets too much."

His hips lift off the bed for a moment as he picks up his pace. I let him do whatever he wants, whatever he needs, while I watch his every reaction in fascination. He's fucking my mouth, and I'm loving every filthy second of it. The knowledge that I'm the one making Beck lose control like this makes between my legs throb even more. I rub my thighs together as I continue to take as many inches of him as I can. I can feel the wetness from my arousal coating my thighs as I try to find my own friction.

With each pump of his thick cock in my mouth, the tip of him hitting the back of my throat, more tears gather in my eyelids. Eventually I can't fight them any longer, the tears from the pressure fall down my cheeks but I don't make any move to stop. I'm loving watching him unravel too much to do anything but let him continue to take what he needs from me.

My jaw and lips hurt from stretching to fit him, but I won't stop. I continue to work with my mouth and hand in unison. A low moan escapes from his lips, egging me on.

I want to make Beckham Sinclair come. I think I'm close to getting my way when he frees his cock from my mouth. My eyes find his. I'm ready to complain until I see the desperate look in his eyes.

"As much as I fucking love fucking that smart mouth of yours, I need inside you."

My bottom lip juts out. As horny as I am for him, desperate to feel him bury himself inside me, I wanted to make him fall apart just by using my mouth and hand.

It'll have to wait. Before I can tell him I wasn't finished, he's lifting me off the ground and pulling me to him.

His hands roughly grab my face, pulling me closer until we're nose to nose. At the moment, it's not being naked that makes me feel exposed and vulnerable. It's the way Beck seems to stare deeply into my soul, seeing things I'm not sure I want him to see, that makes this moment feel heavy. The heaviness doesn't feel bad, it feels the opposite actually, but that realization is terrifying.

"What the hell am I going to do with you?" he asks, his voice hoarse. His eyes roam over my face, his fingers gentle as they lazily rub over my cheekbones. The gesture is sweet considering moments ago he was pounding his cock down my throat until tears streamed down my face.

"Fuck me," I answer, the words coming out more as a plea. Lifting my legs, I climb on top of his lap until I'm straddling him. His cock brushes against my ass, causing shivers to run down my spine.

His grip on my cheeks doesn't loosen. If anything, it gets tighter as he brushes his nose over my ear. "Oh don't worry, baby. I plan on fucking you over and over until your body can no longer take me. And then I plan on doing it all over because you've completely deprived me of you for too long. I was asking what I'm going to do *after.*"

"After?" My hips begin to work against him. I'm so wet that I glide over him effortlessly. If I lined us up perfectly, it'd only take one movement of my hips to slide down on him.

He kisses my neck. His tongue massaging the parts his teeth nip at. It seems like this is how it'll be with Beck. He's hard and then soft, punishing before he pleasures. It makes my head spin with bliss. It's like I'm high without ever touching a drug.

His breath is hot on my neck when he pulls away slightly. "Yes, after. After tonight. After we leave this hotel room. This can't be just a tonight thing. I'll go absolutely mad if I don't get to fucking make a home out of your pussy—out of you—every god damn day from now until forever."

My insides clench at his words. God, they're so beautiful. I don't know how his words can be so dirty yet also be so poetic.

"Beck," I moan. I'm desperate for him. His cock presses against my entrance, just enough to have me needing more. I want him terribly. I need him desperately.

He takes one of my nipples in his mouth, rubbing the tip of himself through my wetness. The feeling against my sensitive clit has me moaning in ecstasy. When he pulls away cold air meets the wet spot left by his mouth. "Margo," he says, his tone warning.

"Hm?" I rock my hips against him. Every time I think I'll be able to slide myself over him, to slide him in me, he shifts his hips away from me and stops me from taking exactly what I want.

"Swear to me that you won't deprive me again. Tell me that sweet little cunt of yours is as desperate for me as I am it. Swear to me that after we leave this hellhole it'll still be mine. Promise me you'll still be mine tomorrow."

I sit down deeper, pressing the head of his cock against my clit. Swiveling my hips, I grab his face and make him look at me. "Only if you'll beg for it," I tease, reminiscing on how he made me beg. I won't actually make him beg, but it's fun to pretend.

His eyes flash with desire. He smiles widely. "You can bring me to my knees any time you want, Margo. Matter of fact, I think I've been on them from the moment we met."

"Not the moment we met," I remind him. He's apparently lost his memory of the time we met at his family's vacation home, when I'd regrettably been on Carter's arm instead of his.

He pulls us down, our bodies colliding with the soft comforter. "From the very first fucking moment."

33

Beck

I don't give her time to ask any questions. The words slipped from my mouth before I could think better of them.

With her on top of me, I grab her hips, no longer letting her take the lead. She had her fun when she rubbed her wetness up and down my straining cock. It'd taken everything in me not to push inside and slam into her. I've never wanted to get lost in someone else as much as I want to lose myself in her.

Her pussy had squeezed my finger when I'd been licking her. She clenched around me, showing how tight she was. I can feel how wet she is against the tip of my cock, but I want to make sure she's nice and prepared for me. When I slide in her, I won't be able to restrain myself. When I finally enter her, I need to know that pussy is as ready for me as it ever will be.

I grab her by the hips, pulling her entire body up my own.

Her hands fall to my chest. "What are you doing?"

"I want to get you nice and primed for my cock."

She squirms, rubbing her arousal up and down me. I love how much the words I use affect her. It's hot as fuck how I don't even need to touch her and she's hot and needy for me. "I am ready. I need you, Beck."

I growl. I don't know how the fuck I'm supposed to do anything else but memorize every god damn perfect inch of her. I could spend eternity inside her, making sure to remind her while she may have been with men before me, there's no fucking chance there'll be another man after me.

"I need you too. More than I've ever needed anything. But I want to make you ready so you can take all of me."

Her hips buck at the same moment she moans loudly. "I can take it. *Please*, Beck."

"Fuck, Margo, I love it when you beg."

"Then fuck me."

The push and pull between us is almost as hot as the moans that fall from her lips. Our verbal sparring just as much foreplay as my tongue against her clit or my cock buried in her mouth.

"I have every intention of fucking you, baby. You can count on that. But first, you're going to fuck my face until I can't breathe anything in except you."

My words make her pause, her hips no longer rocking back and forth. Her lips part. "What?"

My hands fall to the small of her waist, lifting and pulling her at the same time. "I want you to sit on my face," I say slowly.

She shakes her head, her eyes wide. "I can't. I mean I've never—"

I lick my lips, looking down at her pussy that's getting closer to where I want it. "Even more of a reason to bring it to me. I'll prove to you just how much it's fucking mine."

She watches me hesitantly. "Are you sure?"

"That's a terrible question. Of course I'm fucking sure."

I yank her up my body, lining my mouth with her swollen, wet pussy. My tongue runs over my bottom lip. It hasn't been long since I last tasted her, yet I still feel fucking starved.

She clutches the headboard to have something to hold onto. Her pussy hovers just above my tongue, I try to pull her all the way down before I circle her clit with my tongue, but she keeps a good grip on the bed, not allowing her body down anymore.

"Fuck my face, baby," I demand, pulling on her again. I swipe my tongue across her, hoping that'll convince her to get totally comfortable.

She moans but doesn't let her body fully relax. I hook my arms over the tops of her thighs, pulling her down.

"Beck," she moans as I stick my tongue in her. "I'm going to suffocate you."

I spread her thighs even wider for me, opening up even more of her for me to ravish. "That's the point. I want to suffocate in your dripping wet pussy, knowing it's me who made it that way. When you come, I want to feel it against me, Violet. I want to feel every squirm, spasm, and everything else in between. And once I've done that, I'm going to know that sweet little cunt of yours is ready to take every inch of me."

Finally, her body goes lax, my face becoming buried in her wetness. "Such a good girl."

I lick and lap at her, my fingers running up and down the seam of her ass. Her moans get loud, her hips bucking up and down. My tongue is relentless against the most sensitive spots of her until I'm confident she has to be close. I love that she's no longer holding back. All her weight comes down onto my face, and I relish every second of it.

A loud moan erupts from her chest as she does just what I asked of her—she fucks my face beautifully—her hips moving in a chaotic motion as she chooses the pace that feels the best.

"Oh Beck, I'm coming," she screams. Her fingers clutch onto the headboard as she rides my face.

I don't stop licking until she moves her hips from me. She crawls off, sliding down my body until I come face-to-face with her once again.

"I didn't know that could feel so…"

Quickly, I come out from underneath her and spin our bodies. With her now lying underneath me, I take a moment to appreciate the woman who has brought me to my knees. She looks exquisite with her hair wildly outstretched in every direction, some of the pieces framing her cheeks that are hot with desire. Margo looks like she's been properly fucked and my cock hasn't even been inside her yet.

I can't fucking wait to see what she looks like once I'm done with her. I can already tell it'll be burned in my mind forever. The image of her watching me curiously as she wonders what I'll do next. I remember a similar look on her face that night at my parents. That time we weren't naked, our bodies barely touching, but I wanted her as desperately then as I do now.

Her eyes roam over my face. She reaches up, swiping her finger over my lip. "I'm all over your face."

She doesn't look embarrassed by it, or unsure about it at all. In fact, she squirms her hips against my straining cock as she looks hungrily at my lips. "Does it turn you on to see your cum on my face?"

Her eyes roll back in her head, her body trembling at my words.

I lean in close, brushing my lips against hers. "If it turns you on to see yourself on my lips, I wonder how much it'll drive you wild to taste yourself on my tongue?" I stick my tongue in her mouth, licking the seam of her lips like a man who's been starved.

She rocks against me, almost perfectly lining up my erection with her entrance. If I just applied pressure, I'd be stretching her wide for me.

I look at her pussy. "God, Margo, you're dripping wet for me, baby."

Her back arches off the bed. "Beck, if you don't fuck me already I'm going to lose it."

I smirk, running the head of my cock through her puffy lips. Fuck, she's so ready for me. This is the most patience I've ever shown in my life. I've fought the urge to plummet inside of her since the moment I saw her lingerie in the shower. Yet by some miracle, I've taken my time.

But the time has finally come.

I'm going to fuck Margo Moretti. The woman who has haunted so many of my dreams. The woman who has been in every fucking fantasy I've had for the past year.

I click my tongue, sticking just the tip inside her. I'm in only an inch, but she moans so loudly I'm dying to know what sounds I can pull from her when I sheath myself all the way inside her. "I won't make you wait any longer for me."

"Thank god," she replies, total ecstasy in her features as she wiggles her hips to try and take me deeper.

I pull out of her, circling her clit with my head. "Remember, Margo, god isn't the one making you feel this way. If you say any other name but mine, I'm going to have to find ways to remind you just who makes you feel this way. And I promise you, if that's what it takes, you won't be able to walk for days."

She moans in frustration—or maybe it's pleasure. Truly, I don't know with her. We seem to be in a constant stream of both when it comes to us. I wouldn't want it any other way. "Is that really a threat?" she fires back at me.

This woman. She'll be my undoing. My ruin. And I'm going to savor every fucking second of it.

34

Margo

Beck clicks his tongue. "Fuck, baby. You can't say things like that."

Hearing him call me baby might be my favorite thing in the world. Finding out why he gave me the nickname Violet did funny things to me, but for some reason, baby has me feeling too much at once.

I arch my hips into him. "I'm just telling you it doesn't sound like much of a threat. In fact, it sounds like a promise you've been making to me for a long time…"

Beck hovers over me, his eyes tracing every inch of my delicate skin. I shift my hips, aching for all of this foreplay to be done with. It's been delicious to have his mouth consume me the way he has, but now I'm ready to feel him inside me. I want to feel myself stretch around him, to mold perfectly to him and only him. I want him to push me to my limits, trusting him completely to do it in a way that'll ruin me for anyone but him.

"Threat or promise, it's time for me to stick to my word, isn't it?" Just from the look in his eyes, I know he'll keep that unspoken promise. He said it earlier. He hasn't even pushed inside me yet, and I'm scared that he's right—I'm his. At least in the sense that it'll never be like this with anyone else. How could it be? No one else has ever looked at me with the pure need that he looks at me with now. I don't think anyone but him ever will again.

I nod my head up and down enthusiastically. He's about to push in when his hips pause. "I need a condom."

"I'm on the pill. Please don't." My words come out more pleading than I expected them to. "I just mean, I want to feel all of you. Nothing in between."

His eyes darken as his jaw clenches. "Margo..." My name comes out of his mouth sounding like a warning.

"I mean, we don't have to," I hurriedly get out.

He glides his tip through my wetness. "I've always had a rule to never."

He looks up from between my legs, a vulnerable look in his eyes. I open my mouth to tell him to just grab a condom. He speaks before I can say anything. "I don't want to feel anything between us either."

Words are no longer needed. With an understanding between us, he pushes into me. I moan, half from the pleasure of finally knowing we're going to join our bodies, half from the pain of stretching enough to be able to take him.

"I've made you as ready as I can, baby," he says through clenched teeth. "Now it's time for you to be a good girl and take all of me."

He sheaths himself in me, filling me completely with him. I feel full, the pain only a dull throb compared to the euphoria of the feeling of the head of his cock bumping the spot where it feels the best.

"I can feel you stretching around me, molding perfectly to my cock."

"More," I plead, my hands finding the muscles at his back. I scratch at him, trying to bring him even deeper inside me.

He slowly pushes in and out, leaning down to lay light kisses on my chin. His hand snakes up, his fingers pinching one of my nipples before he cradles my face. "I want to go slow for you," he says, his lips moving against my mouth. "But fuck baby, I need faster. I need it harder. I can't help myself."

My hips buck, my body desperate for the same things he wants.

"That's what I want," I mutter. "I can take it."

A loud growl erupts from his chest as he jerks his hips into me, forcing me to take all of him. My fingertips dig into the taut muscles of his back as he rails into me. The bed shakes underneath his power. The backs of my thighs hit his torso, a smacking sound filling the room.

His hips are punishing, but his tongue in my mouth is sweet. The perfect combination to have pressure building low in my stomach. My eyes open, needing confirmation that he's as affected by what's happening right now as I am. I've never felt the desperate need for someone as I do right now. I want to claw at his back, to mark my territory, to take him and mold to him perfectly so I won't fit with anyone else.

My hand trails up his back, my fingers tangling in the dirty blond locks of his hair. The perfectly styled straight tendrils became tousled hours ago when we first got stuck in the snowstorm, but it becomes my mission to mess them up even more. I want to break every perfect composure of Beck, to shatter the facade he puts on for the rest of the world and see what's underneath.

I pull at his hair, needing something to hold on to as he continuously pushes into me so deep I feel like I might break.

He slows down, pulling himself out until only the head of his cock remains. It's like he knew I was on the brink of coming and he wanted to prolong the feeling of almost falling over the edge even longer.

In one easy motion, he takes the hand that plays with his hair and shoves it into the pillow above my head. He repeats the same thing with my other arm, shoving both above my head until he holds both my wrists in one hand. He shoves them into the pillow, taking all of the control.

All I'm left to do is let him have his way, reveling in every movement of his hips.

"Look at you," he muses. "Taking every inch of me like the good girl you are."

I moan, my back coming off the comforter. His words mixed with the punishing push of hips is pure ecstasy. I never want to stop. I'd gladly beg over and over if it meant I got to feel like this.

"Do you like giving me the power to fuck you however I want, Margo?"

All I can do is nod. Words fail me. I'm so close to coming that I can't do anything but focus on the buildup between my legs.

I try to free my wrists from his grip, needing to touch him somehow, to hold onto something before the orgasm rips through me. His fingers tighten around me, not allowing me to do anything but relinquish all control to him.

"Just imagine how many times you could've felt that sweet pussy of yours greedily take me if you hadn't fought this attraction between us for so long."

I moan. I hate every second I lied to myself and pretended that this wasn't going to happen. If I knew my body would feel like it could combust at any second underneath his touch, I probably would've accepted the inevitable a month ago.

"I could've made you feel *so* good for *so* long," he says, his voice low.

Leaning down, he blows air onto my nipple, sending my sensitive flesh into overdrive. His tongue caresses the skin around the peaked flesh. It's like he's everywhere at once. It suddenly becomes too much, and I can't hold on any longer. A moan erupts from my chest as my entire body erupts into fireworks.

Beck continues to push into me, milking every last second of the orgasm from me. I can feel my muscles clench around him, wrapping around him tightly as he chases his own release.

"You're so god damn sexy when you come on my cock," he growls, his lips still right next to my nipple. He bites the fleshy part of my breast. "I'm going to become fucking obsessed with feeling that pretty pussy of yours hold me tight."

My body should be spent. He's already managed three orgasms from me, something I've only done once thanks to a special little purple friend. I can already feel a dull ache between my legs, but I don't want to stop.

The look on Beck's face proves to me that he isn't done either. He smirks, the sight of him hovering between my breasts as he slowly pushes in and out of me something I'll commit to memory forever.

"I've only just begun making good on my promises."

35

Beck

knew finally fucking Margo would change things for me, but I hadn't thought it'd feel so catastrophic. The way she wraps around me perfectly fools my brain into thinking she was made for me. That we're perfect together. It's a shame she's only promised me a year. I'll do everything in my power to keep our charade—if you can even call it that—going for as long as possible. I'm fairly confident I'd spend forever fighting with her just to fuck her after if she'd let me.

Once I feel her body relax underneath mine, I flip her over until her front presses into the comforter. Lifting her hips up, I line myself up with her soaking wet pussy once again. There are little red marks on the backs of her thighs from where my hips have slapped against her. I like the idea of the physical reminders of what's happening between us. I feel it, she better fucking feel it, but there's nothing wrong with leaving harmless little marks on her. To leave it as proof to anyone who'd dare to look at her that she's mine.

"You were sexy as hell crawling on your knees to me. Even sexier on your knees as you gagged on my cock." My palm rubs over the curve of her ass. "But fuck, baby, you on your knees with your ass in the air, your cunt dripping in anticipation to take me again, might be my favorite view of you on your knees."

Even with her face pushing into the pillows, her moan ricochets off the walls. I fucking love how much my words get her off.

My fingertip runs over the seam between her asscheeks. She flinches, making me wonder if I've found a spot she's never been touched. Not wanting to be outside of her for another moment, I plunge into her once again, reveling in the loud gasp that leaves her body.

She's so reactive to my words, my touch, my cock; I'm addicted to it. I press one hand into her back, pushing her into the mattress as I fuck her from behind. Her moans get louder and louder, sending me close to my own release.

One arm snakes underneath her, pulling her body flush against mine. The new position somehow seats me even deeper inside her. Margo wraps her arms around the back of my neck, her tits bouncing as I continue to plunge in and out of her. The bed squeaks underneath us, the creaking a threat that the bed could break at any moment from the punishing rhythm I've set.

Her knees overlap mine as I take her from behind, her back against my front. I reach around her, my finger finding her clit. I can feel myself push in and out of her as I rub the sensitive bud. Needing as much of her as possible, my free hand reaches up to pinch her perfect pink nipples. I'm so fucking close at this point, and I know by her muscles clenching around me and the mewls and moans falling from her lips that she's chasing yet another orgasm.

I want this to be her best yet. I want to hear her scream my name as my cum coats her naked skin. It's my duty to stimulate every inch of her possible, to prove to her how perfect we are together.

My lips kiss the side of her neck as her head falls back to rest against my chest.

"Scream my name again," I say against her tender skin. "Scream it so every damn person in this place knows who you belong to."

"No."

My teeth scrape against her neck in disapproval of her answer. I pick up the pace, bracing her body against mine to keep her upright. The sound of skin slapping against skin fills the room. As her spine arches, her pussy wraps even tighter around my cock. The feeling of her clinging to me so perfectly has me reaching the brink of my release. My spine tingles as I pump into her faster and faster, desperate to be sent over the edge.

"One more, baby," I growl next to her ear. "One more to prove just how fucking wrecked you are for me like I am you."

"Beck!" she screams. Her nails bite into the back of my neck as she comes all over my cock. This time, I can feel the proof of her arousal drip down my shaft. That feeling coupled with her screaming my name is what does me in.

Now knowing she's come again, I pull out of her. She falls into the comforter, moans still ricocheting from her chest as she comes down from her orgasm. Grabbing onto her ankle, I flip her body over until I can see that perfect face of hers.

My hand falls to my cock, pumping up and down until hot liquid spills out. I watch as it coats her body, her eyes wide and lustful as she watches the proof of my desperation for her. I continue to work my shaft as I come back down. The entire time, Margo watches me with lust in her eyes.

I look down at my cum all over her. "You look good marked with the signs of how crazy you drive me." I run my fingertip through drops of cum that sit between her thighs. I trail the wet finger up her inner thigh, stopping when I softly circle her swollen clit.

Margo jerks. "Beck, I can hardly move," she whines. "As mind-blowing as those felt, I need like two seconds to recover."

I smirk, pulling her body off the comforter and wrapping my arms around her. She shrieks with the sudden movement. "I'm going to get you all dirty," she says against my chest.

My fingers move her tangled hair out of her face. I brush my thumb over her flushed cheek. "I don't give a damn about that," I mutter, taking in her utter beauty. I've always thought she was breathtakingly stunning, but I hadn't imagined how much she'd take my breath away after she'd been thoroughly fucked.

I'm lost in my mind thinking how it's a view I could get way too used to when she pulls away from me. Her knees sit on either side of my hips as she straddles me. My still erect cock pushes up against her wetness, but I know she needs a break, so I don't press anything.

It doesn't stop me from still leaning in and sealing her lips to mine. The kiss is slow and drawn out, the both of us tired from the tension between us finally snapping. Her tongue brushes against mine, her fingers finding the nape of my neck.

Somehow the kiss now feels more intimate than anything we just did. I've never kissed a woman after sex. Most of the time I preferred not to even look at a woman after we'd slept together. I didn't find it necessary. I wasn't interested in small talk after. I didn't want them to take me speaking, or looking at them, as interest in ever doing it again. Women in my circle were great at misinterpreting things. They spun and twisted reality into a warped truth of their own.

I thought I'd been doing the right thing by never sleeping with the same woman twice. I thought it was the gentleman thing to do to make it seem like I was never making them false promises, but it'd been the fact that I'd been seen with numerous different women—some I'd never ever slept with—that got me in the situation with Margo in the first place. Not that I'm going to complain about it. In fact, I might send the author of the article that was supposed to expose me as some terrible playboy billionaire some flowers as a thank you.

The article is what led Margo to me, or if we're talking semantics, what led me to Margo. Either way, I can't be upset with something that brought me her.

We kiss like we have all the time in the world. In this inn in the middle of bumfuck Colorado, it almost seems like we do. Eventually, she pulls away, smiling softly as she presses her forehead into my lips. I give her a tender kiss there, seemingly needing to have my lips on various parts of her at all times.

"I can't believe we did that," she says softly.

"Did what?"

"Had sex. Oh my god, I just had sex with my boss. Shit, I just had sex with Carter's brother and—"

I rip my face away from hers, looking down at her angrily. "You're really going to say his name while my cum dries on your skin?"

Her full lips form a small *O*. The regret in her eyes is the only thing stopping me from plummeting into her once again just to prove to the both of us that the only Sinclair brother that matters is *me*. She reaches up, her fingers cupping the side of my face. "Before you interrupted me, you asshole, I was going to say how I had sex with my ex-boyfriend's brother, and I loved every single second of it."

The jealousy flaring in my chest slightly dulls. She runs her thumb over my bottom lip. I nip at it, making her smile and easing some of the tension between us. "I just fucking hate that he ever had the chance to have you like that."

Her eyes soften as she stares into my eyes. "I probably shouldn't admit this, but it's not like we really... you know"— she looks uncomfortable for a moment—"did much. Maybe when we first started dating, but I can pinpoint the moment he found pleasure with other people. He became less interested in me."

I grab her hips. I want to be gentle with her, but I know the way my fingertips press into her delicate skin, that gentle is not an adjective to describe the way I hold her body against mine. "His fucking loss," I whisper against her lips.

Unable to stop myself, I kiss her again, not wanting to go long without tasting her. I only pull away far enough to say what else is on my mind. "No matter how much I hate him for ever having you, I'm fucking thrilled that he was dumb enough to not keep you."

"Why?"

"Because now I have you."

"We have each other. For a year at least."

I brush off her comment. If it were up to me, I'd have her longer. I just have to find a way to make that happen. I heave her up off the bed, wrapping her legs around my middle. She squeals but doesn't protest at all as I walk us to the bathroom. Setting her down on the lip of the large clawfoot tub, I turn the knobs to begin to fill the bath. Hot water cascades from the faucets, covering the red roses the hotel staff had lined the tub with.

Margo watches me carefully, her lips pressed together as steam begins to billow around us once again. Once the water fills the bottom, I silently gesture for her to get in. She hesitantly dips one toe in, testing the temperature before stepping all the way in. I follow her. We find a comfortable position with my back against the end of the tub and her back to me.

She finds a bottle of bubbles on the edge of the tub, pouring almost half of it in as the water rises around us. Our bodies become fully submerged until bubbles threaten to spill over the sides.

Margo plays with the bubbles, letting them run through her fingers. "You're quiet. What are you thinking about?"

"Just our earlier conversation."

"About Carter?"

"I think you're saying his name because you want to be punished for saying it…"

She shrugs against me. "*Maybe*."

"I'll remember that."

Margo settles deeper into me. "Okay but really, tell me what you were thinking. You're always so in your head. I want to see into it, to know what's going through that brilliant mind of yours."

I hold my tongue. I doubt she wants to know how much my "*brilliant mind*" has been muddled with thoughts of her recently. Way more than what's acceptable for someone who's supposed to only end up pretending to be engaged.

I trace the delicate slope of her shoulder. Her skin is so tan compared to mine. "You really want to know?"

She nods.

"I was just thinking about how I've never really cared that you weren't mine. It didn't matter to me that you were my brother's. It didn't stop me from wanting you. And deep down, I always knew eventually I'd stop at nothing to have you."

36

Margo

My body stills against his. I turn my head, needing to look at him. I expect to find his usual smirk on his mouth. One that would tell me that he was joking, but I don't find it. He looks right back at me, his eyebrows raised slightly, like he wants me to call him out.

"You didn't," I breathe.

"You telling me that I'm lying?" he challenges.

I shake my head. "I just…"

Beck moves a wet piece of hair from my face. "Deep down, I think you knew there was something between us back then. I just think you didn't want to admit it to yourself."

My mind catapults to a memory I've worked hard at trying to forget. To one that wouldn't ever truly go away, no matter how hard I tried.

I toss in bed, letting out an aggravated sigh that I haven't been able to fall asleep. I spent an entire day in the sun, sleep should be reaching me easily. And yet it doesn't.

Carter lets out a snore from behind me. I roll my eyes, annoyed he was able to fall asleep so quickly. Or maybe it's the fact that he'd come in with promises of having sex with me. I argued at first, telling him we couldn't possibly sleep together in the same house as the rest of the family. He had a good point when he said the beach house was fairly large. They wouldn't be able to hear us. After his persistence, I agreed to it. It seemed like forever since we'd been intimate, and I missed my boyfriend.

Too bad he spent a few minutes fingering me and the moment I reached to return the favor, he stopped and complained of a headache from drinking all day. I hadn't had an orgasm, and I nowhere near felt comfortable doing it myself with him snoring next to me.

The inability to fall asleep mixed with the tightness in my stomach from being brought to the brink of release and not being able to get it has me throwing the soft sheet from my feet and getting up.

Carter doesn't move an inch, too deep in sleep to notice his girlfriend leave the bed. I search for my things in the dark, sliding my flip-flops on and grabbing my bag full of art supplies off the chair in the corner.

Stepping in front of the door, I take one last peek at Carter. Deep down, I think I'm hoping for him to wake up and ask me to come back to bed. I want the boyfriend who used to care about me back. Now, he seems disinterested in me, like I'm more of a nuisance than someone he loves. Every time I bring it up, he blames it on the stress of starting his first real job out of college. He keeps promising once he gets settled in there that things will change.

I won't hold my breath. We've been making long distance work, but I'm moving out to California to be closer to him. Maybe that will change things. Deep down I'm worried that it won't matter. Him wanting almost nothing to do with me anymore when we actually are together isn't very promising. I still hold *onto hope. He's the only real boyfriend I've ever known, the only man I've ever loved. I want to cling to what we used to be—what we could be again—for as long as possible.*

I stare at his sleeping form for a few more seconds before slipping out the bedroom door. I've luckily been able to memorize the layout of the house in the few days we've been staying with Carter's family. Their vacation home is loads nicer than the actual home I grew up in. Just another reminder of how different the world I grew up in is from Carter's.

In my few days of staying here, I've learned which floorboards creak and which ones don't. I navigate them carefully, although I'm not sure it's necessary. From Carter's point earlier, I don't think anyone in the house could hear me.

When I finally reach the backdoor of the kitchen, I let out the breath I was holding. I'm not sure if anyone in the Sinclair family would really care that I'm wandering their house in the middle of the night, but I'm not trying to figure it out either.

I hold the strap of my art bag tightly as I sprint toward the crashing waves of the ocean. As someone who grew up without anything scenic enough to stare at, the ocean has completely captivated me throughout this trip. While it wasn't my first time seeing an ocean, it was my first time at a beach. From the moment my toes hit the sand, I dreamt about sitting in it and getting lost in my sketchbook.

I hadn't exactly pictured doing it while I was reeling from another rejection from my boyfriend, but it didn't matter. For a few peaceful hours, I don't want to think of anything—including Carter.

I pull a towel I'd snatched from one of the pool chairs off my shoulder and lay it over the sand. Taking a seat, I open my bag and neatly place my supplies around me. I treated myself to a brand-new set of drawing pencils before the trip, and I've been itching to put them to use. I'd attempted to draw by the pool today, but Carter kept bothering me, his wet body threatening to drip all over my favorite sketchbook.

Once everything is neatly laid out, I place my sketchbook in my lap. I'd begun a drawing earlier in the thirty minutes of peace I got when Carter fell asleep on one of the pool loungers. Since the moment I had to stop sketching to get ready for a fancy dinner with the Sinclair family, I've been dying to get back to it.

Call me inspired. I found a muse, and now with just the moon as my witness, I can get to sketching without anyone interrupting me.

I turn the pages in my book, admiring the past work I've kept in there. There are rushed, rough sketches and one I've taken my time on, all works I'm still proud of deep down. One day, I'd give anything to see my very own drawings on display in a gallery, until then, me appreciating what I've worked on is enough.

Stopping on the one I was working on earlier, I trace my finger over the pencil strokes I've already created. My cheeks flush slightly at what my inspiration was—or who for that matter. The detail of the muscles is something I wish I could show somebody else. I'm impressed with my attention to detail on them.

I pick up one of my pencils, continuing to shade the perfect ridges of the abs I was working on. With the sound of crashing waves surrounding me, I get lost in the drawing. I don't know how much time has passed when I suddenly feel hot.

My head shoots up, my eyes connecting with the very person I've spent god knows how long drawing in precise detail.

"Beck?" I ask in disbelief, snapping the book closed before he can get a look at what I've been working on. My neck prickles with heat as I pray in my head he didn't see what I'd been drawing.

Carter's elusive older brother stares down at me, no hint of emotion on his face. His lips are set in a scowl that I've learned in a very short amount of time he wears often. He keeps his hands tucked in the pockets of his nicely pressed shorts.

"You shouldn't be out here alone." His voice is rough, that one sentence almost more words than he'd uttered to me this entire weekend with his family.

I look up and down the beach, raising an eyebrow at him. "I don't see any threats around here."

He grunts, taking me by surprise when he takes a seat next to me. He carefully moves a few of my supplies out of the way, his huge body way too close to mine as we share the towel I'd snatched.

"What are you doing?" I hiss. My arms clutch my sketchbook to my chest for dear life. I hate to admit it to myself, but there's a good chance he's already seen what I was working on. I'm going to live in denial until he gives any indication he's seen what's inside.

Beck brings his knees to his chest, looping his arms around his legs and looking way too easy-going for this persona I've made up for him in my head. "I'm not leaving you out here alone," he states. The abrasive tone of his voice makes it clear he's not interested in me arguing.

I do it anyway.

"We're on a private beach. I'm fine. I came out here to be alone, and you're ruining that."

He effortlessly reaches out and plucks the sketchbook from my arms. I screech, reaching across the towel to try and steal back my own property.

"Give that back right now!" I yell, my hand trying to yank the book free from his grasp.

He holds the book on the opposite side of him, pinning me with a stare that dares me to try and get it from him. I know it's probably no use, but I'm going to melt into a puddle of embarrassment if he looks at what I've been drawing. I have to do everything in my power to get it from him.

My hands fall to my lap as I pretend to be disinterested in getting it back for the time being. "Has anyone ever told you it's rude to steal someone else's things?"

The only response I get from him is an amused chuckle under his breath.

Why does the tiniest twitch of his lip, the movement not even forming a smile, have heat washing over my entire body? I could blame it on embarrassment for what he might find, but I know it's not that.

Beckham Sinclair is staring at me. It feels like he's leaving so much unsaid with the way his eyes take their time running over my features.

My eyes flick to the sketchbook in his hands. "If I wanted to show you what I was drawing, I would. You have no right stealing it from me."

"Don't I?" His challenging stare says everything it needs to. The asshole definitely saw.

"First, you hijack the first chance at alone time I've had this weekend, and then you have the nerve to steal something that's meant to be private. Are you always like this, Beckham?"

"It's Beck."

I roll my eyes. "Oh excuse me, Beckham." I use the name on purpose just to annoy him. "I'll get the memo to call you that when you stop being an ass and give me my drawings back."

My stomach plummets when he lifts the cardboard cover of the book. At least there's a small grace in the fact he doesn't automatically flip to the newest page. He starts with the first page, his eyes raking over every pencil stroke I'd drawn.

He's silent, taking his time looking over each drawing before flipping to the next. Eventually, he looks up at one I'd drawn of a man I'd seen eating alone at a cafe. One page had him seated at the table exactly as I'd seen him that early morning. The page after it was the life I'd made up in my head for him. He was walking through a Brownstone neighborhood in New York with his arm looped through a woman's. In my head, this was the life he used to live before whatever transpired to have him eating alone that morning. I'd drawn him happily in love with the woman next to him, the two of them on a morning stroll with their tiny, yappy dog.

Beck pauses on the picture for a long time, flipping back to the previous page of the man before focusing on my re-imagined one again. His eyes look up to mine. There's no longer humor in them. They're serious, and I wish I knew him better to know what secrets lay beyond that penetrating indigo gaze of his. "These are breathtaking."

I try to hide my gasp at his compliment. I've had plenty of people in my life tell me I'm talented, but for some reason, none of their opinions affected me the way his just did.

His stare is too much. It's too intense. I have to look away, afraid the look on my face may show too much vulnerability to a man I barely know. "Thank you," I mumble, brushing sand off the towel to give myself something to do.

I allow him to flip through the subsequent drawings, knowing there's still a good amount left before he reaches the one I've drawn of him.

Once I'm confident he's too focused on what he's looking at in the book to pay attention to me, I make my move. Springing off the towel, I lunge for the book, attempting to snatch it from his unexpecting hands.

If it took him off guard, you'd never know. He easily rips the book from my grasp. I refuse to let go, resulting in him pulling me along with it. One large tug from him has the book coming free from my hands, but not at the expense of my body jerking into his lap in the process.

My hands find his body, running over his rock-hard abs, as I attempt to steady myself and prevent my body from crashing on top of his. The sudden movement has one of my thighs hiking over his, causing me to straddle him in a compromising position.

I should move.

If anyone were to happen on Beck and me right now, this position would have people automatically thinking the worst.

The problem is, I can't. I'm stuck staring at him, marveling at the way his body feels underneath mine.

He lets the sketchbook fall from his hand. It lands next to him with a soft thud. *With it no longer in his grip, I should feel safe. He isn't focused on sorting through my drawings any longer, at least for the time being.*

He's focused on something much worse—me.

One of his large hands comes up to rest at the small of my back. It only hovers there, more of a tease of a touch than an actual touch. Still, it ignites fireworks low in my belly.

I come to the realization that I feel an intense need to kiss my boyfriend's brother.

Maybe it's still the lust from earlier rolling through my veins. Carter had gotten me so close to an orgasm before leaving me high and dry. I can blame the feelings passing through my body on that. But I know it really isn't that. My body feels like a rubber band that's been pulled taut, ready to snap from the tension at any moment. It doesn't have anything to do with my boyfriend. It has everything to do with his brother.

In the company of the moonlight and the crashing waves, I can admit to myself I want Beckham Sinclair. Wholly, desperately, in a way so fiercely that I don't care that I'm in a relationship with his brother.

His stare is so intense I'm wondering if he wants the same thing...

My gaze flicks to his lips. They're so perfect, I want to know what they taste like. Is his kiss as demanding as his personality or is he softer when his lips press against another's?

"Careful, Violet," he warns. His hand moves from the small of my back, wrapping around my bicep. His grip is tight, his fingertips pressing into my tender skin. It's almost like he's trying to restrain himself. I could trick myself into thinking he's a coiled rubber band about to snap as well.

My tongue peeks out to wet my lips. They suddenly feel dry under the intensity of his gaze. "Careful how?" He didn't use the right name, but it doesn't matter. It sounds phenomenal coming from his lips. Even if he has my name wrong, there's no misinterpretation of who he wants at the moment. I can feel him stiffen underneath me. It's clear what he wants. Me.

I don't realize I'm doing it until he latches onto my hips, causing them to stop the rocking motion I'd begun. "Because I'm nowhere near good enough a man to deny my little brother's girlfriend when her hips are moving against me like that."

The moan that falls from my lips takes both of us off guard.

No, Margo. No.

I rip myself from his lap, falling onto the towel with an aggravated sigh.

What in the hell just happened?

My chest heaves, lust coursing through my veins. My body protests breaking the connection with Beck while my head scolds me for allowing it to happen.

What did his words mean?

I cover my eyes with my hands, letting out a groan. I don't know how much time passes as I lie there, wondering why I don't feel as regretful as I should. Instead of feeling remorse for wanting to kiss Carter's brother, I feel aggravated that I stopped myself.

Only the sound of Beck clearing his throat could break me from my self-conflict.

"Your attention to detail is top-notch, Violet."

My eyes widen as I quickly push myself up from the towel. "No," I plead, only now remembering the thing that got me straddling Beck's lap to begin with.

My sketchbook.

It's too late. I find Beck staring at the picture I'd drawn the first day he arrived.

This one is much more innocent than the one he'll find next.

I hadn't felt as weird drawing this one sitting in the breakfast nook of the Sinclair house. Carter had left halfway right as I started it, saying he had to run into town. I hadn't thought too deeply about why he was leaving me alone when he begged me to visit with him to begin with. It hadn't mattered. My brain was focused on Beck sitting at the counter with his laptop, phone pressed to his ear as he discussed business with someone on the other line.

There were so many things I could've focused on as he sat working on the counter, but what I couldn't stop looking at were his hands. He had defined veins on the top of them. Ones that rippled with every single one of his movements.

I told myself it was purely innocent as I'd begun to sketch the one whose fingers wrapped around the handle of a coffee mug. Hands are hands. I hadn't wondered what those strong fingers felt like on intimate parts of me. Or what it'd feel like to have his fingers wrap around my throat the same way they did the mug.

I hadn't thought of any of that. Or maybe I had. Either way, I spent an hour sketching the stupid Greetings From The Hamptons *mug.*

"That's my favorite mug," he quips, pinning me with a sultry smirk.

"A weird coincidence that I saw someone else with the exact same one," I lie.

He gives me a knowing look. He knows I'm lying through my teeth. But he lets me have the lie. At least for the moment. When he turns the page, there won't be any more pretending.

He prolongs the inevitable, letting me linger in the anticipation of him finding the more intimate sketch I'd drawn of him. I wait with bated breath until he finally turns the page, his lips turning into a frown when he takes in the picture I'd drawn of him.

He'd been lying by the pool, not working for the first time that weekend. The hard planes of muscles had caught me off guard when he walked out that afternoon. His swimming trunks had fit him perfectly, showing off a perfect ass. I'd never been more thankful for a pair of oversized sunglasses in my life. They allowed me to check him out without anyone seeing.

It may have been the backward baseball hat over his blond hair that threw me over the edge.

I'd never wanted to draw a human being more than I had in that moment.

The thing was, I didn't want to create some other scenario for him for me to draw. I wanted to draw him exactly as he was, casually lounging by the pool. The moment was perfect enough as it was. He was perfect enough. I didn't have to come up with some alternate life for him, because I couldn't imagine him any other way than how he was at that moment.

It still started out fairly innocent when I had the time to draw him. I started with the tendril of hair that peeked out from underneath his hat. He had a pair of wayfarer sunglasses covering his eyes that I'd drawn. I'd taken my time sketching the hard set of his jaw, his perfectly straight nose and the curve of his defined Adam's apple.

Then things got a bit more…not innocent.

I stared at his defined pecs, wondering what they'd feel like to the touch. I'd been finishing the slopes and planes of his abs when Beck happened upon me tonight.

He takes me by surprise by placing the book back into my lap. I expected him to spend more time looking at the picture I'd drawn of him, or at least for him to give me shit about it. He does neither of those things.

I can't move as he watches me. I wonder how often he uses that same stare in a boardroom. It's commanding. With one look, he can pin you to your spot.

His fingers find the collar of his shirt. In one fluid movement, he tugs the shirt off. He balls up the fabric and throws it next to him.

"What are you doing?" I whisper. My voice betrays me. I can't say anything more, too caught up in staring at the skin he just bared to me.

He leans back, propping himself up by the elbows. I only last a few seconds staring into his eyes until I can't help but look at his perfectly sculpted muscles.

"Beck?" My voice comes out as a squeak. I hate that he's not a man of many words. I'm left wondering what he's thinking. I wished he'd say whatever was on his mind so I didn't have to fill in the blanks.

"Finish it," he clips.

I pull my gaze from the splatter of hair above the waistband of his shorts. "What?"

He growls, his eyes ushering to the picture in my lap. "You don't have to study me from afar. I'm right here, Violet. Finish it for me."

I'm right here, Violet. Words have never been hotter, and he didn't even have my name right.

I bite my tongue, not wanting to correct him. I don't know where he got the impression that was my name, but I don't hate it coming from his lips. Telling him he's got the wrong person would ruin whatever is happening between us right now. The last thing I want to do is break what is happening between us, no matter how wrong it is.

He shifts on the towel. It feels weird to be allowed free rein of staring at the way his muscles flex with each movement.

I stare at him, unsure. It feels way less innocent than it did earlier today with him laid out in front of me, a willing participant. "I um…" I don't know what to say. This was the last thing I expected.

The confident look on his face has me picking up my pencil. He seems so sure, it's like through his concrete resolve that I have no option but to do as he wishes.

This should feel weird. It should feel off. Neither of those are how it feels. It's thrilling. It feels right. It's like there's nothing else I should be doing under the moonlight than sketching every perfect inch of Beckham Sinclair.

My fingers clutch the pencil for dear life. I have to erase something almost immediately after picking back up, my nerves getting the better of me.

I can feel his gaze hot on me as I study him. I've already drawn his face, so I don't have to look him in the eyes. But it doesn't stop me from feeling him look at me. I want to ask him what he's thinking. Or how he knew I was out here to begin with, but my mouth stays shut.

Right now, it feels like things should be silent. That the only sounds around us should be the scratch of my pencil on paper mixing with the sound of the waves. It's incredibly peaceful.

I work on getting a rough sketch of the muscles along his hips. They're huge. I don't know what he does to get them so defined, but whatever it is, it's working. As I bring the muscles to life, shading in different colors, I can't help but think about where the muscles lead to. They dip into his shorts, leading to something forbidden.

In the silence of the moment, I want to know what Beck looks like underneath. I shouldn't, but I can't help myself. Does that dirty blond hair go all the way down? Are there muscles hiding underneath his shorts that I need to pay attention to?

Beck breaks me from my dirty thoughts. He adjusts the waistband of his shorts, pulling it down slightly to show off even more of his skin. With his pants lowered an inch, I can see that the newly exposed skin is a shade lighter than the rest of him. It isn't as pink from the burn of the sun.

Neither one of us speak for minutes, maybe even hours. I don't know exactly how long we spend out there. By the time I'm done drawing him, the sun has barely begun to rise. It's pretty, pink and orange bleeding into the dark blue of the night sky.

The deep color of the ocean reminds me of the indigo color of his eyes.

I lean in, blowing some pencil shavings off the piece of paper. "It's done," I tell him quietly, shy being in his presence all over again. Soon he'll realize that I started completely over. I couldn't help myself. I wanted to capture the look on his face in this moment, the two of us alone under the moonlight, so I could keep it and remember it forever.

He sits up. Part of me hopes that he'll immediately put his shirt on so I can stop fantasizing about the muscles I just spent hours drawing. He doesn't allow me the mercy. His shirt remains off. Worse, he brings his body close to mine to look at the sketchbook in my lap.

His breath tickles my neck as he inspects it. It's an excruciating few seconds of silence as he observes what I spent so long working on. I begin to panic that he hates it, that I've done something wrong when he lets out a long sigh.

"Your talent is unbelievable. You're unbelievable."

I fight the urge to tell him it wasn't hard when the subject was someone as perfect as him. All I manage is a small thank you.

I look down, proud of what I've created. It's probably my best work, the details perfect.

Beck's fingers grab my chin, lifting my face to stare at his.

For the briefest moment, I wonder if something like desire flashes through his eyes. I tell myself I'm making it up. This is Beckham Sinclair, Carter's older brother. I'm probably the last person that could elicit a look of desire from him.

But...

The way he looks at me, his cold stare softening has me wondering. His lips press into a thin line, his jaw clenching. It's like he's working hard at keeping his mouth shut to keep himself from saying whatever is on his mind.

He traces over my lip with the pad of his thumb, leaning in a fraction of an inch.

He leans in closer. I lean in closer. Our breaths mingle.

I want him to kiss me.

I snap back to reality at the thought.

I scurry away from him, putting as much space between us as possible. I carelessly throw my art supplies into a bag, needing to get back to the house.

To get back to my boyfriend.

I'm trying to shove my box of pencils into the bag when it snaps open, pencils tumbling to the towel. I reach to grab them when he beats me to it.

"Look at me," he demands. I do no such thing.

I can't. Tears prick my eyes as I think about what I almost did. What I wanted to do.

What I still *want to do.*

When I shake my head, he stays quiet, although I can feel his stare boring into mine. If I looked up, I bet I'd find his normal, angry scowl on his face.

I swallow, feeling incredibly guilty. I look at my open sketchbook on the towel. With one loud rip, I tear what I'd just drawn and shove it into Beck's naked chest.

"This is yours," I force out. I don't wait for any kind of response. I shove the book into my bag and leap to my feet.

I rush back toward the house when he grabs my elbow, spinning me to face him.

I was right. He looks angry. The muscle in his jaw feathers as he clenches his teeth. I look down to where he holds me. His hand is warm and firm against my skin. He takes the paper I tossed to him and hands it back to me. He pushes it into my chest, keeping his hand over mine to ensure I keep it there.

"Keep it as a reminder."

"A reminder of what?"

"Of unfinished business. A reminder of the night you realized that things might not be as perfect with my brother as they seem."

He leaves me standing there alone, holding the finished drawing of him. I stare at his retreating back, obsessing over the hidden meanings in every one of his words.

37

Beck

I let her think about my words for as long as she needs. It's a fact I've been sitting on for over a year now. I've had all the time in the world for it to sink in. She hasn't. Her distant stare tells me all I need to know. She's remembering that summer night.

Good. I love that she's recalling it. It's been all I've thought about for over a year now.

"What do you mean it didn't stop that you wanted me?"

My hands wrap around her, pulling her into my body. So much has changed from the moment we stepped into this inn. We showed up here at each other's throats, doing nothing but arguing. The tables have turned. We finally gave into each other and fuck did it feel good. Holding her in my arms, doing something as simple as taking a bath almost feels even better.

"Margo," I say, my tone almost a warning. "I think you know *exactly* what it means."

She spins in the bathtub, water and bubbles sloshing over the edges with the movement. Her knees stay between my legs as she sits on them, her eyes pinned on me. "You wanted me then?"

I scoff. "Don't act like you didn't know that."

Her eyes search mine. I don't know if she finds what she's looking for as I stare back at her. Regardless, I don't back down. I've wanted to talk about that night since the moment it happened. I'm ready to lay it all out on the table now, to tell her how much I fucking hated the fact she crawled back into my brother's bed that night. He spent the weekend sneaking away from her whenever he could, fucking the staff in the pool house whenever Margo was busy.

I wanted to punch my brother when I happened upon him plowing into one of the housekeepers. I saw red when I realized he was being unfaithful to her. I'd never been in a serious monogamous relationship, but I'd never pretended to be either. He, on the other hand, had been with her for years. She deserved his loyalty—his faithfulness—and the piece of shit couldn't even give her that.

"I always wondered…"

"Wondered what?"

"If you wanted to kiss me on that beach."

I lean in close to her, needing to feel the press of her forehead against mine. "Want is a terrible word for it. I didn't just want you that night. I needed you. Desperately. I coveted my brother's girlfriend, and I didn't give a damn that you were his. There was nothing more I wanted to do than prove to you how terrible of a fit the two of you were."

I can feel her erratic pulse thump against the fingertips that press into her neck. "Why didn't you then?"

"Because you ran. You went back to his bed, and I fucking hated the idea of it. It'd already been horrible enough that I heard your soft little moans coming through the door as I walked by that night, unable to sleep. It was worse knowing you crawled back in bed with him. That he could do whatever he wanted with you because you were *his*."

"You heard us that night?" She looks shocked by the realization.

I grimace, remembering how livid I'd been that night. It was the first time a woman had ever captivated my attention—my affection—and it happened to be the girl my brother brought home to meet the family. "Yes," I spit. "My room was the one next to yours, it was easy to hear."

"Carter told me no one would."

"He lied. He probably wanted me to hear. I'm sure he saw the way I looked at you."

I can tell she wants to ask more questions, she just doesn't know where to start. I'll answer whatever she wants. I've already admitted to this much, might as well be upfront about whatever she wants to know.

Water splashes as she leans in closer to me. I hold all of her weight, wrapping my arms around her waist. She rests her chin on my chest, looking up at me with her wide green eyes. "That night, he never," she pauses looking around the room as she gathers her thoughts. "I mean I never you know…"

"No, I don't know."

"He didn't make me…finish."

I'm both relieved and angry. Relieved because lying in bed, listening to the sounds coming from her…it made me want to vomit. I couldn't bare another second of being in that room next to them, imagining him fucking her, so I got out of the house. I'd been shocked to find her sitting on the beach—totally alone. Yet, I'm angry at how much of a selfish prick my brother was.

"I don't want to think about that," I confess. Even if she didn't that one time, I still see red at the fact my brother *ever* had her. That she was his before she was ever mine. Deep down, I'm livid that I don't even know if she is or ever will be truly mine.

Everyone will think she is with the fake engagement, but that isn't what matters. What matters is I want *her* to feel like she's mine.

And I don't know what to do with that fucking feeling.

It's as if she's completely in tune with me, knowing exactly how to tame the storm that brews inside my chest. She lays a chaste kiss on my lips. When she pulls away, I see the confirmation that neither one of us is willing to say out loud in her eyes. She may have been with him at one point, but right now, she's here with me.

Turning around, she settles back into the tub, pressing her body against mine until it's as if we're almost glued together. I hold her tight, unknowing if I'll be able to do this again once we leave the inn.

"I did crawl back in bed with him," she begins. Her fingers stroke the top of my hand, her fingertip tracing the veins that travel up it.

I wince, loosening my hold on her for a moment. "Margo I—"

"Let me finish," she snaps. "But that was after I snuck into the shower and touched myself thinking about…"

"Thinking about what?"

"Not *what*, but *who*…"

My chest squeezes. I hate it, knowing this woman has more of an effect on me than anyone has before. And more of one than anyone will ever be able to have again. "I'm hanging on by a thin thread here. Stop being vague. Who did you touch yourself thinking about?" I let the tip of my finger brush against the sensitive flesh between her legs.

She moans. "*You*, Beck. Not Carter, not anyone else. It was just you."

Her body molds into mine in pleasure as I inch my finger

in her as a reward for the truth. "It could've been me doing it, Violet, if you hadn't gone back to him."

"I never told anyone else that," she confesses, wriggling against me as I remind her who exactly makes her lose control like this. "I never really even admitted it to myself," she continues.

"Oh, but you've told me. And now I won't ever let you forget it."

"Beck," she moans as I coax two fingers inside her.

"It should've been me that took care of you that night. Not my selfish brother who couldn't get the fucking job done. And not you, either. It should've been *me*. You denied yourself *and* me by walking away."

My thumb presses into her clit. "I couldn't—"

I nod, my chin hitting her shoulder. "I know, baby. That's why I didn't blame you for it. But I couldn't stay there any longer knowing he had you."

"That's why you left…" Whatever else she was going to say gets lost in the bliss of her orgasm. Her moans are loud, echoing off the small space of the bathroom.

I rub her until her fingers wrap around my wrist, stopping me. I place a kiss on the back of her neck, needing the connection. "Yes, that's why I left unexpectedly that morning. I blamed it on a meeting, but the reality was, I didn't want to see you with him. It was past that I didn't want to see you with him, it was more that I couldn't without feeling sick."

She spins around again, taking my face between her hands. The gesture seems far more meaningful than anything between us before. It doesn't feel fake or out of lust. It feels real, and the thought disarms me.

"Never again," she promises.

I smirk, mimicking the way she holds my face by placing both my hands on her cheeks. "Well, that part is fucking obvious."

She giggles, shaking her head at me. I lean in, playfully nipping at the tip of her nose. She squirms on top of me, the movement sending another round of bubbles and water over the edge of the tub. Then I emphasize my words by kissing the woman who has found a place in my heart, wondering in the back of my mind how long I'll get to keep her.

38

Margo

Beck stands in front of the hotel room phone with a towel precariously wrapped around his waist. With one small tug I'd be met with the sight of every perfect inch of him. I smile at the thought, knowing how easy it would be to strip him completely and let him have his way with me all over again.

"Stop staring at me like that," he warns, the phone pressed to his ear.

I bite my lip, shaking my head at him. "I have no idea what you're talking about."

He grunts, gesturing to the bed in the middle of the room. "You're eye fucking the hell out of me. If you aren't careful, I'll end this call right now and fuck you on top of the sheets I'm trying to replace."

I open my mouth to respond, but he holds up a finger. "Oh hi," he begins, clearing his throat. "Uh yes, we do need new sheets."

My eyes bug as I realize whoever is on the other line with him definitely heard the threat he just gave me. I know I should be embarrassed, but instead I find it hilarious that Beck is clearly uncomfortable talking to whoever answered. His pale cheeks fill with color, something I haven't seen before.

I have to stifle a giggle as he places the phone back on its station. When he looks at me with a menacing grin, I know I'm in trouble.

"You find that funny?" he taunts, taking a step closer to me. I take a step backward, trying to escape the wrath in his eyes. The plush hotel robe is way too long on me, causing me to almost trip over my feet with the backward movement.

I shake my head at him, hating that my lips betray me by curing up in a smile. "Nope," I answer, popping the *P* for dramatics.

He raises his eyebrows, adjusting the towel on his waist. "You're lying," he drawls.

My calves hit the back of a chaise lounge, giving me no place else to go. He knows I'm cornered by the Cheshire cat grin on his face. "Do you find it amusing that a poor old woman just heard me threaten to fuck you?"

"I mean, she probably would have gathered anyway when you asked for new sheets."

He hums, closing the distance between us and pulling me toward him by the lapels of my robe. "You have a point there, Miss Moretti."

Standing on my tiptoes, I loop my arms around his neck. He smells delicious. The vanilla and sage soap the hotel provided is a scent I've become obsessed with. "Soon to be Mrs. Sinclair," the words fall from my mouth before I can think better of them. The moment they're out, I wonder if I've said too much. "You know, with our agreement and everything. I didn't know if it was now time for *that*," I add last minute, internally wishing I would've just kept my mouth shut.

Now that we've slept together, I don't know what it means

for our arrangement. I'd imagine it's still on, but things do seem more...*complicated* now.

"I'm the one who mentioned it to begin with. Tell me when and where and we'll make it official."

My heart flutters in my chest, something it shouldn't be doing. While we may be intimate now, it doesn't change the fact that our engagement will be a lie. When he says, "make it official," it isn't in a romantic way. At the end of the day, it's a business arrangement for him, and I need to keep reminding my heart of that fact.

I run my fingers over the hard planes of his muscles. For the time being, all of this is mine. We'd also come to that agreement. We'd have each other and nobody else for the year while we pretended to be in love. It'll undoubtedly hurt at the end of this when we stop pretending, but it doesn't mean I can't enjoy him for as long as I have him.

Any amount of time I can have Beck looking at me the way he is right now will have to be enough for me. Women would kill to have one night with him. I get an entire year.

"You did say people would believe us after a month of me working for you..."

His hands drift underneath my robe, running over my ass. "Are you saying you'll be my fiancée?"

"I'm saying whenever you decide to ask, I'll say yes. Don't forget I want a big ass ring Mr. Sinclair. It has to be believable, of course."

He kisses the tip of my nose. The gesture makes me feel warm all over. He's so commanding and scary at work, when he does soft things like kiss the tip of my nose or run his thumb along the top of my hand, I can almost convince myself that this isn't all just for show. That we did develop feelings while working with each other, and that none of this is pretend. That everything between us is raw and real.

"Noted." The tone of his voice makes me wonder if there's more he wants to say, but I don't push it. I've already tested my luck by bringing up the impending fake engagement.

A knock sounds at our door, bringing a halt to our conversation. I miss the warmth of his body the moment he pulls away. Taking long strides to the door, he peeks out the hole, standing there and watching whatever he can see on the other side. He waits there for a few moments before opening it.

He grabs a paper bag identical to the ones we got in the gift shop from the ground. Smirking, he shuts the door. "Looks like our new sheets came."

"I don't know if I'll be able to look that nice woman in the face again tomorrow morning." She seemed so sweet, like my grandmother. The fact she knows that Beck and I clearly put the honeymoon suite to good use—even after admitting we work together—mortifies me. I'm fairly confident my grandmother still thinks I've never kissed anyone. She'd probably faint if she knew all the filthy things my boss just did to me here.

Beck sets the bag on the top of the bed. Walking over to our stuff from earlier, he pulls out the clothes we bought at the gift shop and throws them over to me. "Put these on before I strip you of that robe and sink inside you again."

"That doesn't sound so terrible."

His returning look is heated. "As much as I want to do that, you need rest. You need to eat. So put some god damn clothes on so I can think straight."

Teasing him, I slip my arms out of the sleeves of the robe. It's so oversized that it slips to the ground now that my arms and shoulders no longer keep it secure on my body.

I don't think I could ever get used to the way Beck looks at my naked body. I've never had anyone look at every part of me with such primal need. When he looks at me, I don't think of the flaws of mine he could notice. No. Under his stare, I feel like the most beautiful woman in the world.

He licks his lips, letting his towel fall to the ground. "Two can play that game, baby."

He's rock hard, his cock standing at attention. I know if I closed the distance between us and touched him, he'd forget about his insistence on giving me a break. At least I think he would. I resist the urge to test my theory, because he's right. I'm starving and my muscles are already sore despite the warm bath.

It doesn't mean I can't have a little fun with him, however. I turn around, giving him a perfect view of my ass as I bend to the ground to pick up the clothes he'd thrown at me earlier. I stay bent over a little longer than necessary, arching my back in hopes of driving him wild.

"One day I'm going to put a perfect handprint on that ass."

"What for?" I slide one foot and then the other into the pant legs of the pants he bought.

"For all the times you've been a pain in my ass."

"Me?" I mock. "*Never.*"

He lets out a deep, rumbly laugh. "Being a pain in my ass is like a personality trait for you, Margo."

I slide my arms through the sleeves of the oversized hoodie he'd picked out for me in the store. It's warm in here, I could've totally picked out something else so he could have the hoodie. But I don't say anything. When I turn around, I much prefer the view of him in a pair of pajama pants and no shirt at all.

"Name one time I've been a pain in your ass." The both of us are now dressed. Well, me all the way and him partly. He begins to strip the sheets off the bed, throwing them into an empty corner of the room.

"I could name way more than one."

"Then do it," I challenge, stepping up to the opposite side of the bed as him. When he tosses the fitted sheet on top of the bed, I do my best to lay it out and hook one of the corners of the mattress.

We work in unison putting the fitted sheet on followed by the rest of the sheets. They smell nice and fresh. Part of me hopes we'll dirty them all over again tonight.

"Well for starters, you were a pain in the ass from the moment I met you. I'd been on an important business call when I walked in the door of the beach house and found you standing in the kitchen in nothing but a string bikini."

My eyes go wide in shock, remembering the exact moment. "That doesn't count, I didn't even do anything," I argue.

"Doesn't matter. You were a pain in my ass because you had the nerve to be so fucking sexy while also dating my brother."

"Name another time," I counter.

"When you wouldn't answer your damn phone when I was trying to reach out about the agreement."

"Again, not my fault. I thought you were calling about Carter."

"The fact you thought I'd be calling you to try and convince you to get back with him only furthers my point of you being a pain in my ass."

My eyes narrow. No matter how hard I try, I don't think I'll win this argument with him. I understand how he gets whatever he wants at work. He's relentless. An expert at twisting things until he's right.

"Name something else."

An aggravated growl passes through his lips. "What about the time I had to *beg* you just to take *one bite* of my homemade chicken alfredo?"

My nose scrunches. "Listen. No alfredo could ever come *close* to the one I grew up eating in my grandmother's kitchen. I was just trying to do you a favor."

His lips twitch as he fights a smile. "If I remember correctly, you said it wasn't half bad."

I scoff. "Because you didn't add cream. People here don't know authentic alfredo. It's never the same as the way my grandma who was born and raised in Italy makes it."

"My point still stands. It took thirty minutes of convincing just for you to taste one noodle."

"We'll have to agree to disagree," I get out.

He hits the bed softly with his hand. "Sit."

"Why?"

"Do you always have a question for everything?"

Proving him wrong, I take a seat while sealing my lips shut. I back up until my back hits the soft pillows against the headboard. I hold my lips together, fighting the urge to ask him why again.

He walks and grabs the bag of snacks I picked out. I guess that answers my question. Turning the bag over, he dumps out all of the food, his eyes running over my decisions. He picks up the bag of Twizzlers, holding them with a confused look on his face. "Out of all the candy you could choose from, you picked *these*?"

I gasp. Reaching across the bed, I swipe the candy from his grasp and hold it protectively against my chest. "These are the supreme candy, *thank you very much*."

His nose wrinkles in disgust. "They taste artificial as fuck."

I rip the bag open, sticking one end of the candy vines between my teeth and taking a bite. "I don't care what you say.

They're my favorite and you being a Twizzler hater won't change my mind."

He shakes his head at me, opening the bag of beef jerky and taking a bite. We settle into a comfortable conversation the rest of the night. When he turns off the lights and climbs into bed next to me, I wonder what to do next.

Should we cuddle?

Do I stuff a pillow between us and tell him to stay on his side?

Before I can worry too much about what the etiquette is for sharing a bed in this situation, he makes the decision for me. Reaching across the bed, he loops his arm around my middle and pulls me against his chest. Beck tucks his chin between my neck and shoulder, our bodies connected from that point all the way down to our feet.

It takes no time for me to fall asleep, feeling more peaceful in his arms than I ever have before.

39

Beck

"I never thought I'd say this, but I've never been more excited to see Ezra in my life," Margo says with enthusiasm as she bounces up and down to stay warm. I look to my side at her, a growl rumbling low in my throat. "Careful sounding so excited when speaking of my driver. He's worked for me for years but make me too jealous when it comes to him and he might just lose his job."

The eye roll she gives me tells me she doesn't believe me in the slightest. She practically skips across the parking lot toward Ezra, leaping into his arms and enveloping him in a large hug.

If he didn't hover his arms over a safe spot on her back, he'd already be fired, our friendship be damned. I stop in front of them, raising my eyebrows as Ezra looks at me with an amused smile. Margo steps from his arms, looking at the waiting car behind him. "I thought we'd be stuck here forever."

"Was it really such a *terrible* time?" I question, giving her a knowing look. While what happened last night was nowhere near planned, it wasn't the worst turn of events I could imagine. In fact, in my personal opinion, it turned out more than perfect.

A blush creeps to her cheeks. She looks from me to Ezra and back again. A frigid breeze picks up around us, a bite to it as it hits us all in the face. Margo fixes the hair that blows with the wind, a gleam in her eyes as she looks between Ezra and I. "Awful. The worst." She tries hard to fight a smile, but eventually she can't any longer. She winks as a breathtaking smile overtakes her face.

"Why don't you tell your new best friend Ezra how we passed the time?" I challenge.

Her eyebrows raise to her hairline as her stained cheeks get even darker. Margo always has such a smart mouth and no filter. I love it when I'm able to push her buttons enough to get her to blush. Especially in the presence of others.

Ezra whistles before he leaps forward and grabs the paper bags from my hand. "Now that you've mentioned it, I think I'd rather not know the details."

"The *dirty* details," I correct, still staring at Margo. I'd been pissed when our car got stuck in the snow. Livid when I thought I'd be tormented by sleeping next to her all night without being able to have her. Now I'm grateful for the snowstorm, for how much things have changed between Margo and I from yesterday to today.

"Beck!" Margo shrieks, hitting me in the arm.

Ezra loads our small amount of belongings into the back of the car, shaking his head at both of us as he tries his best to ignore us.

"Thank you for sorting out the car situation," I tell him. It seems that not only did he spend his morning getting the car towed for us, but he even took the time to get the rental washed. Scanning the trunk, it appears that all of our luggage stayed safe despite the car being left on the side of the road.

"Just doing my job," he responds, closing the trunk.

Margo busies herself by typing something on her phone. If I had to guess, it's something to do with those friends of hers she's always adamant about speaking with. Walking up to her, I put an arm around her shoulder and pull her into my side. I kiss the top of her head. At first she looks shocked by the PDA. She aims a hesitant glance at Ezra, who's already gotten into the car and isn't paying attention. Even if he was, it wouldn't matter.

Something changed between Margo and I last night. I'm not taking a step backward. Now that I've had her, I won't let her go. I don't care who's looking, if I want to touch her, kiss her, or anything else, I'll do it.

"Ready to go back to New York?" I ask, letting her slide into the backseat.

"I'm *so* ready to go home."

I nod, my throat feeling tight. *Home.* It was a simple sentence and yet to me it holds so much more meaning. She doesn't realize the weight of her words, the effect they've had on me.

She called New York her home. She called the place we live together her home. Not a house, not some place she's staying for a year while she fulfills her end of the agreement.

No, in her mind it's her home, and I've never loved the penthouse I reside in so much.

Because if she views it as her home, maybe she'll never want to leave it.

Maybe she'll never want to leave *me*.

• • •

My knuckle softly brushes over her cheek. I wish I didn't have to wake her up, but we've arrived at the private airport. It's time for us to get on the jet and fly back to the city. Margo had fallen asleep five minutes into the car ride. It wasn't too shocking considering how much of the night I kept her awake.

I'd intended on sleeping, but I couldn't resist her. I couldn't get enough of her last night. Anytime we'd drift off to sleep it wouldn't be long before we'd wake up again and get lost in one another. It was the first night in I don't know how long that I hadn't woken up to check my phone multiple times. In fact, the only reason I'd woken up this morning was thanks to the sound of my vibrating phone on the nightstand.

I've never had such great sleep, even with all of the late-night interruptions. It seems that Margo may need a bit more sleep than I'm used to by the way, even as I run my fingers over her face, she doesn't move a muscle.

She nestles even deeper into my side, giving no indication of waking up.

Ezra opens his door, returning from talking to the pilot and crew. I'd sent him to go check in with the crew, wanting to give Margo as much time to catch up on sleep as possible.

"They're almost ready to take off," he whispers, his eyes looking at Margo. If he's wondering what transpired between Margo and I in the time since he last saw us yesterday, he hasn't asked.

I nod before quietly opening my door. Ezra grabs it, holding it open for me. My hands slip underneath Margo's thighs as I lift her to my chest. Her body is limp, the movement not jolting her from her sleep. I cradle her against me as I slip out of the car, mouthing my thanks to Ezra as I walk down the tarmac.

I'm expecting Margo to wake up. Between the cold air hitting us, despite my attempts to shield her from the bitter air with my body, and the sun beating down on us and shining brightly against the snow, I don't know how she still sleeps so peacefully against me. Apparently last night had taken more energy from her than I'd even expected.

A flight attendant smiles at me from the bottom of the stairs leading to the jet. I nod before I follow her up, mumbling a good morning to the crew who wait inside for us. Without saying anything else to anyone, I go straight to the back of the plane where a private room waits behind a small door. I try to carefully place Margo atop the covers, being as gentle as possible. Careful to not wake her, I pull each of her boots off and set them on the ground by my feet. Once I feel like she should be comfortable enough to sleep, I pull the covers over her to keep her warm.

For a few moments I watch her sleep. I can't fight the urge to lean down and press my lips to her forehead. She lets out a content sleepy sigh, the sound making my heart constrict in my chest. It takes everything in me to leave her sleeping alone in the room and talk to the crew who will be taking us to New York.

There's a split second where I consider saying fuck it and just climb into bed with her. I plan on returning in a bit to check in on her, but I do need to speak with Ezra and answer a few work calls.

Taking one last look at her, I softly shut the door and leave her in peace to sleep.

Earlier she'd said that New York City was her home. I loved the sound of it coming from her lips. It was that moment that I realized Manhattan was no longer the place I call home. I'd call anywhere home if it meant I was with her, because my home is no longer a physical place. My home is *her*.

I've made a home out of Margo, even at the risk of knowing she may never find a home in me.

40

Margo

The feeling of warm lips pressing to the inside of my wrist pulls me from a deep sleep. My feet stretch underneath a soft, heavy blanket as my eyes drift open. I feel the tender caress of lips against my palm at the same moment I register Beck's figure kneeling on the side of the bed.

I smile, feeling hot from the intense gaze in his eyes. "Hi," I mumble, still trying to fully wake up.

His eyes soften the same moment his fingers run softly over my forehead. "Hi, baby." Pet names always seemed overused and cliché until I heard the word *baby* fall from his mouth. Now I'd willingly never hear my own name again if it meant he'd keep calling me it. I thought it may be something he said in the throes of passion, but his use of it now says something different.

He keeps a hold on my hand, laying gentle kisses on it. The gesture does so much to my fragile heart, making it hope for something that isn't in the cards for us.

"How long have I been asleep?" I roll to face him, his grip holding true around my wrist. My eyes travel down his body, realizing he's changed into a custom suit. Apparently I've been asleep long enough for him to get cleaned up. It was amusing to see him in the clothing from the inn but disarming to see him back in a suit that was custom-made for his body.

It's only when he presses a kiss to the knuckle of my ring finger that I notice something new. Gasping, I sit up in the bed, tearing my hand from his grip and holding it in front of my face.

I focus on the enormous oval diamond ring on my finger. It's the biggest diamond I've ever seen, and it sits on *my* ring finger.

"Beck," I say cautiously. "What is this?" I can't stop staring at the beauty of the simple gold band with the stunning, flawless diamond that's perched atop it.

He reaches for my hand, pulling it to his lips once again. "It's an engagement ring, Violet. One I picked out for you."

I stare at it. It's classic yet modern. Definitely gaudy, but I was the one who told him I wanted a massive ring. He delivered on that, even if I'd been only halfway kidding when I said it.

"I've never seen something more stunning," I marvel, not knowing if I should look at him or the ring.

"I have." The deepness in the tone of his voice and the intense look in his eyes has my stomach dropping. No one has even been able to make me melt into a puddle just by one look except him. He's able to say so much without ever uttering a word, yet still leave my mind racing with what lies behind his fervent indigo gaze.

My thumb runs over the metal, the feeling of something on my finger foreign. "Is this a proposal?"

He lifts my chin, making me look away from the ring and look at him. "I will get down on one knee right here and do the proposal thing if that's what you want, Margo. I have plenty of elaborate and extravagant ideas of ways I could ask you to marry me. I've thought of how I'd ask you countless times as I carried this ring in my pocket, always wondering when the time would be right to ask you. But none of it would be as special as you deserve. Truth be told, I fucking hate saying this, but I don't want to take the special feeling away from you when someone gets down on their knee and asks you for real. You've agreed to be my fiancée for a year, but only for a year. If I were to propose to you the way you deserve, the way I want to, I'd make damn sure no other man could ever compete with it. So I've waited on the whole typical proposal thing, only to be fair to the next guy."

I swallow, trying to hide the tears that threaten to spill from my eyes. "You're probably right," I croak, emotion welling in my throat. No matter how hard it is to hear his words, I understand his point. I can't imagine ever wanting to say yes to another man after the way Beck has unintentionally laid claim to my body and heart recently. I try not to think about the expiration date of our agreement, of the day he won't look at me with the same heated stare he does right now.

His mouth parts like he wants to say something. For a fleeting moment, I let myself hope for something I know won't happen. The look in his eyes gives me a brief moment of longing that he's beginning to feel the same things I do. That the moments we shared last night had meant something to him like they'd meant something to me.

Beck runs a finger over my eyebrow. "I wish I knew what was going on in that head of yours," he mutters, his voice hoarse.

"I could ask you the same thing."

"Ask me anything, and I'll tell you."

It's on the tip of my tongue to ask him if things have changed for him. If he feels anything for me, even in the slightest. I almost ask it, but I manage to keep my questions to myself. The truth is, I don't want to know the truth. Ultimately, I'm riding false hope that I could change Beck. The whole reason I'm agreeing to be his fake fiancée is because of his love to not settle down or commit to one woman. I'm not naive enough to think one heated night between us would change anything. I wouldn't even dare think it possible if it weren't for the unreadable look in his eyes. A look that says so much and nothing all at once.

"Do you want to kiss me?"

"I want to do so much more to you. But that's a good start."

He closes the distance between us, melding his mouth to mine in a way I could never grow tired of. I run my fingers through the neatly styled tendrils of his hair, using them as leverage to pull him closer to me. I leave every question I have unasked, deciding to soak in the feeling of his lips pressed to mine instead.

Beck rises from his knees, crawling onto the bed and pressing his body to mine. I love feeling the weight of him on top of me, of sliding my hands underneath his suit jacket and feeling his muscles tense beneath my touch.

He stuns me with his kiss, making me desperate for anything he's willing to give me. The kiss makes me forget a crew full of people wait on the other side of the thin door. I hadn't been awake when we'd gotten on the plane, but if it's the same crew from when we flew out for the business trip, there are plenty of people waiting on the other side.

Beck's hand finds my left hand, pushing it up the bed while still kissing me. He intertwines his fingers with mine, brushing his thumb over the diamond. "So, is that a yes?"

His lips move from my mouth to my neck. He sucks at the tender skin, making my entire body break out in goosebumps. "You already know the answer," I tell him, trying to keep my voice steady as he pushes the sweatshirt up, finding me in the same lingerie from yesterday.

"I'm going to buy you many more of these."

"You've already bought me plenty." I moan as his tongue works over my nipple through the fabric of the bra.

He looks at me, his face between my breasts, with a daunting smile. "I want to see you in every single color possible. *Every* fabric. *Every* style. Then I can find out how good they look on the floor."

My back arches from the bed as his warm mouth kisses over the skin of my ribcage. I'm already wet, my body anticipating exactly where his tongue is heading. "There's many more where these came from." Even though I know there's a crowd of people close to us, when he loops his fingers through the waistband of my pants, I find myself lifting my hips to allow him to strip me of them.

"I can't fucking wait to see every last one of them."

I hadn't bothered putting on any underwear when I'd gotten dressed this morning. There wasn't any need with the pants I picked out and the oversized sweatshirt. Instead, I stashed my panties in the bottom of one of the bags and went without.

"God, baby, I haven't even touched you yet and you're already so soaked and swollen for me."

"Beck," I moan as he kisses below my belly button. "What if they hear us?"

I feel the breath from his laugh against my skin. "Then they'll know how well I take care of my girl."

I'm internally freaking out at the way *my girl* sounds coming from his mouth when he runs a finger through my wetness. "Or should I say, my fiancée."

Never once have I done anything if I knew other people could hear me. I guess I've never wanted someone bad enough to not be able to wait until we were alone. But right now, I'm right there with Beck. I don't care if they hear. After it's all said and done maybe I'll be embarrassed to look Ezra or the flight attendants in the eye, but for right now, I'm too desperate to feel his mouth against me again to care.

Before he places his mouth exactly where I want him, he makes his way up my body and kisses me softly on the lips. I want to ask him why he stopped when his fingers wrap around the bottom of the sweatshirt. He lifts up, pulling the fabric over my head and throwing it onto the mattress next to us.

I'm left in nothing but a bra while he's still fully dressed in his suit. "As much as I love this," his fingers drift underneath the band of the bra, "it's got to go." It doesn't take him long to reach behind me and unclasp it from my body. The fabric gets discarded with the rest of my clothes next to us.

Now it really feels off balance. Me totally naked while he hovers over me in a three-piece suit. It might be wrong that I like the feeling of it, for me to have not a hint of fabric on while his presence screams business with the formal attire.

"Do you know how beautiful you are?" he utters, looking at me with so much admiration.

"Beck," I whisper, his words doing much more than turning me on. I'm wet and ready for him, but my heart's also joined the fun, leaping at hearing him call me beautiful.

"Every fucking inch of you is stunning. There's not a fucking flaw on you."

I yelp when his fingers wrap around my ankle and he pulls me down the mattress until my legs almost hang off the bed. He drops to his knees, seating himself between my legs.

"I know I made you beg for me, but I'd kneel and plead every damn day for you." He spreads my thighs, his hands digging into my skin to keep them open. "For this." His tongue licks me from top to bottom. I squirm, relishing how the gentleness of his tongue eases the sting from between my legs that still lingers from last night. "I'd beg and plead, ready to do whatever it takes."

If anyone were to open the door behind him, they'd be met with the sight of me spread wide open for Beck. His hands stay pressed into the muscles of my thighs, keeping me exactly how he wants me as he kisses my core with the same expertise as he kisses my mouth.

Eventually one of his hands no longer holds my thighs open. It isn't needed. I'd keep my legs in whatever position he wanted to keep his tongue working against my clit with such precision. He slowly pushes two of his fingers inside me, hooking them slightly in a way that drives me wild.

There's no way people don't hear me. I can't help it, the feeling wreaking havoc through my body is too much for me to be able to stay quiet and I haven't even come yet. Although, with the rate his fingers work inside me and the feeling of his tongue circling my clit, it won't be long until everyone on this jet knows exactly how Beck and I are keeping busy.

I grab a fistful of Beck's hair, my hips moving against his mouth in pure heaven. I don't hide my groans of annoyance when he pulls his mouth away, his fingers still working in and out of me. He smiles, around his mouth wet from me. "When you come, I want every damn person on this plane to hear it. You got that, baby?"

My head falls into the pillow, my eyes squeezing shut in arousal. I shouldn't find it so hot that he wants everyone to hear me. In fact, the possessiveness and his desire for everyone to know we're hooking up should be a turn-off. It isn't. I want to please him. I want everyone to know how he pleases me, how unhinged I become underneath his touch.

He slides his fingers out of me. "It's fine if you don't want people to hear. We can try something else. But if that's the case, I want to because while I eat this sweet little pussy of yours, my cock will be so far down your throat you can't make any noise."

His fingertip runs from my clit down to another part of me that no man has ever touched. A place I haven't even explored anytime I've made myself come either. "Choose one or I'll choose for you."

"I want them to hear," I pant.

"Good girl," he says, lining his mouth up with me once again. "I want them all to fucking hear too. My ring is on your finger and my mouth is on your pussy. You're *mine*."

Then Beck proves his point by making me scream his name not just once but three times.

41

Beck

M argo's head falls to my shoulder as we ride the elevator up to the penthouse. We lean against the back wall, both of us tired from the past twenty-four hours. "I'm so happy to be home," she speaks up, breaking the silence.

I have to swallow the growing lump of emotion in my throat. "Me too," I get out, not elaborating that I felt more at home in bed with her at that inn than I've felt here at my own place alone. Truth be told, I'm happy to get back to our own space, to the mundaneness we've created in the past month. Nothing has really felt like home until her, but I'm excited at the thought of this penthouse slowly becoming one because of her.

Her stomach growls loudly, making her giggle as she covers it with her hand, a bashful look on her face. "Clearly I'm starving." She laughs again, shrugging.

The elevator chimes, the doors to the penthouse opening wide. The usual smell of the cleaning solution the cleaning service typically uses hits my nostrils. As I roll our suitcases in, the both of us stopping in the gallery, a different smell hits our nostrils.

Margo looks at me, excitement lighting in her eyes. "Do I smell Chinese food?"

I can't help but smirk at her excitement as she beelines for the kitchen, not bothering to take off her shoes. "Oh my god, I've never been more excited to see takeout in my life!"

Following the sound of her voice, I find her already tearing into a white plastic takeout bag that sits on the edge of the kitchen island. She pulls out two containers of soup, a small box of egg rolls and then two large boxes with our entrees.

She wastes no time tearing open a packet of chopsticks, opening one of the bigger boxes and popping a piece of chicken in her mouth. She moans loudly, her eyes rolling back in her head. "Holy shit. I forgot how much I missed New York takeout."

I pull my phone out of my pocket, firing off a text to my house manager to thank them for running the food by. I watch her shove a large bite of chow mein into her mouth, noodles dangling by her chin before talking. "We had it like two weeks ago after you begged me for it."

She smiles at me through a mouthful of food. If anyone else did it, I'd find it revolting, but with her it's endearing and cute. Every little nuance of her is. She swallows the food in her mouth. "Exactly. It's been *way* too long."

I roll my eyes at her dramatics, pulling my arms from the sleeves of my jacket and tossing it over the far edge of the island. "I'm sorry that the home-cooked meals you've been living off of have been so awful."

She slurps a noodle into her mouth. "I never said they were awful. But you're talking to a girl who was broke in college who collectively shared one pot and one pan with her two other roommates. We never cooked for ourselves and we could make Chinese leftovers last for days. You cook almost as good as you fuck, Beck, but that doesn't mean I don't miss some overly GMO sesame chicken from time to time."

Her uttering the word fuck brings my mind back to the plane ride, how it felt to bury myself inside her while my staff waited for us. It hadn't been my intention to fuck her on the plane. I really just wanted to slip the ring on her finger and know the world viewed her as my fiancée, but I got carried away. I seem to be doing that a lot when it comes to her. Not that I really mind it.

She manages to shove a few more bites into her mouth before I point to the chairs at the island. "Would you like to maybe actually take a seat and eat your food?"

Her eyes widen, like it just occurred to her that we could sit and eat like civilized people. She'd eaten on the plane, but apparently she was still starved. Margo keeps the box of sesame chicken close to her as she slides it across the countertop until it's placed in front of one of the chairs.

As soon as her ass is planted in the chair, she's back to funneling food into her mouth. Taking a seat next to her, I begin to take my own bites of the dinner. Chinese food is probably last on my list of things I enjoy, but she doesn't have to know that. When she asked if I liked it the first time she admitted to craving it, I lied, telling her it was my guilty pleasure. My guilty pleasure is in the form of a Brooklyn-style slice of pizza or gelato from a little unknown market, not Chinese food.

The light hits the diamond on her finger just right, bringing my attention to it. "I like the look of that ring on your finger," I tell her, standing up to get us both some water.

She lays her chopsticks on the corner of the box, lifting her hand to admire the ring. The setting evening sun hits it just enough to make sparkles appear on the wall and counter. "Having me scream your name while your whole team listens on isn't enough for people to know I'm yours?"

"Not even close."

"But this helps?" She flashes the ring in my direction.

"You're damn right it does. With that on your finger no man should dare to look twice at you."

"Since when did a ring on a woman's finger stop a man from going for what he wants?"

Jealousy burns wildly in my chest. One, at the thought of another man's ring on her finger, and two, of any man even sparing a second look at her to begin with. "I'd love to see anybody try."

"That sounds scary," she quips, taking a small bite of her food.

"You're damn right it does."

We both fall into silence as we eat our food. It's not that I don't want to have dinner conversation with her. In fact, one of my favorite things since she's moved in has been the time we've spent chatting as I prepared dinner, the conversation continuing even after she's cleared our plates and washed up. But the topic of her wearing the engagement ring I gave her, knowing it's not one she plans to keep on her finger forever, makes the food taste bitter in my mouth. The thought of her with any other man has me burning hot with rage.

"Speaking of the engagement, when are we going to tell people? My friends will kill me if they find out I've already kept it from them for this long. Even if it isn't—"

"Don't say it," I hiss before thinking better of it. I'm tired of her calling it fake, even though that's exactly what it is. I knead my fingers into my temple, trying to stifle the headache that's come out of nowhere. "Sorry, I think I'm just tired. I actually figured we could tell my family tomorrow night. My dad called when you were asleep on the plane. They're going to be in the city for business and want to have dinner to celebrate an early Thanksgiving. If that's okay with you, I figured we could just tell them then. And anyone else you want to tell after."

She thinks through my words for a moment, twirling the noodles with her chopsticks. "Yeah, that sounds good. I'll tell my friends around then too." Her voice sounds uneasy, the pitch changing from the beginning of her sentence to the end.

I slide the box of food away from me, reaching out to move her hair from her face. "You okay?" I ask. Hopefully she isn't having second thoughts about our arrangement. In my mind I have a year with her. I'm not ready to give her up just yet. I won't ever be ready, but I'm certainly not ready now.

She mimics my motion, moving the food from in front of her. Her fingers wrap around the crystal glass I placed in front of her. My heart beats erratically as she takes a long gulp of water, my mind racing with what she's going to say.

I'm preparing myself for the worst—that she no longer wants to tell people we're engaged. I'm already thinking about what I'll do if she slides that ring off her finger without even wearing it for twelve hours when she looks up at me, her green eyes roaming my face. "I'm fine. I'm just a little nervous about what your mom and dad will think of me knowing I'm with you after dating your brother."

"They aren't going to think ill of you, Margo. They're aware of how much Carter fucked up. Truthfully, I think they'll be thrilled to see you again."

"Will Carter be there?"

"Doubtful." He hasn't faltered in telling me how he still wants Margo back. I'd rather keep him far away from her. Not that I think she'd ever do it. But I'd rather not even test it. I'm fucked up enough that I'd actually love for him to see her with me now. For him to know he has no chance with ever getting back with her. She's mine just as much as I am hers.

I watch her face carefully, trying to read her facial expression and body language for any hints on how she feels about the situation. Even if Carter isn't at the dinner, Mom and Dad will most likely tell him of the engagement right after. If she's regretting the entire plan, she doesn't give any indication.

"I was also thinking we could do an engagement party. You haven't seen your friends in a while, so we could fly them in for it. Your family, too. Really whoever you want. It's how we could announce to the rest of New York society our intentions to marry."

Her eyes light up. "Really? I'd love that. A fancy Manhattan event all about me? Sign me up."

I chuckle. This woman. I love how she's not afraid to say exactly what's on her mind. "I'll look over my calendar to pick a date."

When she looks up at me, her large eyes filled with excitement, I can almost trick myself into thinking she actually wants to marry me. Almost. Her smile is wide and bright and so fucking beautiful it makes my heart hammer in my chest. "I'll be there."

42

Margo

"I think I'm going to go to bed," I announce, fighting a yawn as I push the knit blanket from my lap. Beck and I had settled in to watch some TV and relax after a busy day of getting back to Manhattan. Well, I relaxed, spacing off while sketching in my notebook while the TV played in the background. Beck however worked on his laptop and phone the entire time. I tried telling him he could go to his office to work, but he insisted on staying in the living room with me. Not that I put up much of an argument after that.

Beck's thumb brushes over the inside of my ankle as his eyes stay scanning whatever is on his laptop. During one of his business calls he grabbed my feet that'd been resting against his thigh and began to rub them, all while his phone was on speaker and he talked business with one of his investors.

I don't think he even realized how tender the moment was, how much it meant to me.

"I was wondering if you were going to doze off on me," Beck responds, looking at me from over his laptop screen. I carefully set my sketchbook between us. For the last thirty minutes I hadn't drawn a thing because the feeling of his strong thumbs pushing into the soles of my feet was enough to almost put me to sleep.

"I was definitely close."

"I'll probably head to bed soon, too." His laptop snaps shut as he stands up, stretching his arms above his head. A small amount of skin peeks out from above the waistband of his joggers, giving me a glimpse of his hardened oblique muscles I'm so damn turned on by.

I stand up, neatly folding the blanket I'd been using even though I know the house cleaning staff will redo it tomorrow. "Thank you for you know, hanging out," I get out awkwardly.

Hanging out? What the hell is wrong with me? Beck isn't the type of man to ever use the word hanging out.

I'm even more mortified by my words when he doesn't respond at all. Sheepishly, cursing myself for my juvenile choice of words, I swipe my sketchbook from the kitchen and beeline for the stairs. "Goodnight!" I yell, not bothering to look behind me. All I want to do is go to sleep and pretend I didn't thank the man for hanging out with me like we were making friendship bracelets or gossiping away like a pair of teenage girls.

My feet barely hit the first stair when a strong arm snakes around my waist. Beck pulls me against his hard body, his lips right next to my ear. There's a loud smacking sound as my sketchbook falls to the ground.

"And where do you think you're going?" He nips at my neck angrily.

My mouth opens and shuts as I try to form words. I'm still reeling from the embarrassment of my word choice earlier and now he's taken me by surprise by locking me in an embrace.

"G-going to bed," I stutter.

"Your bed is no longer upstairs."

"It's not?"

Beck's large hands grab me by the waist as he spins me to face him. "You're my fiancée," he growls. "The only bed you'll be sleeping in is the one in my room."

I'm stunned, unable to think of a response to him. I hated the thought of going upstairs to an empty bed after having the luxury of feeling his warm body next to mine last night. But it didn't stop me from accepting that was how it was going to be. At least that's how I thought it'd be, but the angry look in Beck's eyes tells me I must be mistaken.

"Get whatever you need upstairs right now and then meet me back here. I've had the taste of having you sleep next to me. As long as you're under this roof, there's no going back. I want to be able to reach across the mattress and run my fingers through your hair. I want to wake up and be surrounded by the smell of you. I want to wake you up with my mouth on your pussy, to see how close I am to getting you to come on my tongue before your eyes even open. There's so much more I want to do with sleeping next to you every night, but it starts with you getting the stupid idea out of your head that your place is in any other bed but mine."

I've never met someone who can say the sweetest yet dirtiest things all in one speech. It's a talent, the way he can make me melt into a puddle at his feet with his lust-filled words.

"You have two seconds to turn around and get whatever the hell it is that you need before I say fuck it and throw you over my shoulder. I'm pissed at you for even thinking that you wouldn't be joining me in bed tonight. If you don't move fast baby, I'll be pulling you back to my room and making you pay for it."

I yelp, turning around and running up the stairs as fast as my legs will take me. My clit throbs at his words. His threats have never once actually felt like a threat. They've always felt like a promise. And for some twisted reason, I can't wait to take my time up here. To make him wait. I want to see how long it takes for him to come looking for me, how solid his patience is.

"I'll be a minute!" I yell as I run down the hallway to my room. I'll be way longer than a minute. He doesn't have to know how eager I am to climb into bed with him and feel his strong arms around me all night, but first, I want to tease him a little.

As soon as I'm in my room, I slam the door and turn the lock. I don't know if he'll come upstairs and look for me, but it'd be fun to see his reaction—his threats—if he were to come upstairs and find the door locked.

I'm tearing through my drawer of lingerie when I feel my phone vibrate in my pocket. Pulling it out, I see a video call coming in from Winnie. I tried calling both her and Emma earlier to tell them the news of the engagement, but neither had answered.

I swipe to answer the call immediately. The moment I see both my best friends' heads jammed together to fit in the camera view, my heart swells. I can't freaking wait for our engagement party if it means I get to see them.

"Where the fuck have you been?" Emma scolds, grabbing the phone from Winnie and holding it so she's the only one in view.

I smile. God, I missed her.

"Well, Beck and I got stuck in the middle of nowhere Colorado in a snowstorm after a business meeting. I had spotty service there."

Emma gives me a beaming smile. "Oh my god, did you guys have to bone to stay warm?"

I bite my lip, unsure how to even begin to tell them how much has changed. At least they'll take it as a lot changing. They don't know it's been the plan all along.

"Holy shit. YOU FUCKED!" Emma shouts, the screen going blurry as she jumps up and down in excitement.

I'm fighting the urge to throw up from motion sickness with how much the phone is being thrown around when Winnie's face pops into view once again. She and Emma fight over the phone, the two of them both coming into view finally as the phone settles.

"Is Emma being her typical dramatic self or did you really sleep with Beckham Sinclair?"

"Well…" I begin, propping them on a shelf in my closet. Taking a deep breath, I lift my hand and wiggle my fingers at the camera.

"WHAT THE ACTUAL FUCK!" Emma screams while Winnie lets out an audible gasp.

"Is that what I think it is?" Emma questions, her voice rushed as she leans so close to the camera all I can see is her eyeball.

"Mar, are you engaged?" Winnie asks, her voice full of disbelief.

I move my hand from the camera, smiling at both of them. "Yes," I answer smugly. "To *both* of your questions."

They scream in unison, both of them taking turns to grab the phone to talk to me. "I'm going to fucking bow down to you queen," Emma begins. "When one brother breaks your heart, fuck the other one and get engaged to him as payback. You're a fucking icon."

I shake my head. "It's not like that, Em. It started out as us working together and then it just became…*more*." Nothing of what I said is a lie. Beck and I did start working together, but now it does seem like more. I just don't know if he sees it that way too.

"So this has nothing to do with Carter?" Emma's question is

innocent, but it catches me off guard. For the first time, I realize I could've taken this opportunity as a way to get back at Carter for everything he's done to me, but never once since I moved in with Beck have I thought about it that way. It was always about Beck. It was never about Carter.

"Nothing," I answer, lacing convention in my voice.

"Every heiress in Manhattan is going to be so pissed," Winnie mutters, a sly smile on her face. "I think half of the Manhattan socialites have gone their entire adult life thinking they'd be the one he finally settled down with."

They still might, I think sadly, knowing there will come a day where I won't be his anymore.

Emma wraps her arm around Winnie's shoulders, pulling her into her side. "Well they can all back off because of course it was our girl who got the playboy billionaire to settle."

I laugh, wishing that would forever be the case. "Speaking of, Beck and I are going to have an engagement party soon and you both *have* to be there."

"Obviously!" Winnie cheers, rolling her eyes at me. "Tell us when and where and we'll be there in a heartbeat."

"Beck and I are still nailing down the details but it'll be pretty soon, I think."

"Good! I can't wait to see that boulder on your finger in person," Emma says proudly.

I spend another five minutes talking to them, coming up with a more acceptable story about how Beck and I ended up engaged. Eventually, I tell them I have to go, although I'd love to sit up and talk with them all night like we used to do when we lived together. Even though I've been engaged in a conversation with my best friends, I haven't forgotten the reason I came up here in the first place.

I haven't forgotten who I left waiting for me, undoubtedly getting angrier with each second that I make him wait.

After saying goodbye to my best friends and promising them I'll tell them when the party will be, I hang up the phone and get busy getting ready for bed.

Even though we may be going to bed, it doesn't mean I can't look good doing it. If he's going to make good on his threat, why not push his buttons even more?

I pull out a short lavender negligee. It leaves absolutely nothing to the imagination, but that's how I prefer it. He's already seen it all, but it does the job and will surely tease him. I smile, pulling it on. The lavender color looks good against my olive skin tone. Twirling in front of the full-length mirror, I grin in anticipation of what Beck's reaction will be to it.

Walking to my bathroom, I find a scrunchie and pull my hair up into a bun on top of my head. Beck seems to always be kissing and staring at the skin of my neck, with my hair now up, it brings attention to the small love bites he's left all over my skin.

I grab my toothbrush, phone charger, and a few other necessities before throwing them into a small bag. My stomach jumps eagerly as I confirm I have everything I'll need to switch rooms for the night. If he's serious about wanting me in there with him every night from now on, I'll have to move some more things to his room, but these things will do for the time being.

I'm lost in the thrill of seeing him downstairs when I open my door, my face colliding with a hard chest. I look up, finding a scowling Beck waiting for me like a predator waiting for his prey. He grabs the top of my doorframe, a storm brewing in his eyes as he stares daggers at me.

"That was far more than a minute." His voice is rough, causing shivers to move down my spine. They could also be by the way he takes his time looking down my body, the longing in his eyes unable to hide even behind the anger as he takes in what I wear.

I pull at the sheer fabric that sits high on my thighs. "I had to get ready," I explain, feigning innocence.

His hold tightens on the frame above my head, the wood making a straining sound under his viselike grip. "If that's what you wear to bed every night then you're only furthering the fact that there's not a chance in hell that you'll ever be sleeping *anywhere* but my bed."

I take a step closer to him, running my hands over the soft fabric of his T-shirt. Even through the cotton I can feel how tense he is, how hard his muscles are underneath my fingertips. "It's what I'll wear from now on," I say quietly. "For *you*."

The growl that rumbles through his chest is visceral as he rips his body from the doorframe and pulls me against him. His lips have only been pressed to mine for a second when he heaves me up by my bottom, giving me a better position to kiss him.

He walks us into my room, not even bothering with taking us to his before he throws me down on the bed, his body following suit shortly after. With one easy motion, he rips his shirt off and throws it to the ground.

His eyes travel over my body as he appreciates the outfit he bought me. The one I put on just for him.

"I planned on just letting you sleep tonight," he begins, taking my leg from the mattress and kissing the inside of my calf. His mouth is so far away from the spot that throbs between my legs, but yet it feels like he's licking me right there with how I feel him everywhere as his wet mouth travels up my leg. "But then you had the nerve to act like we wouldn't be waking up every morning with our limbs tangled together, and that just isn't okay with me."

"I didn't realize it'd make you so upset." I roll my hips, trying to produce some sort of friction as he plants a kiss on the inside of my knee.

Fire flashes in his eyes as he looks down at me from between my legs. "Of course it'd fucking make me upset. You think I'd have one night of you and that'd be enough?"

I'm hoping he'll never have enough of me, but I don't say it out loud. Instead, I feed into his anger a bit more, loving how he takes out his frustrations on me. "Maybe. I thought you grew tired of women after one time."

In an instant, he's on top of me, his face a few inches from mine. His fingers tangle in my hair, pulling me by it so our lips almost touch. "I never want you to compare yourself to other women again. You're not like other women."

I lean forward, catching his bottom lip between my teeth and tugging on it. "Prove it."

43

Margo

To: MargoMoretti@SintechCyberSecurity.com
From: BeckhamSinclair@SintechCyberSecurity.com

Violet,

I'd be upset by how sweet my coffee tastes this morning but I don't know if it's from you adding a bit of the west coast to it or if it's because the taste of your sweet pussy still coats my tongue from this morning. Either way, I don't hate it.

Sincerely,

The man who is dying to bend you over his desk and take you again after watching you walk around in that skirt all damn day

    I stare at my computer screen, reading his message three more times while pressing my thighs together to try and stifle the wave of arousal from reading his email. My fingers tap the keys of my keyboard as I think of a good response. I look out the open door of my office. From my spot, I can see Beck sitting at the head of the conference table, somehow managing to fire off a filthy email while the board members sitting around the table seem to be locked in a heated conversation. And not the same kind of heated I feel. They look angry, I feel hot with lust and need.

I shouldn't find it so hot, yet here I am, soaked for him from a freaking email.

To: BeckhamSinclair@SintechCyberSecurity.com
From: MargoMoretti@SintechCyberSecurity.com

Beck,

What a shame you're in a meeting. I'm still ready for my own taste.

With regret,

The woman who was desperate to return the favor before she was denied :(

I watch him from my desk. It takes a minute or two for him to read the email, but I can tell the moment he does when his back straightens. I stare at his profile, appreciating the view. It was surreal to go about a normal morning routine with him this morning for the first time. I watched him shave the blond stubble that'd grown overnight. When he stepped out of his closet, he held up two ties and told me to choose one for him to wear.

It felt so normal, yet perfect. I know already I could get a little too used to waking up and getting ready with him only for us to still be late meeting Ezra in the gallery because Beck insists on me starting the morning with an orgasm.

An email chimes from my desktop in front of me.

To: MargoMoretti@SintechCyberSecurity.com
From: BeckhamSinclair@SintechCyberSecurity.com

I don't know what I was thinking. I'm going to end this meeting within five minutes. Your throat better be ready for me, baby.

My eyes pop open as I take in the words he wrote. When I look back at him, I find him leaning forward, his laptop already shut. He hadn't even wasted time with a closing statement in the email.

Shit.

I don't think he's kidding. My ass flies out of my office chair as I scurry through the door that connects our two offices. I close it behind me. Now that we've switched offices, he has one that's a bit more private, whereas mine is more like a fishbowl with windows. With the door shut that connects our offices, we'll be relatively secluded from the prying eyes of our coworkers.

It's probably a terrible idea to hook up at work, but I'm not thinking clearly right now. The two of us probably have a mile-long list of things that HR would lose their minds over if they knew, what's one more to add to it?

Taking a seat on the corner of his desk, I begin to unbutton my sweater. Once the last button is undone, my shirt hangs open, my bra on full display. In two minutes time, Beck comes rushing through the door, his footsteps heavy as he slams the door behind him. I yelp at the sound, knowing a lot of the office probably heard it as well.

They'll probably just assume he's pissed about something. He's known to be cold and have a temper, it isn't too far-fetched of an excuse. Plus, we were waiting until we told his family tonight to announce that we're engaged. Once the world knows we're engaged, we'll have to restructure my position working for him a bit since he's technically my superior. It's all a bunch of serious stuff I don't quite understand, and don't really care to.

He'll handle it and I'll follow, too engrossed in what's going on between us behind closed doors to truly care about my job title. In the end, I'm still after that meeting with Camden.

Now alone with me in this office, Beck's footsteps slow and then stop altogether as he comes to a halt in the middle of the space. "You have me acting *very* unprofessional by walking out of that meeting."

I lick my lips, probably ruining my freshly applied lipstick. "Do you want me to say sorry?" I counter, spreading my legs slightly on top of his desk.

His gaze zeroes in on my panties underneath my skirt. They're my second pair of the day. The first got soaked before he gave me an orgasm over our morning yogurt parfaits.

The veins on his hand ripple as he reaches up and loosens the tie I picked out for him. "No. I want you to do as you're told and suck this cock like you'd promised. You wanted my attention? You've got it, Margo. I just left a very important meeting with my cock hard as a rock. It's time you do something about it."

He circles his desk and takes a seat in his oversized, leather office chair. I look at him over my shoulder, incredibly turned on by the brashness of his words. I slide off his desk, pushing my sweater off my shoulders and tossing it on a chair reserved for when he has one-on-one meetings.

"I wouldn't have had to ruin your meeting if you'd just let me taste you this morning," I point out, taking my time making my way to him.

He looks sexy as sin, his silhouette framed by the New York City skyline behind him. "We only had time for you, baby. I had that important meeting to get to."

I shrug, coming to a stop in front of him. "Apparently it wasn't *too* important considering you left early."

His lip twitches as he fights a smile. "I told them I had a *very* important phone call to get to."

Even through the black of his slacks, I can see he wasn't lying. The thick outline of his cock is obvious. I'm eager to feel the weight of him against my tongue. To trace the thick line of his vein with my tongue, to feel him come apart because of me.

Grabbing him by the tie, I step between his legs. I yank on it, pulling his shoulders from the back of the chair so his lips are close to mine. "A *very, very* important call." I lean in to kiss him, missing the feeling of his full lips against mine since I last felt them before we got out of the car this morning.

Once I'm satisfied by the taste of his lips, I move on to his neck, kissing the same spots he kisses me that drive me wild. My red lips accidentally hit the collar of his stark white dress shirt. "Oops." I laugh, trying to rub the red stain off. "I didn't mean to."

He hums in disapproval. "Sure you didn't, Violet. You like the idea of seeing it there, that you've marked your territory."

I drop to my knees, looking up at him through my lashes. It doesn't take me long to undo the fly of his zipper and free his cock from his boxers. I lean down, taking all of him down my throat once before pulling away. My eyes look from him to his cock, focusing on the red lipstick stain that runs down his shaft. "Now I've marked my territory," I answer proudly.

With a wild desire in his eyes, he throws his head back against his chair. "Fuck, Margo. It's yours. *I'm* yours, baby. Now take me in your mouth like a good girl and remind me why I'd drop every fucking important meeting I'd ever have for you."

He doesn't have to ask me twice. I run my tongue down his length before taking him in my mouth. Opening the back of my throat, I slide him in as far as I can take him. It takes everything in me not to gag. He stretches my mouth, my throat, but I relish the feeling of it. The knowledge of how good it must feel for him.

His fingers tangle in my hair as he pushes me down a little further. "You suck my cock so fucking good, baby," he says through clenched teeth. "That's it." He swallows loudly as his head falls to the back of the chair. "Gag on me, baby."

I moan, the sound loud as I happily attempt to take every inch of him. I'm running my tongue over his head when a loud knock sounds at his door.

I jump at the same moment he curses. "Busy!" he barks, applying pressure to my scalp so I can't go anywhere.

"Like I give a shit," a familiar voice says from the other side.

I look up at Beck, eyes wide as we both realize who's standing on the other side of his office door. At this point, Carter should know I work for Beck, but my shirt is halfway across the room and I'm not sure I have time to grab it before he pushes through the door. I don't have time to hide the evidence of what we've been up to.

Scooting backward, I climb underneath Beck's desk. Beck catches onto my plan, inching his chair forward until he sits as close to the desk as it allows with my body stuffed underneath. I'm able to get hidden just in time for the door to bust open.

"Carter, I told you I'm busy," Beck growls. The anger in his voice is clear as day. A lot of it probably stemming from the fact that his cock is still out and wet from my saliva, still hard as a rock because I didn't have time to make him come yet.

"You're never too busy for family," Carter responds, his voice a bit closer.

Beck grunts a response, his cock jerking with motion. His hand reaches underneath the desk, palming his length for some sort of relief.

"We'll talk later," Beck all but barks. "I'm on an important call."

"Doesn't look like it," Carter fires back.

Knowing Carter, he won't leave until he gets whatever he came here for. Beck must come to the same realization as me because he lets out a resigned sigh. "What the fuck do you want?"

When Beck runs his hand over his cock once again, I get an idea. A wild one, one that makes liquid form between my legs.

Leaning forward, making sure to stay underneath the desk, I wrap my hand around the base of him. His hips jerk underneath the desk as he places his hand on top of mine.

"I was hoping to catch Margo," Carter explains, his voice still somewhat of a distance away.

"She's also busy," Beck quips at the same time my hand starts to move up and down his shaft. He keeps his hand on top of mine, not stopping me from touching him while his brother— my ex-boyfriend—stands on the other side of his office.

Technically, Beck isn't lying. I *am* busy. I've been given a work task of utmost importance. Just not in the way Carter would ever expect.

I slowly lean all the way forward until my mouth is inches away from the tip of Beck's cock. It's still wet from being in my mouth just minutes ago, a red stain coating the tip. I lick my lips, ready to take all of him again, no matter who else we have in here.

"When will she be back?" Carter presses.

I shove Beck all the way down my throat. When he sits forward slightly, forcing more of him into my mouth, I have to fight the urge to gag. Tears prick my eyes as I fight back the urge to make any noise. It's intoxicating, knowing how taboo the situation is.

"It shouldn't matter to you," Beck's deep voice responds. I have to hand it to him; he's managing his composure better than I'd be able to if the roles were reversed.

Part of me wants to push the limits, to make him break his resolve with Carter here with us. How far will he let me go while we have an audience? Never in my life did I imagine myself sucking Beck's cock while his brother was in the room. But it might be one of the hottest experiences of my life and Beck's not even touching me.

I push his hand away, making sure it's known that right now it's *me* that's in control, not him. He lets me, pulling his hand out from underneath the desk, doing something with it I can't see.

"She was my girlfriend before she was ever your employee, you know. You better remember that."

I smile, wrapping my fingers around the base of him as I greedily take every inch of him I can manage. I may have once been Carter's girlfriend, but I want to remind Beck that's no longer the case. It's him I want, him that I'm so desperate for I'd do something as risky as this, loving every filthy second of it.

"She doesn't belong to you. You better remember that," Beck jabs. I prove his point by slowly bobbing up and down his length.

He's right. I don't belong to Carter. I belong to Beck. Whether he wants me to or not.

44

Beck

My brother watches me closely through narrowed eyes. It takes all of my restraint to not clench my teeth, to show a reaction to the way Margo expertly takes me in her mouth. She blows me with such enthusiasm, it's a damn miracle I've been able to keep my cool with my brother standing a few feet away from me. I'm shocked she isn't making gagging noises with how far down her throat she's taking me.

"You'll tell her I stopped by?" he asks steadily, looking out to the city behind me.

"I don't see the reason for it. From the way she's spoken, the two of you are over, Carter. It doesn't seem like she wants to speak to you."

As if Margo is nodding in agreement, she twirls her tongue around my head as her small hand works up and down my length. It's like she's egging me on, confirming my words without saying a thing.

"You're lying," he seethes. He runs a hand through the stubble on his chin. I fight the urge to tell him how terrible the new look is. His dark hair is unforgiving, the patches obvious on his cheeks where he can't grow a full beard. Even if I was kind enough to tell him, he wouldn't believe me. He's too full of himself.

My teeth dig into my lip as Margo picks the pace up underneath the desk. The moment my brother leaves, I'm going to pull her up and fuck her senseless. It's incredibly risky for her to be taking my cock so well while I talk with my brother, and I fucking love her for doing it. She's always surprising me, and the eagerness with which she shoves all of me down her throat has me ravenous to plow into her.

"Are we done here?" I ask through gritted teeth, my balls tightening.

I swallow, not wanting to come. *Not yet.* Not with Carter here, not before I fuck her up against the windows of this office, letting her look out at the city she loves so much.

Carter runs a finger over the leaf of a tree that Polly works so hard at taking care of. "Yes. Tell Margo I stopped by."

He begins walking back toward the door, thank fuck.

I'm about to pull Margo up by the hair and bury myself in her when he turns around to face me once again. "Better yet, maybe I'll hang out for a bit. She's bound to show up eventually, isn't she?"

"Goodbye, Carter," I clip, hating the fact that he's here to begin with. He hates Manhattan. Says it's too dirty and busy for his taste.

Carter opens the door, his eyes scanning the room one last time before walking out. He's almost scanned the entire room when his eyes land on Margo's discarded sweater.

Fuck.

He zeroes in on it, looking from the sweater, to me, and back again.

Margo continues to suck me perfectly while I see the gears in my brother's head turn. "Remember what we talked about Beckham," he warns, pulling the door shut behind him. "Remember who had her first."

Oh, I remember. I just don't give a fuck.

Margo was never truly his. She was always meant to be mine.

The moment I hear the door seal shut, I'm pushing my chair back and pulling my cock from her warm mouth. It's a sight to see, seeing her crammed underneath my desk, her lipstick smudged all around her mouth. God, she's fucking hot. My brother made the mistake of his life by letting her go. I don't intend to make the same one.

I hold my hand out, pulling her from underneath the desk. Her knees are red from rubbing against the floor, her eyes watery from how well she took me. "That was unexpected," she says, smiling at me.

"He's a fucking bother."

Both of us stand up, her back resting against the corner of the desk. "Well, he didn't bother *too* much," she muses. "Although, I was kind of hoping I'd get you to finish."

"Oh I'll come," I assure her, spreading her thighs open so I can step between them. "It's just going to be after I've felt you come on my cock a time or two."

Her bottom lip juts out in a pout. "This was supposed to be my turn to do you. To swallow…"

I take her next words away, needing to feel her lips against mine. Needing to taste her and feel her come undone underneath my touch. The kiss isn't gentle or loving, it's filled with feral need and longing. I've never wished to be back home in my life, at a place where I could take her as long and as loudly as I want.

After seeing Carter, seeing the look in his eyes that assures me he thinks he isn't done with Margo, I need to feel close to her. I need the reassurance that she's mine just as much as I'm hers.

Margo doesn't hold back as she kisses me back. She puts everything into it, more than reassuring me it isn't Carter she wants anymore. I can't fight the jealousy that still rages in my chest, despite the reverence she kisses me with.

I pick her up by the hips, walking us to the floor-to-ceiling window of the office space. It isn't the same view as the one offered in the one I gave her, but it still works. "Is it bad I wouldn't have cared if my brother caught you underneath there?" My hips keep her pinned against the glass, her legs wrapping around my middle to secure her position.

She moans as she sticks her hands underneath my jacket. Her hands fist in the dress shirt I wear underneath as she attempts to untuck it. "No." She tilts her head back as I kiss down her throat. "I didn't care either."

I laugh against her sensitive skin, marveling at the goosebumps that raise all over her skin. "I know you didn't care. You were taking my cock so greedily down your mouth I could barely think straight. I was so close to letting my brother watch you gag yourself on me, just to prove to him how little you want to speak with him."

I pop her breast from the cup of her bra, sucking her nipple into my mouth. "Would you have done it?"

I lift her skirt until it bunches around her waist. While the panties she slipped on this morning after I had her for breakfast are sexy as fuck, I rip each thin side and stuff them in my pocket. They're in the way and I don't want to lose connection with her even for a second for her to take them off properly.

"I liked those."

"So did I." Her thighs tighten around me as her heels dig into my back. She's trying to line herself up with my erection, but she's just out of reach to accomplish it.

"You didn't answer my question," I continue, reaching between us to feel her absolutely soaked. Her breath hitches as my fingers slide over her.

"Remind me what it was."

I inch my finger inside her, going as far as I can. Her eyes roll back in pleasure. "Would you have continued to greedily take my cock if your ex-boyfriend looked on? Would you be as determined to fit every inch of me down that throat of yours if you knew my brother was watching you do it?"

Her head nods up and down enthusiastically. "Yes," she mewls, grinding against me.

"Good answer." Taking a step back, I let her feet fall to the ground. Instantly, I spin her body around, pressing her cheek into the cold glass. I allow myself a moment to take in the view. Her dark hair spills down her slightly arched back. Her skirt bunches around her waist, allowing me the perfect view of her round ass.

I place my foot between her legs, forcing her to open her legs wider for me. If the glass is too cold against her skin, she doesn't say anything about it. In fact, she presses even deeper into it when I run my fingertip down her spine. "You did so good sucking my cock, baby," I praise. "But I can't resist taking the chance to fuck you right here in this office." I run my head over the seam of her asscheeks, loving how loud she moans from the motion.

"I want to fuck you while you look down at the city you love so much." I slide into her from behind. "Now you won't be able to look at the busy street below without thinking of the time I fucked you so good while everyone below went about their day."

I set a punishing pace for the both of us, slamming my hips against her ass. Her moans come louder and quicker. Reaching around her, I cover her mouth with my hand. "As much as I love to hear you scream, baby, I'm going to need you to be quiet this time. Soon everyone in this office will know we're together, but not just yet."

Her body slackens, melting to the window as I pump in and out of her. She feels so fucking good in this position. She'd already worked hard at getting me close to coming while blowing me, now with her pussy clenching around me, I know it won't be long before her efforts will pay off.

I pump into her quick and hard at a pace I've learned drives her wild. The moans vibrating against my hand are a clear indicator that it feels just as good for her as it does for me. She surprises me by staying quiet, at least quiet enough for no one else to hear. It might be because my fingers push into her mouth, gagging her to keep her quiet as I keep the punishing pace between us.

While I relish the thought of every last man in this office knowing she's off-limits, I should probably have a conversation with HR first. They probably wouldn't love to find out about us by hearing us fucking in my office, especially if they were to know I left an important meeting to do so.

Her eyes stare down at the city below her. We're so high up there's no way anyone on the ground could see us, but that doesn't mean someone in the building next to ours isn't looking out their office window right now and seeing way more than they expected.

"Does it turn you on to think that someone could be staring at us right now through the window? That they'd see your tits bouncing as I bury myself in you? That they could see you greedily take every inch of me? That they'd think you were my dirty little slut?"

She mumbles something against my fingers, but it's muffled and unintelligible. My fingers sneak deeper into her mouth, her lips closing around them the same way they did around my cock. Her tongue against them as I push deeper into her, making her feel me everywhere. Even with her mouth full, she moans loudly, her eyes fluttering open and shut with pleasure.

"You're so full of me right now." I thrust harder into her. There will be a time and a place where I can gently push in and out of her, taking my time plucking an orgasm from her. That time is not now. This is hurried, raw and full of ravenous passion. "Do you enjoy sucking on my fingers the same way you do my cock? Knowing that you're feeling me everywhere?"

She clenches around me, her back arching as a moan ricochets around my fingers. I cover her mouth once again, knowing I'm about to fall over the edge with her. A few more thrusts and I fall against her as cum spills from me.

We stay pressed together, her body against the window and my body against her for a few moments. Our chests heave in perfect unison. My hand slips from her mouth, falling to her hips as I lean in and kiss the back of her neck.

She sighs, letting her head fall to the back of my shoulder. She tilts her head to face me with a satisfied smile on her lips. "That was the most perfect view of New York."

I laugh, slowly freeing my cock from her. There are still red spots on the base of it from her lipstick, now completely coated in both of our cum.

When I look between her thighs, I find my cum dripping down between them. I smile in satisfaction, leaning down to kiss the top of her nose before I find something to help get both of us cleaned up.

Returning with some tissues, I help her clean between her thighs and straighten her skirt back out. Before she can leave the window and retrieve her shirt, I pin her against the cold glass one more time.

My fingers skirt against the bare skin of her inner thigh. I run my nose over her chin, leaning in close until my lips press to her ear. My fingertips dig into her smooth skin with my next words. "When my brother finds you and tries to win you back, remember that it's *my* cum leaking out of you."

45

Margo

"Maybe this isn't the best idea," I say in a rush, my words coming out jumbled.

Beck stops in the middle of the sidewalk. His hand tightens around mine as he pulls me through the crowd of people walking, stopping us in a secure nook between two shops. His eyebrows knit together in a frown. "Why are you saying this?"

I take a deep breath, wondering if the outfit I picked out was a good idea. I opted for a jumper I got from the shopping spree I had with Beck. It's a plaid pattern with black and emerald-green details. Underneath, I wear a sheer black bodysuit with a high neckline, and I paired it with a long camel-colored trench coat to stay warm in the brisk night air. To cover my legs, I chose a pair of sheer black stockings and a pair of kitten heels. I adore everything about the outfit, and so had Emma and Winnie when I'd spoken to them on FaceTime and asked if it was worthy for meeting the parents. It's just now that I'm moments away from coming face to face with my ex's parents only to tell them I'm now engaged to their other son, it seems weird. How the hell does one dress for that occasion?

"I'm just worried that the outfit screams Catholic school girl and not billionaire's wife," I explain, running my hands down the front.

Beck literally laughs out loud, apparently finding my inner turmoil hilarious.

"Beck," I whine, adjusting the headband in my hair. "It's not funny. I just want to look good when meeting the parents of my fiancé to announce to them that we're engaged."

His eyes soften as his face becomes serious again. He wraps his arms around me, pulling me against his warm body. Of course he never has the problem of looking too naive or silly in an outfit. Anything he puts on he looks like a model straight from a catalog. Tonight is no different in a suit that isn't as formal as the ones he wears to work, but one he looks delicious in either way.

"If we're being technical, this isn't you meeting them for the first time. So you don't have to worry about first impressions at all. Which even if you did, you'd kill it because you look absolutely breathtakingly beautiful tonight, Violet. Have I not told you that enough?"

I sigh, playing with the zipper of his coat. He had told me I looked beautiful countless times from the time I slipped the outfit on until the moment we stepped out of the car. I'm just so full of nerves I keep wondering if it's something he's just saying to make me feel better.

My nose scrunches. "I think the first impression comment makes me feel even worse." I crane my neck to look up at him. He's so handsome it makes my chest hurt. Every single one of his features are perfect, all things I've been obsessed with sketching as of late.

"Trust me. It won't be weird. They'll be excited. Our story seems natural. You worked for me, we were together a lot and then we fell in love. They know my personality. I always go all in when I want something. It won't seem too far off that we got engaged quickly."

His fingers brush against my temple tenderly. When he does simple things like this, it makes my heart long for things it shouldn't. Things like I wish this was actually real, that he wasn't known to be so closed off and that we weren't just pretending.

Well at least that he wasn't pretending, I often wonder if I've reached the point where I no longer have to fake it.

I think I've caught feelings for Beckham Sinclair. Terrifying, massive, *powerful* feelings. The kind that have overtaken my every thought, every feeling, my entire being. I'm afraid I've done the one thing I told him I couldn't do, allow myself to blur the line. I need to reign myself in some, to have a reality check. Tonight won't be the night, however, because I need to play the lovesick fiancée to Beck to make it believable. It won't be that hard, considering it's not really faking it when it feels so incredibly real.

His indigo eyes search my face. He seems worried. Not about seeing his parents, but maybe it's the caution in my eyes making him look more apprehensive than normal.

"You're not embarrassed to be telling them you're engaged to me? I hear you could've had the pick of an oil or jewelry heiress, not a girl born to a preschool teacher and an electrician."

He cradles my face in his hands, the leather of his gloves soft against my cheeks. "I've never been more proud."

My stupid, pathetic heart cartwheels at his words. It clearly has no idea that his words don't mean what we hope. They couldn't...

But what if they did?

His stare is so intent, his gaze so deep that not for the first time, I wonder if somehow Beck is falling like I'm falling. Have things changed for him like they have me? A girl can dream.

"Beck," I start, needing to tell him that I think I might be falling for him.

He leans down, pressing his lips to my forehead. He does it so often I've become used to it. I've grown so accustomed to it; it makes me ache to think of the day I won't feel the press of his full lips above my eyebrow. "Shhh," he says against my skin. "I know, Violet."

You know what? I want to ask.

I'm about to do just that when he slides his phone from his pocket, looking down at the name on the screen. I look too, finding his dad's name glowing on the front. One hand stays on my cheek, his thumb absentmindedly brushing over my cheekbone as he answers the call.

"Hey, Dad."

There are a few silent seconds as he listens to whatever his dad says on the other line. "Yeah, we'll be there in a few minutes. We're just down the block."

He hangs up the phone, tucking it back in his pocket before giving me a wide smile.

"I'm nervous," I admit, the words tumbling from my mouth.

Beck intertwines our fingers once again continuing down our path from earlier. We get so many looks, mostly from women. They watch us with curious envy, like they're trying to figure out how I managed to get a man like him to walk down the busy sidewalk with me hand in hand.

"You have no reason to be." He comes to a halt, stopping behind a crowd of people as we wait for the light to tell us we can cross the street.

"I have every reason to be, Beck. I wasn't bred to marry into money like every other woman you've brought home to your family. And I certainly don't think those girls have also met your family when dating your brother."

"That's the thing. I've never brought a woman to meet my parents."

I almost trip over my feet as the group of people cross the crosswalk. The only thing that keeps me up is Beck's strong grip on my hand. Once we're safely back on a sidewalk, my face thankfully not against the concrete, I look at him with a stunned expression. *"Never?"*

We come to a stop in front of the restaurant. He turns to face me, shielding my view from the rest of the world. All I see is him. "Never. Until you. Until now."

"Yeah?" I ask hopefully.

He nods his head confidently. He stares at me like he's just waiting for me to ask the countless questions running through my head. I hold them back, knowing we don't have the time.

But later, I might feel confident enough to ask him—to hope—that maybe this has transpired into something more.

"I'll give you something even better," he says hoarsely. "I'm excited to tell them about us, Margo. So the next time you find that you're comparing yourself to other women, don't. There's never been anyone else. Just you."

He doesn't give me room for further questioning. He pulls me into the restaurant, giving my hand a reassuring squeeze as he leads us to the host stand.

"We're here for the Sinclair reservation," he announces smoothly. The hostess looks him up and down with appreciation. I get it. He's hot. But she could put her tongue back in her mouth before she drools all over the menus. It'd be the polite thing to do.

"I'll lead you there."

Beck thanks her politely, keeping a hold of my hand as we're escorted to the back of the dining area.

I notice Beck's parents before they notice us. There's just one minor issue. It's not just Beck's mom and dad at the table. We won't be announcing our engagement face-to-face with only his parents.

We'll also be announcing it to Carter—my ex-boyfriend and Beck's brother.

Oh shit.

46

Beck

Even with his random appearance at the office this morning, I hadn't expected Carter to show up to dinner tonight. Family dinners aren't Carter's thing. They aren't typically mine either, I guess, but they're even less his.

Carter looks straight past me, his eyes zeroing in on Margo behind me, on our clasped hands.

He jumps out of his seat, the chair flying to the ground behind him. "What the fuck?"

My mom's eyes go wide with shock, or maybe it's embarrassment. She looks around the restaurant, giving the innocent bystanders an apologetic smile.

Dad gives me an unreadable look before he reaches up and grabs Carter's shoulder. He pulls on it. "Sit down, son."

Carter's eyes burn with fury as he picks his chair off the floor and follows our father's direction.

"Mom, Dad." I smile softly at my parents. I feel slightly guilty pulling them into the drama that's about to ensue with Carter here. I really hadn't expected him to show up tonight. It was supposed to be an enjoyable pre-Thanksgiving dinner with my parents as I introduced Margo as my fiancée.

Now it's going to be drama-filled. Carter was babied terribly. He's not used to things being taken from him. Add in the fact that he's been extremely competitive from the moment I established my own company, and there's no way this will end well. He's wanted to beat me at everything from the moment Dad off-handedly asked him at a dinner once when Carter was going to do something with his life like I had. I don't think Dad had meant it to be offensive. But Carter took it that way. Since then, he's been trying to win against me when I've never been interested in even playing the game. When he finds out Margo and I are engaged, he's bound to lose his shit. I hoped it would be over a phone call, not in a place that's always packed and takes six months to get a reservation unless you have an in with someone.

"I presume you remember Margo?" I offer, turning my body so she can no longer hide behind me. She pinches my arm, clearly unamused by bringing her into the limelight.

I squeeze her hand, trying my best to reassure her. Neither of us had expected Carter to show up, but that may have been naive of us. She managed to hide from him all day at work. Leave it to Carter to never work hard for anything until now—until it came to winning her back.

My mom stands up with a warm smile on her face. She rounds the table and pulls Margo into an embrace before she's even said hi to me.

"Margo," she says lovingly, petting the back of Margo's head. "It's been so long, sweetie."

Margo hugs her back. It's only because I pay close attention to her every move that I notice how her back is tense and her hands are balled tight. "Yeah, it has," Margo responds uneasily.

As soon as my mom pulls away, my dad is there to pull Margo into a hug. He always had a soft spot for her. Even after Margo called things off with Carter, my dad never stopped asking about how she was doing.

While he and Margo get reacquainted, my mom stops in front of me with a wide smile on her face. "My boy," she says, her voice filled with love. Leaning down, I pull my mom in for an embrace, feeling comforted by the scent of the same perfume she's worn my entire life.

"I missed you," I say against her hair.

My dad reaches out to shake my hand and then we all look at each other, the vibe in the air a little uncomfortable after Carter's outburst. Dad eases the tension by pointing to the table. "Let's take a seat and catch up." The look he aims my way tells me he's full of questions.

I feel Carter's hot glare on me as I pull Margo's chair out from the table. Her smile seems more comfortable than she may seem as she mumbles a small thank you and takes a seat. I take the seat next to her, smiling at my brother, letting him know I'm completely unbothered by the seething glare he's aimed at me.

Carter takes a drink of his bourbon. "I wasn't aware we were bringing *assistants* to the family dinner."

"I wasn't aware you were invited."

"Boys," my mom hisses, the word coming out more pleading than she probably intended.

I look at her, my expression softening. "Sorry, mom. I'm just slightly confused why Carter has decided to grace us with his presence for once." My eyes flash to Margo at my side. I have to hand it to her; you wouldn't ever know how nervous she was just minutes ago. She holds her head high, not an ounce of nerves on her face. "I wonder if it has something to do with my assistant."

It's probably cruel of me to draw out the news of our engagement, but I can't help myself. I like that Carter is uncomfortable across from us, that he's wracking his brain wondering what's going on between Margo and me.

Carter's dark hair gleams underneath the soft yellow lighting. He watches me closely. If he's looking for answers on my face, he won't find them. He leans back in his chair, risking a glance at Margo before looking back to me. "Am I not allowed to join my own family for dinner?"

"You know what?" I pick up the wine menu and pretend to look over it even though I know what to order. "You're right. We're so thrilled to have you join us tonight. Tell me, how's your girlfriend? What was her name again?"

Carter glares at me before looking at Margo. "We broke up," he explains, looking at Margo with want in his eyes.

Margo smiles widely at him. I don't realize how jealous it made me to see them looking at one another until she reaches under the table and places her hand on my thigh. "It doesn't matter to me if you have a girlfriend or not. I would love to meet her if you do."

Fuck. Why am I relieved to hear her say those words?

"She wasn't you," Carter fires back.

Oh, hell no.

I dismissively wave the waiter away when he stops at our table. He scurries away, the jealousy surrounding me probably palpable enough to have him running for his life.

"I've actually got some great news," I announce, jealousy getting the better of me. Underneath the table, I place my hand on top of Margo's, intertwining our fingers.

My mother's eyes light up. She exchanges a look with my father, who looks somewhat relieved by the change of conversation. That face may be wiped right off with my next words.

I look at Margo, my eyes softening as I take in her beauty. She squeezes my hand, prompting me to continue. Looking back to my parents, I take a deep breath. "Margo and I have fallen in love."

"You're fucking lying," Carter spits immediately.

Margo looks at him, not showing a hint of emotion on her face. "Things happen when you work closely together."

I could kiss her in front of all of them for her statement. I hadn't expected her to say much. In fact, I expected her to stay quiet as I explained the change in our relationship. When I saw Carter seated at the table, a small part of me became nervous she wouldn't be able to follow through with him here. She'd been upfront about how much he hurt her. I didn't know how much of it still lingered, if a part of her still wanted him.

The confident set of her features as she stares into his rage-filled eyes tells me everything I need to know. She won't be leaving me for him. He no longer has her—I do.

The entire table is tense as Margo and Carter stare at one another. She's the first to break eye contact, looking away from him to focus on me. Lifting her hand, she brushes my cheek lovingly. "Neither one of us expected it," she lies graciously.

"You whore," Carter snaps, slamming his hand down on the table. The glasses on the table rattle with his sudden movement.

"Carter!" My mom gasps.

"Son," my father growls.

I hold my hand up, stopping my parents from saying anything else. Anger brews in my chest as I fumingly focus on that pathetic excuse of a man I have to call my blood. I can feel Margo watching me carefully from my side. My body is coiled tight with rage. I lean forward, smoothing a wrinkle in the tablecloth.

Every fiber of my being wants to lunge across the table and hit my brother square in the face for having the nerve to call Margo that. My hand flexes underneath the table as I try to keep my composure. The last thing my family needs is to make the headlines for Carter and I getting into a brawl during dinner.

"Carter," I seethe, looking up to look him dead in the eye. I hope he sees the fury raging in my eyes. "Call my fiancée that again and I will fucking ruin your life as you know it. The blood we share be damned."

He rears back, his eyes widening. "Fiancée?"

"Yes, *fiancée*. Apologize for speaking to her like that."

"No," he answers aggressively.

"Carter," our mom pleads. This wasn't how I envisioned sharing the news of our engagement, but then again, I hadn't expected Carter to be here.

Carter looks away from me, to look at Margo. "Just hopping from one brother's cock to another, aren't we?"

I fly out of my chair, rounding the table in an instant. Dishes clatter to the ground as I shove his face into the tablecloth. My mother shrieks. Margo says something, but I don't catch it as I dig Carter's cheek into the stark white tablecloth. Anger courses through my veins as I lean forward, tightening my grip on the back of his neck.

The pleas from my family and musings from other diners go completely unnoticed. All I can focus on is my brother. The piece of shit doesn't deserve to be in Margo's presence, let alone have the right to have ever called her his. My fingertips dig into his neck as I lean close to his ear.

My teeth grind, threatening to shave down from the pressure of the angry set of my jaw. "You're lucky we're in public, brother. If we were in private your face would already be black and blue."

"You wouldn't," he spits.

My fingers thread through his hair, yanking his head up, I turn his head to look at Margo. He tries to push me off him, but his pathetic attempts are useless. My eyes flick to the people around us, all of them gawking at the spectacle we're putting on. I hate the attention, but I despise the words he used against Margo more.

When he tries to turn his head, I use my free hand to clutch his jaw, forcing him to look at Margo. "Apologize to my fiancée, Carter."

He tries to jerk free from my grip but fails. I'm too angry, too filled with rage to let him out of this. He's going to apologize to her. I'll do whatever it takes.

"Fuck no." He yelps like a child when my grip tightens on his jaw.

"Try that again," I demand, moments away from beating his head into the table.

"I'm sorry," Carter mutters, staring at her lap.

"Be a fucking man and apologize to her face."

"I'm sorry!" he shouts. "Ow," he groans as my fingers dig so hard into his neck that his face begins to turn blue.

"While you're at it, tell her how sorry you are for cheating on her. For being stupid and pathetic and walking out on your relationship."

A large hand lands on my bicep. I look back to find my father giving me a warning stare. I ignore it. He's going to have to rip me off Carter if he wants me to stop before Carter does as I ask.

"What the fuck." Carter manages to get out through gasps of air.

Margo is the only one who can pull me from my rage. Her voice breaks through the anger, pulling me out of it. "Beck," she murmurs, "it doesn't matter. I don't care what he thinks of me. It doesn't matter."

I look at her, my fingers applying slightly less pressure to where he can get a deep breath in.

"He doesn't matter," she repeats, giving me a hesitant smile. "All that matters is you."

Relief washes over me as I let go of him. The sudden movement has him lurching forward. He groans, rubbing at the handprint I left on his neck.

Walking up to my mother, I give her a kiss on the top of the head. "I love you, mom. We'll catch up when he's not around. Sorry to ruin our dinner."

My dad and I share a knowing look. He doesn't argue with me or try to convince me to stay. Words aren't needed for us to come to an understanding. We'll talk later. But I can't be in the presence of Carter for another second and keep my temper at bay.

Before going, I stop in front of him and look at him down my nose. "Don't fucking speak to my future wife again. In fact, don't even breathe in her god damn direction unless it's to utter an apology."

47

Margo

"It was good to see you again." My words come out so quickly they sound all jumbled as I stand up from my seat. I give them both an apologetic smile. I was really looking forward to catching up with them, but I'm seconds away from losing Beck's retreating form in the crowd of diners.

"We'll speak with you later, darling," Beck's mom says, giving me a soft smile. I don't even bother to look at Carter. It's beyond me how I gave years of my life to that man. He fails in comparison now that I've gotten to know Beck. It's wild to me that I spent weeks crying over someone who clearly didn't deserve me. Hell, I don't know if any woman deserves him. He's as pathetic as they come.

I give them one last wave before I rush toward the exit. Beck disappeared in the few seconds it took me to say goodbye to his parents. When I fly out the front doors of the building, I'm disappointed when I don't see Beck anywhere. My heart thumps in my chest as I look in every direction, trying to find where he went.

Fighting past the panic of where he went, worried about how angry he was and him being alone, I pick a direction and search for his body through the throng of people. He's nowhere in sight. I stop in front of a narrow alleyway, pulling my phone from my handbag in hopes I'll be able to get ahold of him.

I'm about to click on his name in my contacts when a hand snakes around my waist and pulls me deeper into the alleyway. I let out a loud shriek, gasping for air as I prepare to scream for help. The body engulfs my back, pulling me against a familiar chest. I'd know him anywhere by his smell, the scent I've grown far too attached to.

"Beck." I let out a sigh of relief, only now realizing how worried about him I was.

He turns my body to face his, backing me up until my shoulders hit the brick of a building. I immediately wrap my arms around his middle, going underneath his suit jacket so I can feel the heat of his body as I do my best to comfort him.

His hand comes up to cradle the back of my head, holding it against his chest. "I'm so furious he spoke like that to you, Margo," he admits, his voice hoarse. "I can't begin to apologize enough on his behalf."

I squeeze him tighter, relieved to have found him. His heart beats against my ear, the rhythm wild and untamed. "You don't have to apologize for him."

"He never should have spoken to you like that. Fuck, I could kill him for that."

Pulling away, I cradle his cheeks between my hands. He presses his left cheek deeper into my palm, his eyes searching my face frantically. "Forget about it. It doesn't matter."

"Of course it fucking matters."

I shake my head at him. God, the intensity in his eyes has me locked in a trance. I'm drawn to the pure anger radiating from him. I feel something deep inside that his anger is in defense of me. "It doesn't. Not one bit. We're what matters, Beck. Not him."

A muscle ticks angrily away at his jaw, like a visible countdown before he loses the restraint of his control. He places his forehead against mine, taking a deep breath. For a long moment, we breathe in each other's air. I hope my steady breaths help calm his erratic ones.

"No one gets to talk to you like that. I don't care if you love him or have history. I'm not okay with it."

"Loved."

"Like past tense?"

I could die from the vulnerability in his eyes. The sounds of the city echo in the distance, but I'm lost in his dark eyes, the blue the same color of the ocean from our first night together. I pin my focus on him and only him. "Yes, *past tense*. If you could ever even call it that to begin with."

A shaky breath falls from his lips, tickling my face. "Fuck, you have no idea how much I needed to hear that," he confesses.

My hands tighten on his face, my pulse racing with nerves. "Can I tell you something else?"

"Anything."

"I'm afraid the other Sinclair brother will steal my heart."

"Margo. Don't say things you don't mean."

My hands shake against his cheeks. I'm so nervous to come clean, but I can't hold it back. In the process of working with him, or pretending, I haven't been able to help myself. I've caught feelings for him. "I'm not," I answer with conviction. "Beck," my voice quakes as I stare into his deep-indigo blue eyes. "I think through all the pretending, I've started to wish for all of this to be real. I have feelings for you. The kind of feelings I'm afraid won't fade. The kind that I'm scared that soon will solidify themselves so deep in my soul that I don't know if I'll ever remember what it was like to not have my heart want you desperately."

He lets out a long breath of relief, his entire body visibly showing the tension leaving his body. "I've been waiting so god damn long to hear you say that." His fingers tangle in my hair as he brings his face to mine, kissing me with so much reverence I can't help but think that maybe he feels the same way too.

The sound of a loud whistle a few feet away from us breaks us apart. We pull away, looking toward where the sound came from. We find Ezra pulled up to the curb, his passenger side window rolled down with a smirk on his lips. "Would you two like to get back to get a room?" he asks smoothly, a teasing tone to his voice.

I laugh, pressing my face into Beck's chest. It feels like I'm floating on cloud nine. I couldn't imagine a better place to tell him how suddenly things are changing for me. It doesn't feel fake. It feels incredibly real. I'm falling for him. Fast and hard, no doubt causing me a few bumps and bruises to my heart when this is all said and done. There isn't anywhere else I'd rather confess that to him than with the bustling city behind us. The perfect backdrop for a monumental moment.

Beck wraps his arms around my shoulders, keeping me pressed into his clean dress shirt. "You couldn't have waited a few more minutes?" he yells to his friend.

"Sorry, Mr. Sinclair," Ezra responds. "You told me to hurry when you called all pissed off. I was only following your direction."

Beck scoffs, planting a kiss to my head before he pulls away. As we walk toward the car, he wraps his large hand over mine. I could get used to it. Get used to this with him, just the two of us holding hands through the city.

Before we get into the car, Beck tugs on my hand, pulling me into his hard body. "Hey, Margo?"

"Yeah?"

"I know *technically* you're my fiancée, but will you be my girlfriend?"

I laugh, marveling how five minutes ago he was so mad I was worried that he was going to go back into the restaurant and beat Carter's face in. Now pure happiness shines in his eyes, forming little crinkles next to his eyes.

"Beck, I'm already your fiancée. I think we're past girlfriend." To prove my point, I lay my hand on his chest, the diamond catching both of our attentions.

"Just say yes, Violet."

"I feel myself always saying yes to you."

He leans in, his breath tickling my cheek. He softly tucks my hair that blows in the wind behind my ear. "This one feels so much better."

"Why?"

His smile gets so wide, it takes my breath away. How is he real? How is he mine? *How do I keep him forever?*

"Because it's real."

"Real," I repeat breathlessly, my heart soaring.

"This one is for nobody else but us."

I nod, fighting happy tears. Falling for him may have been putting it lightly. As I slide into the car, a huge grin on my face, I wonder if in a New York minute, I've already fallen.

48

Margo

"Are you sure this looks bridal?" I spin in front of the mirror, catching the eyes of my best friends in the mirror. My hands run down the silk dress, marveling at the way it hugs my curves perfectly, but still leaves a little to the imagination.

"You look hot as fuck," Emma chirps from behind me. She picks up a pair of my red bottoms, raising her eyebrows as she inspects the heel.

"I think you look stunning," Winnie agrees.

"Is it chic enough? Formal enough? I didn't know when Beck suggested an engagement party that it would be this... elaborate."

Emma hums. "Keep telling yourself that, Mar. You're marrying into old money; every occasion is an excuse to throw a party."

I grab a pearl studded headband from the armoire in the far closet. I haven't slept in my bed since the night Beck and I returned from the business trip, but I've been insistent on keeping my closet up here instead of moving all my things in with

Beck. It's nice to have a space that feels like my own, to have a little bit of space away from Beck at times. It feels like we spend every waking second together. We live together, work together, do *everything* together. I wouldn't have it any other way, I love that Beck is always showering me with his attention, even when it's in the smallest of ways. It's just that I think I love it a little too much. The feelings I have for him get stronger every single day, and even though he's steadfast in showing me that he cares for me, I can't help but have doubts.

Everything about us was built on being fake. While things have become real for me, I can't help but wonder where his head is at. Does he still expect us to end after a year? Does he want to see where this leads? I can't get my head on straight when it comes to him. I've been so swept in relishing in his constant attention and affection that I haven't had time to really figure out if we're on the same page. It's messing with my head.

Like right now. If I let myself, this could feel like a real engagement party for Beck and me. I could let myself imagine discussing wedding plans with people and telling them about the actual wedding I envision having one day.

All of it is feeling too real. Beck and I have been swept up in planning an extravagant engagement party in a week that we haven't even stopped to talk about what happened at dinner with his parents last week. We've been in a fog of working, planning and joining our bodies any spare moment we can find. I've never felt so desired in my life. It's like we can't keep our hands off one another. I can't complain about it, but I also feel like once this party is done with, we need to have a serious talk about the feelings that are happening.

I need to know he's as in it as I am.

A hand smacks my butt. "Stop staring at yourself." Emma smiles from behind me, wrapping her arms around my middle and resting her chin on my shoulder. Winnie comes to the other side, all three of us locked in an embrace as we stare at our reflections in the mirror.

"I always thought Winnie would be the first to get married." Emma looks over at Winnie and winks.

"Why? Because you thought my father would marry me off to one of the trust fund babies I grew up with?"

Emma shrugs. "Well *yes*. Too bad your heart—well at least your clit—is preoccupied at the moment."

My jaw drops. "Excuse me, what?" I stare at Winnie through the mirror.

Winnie shoots a dirty look at Emma. "Emma doesn't know what she's talking about," she hisses. "Anyway, tonight isn't about *me*. It's about *you*." She squeezes me harder. "We get to celebrate you getting married!"

I make a mental note to ask her more about what Emma was talking about later. It hurts a little to know that Emma knows something that I don't. I'm used to the three of us sharing everything with one another. I've never been left out when it comes to them. And while I've kept secrets from them when it comes to Beck, I don't like knowing they share a secret that I'm not privy to.

Winnie pulls away, looking at me from head to toe. "Back to your original question, I think this looks incredibly bridal *and* chic. Beck is going to lose his mind when he sees you."

"Beck *always* loses his mind when he sees her," Emma pipes up.

I look down at the halter neck silk dress. I tried on upwards of twenty dresses, none of them feeling right when I finally landed on this one. It didn't even need any alterations; it fit me so perfectly. Beck had surprised me earlier by hiring a team of hair and makeup professionals to help us get glammed up. I'd been upset that my family couldn't make the trip up for the engagement party. My dad got sick last minute, and while he's doing okay, he was advised not to travel.

We had a mini spa day this morning in the loft while Beck took care of last-minute arrangements for the party. It made me feel better, even though I swore up and down to do a video call with my mom later to show her the party. She's mad she has to miss out, she's more fun than I am. Never one to miss a party.

A knock sounds on my bedroom door. Emma races to it. "I'll get it!"

I walk to the edge of my closet, opening up my jewelry organizer. My eyes travel over the different luxurious pieces of jewelry Beck had bought me. I settle on a pair of teardrop diamond earrings that have a halo of sapphires. When Beck had told me to pick out whatever I wanted for the occasion, I knew immediately when I saw these that I wanted them. The deep blue of the gemstone reminded me of his eye color.

"Something blue," he noted, staring at me with an unreadable look. I blushed, imagining not only wearing the earrings at our fake engagement party, but one day to an actual wedding to him.

"Okay, but seriously," Emma comments, walking back into the closet. "Where do I find a man like Beck? *Surely* he has some billionaire friends who will spoil me with gifts and orgasms."

I focus on the nicely wrapped box in her hands. It's wrapped in matte black paper with a white bow neatly tied around it. Emma begins to pull on one strand of the bow before I yank it from her arms. "Hands off," I scold, holding it to my chest. "This is *my* gift."

She playfully sticks her tongue out at me, turning to go into my room. "Well, let's sit down and open it so I can be incredibly jealous of you."

Winnie shows off her perfectly straight and white teeth in a wide smile. "You don't have to open it in front of us if you don't want to. *Although* I do want to see…"

"Speak for yourself!" Emma yells from the room. "I'm dying to know what he got her. Hurry up, ladies."

I laugh, nodding my head to the room. "We can't keep her waiting or she'll come back in here."

Winnie and I take a seat on the bed with Emma, all of us staring at the neatly wrapped box in my lap. Part of me wants to open it alone, to cherish the moment, knowing the gift has to be from Beck. I know there's no way Emma would let me get away with that, and another part of me wants to giggle like a girl in high school with an intense crush with my friends about receiving a present from the boy I like. Beck is no boy, but the feelings coursing through my veins right now have me feeling like a lovesick school girl.

I pull a black envelope from underneath the ribbon. Beck's familiar handwriting is scrawled across the front, spelling out my name. I run my hand over the letters, loving how the loops and lines eloquently form together to spell my name.

Flipping the envelope over, I pull at the monogrammed sticker he used to seal the envelope. There's a white custom card inside. I pull it out, holding it up to my face and looking at my friends from over the top of it as I hide my smile.

"Read it," Winnie encourages, leaning forward in excitement.

I hold it closer to my body. "The note is for me and *only* me. So back off," I tease, scooting back on the bed. Knowing Beck, something dirty could be written on the expensive custom card. I want to read it before either of them have the chance to.

I neatly set the envelope down next to me. I want to keep it nice and safe, to keep everything nice and pristine from this gift so I can stare at it all later. I open the letter, blushing as my eyes roam over the words he's neatly scrawled.

Prepare to wear nothing but these for me.
Love, your fiancé

The blush creeps from my cheeks all the way down to my chest. I meet the eyes of my friends, unable to form words as I recount the simple sentence he'd written. How do only eight words have me wishing our party was already over and he was making good on his promise?

"Is it romantic?" Winnie asks whimsically.

My lips rub together coyly. "You could say that."

In one fluid movement, Emma leans forward and snatches the note from my hands. She quickly reads over the note, throwing it back into my lap with a loud groan. "I get *hey you up* texts and you get shit like this? Not fair," she whines.

Winnie grabs the note from my lap, doing it a lot gentler than our friend just did. Her cheeks get pink immediately as she hands it back, her eyes wide.

"That wasn't for either of you to read," I murmur, pulling the present into my lap.

"I'm glad I did. Next time a man sends me a dick pic as foreplay, I know what I'm missing out on."

I ignore the conversation between the two of them as I pull at the ribbon atop the present. It's wrapped so perfectly that I feel bad tearing into the paper. It doesn't stop me from pushing forward, to see what he's placed inside.

To find what I'll be wearing for him tonight.

Pulling the paper off, I find a Jimmy Choo cloth bag that envelops what must be a shoe box.

"I think I might hate you," Emma pipes up as I open the drawstring bag. I pull the shoebox out, running my hand over the lid.

"Jealous much?" Winnie teases.

"Obviously I'm jealous! I want one. Where do I find one?"

I resist the urge to tell her it wasn't luck or fate that brought Beck and I together. It was him needing his board to think he's settled down and me doing anything to get back to the city that's forever felt like home. Plus, the chance of landing my dream job when this is all said and done.

My fingers carefully pry the lid off the shoe box. All of us gasp in unison as we stare at the pair of shoes nestled inside. I don't know if you can even call them shoes, they look more like art.

"That's it. I'm jealous, too," Winnie states.

"Back off. You can buy your own." Emma shoves Winnie's shoulder playfully.

"Not the same," Winnie responds under her breath.

I stay silent, staring at the beautiful pair of heels inside delicate white tissue paper. I pull one of them out, making sure to treat it with care. It's a beautiful shade of white, matching the fabric that encases my body perfectly. A thin piece of material is meant to buckle around my ankle. The most stunning part is the intricate tulle bows on the shoes. The one in my hand has a large tulle bow at the back of the shoe. The shoe still in the box has one on the tip of the shoe.

"You'll look hot as hell when you're butt ass naked in those," Emma announces out of nowhere.

Her random comment makes me laugh out loud. I'm so happy

they both flew here to help me celebrate. While I've loved being stuck in a bubble with Beck, I'm thankful to have more girl time with them. It's the one thing that's lacking here, spending time with my best friends. I really only ever spend time with Beck and the occasional outings with Ezra.

"Is it wrong if I don't wear these? What if I break the heel or something?" I worry.

Winnie and Emma share a laugh. I narrow my eyes at them as they both look at me unapologetically. "You have a point." Winnie giggles. "You aren't the most graceful in the world, Margie."

"I've been wearing heels every day since I started working for Beck, thank you very much."

Emma's eyebrows raise to her hairline. "Is that why the thought of you in nothing but heels makes him so horny?"

Probably.

I roll my eyes. "I'm not answering that question."

Emma smacks the side of my thigh before she attempts to shove me off the back of the bed.

"Emma!" I yell.

"Get the shoes on. Right now."

I slide off the bed, attempting to not put any new wrinkles in the dress with the movements. Emma hands me one of the shoes, the dainty buckle already undone for me. One of my hands grabs the back of the chaise lounge as I slide my foot into the shoe. I bring the strip around my ankle, fastening it. I repeat with the next one, marveling at how they fit me perfectly.

"God, you look hot as hell," Emma notes.

"I agree." All three of us look toward my open bedroom door, finding Beck leaning in the opening with a smirk on his face.

Emma rolls on the bed, tucking her chin in between her hands. "Hey, Beck, tell me. Do you have any friends?"

His eyes don't leave me. It's like the first time he stared at me all over again, my skin feeling every movement of his gaze. "I have a few. Why?"

"Are they single?"

"They are."

"I need one of you. Margo can't have *all* the fun."

"Something tells me you don't miss out on fun," Beck responds, taking a step into the room. He doesn't look at either Emma or Winnie as he comes to a stop in front of me. He looks me up and down with appreciation.

"I can't fucking wait for everyone in this city to know you're mine."

49

Margo

"Have I told you how stunning you look tonight?" Beck leans in close, planting a kiss right below my ear.

"Many times." His lips travel over the hollow of my throat, making me arch into him in pleasure.

"Good. You deserve to know how I'll be thinking of how sexy you are all fucking night." His hand snakes up my thigh, pulling at the silk fabric of my dress. At first when he told me we'd be taking a private limo without my friends, I was upset. I wanted to spend as much time with them as possible. I didn't put up a fight for long, however. All it took was Beck telling me he had to share me for most of the night, he just wanted a private moment between us before we spent the rest of the night with people. I understood his feelings. I wasn't used to having to share him with so many people. It's as if sometimes I've forgotten how busy his social life really is, how many people crave his attention.

Emma and Winnie seemed just fine riding with Ezra to the event, so I agreed. Something I'm extremely thankful for as I feel Beck's lips press to the delicate skin of my collarbone.

Finally getting the heavy fabric out of the way, Beck slips his hand underneath the dress, running a fingertip along the side of my knee.

"Beck," I moan, knowing where this could lead.

"Yes, baby?"

I look at the open partition of the limo. As if he senses my unease, he pulls away from me, slapping his palm against the button to raise it. It loudly rises, the driver thankfully doesn't look up, keeping his eyes focused on the road as we disappear behind the barrier.

"Better?" he questions, pushing my dress all the way up my leg. His fingertips brush the inside of my thigh. My head falls backward. I should stop him. The last thing I need to do is mess up my hair or makeup before he presents me to the elite society of New York he calls friends and family. Yet, I don't stop him when he bunches the fabric around my waist, no doubt wrinkling the fabric I'd worked so hard to keep wrinkle-free.

"Aren't we going to be at the party soon?"

Beck grabs me by the chin, directing my face to look at him. "We'll be there in about ten minutes. I have *plenty* of time to help ease your nerves."

I suck in air when his finger slips underneath the white lingerie I picked out for the occasion. "You noticed?"

"I notice everything about you, Margo. You've been clutching my arm nervously from the moment we left home. You've also been chewing your lip anxiously. If you're going to ruin your lipstick, we might as well find a much more exciting way to do it."

He dives in, branding my heart with the intensity of his kiss. Kissing should get more boring the more you kiss someone, but not with Beck. Every kiss feels like the first one. He expertly moves his tongue against mine, making sure I feel the press of his lips *everywhere*. The intensity in which we kiss is no doubt ruining my carefully lined lips. For the time being, I can't seem to care if I show up at my own engagement party with unevenly lined lips or smudged lipstick. Every woman there probably wouldn't blame me. If they had Beck at their beck and call, ready to take the nerves away from them in a way that is bound to end in bliss, they'd risk the ruined lipstick as well.

Beck pulls away, his lips stained the same color as mine. He looks down between my legs. "Later tonight, I'm going to fuck you, baby. I'm going to take my time fucking you so hard while you wear nothing but these heels I picked out for you. I don't have that time right now." His fingers hook through my panties, pulling them down my legs. "But I want to make you feel good. To take those nerves from you and make you see stars. My mouth on that sweet little pussy of yours and that ring on your finger are me staking claim to what's mine—*you*."

I should stop him, but I want him too deeply to protest. It's past the point of wanting with him. It's pure need at all times. So when he tucks my panties into the pocket of his suit and looks at my wetness like a man who's starved, I spread my thighs even wider for him.

"That's my girl." He lowers his body to the floor, seating himself between my legs. "Now relax for me. Let me make you feel good."

My fingers grasp his styled hair as his tongue presses against my clit. When the limo comes to a stop minutes later, I've had two orgasms and my nerves have dissipated.

Beck remains on his knees in front of me. His mouth coated with both my lipstick and me. Reaching into his pocket, he pulls my panties back out of his pocket. "As much as I love the thought of you walking around bare, you still wet from coming on my face, I won't be able to think straight if I knew how easy it'd be to push your dress up to your waist and slip inside you all night." He picks one leg up and then the other, slipping the fabric back up my legs. I lift my hips, allowing him to put them neatly back in place.

He adjusts my dress so the fabric falls back to the floor of the limo. I'm impressed to find it relatively wrinkle-free.

His arms rest on either side of my head as he cages me against the seat with his body. I reach up, running my thumb underneath his lip to remove my lipstick. "You've got a little something right there," I joke.

He allows me to wipe it away, warmth in his eyes as he watches me. "You seem less nervous now."

I laugh. "A lot less nervous."

His lips press to my nose for a moment before he pulls away. "Let's go greet our guests then."

50

Beck

As we climb the stairs to the event, I feel an immense amount of pride with Margo on my arm. She's undoubtedly the most beautiful woman here, and I'll be introducing her to everyone as my fiancée. It doesn't get better than that. Nothing could ruin the high I'm feeling.

Planning an engagement party in under a week wasn't ideal, but I didn't want to wait. I was ready for everyone to know about us. I was on cloud nine when she told me she'd be my girlfriend. It meant more to me than I'd care to admit to myself. From the moment I spoke with her in that awful conference room in LA, I'd told myself to be cautious in the coming months. We'd established everything we were on something that wasn't real. At least that's what *she* thought.

Margo slips on one of the stairs, her fingers digging into my black suit as she tries to stay vertical. I wrap my arm around her, making sure she doesn't fall in front of all the eyes watching us.

"I think I just about face-planted in front of all of Manhattan," she mutters under her breath.

I give a courteous nod to those watching us, holding onto her tightly. "I think all of Manhattan is a little bit of a stretch." I place my hand over hers. If she goes down, we'll both go down because there's no way I'm letting her go. "I've got you," I add.

We near the crowd of people waiting at the top of the stairs. I can feel Margo tense underneath me with anxiety. "I worked very hard to get rid of those nerves," I tease.

She almost stumbles again, my words taking her by surprise. "You can't bring that up when so many eyeballs are staring at us."

My response is lost as we reach the top step. Some of our party enjoy cocktails as they wait for our arrival. Instantly people bombard us, all of them offering their congratulations. We politely thank each of them, some of them being the very same board members who'd encouraged me to settle down not too long ago.

We're finishing up a conversation with my CTO when I spot my parents coming out of the large doors. "If you could excuse us," I say, planting my hand on Margo's waist and steering her toward them. It wasn't just my need for the world to know we were together that prompted such a quick turnaround for an engagement party, it was also the fact that my parents were about to embark on a month-long trip abroad. I wanted them to be here to celebrate, especially after what happened at dinner with them over a week ago, so hurrying the planning process seemed like the perfect option.

"I'm ready for a drink," Margo murmurs as we get closer to my parents.

I chuckle, nodding my head. "Ditto."

"You look radiant," my mom tells Margo, pulling her into a hug.

Margo hugs her back, seemingly becoming less nervous speaking with a familiar face. "It's not too much?"

My mom pulls away, her hands still on Margo's arms as she shakes her head. "Never, sweetie. This is your night. You can wear whatever you want."

The two of them begin a conversation as my dad claps his hand down on my shoulder. "I've got to hand it to you, Beckham. I've never seen you this happy."

The four of us make our way deeper into the party, my eyes darting around the crowded space looking for a drink for Margo and I. "Yeah?" I ask. I'm easily happier than I've ever been and it's all because of the woman next to me.

"It's all I've wanted for you—your brother, too. For you to be happy. I'm glad you found it with her." Mom had been insistent that we still invite Carter to the party tonight, and it'd be up to him if he'd come to support Margo and me. I'd much rather him not show up. There isn't any part of me that wishes for his support. I don't give a damn what he thinks. I just don't want him insulting my future wife.

A waiter stops in front of us, smiling at Margo and I. "Champagne for the happy couple?" he asks, offering us crystal champagne flutes.

"Absolutely," Margo says in excitement, hastily grabbing the champagne from his hand and downing it in one gulp.

I quirk an eyebrow at her.

She shrugs. "Guess I was still a little nervous after all." She proceeds to take the second glass from the waiter and takes a small sip from what was supposed to be my glass.

The next hour rushes by in a blur. We're pulled from one group of people to the next, fielding question after question about when the wedding will be, when we plan on having kids, where we plan to honeymoon and everything in between. Margo fields every question with grace. I listen carefully to every answer she gives, taking mental notes on what she envisions for a wedding, cataloging if she wants kids and even finding out a tropical honeymoon is not her dream honeymoon. It's a long trip to Europe.

Eventually, she gets pulled from me by her friends. We share a kiss goodbye and I tell her I'll find her in a bit. It gives me time to make small talk with my board and friends that I haven't caught up with in a while.

I'm navigating through a group of people in search of Margo when a familiar face stops in front of me.

"What a party." Ruby Robinson comes to a stop in front of me. I should've known the press would be here. But I hadn't expected the person behind the most popular gossip site's reporter to attend. Maybe it was ignorant of me to not expect her here. She was the one who ran the piece on me with the many women I'd taken on dates in the city in the first place.

"Ruby," I muse, tucking my hands into my pockets. I have to tread carefully when speaking with her. Piss her off, and she'll be blasting personal things about me to the entire internet by the time I wake up tomorrow morning. "I wasn't expecting you here."

She cocks her head. "That was silly of you. I wouldn't miss the engagement party for the *reformed* playboy billionaire of Manhattan."

Unease sets low in my stomach with the taunting smile she aims my way. She moves a piece of her shoulder-length blonde hair off her face, staring at me as she waits for a response.

"Your invitation must have gotten lost in the mail," I lie, hoping to ease the tension brewing between us.

She watches me carefully. I wish I knew what was going on in that scheming mind of hers. Is she plotting something? With her, it's likely. I just need to ensure whatever she's plotting will work out in my favor.

"You hurt my feelings, you know."

The live band stops playing a slower song and opts to play one with a bit more of a beat. The dance floor fills with more bodies as Ruby and I stare at one another in a battle of wits.

My hand runs over my mouth in discomfort. "And how is that?"

"I thought we were close. I figured you'd give me first dibs on running the news of your engagement."

"It happened quickly."

"Did it now?"

The tone of her voice has me swallowing nervously. "Yep. *Unexpected.*"

She hums. "If you say so." She grabs a drink from a passing waiter, taking a long sip as she stares at me from over the rim. "We'll be talking later, Beckham. Be careful about making me angry. Something tells me there are little details I know about you that you'd hate for your sweet little fiancée to find out about. Better yet, you'd hate for the *entire world* to discover."

My jaw clenches as rage wars inside my chest. "You wouldn't."

She begins to back up, already disappearing into a group of people. "You have no idea what I would or wouldn't do."

Before I can chase after her and threaten her, she disappears. I'm left with unease and anger coursing through my veins, my brain whirling with what her words mean. I'd like to think—to hope—that her threats are empty, but you can never know with her. That's the thing about these seedy gossip writers. They have no true moral compass. They only do what's best for them, what gets them the most views. And I'm afraid that she has something on me that'd certainly catch the attention of many.

A hand presses to my chest, making me flinch.

"Hey, you okay?" Margo asks softly.

I look down to find my fiancée watching me carefully, her eyes full of worry. I try to take a calming breath, to not alarm her more than I already have with the shift in my mood.

My hand clasps hers, holding it against my racing heart. "I'm fine," I lie. I'm nowhere near fine. My body is coiled tight with tension after my conversation with Ruby. She has information on me that could ruin what Margo and I have begun. I'd do anything to keep her quiet.

Margo's eyes search my face. She leans in, running her fingers through my hair. "Who were you talking to?"

"Just an old friend." I've never considered Ruby a friend, and I'd never be clueless enough to ever consider her one.

"Oh." Margo shifts her weight on her feet, looking to the group Ruby disappeared behind. "It just looked a little heated."

I pull her into an embrace, clinging onto her a little too tightly. There's no way I'll let the information Ruby is holding over my head get out. I can't lose Margo. Not now. Not with how I feel about her.

"Your heart is racing so fast," Margo presses. I can tell by the way she watches me that she knows something's up, she just isn't pushing asking why.

A gentle kiss to her is the only answer I give to her statement. I don't have a good enough excuse to give her, so I opt to stay quiet instead.

Margo pulls away from me, staring at something over my shoulder. Her lips purse slightly. I turn around, following her gaze to figure out what she's staring at.

My stomach drops.

In the corner, I find Ruby in deep conversation...with my brother.

Fucking hell.

"Now it makes sense," Margo mutters.

My head snaps to look at her in worry. "What makes sense?"

"You're nervous because Carter's here and brought your old friend as his date."

"They came in together?" I ask tightly. My vision starts to get a little blurry with worry. I need to get out, to gain my composure before I lose my shit in the middle of my own engagement party.

Margo shrugs, not catching on to how much I'm internally freaking out. "I'm pretty sure I saw them walk in together, but I was locked in a conversation with Emma and Winnie. I can't be positive."

"Oh." The tie around my neck suddenly feels too tight. I pull at it, loosening it slightly.

"You look a little pale." Margo's cold hand runs over my forehead. A crease forms on her forehead in worry.

"I think I might go get some air. I just wasn't expecting Carter to show up."

"Want me to go with you?"

I take a deep breath, trying to pull myself together. I plaster on a calm facade, trying not to worry her more than I already have.

It should be fine. Even if Carter came with Ruby, she wouldn't tell him anything. She'd come to me before spilling any information she had on me. She'd want to barter and get something out of me before going forward with it.

"No, I'm good. You enjoy your time, babe." I pull her into me once again, breathing in her familiar scent. I lay a kiss on her lips. "I'll be right back."

I walk away as she watches me with a small frown on her face. Guilt weighs heavy on me as I leave her standing there alone. With a few minutes to myself, getting my head together, I'll come back better than ever. I just need five minutes to figure out what's happening.

I need a few minutes to figure out how to tell Margo about my lies...before Ruby—or Carter—get to her first.

51

Margo

I dodge a few people offering congratulations as I search for Beck. When he ran off at first, I hadn't been too worried. I figured he was set off by Carter showing up. Now I'm not so sure.

My steps are quick as I walk the perimeter of the party, smiling at people I've never met before as they tell me how happy they are for Beck and me. Most of these people were invited by Beck. I recognize some from work, but for the most part, it's all new faces stopping me for a quick chat as I look for my fiancé.

After not finding Beck anywhere in the grand ballroom, I search the small rooms that connect to the main room. I come up empty-handed, having no idea where he ended up. My last-ditch effort is to search the outside terrace after I don't find him out front on the stairs.

I step out onto the terrace. It's eerily quiet. My arms wrap around my middle, trying to keep myself warm in the frigid air. I should've grabbed my coat from the coat check, but I hadn't expected to be out in the air for long enough to need one.

I loop around a corner, disappointed when I don't see him anywhere. Turning around, I decide to go back inside to the party and wait for him to find me. He probably had to end up taking a work call or something like that. There has to be a reason he left me alone at the party far longer than the five minutes he'd originally told me.

A pair of cold hands grab my arms as I walk straight into a warm chest.

"Woah there. Careful, Margo," Carter says, his hands holding my biceps tightly.

I try to pull free from his grip, but it's too tight. Deciding not to cause a scene, or set him off, I allow his hands to stay where they are, no matter how uncomfortable they make me.

"Hi, Carter." I greet him calmly, trying to keep my voice steady even though there's an unhinged look in his eyes as he glares down at me. I can smell alcohol on his breath. It wafts around us. My eyes look over his shoulder, searching for any other person on the terrace. I come up empty, completely alone with my, apparently drunk and angry, ex-boyfriend.

"What are you doing out here alone?" There's a slight slur to his words, but less than I was expecting by the smell surrounding us. Maybe he hasn't had as much to drink as I originally thought.

I attempt to take a step away from him, trying to put some distance between our bodies, but he doesn't allow it. For every step I take backward, he takes one forward, keeping a tight grip on me.

"I was just looking for Beck." I manage to pull one arm from him, his fingers staying locked around my other bicep. Reaching up, I move hair from my face so I can see him better.

His eyes flash when he zeroes in on my hand. Before I can even register the sudden rage in his gaze, he's grabbing my hand and pulling it to his face.

"No he didn't," he spits. He inspects the ring on my finger, sliding his thumb over the large diamond.

I try to pull my hand away, but his icy hands won't let me. They've got a viselike hold on my fingers. "You already knew we were engaged, Carter. I didn't think you'd care. You cheated on me for years, remember?"

Carter laughs. It's cold and daunting, making my spine shiver in fear. It's a sound I've never heard from him. "This is our grandmother's ring. Did he tell you that?"

My lips part. He hadn't told me that at all. I thought it was something he designed himself. Not a family heirloom.

"He didn't," he notes, answering his own question. He clicks his tongue, throwing my hands down roughly.

I scurry backward, relieved he's no longer touching me.

"How do you know?" I ask, my voice hoarse with nerves.

"My grandfather showed it to us all the time. He told us all about how he fell in love with our grandmother. He'd been devastated when she passed away when I was in middle school. From that moment on, he told us that the first woman to steal one of our hearts would have the honor of wearing the ring."

I fight the urge to play with the ring, to inspect it with new eyes. Why would Beck give me something so meaningful if the engagement was supposed to be fake all along?

I'm at a loss for what to say back. Beck never told me that the ring was sentimental. I hadn't ever even asked—the thought never crossed my mind that it could be. It doesn't make sense why he'd give me something so special for something that's meant to be fake. I don't say any of this out loud. Even though my head is reeling, I have my head on straight enough to know that I shouldn't admit anything to Carter and jeopardize everything falling apart.

"It seems there's a lot he hasn't told you, Margo."

He unbuttons the first few buttons of his wrinkled dress shirt. It brings attention to how disheveled he looks.

"Are you okay, Carter?" No matter how much he hurt me in the past, I still care about him. Seeing him like this hurts. Through the years we dated I never saw him look so...tortured.

He laughs again, this time louder, the sound bouncing off the stone exterior wall. It's ominous. My heart beats erratically in fear.

"You're asking the wrong fucking question. Ask me what he *hasn't* told you." He smiles sinisterly. "*C'mon*. I know you want to."

I shake my head, trying to stay calm. If I were to try to walk around him, would he let me? Any other time, I'd be confident that he wouldn't hurt me. But there's unrest in his eyes I've never seen before. It makes me hesitant to do anything sudden.

Why can't someone come out here and find us?

Goosebumps pop up all over my skin thanks to the chill in the air and the ice in Carter's eyes. "You're not making any sense, Carter."

"He's been lying to you."

"Why don't we go inside and talk about this?" I brave trying to step around him, giving him a wide berth. He quickly reaches out and grabs me once again, bringing my body flush to his.

His fingertips press so deep into my forearm it hurts. "You're hurting me," I cry.

"We'll go inside when I've said what I wanted to say," he hisses.

I nod, trying to keep the tears that are welling up in my eyes at bay. I swore I'd never shed another tear for Carter Sinclair, but this shouldn't count. The tears are from fear, from the unease at the unhinged look on his face.

"Tell me," I plead, my voice trembling. I'm willing to do whatever it takes at this point if it means he'll let go. Or better, that he'll let us go back inside where we won't be alone.

Where is Beck?

"How did the two of you even start a relationship?"

"I was—or *am*—his assistant. After working long hours and nights together, it just hap—"

"Lies!" he shouts, shaking my body against his. "You know that's a lie, don't you?"

A tear runs down my cheek as I look at the man I loved for years. For all the ways he betrayed me, we still had some great times together. The late-night study sessions at the library where he'd feed me snacks because my hands were dirty from shading my drawings. The nights we danced the night away with our group of friends, the two of us racing to see who could hail a cab home quicker. Even after finding out how deep his betrayals cut, he still took center stage in some of my favorite memories.

There's not a hint of those happy times in his eyes right now. They're black, a deep void as his lips press into a thin line as he stares coldly back at me. The Carter I thought I knew is all but gone.

"I don't understand," I answer, trying to keep my voice as level as possible despite the fear taking over my body. My legs shake, and one more tug of my arm by him will send my pulse spiraling. "I'm not lying, Carter." I *am* lying, but there's no way he could know that. Plus, it's only a half-lie. The truth is, I did develop feelings for Beckham in the late nights we spent together, the constant work meetings and time spent in his penthouse. All of that led to me falling for him. It really isn't a lie at all.

"Do you remember when we first met?"

I nod my head, trying to keep up with the conversation we're having. He's going from one topic to the next, making it extremely difficult to follow his train of thought. "Of course I do," I answer. "Why?"

He wipes at his face with the back of his forearm, letting out a low laugh. "Because my brother is the one that saw you first that night."

My head rocks back and forth as I stare at him in confusion. "What?" I try to think back to that night, to that bar, but I don't recall Beck even being there that night. "You're not making any sense."

"Beckham had offered for my friends and I to join him and his friends that night at the bar. I said what the hell. He and I weren't close, but we knew it'd make our parents happy to know we went out together."

I wait silently, trying to fit the pieces of his story together. There's no way Beckham was there that night. I would've remembered him there. *Wouldn't I?*

"It was just you," I finally manage to get out.

His fingers tighten around me angrily. "No, it wasn't. I just made you think it was."

My eyebrows pinch together as I stare into the dark abyss of his eyes. The smell of vodka permeating from his mouth makes me want to vomit, the multiple glasses of champagne and the small hors d'oeuvres I snacked on are not settling well in my stomach.

"I hadn't even noticed you that night until I noticed *him* watching you. You were chugging beers with those dumb friends of yours. I'd been having an argument with my buddy about a class we were both taking when I noticed Beckham staring at something. I'd never seen something catch his eye. When I followed his gaze, he was staring at you."

That isn't possible. The first time we ever met, the first time he ever saw me, had to have been when Carter took me home to the Hamptons.

"Carter." My voice trembles, his name coming out shaky and unsure.

He reaches up and pushes hair from my face. The feel of his

fingertips against my skin has me feeling sick. I hate it. I want to get out of here, to get far away from this man who isn't acting like the man I once loved.

"In that moment I knew he wanted you. And I hated my brother. I hated how successful he was. How proud my father was of him. I'd never be able to measure up to him. So I got to you first. It was obvious how interested he was in you. I wanted to take *something* from him. I'd never have my own company—but I could have you."

Words fail me. He seems drunk. He could be making all of this up, but it doesn't seem that way. Not with the taunt in his tone, in the way he watches me with morbid satisfaction with telling me that information.

I try to process what he's saying, what his words mean. Is he telling the truth? "You don't know he wanted me," I accuse, grasping for straws at this point. I don't know why it even matters to begin with. Does he just want to be able to say he stole the woman his brother noticed first? It seems extremely petty and irrelevant because in the end, Beckham still got me.

"Oh, I did. I could tell. He wanted you bad. I wanted to hurt him more."

"Why does any of that matter now?"

"It matters because you should know that Beckham lied to you."

"How?"

"Did you see the woman I showed up with tonight? The hot blonde in the blue dress?"

I think I hear the sound of footsteps behind him, but no one appears before us. Disappointment settles deep in my bones. For a brief moment, I had hope that this confrontation was going to be over.

"Did you?" Carter raises his voice, making me flinch.

"Yes," I yelp.

"Do you know who she is?"

I shake my head, my tongue feeling heavy with nerves.

"She's the top reporter for a gossip site. She knows everything about everyone."

"Good for her," I respond in defeat. At this point I have no idea where any of this is going, what he's trying to achieve with the boomerang of questions.

"She told me something about that fiancé of yours that I think you'd want to know."

Maybe he knows why Beck and I became engaged in the first place. I don't know how he or she could've found out about the agreement, but I guess it's possible. I keep my mouth shut, however, in case that's not where he's going with this.

"I'm sorry, Carter," I apologize, walking on eggshells with his turbulent mood right now. "I don't know where you're going with any of this."

"You might know her for the article she ran on him. The one with all the women. I'm *sure* you saw it."

"I've heard about it."

"Did you know that Beckham paid Ruby to run it?"

My body goes absolutely still with shock. I couldn't have heard him correctly. That'd make no sense. That article was the entire reason Beck was pressured by his board to clean up his image. There's no way he'd be the one to run it in the first place.

My teeth dig into my lip as I try and think of a response. I don't believe Carter's delusions, but he also doesn't seem to be in a stable state of mind. It probably wouldn't be the best idea to tell him he's wrong.

"Why would he do that?"

Carter clicks his tongue disapprovingly. He taps my forehead. "You're smarter than this, Margo. *Think*. What happened after that article ran on Beck?"

I hold my tongue. I know *exactly* what happened. After that article ran, Beck was told by his board he needed to clean up his image or they'd risk losing investors. I knew all of this. It's the entire reason Beck came to me to begin with. But why would Beck ever want it to run in the first place?

He grabs me by the shoulders, bringing his face inches from mine. "You can cut the act. I know that Beck told you he needed a fake fiancée after that article ran to get the board off his back. He deceived you, Margo. The only reason the board was ever after him was *because* of him. He found a way for him to finally have you and he took it."

"No," I whisper, suddenly feeling dizzy. I don't know if it's from fear, shock, or the alcohol, but it feels like I'm moments away from passing out.

"He schemed to get you. He hated knowing that I ever had you, from the moment he first saw you at the bar. All of this was him trying to get back at me. He's been obsessed with it from the moment we met. He doesn't give a shit about you. It's always been that he was jealous I got to you first. He never forgave me for that."

My heart pounds in my chest as I feel like I could throw up. Too much is happening at once. I don't want to believe a word he's saying, but I can't help but question everything now.

"You can ask Ruby if you want," Carter adds, pulling me against him.

His breath hits my face. We're way too close. He's too much in my personal space.

"I need a moment," I beg, pushing against his chest. If anything, it backfires. He takes it as a sign that I want him closer.

He grabs my face, our bodies flush against one another. "Take me back, Margo. Fuck him. It's never been about you for him. He won't love you the way I love you. He's incapable of it."

Tears stream down my face as I shake my head at him. "Carter, no."

It's sickening how one hand holds me so tight it's painful while the other strokes the hair on my face delicately. "I won't ever hurt you again. I *love* you. It's supposed to be us."

I try to turn my head to look away from him. He's delusional. I don't know what's true when it comes to what he's accusing Beck of, but even if everything he's saying that I hope to be false actually is true, I still can't be with him. I have no desire to.

I don't love him anymore.

"I can't." My voice breaks. I hate it. He was never supposed to have power over me again. I've already cried enough over him, yet here I am, falling apart in his grasp.

He roughly grabs my jaw, forcing me to look at him again. "You will," he seethes, his eyes flicking to my lips.

No, no, no.

I attempt to push him off one more time, but it's no use. He's much stronger than I am. His lips press to mine angrily, his tongue swiping over my lips aggressively. I almost throw up, my hands punching at his chest to get him off me.

It doesn't work. It fuels him as he assaults my mouth with his. Not knowing what to do, I bite down on his lip, doing anything to get him away from me.

"You bitch!" he hisses, pulling away and grabbing at his bleeding lip.

I run. Not looking back at him as I stumble on my heels, running toward the doors. He yells after me, but I don't stop until I run right into Beck.

"Margo?" he asks worriedly.

I bury my face against him, letting out a large sob as his arms pull me into his body.

"What is it, baby? You're worrying me."

I hiccup, rocking my face back and forth against him. "Carter, he—"

Beck's entire body tenses as he tenderly cups my face. A horrified look crosses his face. "Where is he?"

I don't have to answer him because something over my shoulder catches his eye. Not something. *Someone.*

"If you fucking touched her," Beck seethes, pulling me into his chest and shielding Carter from my view.

"She fucking bit me."

A loud growl comes from Beck's throat. "What I'll do to you is *much* fucking worse."

"No," I plead, just wanting to leave. To not cause a scene in front of all the people here for the engagement party. "I just want to leave."

Beck doesn't seem to hear me. He's busy glaring over the top of my head at his brother.

"Beck," I plead, grabbing the lapels of his suit to get him to look at me. "I want you to take me home. *Now.*"

His shoulders rise and fall in a deep exhale. The tips of his fingers twitch against my neck as he opens his mouth to speak. "We're not done here," he threatens. "You're lucky my fist isn't already shoved down your throat."

I cry, shaking my head. I look underneath his arm to find all of our guests watching us closely—too closely. Plastering on a fake smile, I try to get my shit together.

I will not fall apart here. I take a calming breath, pulling away from Beck. He doesn't let me go far. His hand stays firmly on my back as I make eye contact with those watching us closely. "I'm suddenly not feeling well," I tell the bystanders. If it were just me standing here, they might actually believe me from all the blood that has drained from my face, but with Carter's bleeding lip and Beck's angry scowl, there's no mistaking something else is happening here.

Emma shoulders through a cluster of people, her eyes pinned on me. She doesn't look at a single soul as she bounds toward me, a determined set to her shoulders. "Mar," she says softly. "Are you okay?"

I look at Beck, unable to wonder if Carter's words were lies or not. "I'll take her home," he announces to the crowd.

"Are you okay with that?" Emma asks cautiously. Winnie stops next to her, watching me with anxious eyes.

I nod up and down, leaning slightly into Beck. I need to know that Carter lied about everything. That us getting in a fake engagement wasn't part of some elaborate scheme of his to get revenge on his brother.

My stomach sinks all over again at the prospect of everything about us being even more fake than I'd already imagined.

We exchange goodbyes with those needed. Beck talking for me the entire time as I try to get my breathing even again.

When we slide into the car to go home, I melt into Beck's arms instantly. I have so many questions for him. But for a few minutes, I want to take comfort in his embrace. I want to pretend none of that just happened, and that Carter hadn't just thrown out accusations that could change everything.

52

Beck

I f it weren't for Margo's desperate plea to leave our party, I'd probably be sitting in jail for assault on my own brother. I don't know what happened between him and Margo, I'm afraid to ask for the risk of going mad with rage. Whatever happened has her messed up.

She doesn't utter a single word to me in the car. Ezra even tries to make a joke as he opens her door in front of our building and she doesn't even crack a smile at him.

I fidget the entire elevator ride up, wondering how to even approach what happened out on that terrace. If I hadn't been so fucking consumed with fear at the sight of Ruby at the party, I wouldn't have ever left Margo alone. None of that would've happened, whatever did transpire. I hate myself for leaving her alone—at our engagement party no less.

As we walk into the penthouse, I lose my grip on patience, needing to know what happened with Carter. "I need you to talk to me, baby," I plead. "I don't want to make you talk about it, but I spent the entire car ride picturing all the worst scenarios about what could've happened. I just need to know…"

She stops in the kitchen, her hands grabbing the lip of the island. For a few agonizing moments, she just stares at me. Her eyes are full of defeat. It kills me I don't know what put it there.

"Who was that woman you were talking to earlier tonight?"

"What?"

"The woman in the blue dress. The blonde. Did you know her?"

My jaw snaps open and closed as I try to piece together what she's getting at. My question had nothing to do with Ruby. I don't know why she answered with a question of her own, especially one like that.

"Beck," she pushes. "Did you know who that was?"

"Yes," I answer. "I told you. She was just an old friend."

"Do you know what she does for a living?"

Where the fuck is this going? A pit forms in my stomach when I come to the realization that Carter had shown up with Ruby. Maybe I should be worried about what he could've shared with Margo. Her line of questioning has me wondering if Carter knows more than I thought.

"No," I lie, taking a step closer into the kitchen. "I don't know off the top of my head."

"You're lying," she accuses.

"Why are you asking?" Nerves replace my anger as my fingers fumble with the knot at my neck. In one swift motion I loosen the tie all the way, pulling it off my neck and throwing it onto the island.

"You know exactly what she is. She's a reporter." Her eyes go wide in realization. "But you know that already."

I sigh in defeat. "Okay, fine. Yes, I know who she is. I don't understand what that has to do with anything. What happened between you and Carter?"

"Would you say you and her talk a lot?"

"Absolutely not."

"Did you pay her to run that article on you?"

My jaw drops. There it is. She knows.

Fuck me.

"No." My answer is half-hearted, not fooling either one of us.

Margo's eyes instantly well up in tears. She screws them together tightly, as if she's trying to hide that they misted up in the first place.

I close the distance between us in a few simple steps. When I try to pull her into me, she stops me. "No!" she yells. "You're lying to me, and I want to know why!"

"Margo," I whisper. I never thought it'd come to this. I'd planned on one day telling her the truth, but not like this. Not in this way.

Mascara streams down her cheeks as she stares up at me. I fucking hate myself for being the reason for the tears, for lying to her. It wasn't ever supposed to happen like this.

"You did," she confirms, biting her trembling lip. "You're the one who did it. You knew your board would see the article and give you an ultimatum. Why'd you do it, Beck?"

My silence only angers her. It's not that I don't want to answer her, it's that I don't know *how.* I don't even know how to begin to give her the answers she's trying to force out of me.

"There's so much you don't know," I answer remorsefully.

"I know everything," she seethes. "Carter told me it all. How you saw me first, wanted me first, and you hated him because he's the one who got me."

"That's a fucking lie," I spit. I want to grab her and make her listen to me, but her body only just stopped trembling from whatever the fuck happened with my brother. I don't want to do anything to startle her, even if my entire body needs to feel her skin against mine. To know she's still here with me.

She laughs sadly. "God, I can't even believe you when you say it is because you've been lying to me this entire time. You just couldn't handle him having something you wanted, could you, Beck? Did you ever *really* want me or was it that you knew it'd piss him off to see me with you?"

"Of course I fucking wanted you!" I shout angrily. "I wanted you from that moment you walked into that grimy fucking bar! You were wearing that terrible NYU sweatshirt, the one from that picture you had in your room. You were the least dressed up person there, and I couldn't stop fucking looking at you."

Her chest heaves. "And then what? Your brother spoke to me first and you couldn't get over the fact I was his?"

"You were never his," I hiss. "You were always meant to be mine."

"I'm not fucking property!" she screams, shouldering past me.

I follow her into the dining room, not letting this conversation end until I've come all the way clean.

"No. You're not property. It doesn't change the fact you were meant to be mine from the moment you walked into that bar. I sure as hell have been yours from that very moment."

She spins on her heel, jabbing her finger into my chest. "Then you should've done something about it."

I grab her wrist. "I did."

She shakes her head. "No, you *lied*. You *schemed*. I still don't even know what to believe. Carter says you hated him for dating me. That you told me your board was on your back because you wanted to rope me into your elaborate plan to get back at him."

I laugh, my fingers letting go of her arm. "And you're going to believe him?"

"So, you're telling me he was wrong about you giving that reporter the green light on running that article?"

"He wasn't wrong about that. But he's wrong about everything else."

"I should've never trusted you," she snaps, climbing the stairs to her old room. I'm her shadow up the stairs, not letting her out of my sight.

"You've got everything wrong. If you'd just fucking let me explain, I can tell you how wrong you are."

"I don't care anymore, Beck." She stomps into her room, half attempting to shut the door in my face. It doesn't work. I push it right open, ambling after her into her room.

She goes straight for her closet, pulling her suitcase from a dark corner.

"What the fuck do you think you're doing?"

She gives me a dirty look. "I'm packing. I'm *leaving*. And you're going to let me. I can't stay here knowing I was some sick sort of revenge on your brother."

My hands grab angrily at my hair. "It was never about Carter!" I roar. I'm completely deranged at this point, but I can't handle the thought of her leaving. I only just got her. There's no way I can let her go now. I wouldn't be able to survive it. Not after knowing what it was like to have her.

"Too bad I can't believe you because everything about us was a lie. God, I fell in love with you, and you were lying the entire time."

My throat clogs with emotion. "You love me?" I ask hoarsely.

"I *thought* I did," she answers quietly, walking past me and throwing the suitcase on her bed. "I thought I loved you more than I've ever loved someone else. Now I don't know what I feel. It's hard to love something when everything's a lie."

I desperately reach for her, needing to cling to her to know that we can salvage this. "It wasn't all a lie," I plead. "All the best parts of us were the truth. Everything between us was the truth, Margo." I press my palm to her racing heart. "In your heart, you know everything was real. The way we feel about each other could never be fake. Could never be a lie." I grab her wrist, holding her palm against my erratic heartbeat to try and prove my point.

She looks up at me sadly. I'll never forgive myself for hurting her. I won't get over it. I just need to know that we can come back from this. That she'll listen to my explanation and understand why I did what I did.

I take a deep breath, my fingers pushing into her chest even harder as I cling to her for dear life. "I'll tell you everything," I promise. "I just need you to let me."

Her only answer is a nod. I don't care that she's silent. It's enough for me.

Pulling in a shaky breath, I try to gather my thoughts, trying to think of the best way to explain the real reason how Margo and I came to be.

"Carter was right about one thing. Like I just told you, I noticed you before he ever did. No person had ever captured my attention like you had that night."

"You didn't do anything."

"You looked so young. So carefree. Like someone who was just starting college and having fun. I didn't have the nerve to speak to you while knowing our lives were vastly different."

"So then you just got angry because Carter got to me?"

"I was fucking furious when I learned of the two of you. I don't think I've ever been as upset as when he'd called me to let me know you'd slept together. That you were his girlfriend."

"Well congratulations, you got your revenge. You put a ring on my finger." She looks down at the ring sadly. She obliterates my aching heart when she slips the ring off her finger. Her eyes are filled with tears as she inspects the ring in her grasp. "You beat him. You won."

I shake my head at her, closing her fingers around the ring before she even gets the idea to try and give it back to me. Our grasped hands shake. I don't know if it's hers or mine that tremble. Maybe it's both of ours. "I don't give a damn about winning. It wasn't about that. It was *never* about that. When he brought you home to the Hamptons, when we finally spoke for the first time, I knew I'd do anything to have you. I'd never once cared what my brother had, yet in that moment I wanted everything he had. I wanted you. When I found you drawing me, when you almost kissed me on that beach, I realized I'd spent my whole life saying I'd never fall in love, only to fall in love in an instant with a woman who wasn't mine."

"You didn't," she breathes, her breath hitching.

"I did. I've been in love with you ever since. Fuck, Margo, I might've fallen in love with you from the moment you walked into that bar. I just didn't know what it was."

"I don't understand."

"I knew Carter was cheating on you that weekend. I wanted to tell you so bad, but I didn't want to hurt you. So I kept my mouth shut."

"Beck..."

"But I knew that weekend that eventually, you'd be mine. That you were never supposed to be his, and if I waited long enough, we'd happen."

"So, you realized you were my new boss and thought hey what the hell, I should tell her I need a fake fiancée?"

"No. I told you I bought the company to have an excuse to talk to you. I didn't lie about that."

Her mouth pops open. She watches me carefully, trying to fit the puzzle pieces together in her mind.

"I tried getting you the old-fashioned way. I contacted you for months and you never answered, so I came up with another way to get your attention. That started with Ruby. I knew if something ran on me being some kind of womanizer instead of attention being me and how I run my company, that it'd sound logical that my board threatened me."

"So even that was a lie?"

I nod. "The board saw it. They told me to be careful, but they never threatened me with investors or anything like that. They just told me to be careful of too much negative attention. I spun it to my advantage, which I know was wrong, but I was forced to do something dramatic to get you to even speak with me. If I came to you asking for help, I put my money on that I thought you wouldn't say no."

"So you manipulated me?"

"Yes," I answer sadly. "I guess you could say I did. At the time, I hadn't thought of it that way. I was so hellbent on getting you in my life that I didn't think of it as manipulation. Every feeling, every moment between us was real. It was for me and I'm pretty fucking convinced it was all real for you too. I didn't see the harm in the way we came together being a lie if it meant everything else was real."

"So the article, the board story, everything was all just some massive scheme made by you so you could corner me into being your fiancée? I can't even leave you right now. Not after all of New York attending our engagement party. You were trying to trap me, Beck."

"No. *Never.* I was just trying to have a shot with you. That's all this was ever supposed to be."

"It doesn't feel like that. It feels wrong and fucked up."

"I'll do whatever it takes for you to trust me. I love you, Margo. I love you so much that I would ruin everything I've ever created just to call you mine. I'm so fucking in love with you."

She sobs. Mascara smudges her face, ruining the makeup that'd been meticulously painted on her skin. I feel like I can't fucking breathe when she pulls her hand from mine. In one gentle motion, she pries my fingers open and sets my grandmother's ring in my palm.

"Please don't," I beg, my voice going hoarse. "Please don't do this."

She closes my fingers around the ring. "This isn't love, Beck. Love shouldn't feel like this. It shouldn't be based on a lie."

"Don't give up on me." My fingers tighten around the ring in my grasp. "Let me fix this, baby. *Please.*"

Her eyes are red from crying so hard. "I should've *never* agreed to be your fiancée. I should've never had anything to do with you after everything happened with Carter."

"Don't bring him into this."

She scoffs, pulling her headband from her hair and throwing it to the ground. "You know you're just like him. I knew not to trust one Sinclair brother, I just hadn't expected I couldn't trust the other."

Her words take me so off guard I take a few steps backward in shocked hurt.

"I want you to leave, Beck." It's like she's pouring salt in an already gaping wound. I can't do anything but grant her wish.

With my heart shredded in my chest, I look at her through bloodshot eyes. "I've only ever loved you, Margo. I couldn't help it. I've always loved you uncontrollably. Maybe a little too much, but everything I've done was always out of love."

53

Margo

It's not the same sleeping alone. I toss and turn all night, unable to turn off my mind with the questions soaring through it. The night wasn't supposed to end the way it did. We were supposed to come home happy. I wanted to finish what we started in the limo. To make do on the promise of me wearing nothing but the heels for him.

I roll over in bed to grab my phone off the nightstand. I look at all of the missed notifications. It seems like a lot more people than I expected saw how off I was after the encounter I had with Carter. A lot of people were reaching out to check in. The only people I respond to are Winnie and Emma in our group chat.

Winnie

> How are you feeling this morning, Margie?

Emma

> I'm feeling hungover. I thought fancy champagne wasn't supposed to make you feel like shit?

Winnie

> I didn't ask about you. ;)

Emma

> I was trying to make Margo not feel awkward about leaving. Thanks for blowing my cover, Winnie Boo Boo.

I laugh at the nickname for Winnie. She hates it when we call her that, but neither one of us can help ourselves. She makes it too easy. My heart twinges with disappointment that I didn't get to spend as much time with them last night as I'd wanted to. I'm a terrible friend for flying them out here and then ditching them.

Margo

> I'm fine! I just let Carter get to me more than he should have. What are you two up to?

Emma

> He's a dick. It seemed like Papa Sinclair laid into him though. They left with things looking very heated between them.

My eyebrows raise at that bit of information. I've always liked Mr. Sinclair. He was always kind to me. It seemed like his boys loved him, even if they didn't seem to love each other. I wonder what all he knows about Carter. If he knows how off he acted last night.

Emma

> I bet Beck reminded you why he was the better brother last night. ;)

Winnie

> We're currently eating room service breakfast. Well I'm eating. Emma is complaining that the smell of pancakes is going to make her throw up.

It's hard not to feel sad reading Emma's text. It's an innocent statement. We should've had the best time ever last night. Instead, I locked myself in my old room and refused to come out. I need some space from Beck, to think about everything I was told by each brother and decide who I believe. I need to figure out the truth, the problem is it's buried so deep between both of their lies that I don't know what the real truth even is.

Margo

> Would you want to grab lunch somewhere?

Winnie

> We'd love that!

Emma

> Obviously, bitch. What time?

Once we plan to get together in a few hours, I feel better. Part of me wants to tell my friends everything that's happened, to get their advice on it all. But I know I signed an NDA. I don't want to get in trouble. More so, I don't want them to think badly of Beck. I'm still protecting him because deep down I want to believe every word he told me last night. I want to know that getting me to agree to be his fake fiancée wasn't some sick scheme of his to get back at Carter. I much prefer the reason he gave for all of this. That he simply wanted me and he'd do anything to have me.

My heart wants to believe he loves me because I know without a shadow of a doubt I've fallen in love with him.

Letting out a deep breath, I get up out of bed. I'm tired, my limbs not wanting to move as I make my way toward the bathroom. It feels off to do a morning routine in here. It feels too quiet. I'm too used to listening to Beck take work calls as I get ready or hearing him listen to some boring podcast while I try to distract him in the shower.

It all feels off and I hate how attached I got to him. It all happened so quickly, despite me swearing I wouldn't let a man become my life again like I had with Carter.

With Beck it hadn't seemed bad because he was just as obsessed with spending time with me as I was him. It seemed healthy. It seemed perfect. In hindsight, maybe it was *too* perfect and maybe I should've known that all along.

My stomach growls, proving I can't stay holed up here for much longer. Luckily, because it's Sunday, I don't have to go into work with Beck. But we do live together. I'm going to have to face him if I want to eat.

I may have a stash of Twizzlers in one of my bags in my closet. Maybe I could live off that for sustenance.

Groaning, I know I need to get it together. I'm going to have to face him, even if my heart is broken from the betrayals of last night.

I yank open the door, thinking of how wrong of a turn last night went, when I come face to face with Beck.

His smell assaults my senses immediately, wrapping me up in a familiar advance. I never want to smell bergamot and jasmine again. Or maybe it's that I never want to stop smelling his signature scent again, becoming all too addicted to everything that is him.

"Good morning," he says gruffly, his eyes scanning my face.

Why does he have to look so good even when he looks so rough? I take in his simple pair of jeans and sweater. He might be dressed nicely, but his eyes are bloodshot and his hair is so disheveled it looks like he's been constantly running his fingers through it. I've never seen him look so worn out.

I look from him to the empty hallway. "What are you doing up here?"

He holds up a coffee cup from our favorite coffee shop in one hand and a paper bag in the other. "I brought you breakfast. And coffee."

He gives me an apologetic smile and I almost forget every piece of information Carter told me. It's easy in Beck's presence, with the remorse dripping from his body. If it wasn't for the ache still in my chest, it all may have already been forgotten.

Beck hands me the coffee. "I got you your favorite."

I press the straw to my lips, taking a long sip. It's exactly right. I hate how he's memorized it, despite the fact it's always been me who picked up our coffees. The fact he still remembers my order isn't lost on me.

"Thank you," I answer, trying not to let my words come out too harsh. I'm so angry at him for lying to me, for keeping so many secrets. But he's also become my best friend, my safe place, and I miss him. I miss talking to him, cuddling with him, doing the most mundane things with him, and I hate him for spinning lies to get us to this point in the first place.

"There's also a few different pastries in the bag. I got you all of your favorites. And if none of these sound good then I can have Ezra stop and grab you something else before taking me to the airport."

I pause opening the bag, looking up at him in confusion. "You're leaving?"

He scratches his chin, pinning me with his indigo stare. "Yeah. A last-minute thing came up. I have to fly to San Jose for three days. I didn't figure you'd want to make the trip."

"I'm your assistant. You pay me to go to these things with you." I turn to step back into the room, but he grabs me, turning me to face him.

He manages to still keep space between us as he looks down at me unsure. "I'm not talking to my assistant right now," he begins.

"I *am* your assistant," I correct, looking down to the spot he's touching me.

He waits until I look back up at him to speak. "Then you're fired. Because right now I'm talking to the woman I love, not the one who works for me."

My heart flip-flops dramatically in my chest. Why does it seem like he always says all the right things to make me melt into a puddle at his feet? It's like he knows exactly what to say to remind me that I love him. I just don't know if that's all part of his act or if it's genuine. My head is all sorts of fucked up after last night. I don't know who—or what—to believe. And it's left me reeling ever since.

"Margo," he pleads, gently running his fingertip over my cheek. "Please, just listen to me for a moment, okay?"

I nod, having to swallow back emotion. All of a sudden, I can feel tears pricking at my eyes and there's a lump in my throat. It's the tone of his voice. It matches mine—filled with sadness and remorse. It has me seconds away from telling him I believe him, or at least I don't care if it was fake to start with. As long as it's real now, that's all I need. I hold myself back from saying any of that because the truth of it is, I need to be confident it's real now before I promise him anything. And I'm just not there yet. It's why I couldn't continue to wear his grandmother's ring. It doesn't feel right to wear something with so much sentiment when things between us have gone so wrong.

"I'm going to go on this trip. *Alone*. I know you need space to think through everything I told you last night, and I want to give you that."

"This is your house, Beck," I interject. "I can go somewhere else for space. You don't have to leave because of me."

"I hope you think of this as *our* home, because that's what it is to me. Well truthfully, I think of *you* as my home. I meant every word I told you last night, Margo. If you think long and hard about it all, I think you'll know I didn't utter a single lie last night. But I need to go on this trip. I hope—I fucking pray—that you'll be waiting for me when I get back. And that you'll be ready to put that ring on your finger—where it belongs for the rest of our lives."

"I'm not going anywhere for now," I say softly. My voice sounds weak but I can't seem to care. Even if everything he told me was a lie to begin with, the look in his eyes right now isn't one I believe is fake. The hurt and longing aren't things someone could pretend. "I just have to wrap my head around everything you said. I just don't get—"

"Take the time you need, baby. I'm going to give you three days. But please, when I get back, be mine again. Be confident in how I feel about you—in what we've created." He wraps me in his arms, pulling me into his chest. I breathe in his smell, while it seems like he does the same with his face pressed to my hair. Surely his words are true. This feels too right for it all to be based off some personal vendetta he has against his brother. "I know I've lied to you, and I'll never forgive myself for it. But it still brought us together. I won't forgive myself for it, but I can't regret it either. I'll never regret anything that brought you to me."

Tears stream down my cheeks all over again. I wrap my arms around him, awkwardly trying to bring him closer while still holding my coffee and food. "It's just a lot to think about. Everything about us is a lie."

He jerks his body away from mine, bringing our foreheads close together. "*Nothing* about us is a lie," he demands, a commanding tone to his voice. He presses his palm to my heart. "You know deep in here that nothing we feel is a lie." He then taps my temple. "We just have to get this to realize that, too."

I look down at the ground sadly. If I look into his eyes any longer, I'll beg him to stay. As much as I want that to happen, he's right. We need a little bit of space. I don't want to rush into anything. I need to feel confident in Beck's version of the story instead of Carter's before anything else happens.

"Okay," I say into his chest. I let my arms fall to my sides as I break the contact, needing to put space between us before I cling to him and never let go.

Beck and I stand in the hallway staring at one another, the two of us completely silent. It's awkward. I don't know what else to say to him. I can't get Carter's words out of my head.

Beck's eyes drift down the hallway. He looks at it with regret, taking a step away from me he takes a deep breath. "I'm so fucking sorry, Margo. I need you to at least believe me on that."

I don't even try to hide the tears that wet my cheeks from him. My chest shakes as I take a breath in, trying to keep the last bit of myself together. "I know," I answer shakily. "I do believe you."

He looks at me sadly. "Promise?"

I nod, wiping the tears from my cheeks. "I promise, Beck. We'll talk when you get back."

His mouth opens and closes. If he was about to say something, it never passes his lips. With a loud exhale, he turns and retreats down the hallway. I watch him go, already missing him like crazy.

54

Margo

I t turns out I'm terrible at being alone. I've never really been alone since I started college. I was always either with my friends or Carter. When I moved to LA, I was always with Winnie and Emma. If one wasn't home, the other was. It wasn't often that any of us were alone.

And then I moved out here with Beck. It seemed like we spent every second together. I loved it. It felt right.

Maybe that's why I find myself walking down a busy New York street in the middle of the day on a Monday. Typically I'd be at work, but with Beck gone, there isn't much for me to do. I'd gotten ready this morning as if I was going to go to work. Ezra had told me when I came downstairs that Beck had already given me the week off.

I didn't need the week, but I couldn't argue. I already lost the argument the day before when I attempted to hail a cab to meet Winnie and Emma for lunch and Ezra popped out all angry at me. I really did figure he'd be traveling with Beck, but he said Beck wouldn't have it. After Ezra had dropped Beck off at the airport, he was told to report back to our building to see what I needed.

After Ezra told me I wasn't going into the office today, I told him I wanted to explore the city. I had him drop me off somewhere random so he wouldn't catch on to what I'd been planning.

So that's what I've been doing for an hour when I come to a stop in front of a building I've never had the nerve to step foot in.

Camden Hunter's art gallery. I can't help but stare in awe of the building. The iridescent glass catches the eye immediately. It's like the building itself is a piece of art. My legs shake as I stare at the building, wondering if I'm really about to do this.

I thought of the idea last night in my time alone. Beck had told me he'd get an interview with his friend, and I know he'd stay true to his word. But I'm being stubborn. I don't want his help. If Camden Hunter even looks at my drawings, I'll feel like I've made it. My dreams would be made if they made it into his gallery, but I won't hold my breath.

Either way, I want to do it on my terms. Not because Beck's calling in a favor. As much as I'd like to believe Camden wouldn't do his best friend a solid by putting my art in his gallery, I can't guarantee anything.

So, I'm taking matters into my own hands. It's why I've pulled on a large knit beanie, one that hides half my face and have wrapped a giant scarf around my neck. I'm hoping I'm not too recognizable. I hadn't had the chance to meet Camden at our engagement party. He'd been running late, and by the time he showed up, I was too busy with the Carter drama. But I wouldn't be shocked if he still recognized me. Right now, I hope to be unrecognizable.

A shoulder bumps into mine. I look over to apologize but lose all normal train of thought when I lock eyes with the man I came to see.

Camden Hunter is as beautiful as the art he displays. He looks like he walked right off the pages of a catalog. With two artist parents, it's like they couldn't produce anything that wasn't anything less than a work of art—their son included.

"What are we looking at?" he asks, his voice harsh despite the words being cordial. The hard set of his jaw plays into the ruthless picture Beck had painted of his friend. Camden comes off as rough and isolated from the world. Like engaging in conversation is a chore. I guess that's what I should expect from someone who enjoys spending time confined between masterpieces rather than in groups of people.

"The building," I answer honestly. My heart picks up in my chest from nerves. I thought I had time to think about how I wanted to pitch my art to him, but now I have no time to think it over.

Camden quirks his head, hitching his messenger bag up onto his shoulder. "What about the building?"

I have to look away from him so I don't pass out from my nerves. This is *the* Camden Hunter. Everybody in the art world knows his name, his parents' names. He's a celebrity in this world, and here he is casually standing next to me talking about his building.

"I was thinking that it looks like a piece of art itself."

He's silent next to me. So quiet that if I didn't physically feel his presence next to me, I'd be worried that he ditched me.

"I love that part of it. That even though it houses art inside of it, that it wants to steal the show itself with the sleek architecture," I continue.

"What do you notice about the architecture?"

"It's a mix of different styles. It's modern with the glass, but still very classic and traditional with the lines of the building."

I smile bashfully as he remains quiet next to me. "I'm probably not making any sense. I just meant I love the fact that it's like you can't put the building in one category. It stands out next to everything else here in Manhattan. I love it."

When I get the nerve to look over at Camden, I find him watching me with a quirked eyebrow. "You're the first person to ever *really* get my vision for it." He turns to look at the building in front of him. The way he stares at it so proudly warms my heart. One day I hope to look at my own art in a gallery the same way he looks at the gallery that houses all the art.

"Well, the first person to get it without me having to explain it to them first," he adds.

I turn to face him, taking a deep breath to calm my nerves. "I'm honored. But I think it's cool that people could also get other vibes from it. That's the whole idea of art, right? It's subjective. Art is in the eye of the beholder and all..."

His eyes flick to the bag on my arm. Or more specifically, the rolls of my own artwork that peek out of it. "Let me guess, you're an artist."

I shrug. At least it seems like he hasn't caught on that I'm the fiancée to his best friend. Or if he had caught on, he hasn't let it slip. "It's the beanie that gives it away, isn't it?"

He lets out the smallest of laughs. It's quiet but confident. "*Definitely* the beanie."

"Does your art suck?"

I'm taken aback by the bluntness of his words. I fumble with my words for a moment before I get out something coherent. "I'd like to think it doesn't."

He narrows his eyes at me. "What is it about you?"

"I uh..."

He talks over me, clearly not actually wanting an answer to his question. "Never do I stop and talk to anyone. Small talk gives me hives. But something about the way you looked at the building had me stopping."

His head tilts to the side as he looks over my shoulder to the transport tube I have with one of my pieces in it. "Do you have your work with you?"

"Yes," I rush out, maybe a little too eagerly.

Camden takes a step toward the building. "I've got a private client meeting in an hour. You can show me your work. If it sucks, I'll tell you, so if you aren't up for criticism, turn around now."

All I do is nod.

And just like that, I have my in. I almost blow it because it takes me a few long, drawn out seconds to come up with a response.

Is this really happening?

Finally, I nod my head enthusiastically, almost tripping over my feet in the process. "I'd love that," I say hurriedly.

"Don't ever tell anyone about this," he barks, heading towards the building. "The last thing I want is for people to show up and bother me."

He doesn't give me a chance to respond. His long legs have him already a good amount ahead of me. I scurry after him, not wanting to miss my chance.

Camden Hunter is about to look at my work.

Holy. Shit. Balls.

55

Beck

I step out of the rental car, pressing my phone to my ear as I look up at the building in front of me. "How's she doing?"

Ezra sighs on the other line. "Not great, Mr. Sinclair. She's out for a walk right now, but she isn't herself."

"She's walking alone?"

"You'd think I'd let her roam alone?" he asks, his tone offended. "No, I've followed her. She just doesn't know it."

I let out a hum of approval. "Thanks, Ezra. I appreciate it."

"Want to talk about what happened?"

I scoff, shielding my eyes from the California sun. "Absolutely not."

"Understood," he clips. "Is there a reason Miss Moretti is talking to your friend Camden?"

I smile, despite how hollow I feel inside. *That's my girl.* It doesn't shock me that she'd use this time away from me to follow her dreams. There's nothing I want more for her than that. I just hope her dreams still lead back to me. "Because she's stubborn as hell," I answer truthfully.

Even if Camden gave her a chance to speak with him as a

favor to me, that'd be as far as a favor would go from him. Her work would have to do the talking to keep him interested. It appears she got rid of the middle man—me—and found a way to get Camden's attention herself.

"Got it. I'll make sure she makes it back to your place safely, Mr. Sinclair."

"Thank you, Ezra. I'll check back in later."

I end the call and slide the phone into the inner pocket of my suit. My eyes focus on the brick building in front of me. It doesn't take long for my footsteps to eat the distance from my parking spot to the entrance.

A brunette sits at a large desk. She smiles appreciatively at me. "Welcome to Booth and Associates. How can I help you?"

I give her my most charming smile. "I'm actually here for a meeting. I'm running a few minutes behind so you wouldn't mind if I rushed back there, would you?"

She looks uneasy at first, her eyes glancing at her computer monitor. "If I could just know who you're seeing, I could call them and let them know you've arrived..."

"I'd really appreciate it if you just let me go back."

She nods, flipping her hair over her shoulder. "Okay," she responds anxiously. "As long as they're already aware you were coming."

I don't wait for her to change her mind. People watch me carefully as I look for a familiar face. I hadn't lied when I said had business here in San Jose. I do have a meeting for Sintech. It just isn't until this afternoon.

More importantly—it's time I pay my little brother a visit.

I haven't forgotten the reason shit hit the fan the way it did. He's got some sins it's time for him to atone for.

I hear him before I see him. He laughs with a group of men.

His laugh is too fake—like he's trying too hard. Trying too hard is really the story of his life.

He stops laughing the moment his eyes land on me. I give him a sinister smile.

This will be fun.

"Hey, brother," I say smoothly, coming to a stop in front of his group. I tuck my hands into my pockets, giving him a nonchalant grin. "Miss me?"

Carter gives the men surrounding him a cautious look. *Good.* It's best he's anxious about how unhinged I can become. One simple slip of a comment from my mouth and I could ruin the reputation he's created.

"Beckham," he says through a tight-lipped smile. "What brings you to California?"

I give the men a knowing smile. "Business." As if any of them have any fucking clue what it takes to run a business. This office is filled with men with rich daddies whose last name got them their positions. It certainly wasn't their work ethic.

"Let's have a chat," I tell Carter, nodding my head in the direction of a small office with his name on the door. "We've got *lots* to catch up on."

His fingers clench at his sides. If he tries to give me some kind of smart-ass response to impress his friends, I'll make him regret it.

He chooses wisely. He looks to his friends, "We'll finish this later."

I follow behind as he leads me into his office. The moment the door closes behind me, I shove him into the wall, grasping at the collar of his dress shirt.

"It's about fucking time we talk, Carter," I bite, pushing into his neck.

He lets out a surprised grunt, his beady eyes flashing with fear. "What the fuck," he growls, attempting to shove me off.

His attempts are pathetic. He's got no muscle on me. I could keep him pressed against the wall for as long as I desired.

"Did you think you wouldn't have to pay for all the trouble you've caused?" I growl, looking down my nose at him.

His mouth opens and closes like a fucking fish. How the hell are we related?

I pull my fist back, my knuckles connecting with his jaw with a loud *smack*.

He yelps like a child. As quick as it happened, I let go and take a few steps back, stretching my fingers at my side. "That's for scaring, Margo," I seethe. "And touching what's *mine*."

I look at his desk. "Sit."

Carter looks at me manically. "You just assaulted me," he screeches.

I roll my eyes, unbuttoning my jacket and taking a seat in *his* office chair. He glares at me when he takes a seat in the small chair on the other side of his desk.

"That punch was nothing compared to what I want to do to you."

He rubs his jaw dramatically. "Say what you came to say."

I smile. "You know me so well."

He watches me cautiously. I don't blame him. I've had time for my anger to marinate. It would've fared far better for him if I'd just taken my anger out on him at the engagement party. This is *far* worse. I've had time to plan what I'll do to keep my brother far a-fucking-way from the woman I love. Plus, he's got to pay for the rest of his actions as well.

"On with it," he pushes, sitting back in his chair.

My eyes roam over his tiny office. It's unkept and quite frankly gross. There's a takeout box that has to be days old as well as gum wrappers. He's a grown-ass man. He should take care of his space more. What if a client had come to see him?

"I'm going to cut right to the chase," I begin. "I don't want to spend any more time here than I have to."

His only response is a grunt.

"For starters, if you ever fucking *think* about touching my future wife again, that punch will be nothing compared to what I'll do to you."

"She deserved to know your lies," he spits.

My fingers steeple underneath my chin. "You're right. But that doesn't concern you. Going forward, nothing about Margo should concern you *ever* again."

"That seems like that's up to her, not you."

"One thing I can guarantee is the fact Margo never wants to see you again."

"And how will you stop me if I decide I'm not done with her?"

This makes me smile. Reaching into my pocket, I pull out my phone and scroll until I find what I need. I lay my phone out on the desk between us, directing his attention to it. "Because if you even think about speaking with her again, I'll have no choice but to bring all the debt you've developed to light."

Carter's eyes go wide with fear. He snatches the phone from the desk, scrolling through all the proof I have of his immense gambling debts. "How did you find out?" he says accusingly.

"Threaten what's mine and I'll discover every dirty secret you have. Don't ever forget that."

He continues to scroll through what I have on him. I had to admit, when I realized just how in debt he was, I was shocked myself. If there was anything my father hated, it was men who gambled their money away. As teenagers, we'd get lectures from Dad to never risk losing money. *"Why gamble when you could invest wisely?"* he'd say. The warnings stuck with me, but apparently not with Carter.

I hadn't expected for Carter to develop a nasty little habit of doing it. I especially didn't expect him to gamble away almost every dollar to his name—including the generous inheritance from our father. Mine still sits in the account, completely untouched. Carter's is almost depleted, and he's had his far less time than I've had mine.

Reaching across the desk, I pluck the phone from his hands and tuck it back into my pocket. "I don't want to see your fucking face again unless it's at a family function. And even then, I'm allowing your pathetic presence for our parents and our parents *only*. Don't talk to me. Especially don't talk to Margo. Or I'll have to let Dad know how much of a disappointment his younger son is. It'd be tragic really, considering how much of a let-down you already are to him."

Any nasty remark he wants to say to me is left unsaid. The fury still rages in his eyes. At least he's not dumb enough to say any of the thoughts running through his head.

I clap my hands together, standing up and hovering over him. "We're done here. I've said what I have to say."

I'm standing in front of the door when Carter finally speaks up. "Wait," he calls, turning to face me. "If I do as you say. If I disappear—you won't tell him?"

I give a curt nod. "I'm being gracious to you, brother. You deserve much worse than what I've done. It's best you remember that."

Pulling the door open, I escort myself out of his office.

Now that that's handled, I can only hope that it's only Carter who's out of Margo's life. I don't know if I'll be able to handle it if I'm also cut out of her life as well.

56

Margo

'm reeling from excitement when I walk back into the penthouse. I was seconds away from spilling the good news to Ezra in the car when I thought better of it.

No matter how upset or disappointed I was with Beck, he was still the first person I wanted to call when Camden Hunter agreed to display one of my pieces.

My work is going into Camden's gallery. I'm still too stunned to believe it. There's a red mark on my arm from where I pinched myself the entire car ride home to make sure I wasn't in some elaborate dream.

It's a miracle he even got to see my work after I fumbled for so long as I tried to get the paper to lay flat. He eventually put me out of my misery and put paperweights on the corners so he could see the piece.

When he asked for details on the piece, I stuttered and jumbled my words, but my point got across.

He'd shockingly been really impressed with the concept.

I shown him one I created almost a year ago when I'd been visiting New York with Emma and Winnie. We'd been walking and gossiping about one of the girls who lived in our dorm who was about to be on some reality TV show. I'd been listening to Emma rattle on about how she may give a reality dating show a go when I noticed this man reading a newspaper on a bench.

He was elderly, his hands wrinkly and almost purple. He worn a newspaper hat and a coat with coattails. He even had a pipe slid in his mouth. Next to him sat a fresh bouquet of flowers neatly wrapped in tan butcher paper. I wondered why he was alone and I couldn't stop thinking about him. I obsessed over him so much that I eventually returned to the bench, wondering if I'd find him there again. I wanted to ask him everything about his life, to figure out why he was sitting there alone with the flowers.

When I returned, I was disappointed he wasn't there. I felt sad and defeated. I wanted to know everything about him. Why was he always alone? Who were the flowers for? I became obsessed with creating a new life for him in my head. One where he didn't sit alone. One where he had a partner sitting next to him holding the flowers.

In my rush of sadness, I almost missed the plaque that was on the back of the bench. I leaned in and read the name and dedication over and over. It was for someone who had passed away—a memory bench. I read everything on the internet there was to know about the woman whose name was forever etched in stone.

Come to find out, the man sitting there was her husband. They'd been married fifteen years before the woman passed away in a car accident. He later found out she was pregnant with their first child together after they'd tried for countless years to have a child. He'd been a billionaire, heir to one of the top communication companies in the world and had sold some of his share in the company to his brother after the accident. He still partially owned it, but he didn't want the control he had before. The man never remarried. Apparently, every Saturday he'd sit on the bench and buy her flowers, claiming Saturday was always her favorite day of the week, and she wouldn't go a week without getting fresh flowers throughout their house.

I mourned the loss of his wife with him, even though we were complete strangers.

I hadn't talked to Emma or Winnie for a week when I'd drawn the piece. On one side, there's the man on the bench with his flowers sketched in pencil. The other side I completed by painting it, bringing it to life with the colors.

It was the life I imagined for this man—for his wife and their unborn child—if only reality hadn't been so harsh.

The bench had been continued from the black and white sketch to the painted portion. In black and white he read the newspaper alone, but in color, his wife sat next to him, holding a bouquet of flowers. They both looked down at their grandchildren playing at their feet.

Camden said he loved it. He asked so many questions about the man, about the concept of me reimagining a life for the man who was a stranger to me. It sparked a conversation about most of my work. How I take someone I see, someone who's a complete stranger, and imagine what their life is outside of that moment in time that I saw them.

He said he wants to eventually discuss the opportunity to do an entire show based around my concept.

I still can't believe it.

I'm so lost in the excitement for the day that I almost call out for Beck to tell him the good news. I stop myself, realizing that I'm alone in the large space. It seems eerily quiet. My feet start walking toward the room Beck and I shared on their own accord.

I just want to spend a few minutes there. To see if it still smells like him despite the fact the house cleaners had already come by for the day and cleaned.

I'm about to step into the room when I notice a door a few feet away from the bedroom left slightly ajar. I've never gone into the room. Beck said it was an office he never used, so it never interested me. But now with him gone, I'm curious what's in the space and why he doesn't use it often. Whatever it is, the house cleaners must've been cleaning in there and forgot to close the door all the way.

I can't help myself. My curiosity gets the best of me as my fingers push against the wooden door, pushing it open. I take a cautious step inside.

I'm taken aback by what I see.

This room isn't an office. At least not in the stereotypical way. It's a studio.

An *art* studio.

"Oh my god," I whisper in awe, taking steps deeper into the room. My eyes don't know what to land on first. I marvel at the scene in front of me, wondering how long it's been the dream studio for an artist. And *why* Beck has a state-of-the-art studio when he's not artistic in the slightest.

The lighting in here is enough to take one's breath away. The open windows that take up half the far wall are a dream. A drafter's table sits right in front of it, the perfect location to get daylight and the sun on your face while also getting to stay inside.

"What is all this?" I mutter, looking around to take in the beauty of the space. I had no idea this was in here, and I don't know how long it's been this way. Has Beck always had an art studio hidden away? Why did he never mention it?

There's a shelf that's taller than me filled with art supplies. Some of my favorite brands sit on the shelf, even equipped with brands I've never used because they were too expensive, but ones I dreamed of creating art with one day.

It's a dream. And I have no idea why he has it here, or why he's never mentioned it to me.

I'm about to break and call him when something catches my eye.

On one of the walls, I spot a neatly framed picture. It's the only thing hanging on the wall, looking almost out of place with how small it is compared to the empty space around it.

I hurry to take a closer look, gasping when I come face to face with what is hung on the wall.

It's a picture of Beck. *The* picture of Beck. The one I'd drawn on the beach two summers ago.

I'd been distraught when I couldn't find it the morning we left the Hamptons, but I couldn't really tell Carter. I didn't know how I'd explain to him that I couldn't find a portrait I'd drawn of his brother, so I had to forget about it.

But I never *really* forgot.

All this time, Beck had it. Not only had he stolen it, he'd hung it up in his house.

As I look from the picture to the room, pieces start falling together. I realize that Beck may have lied to me from the very beginning, but deep down, I know I believe every word he told me the night of our engagement party.

He wouldn't have done all of this if he was trying to get back at Carter.

I know deep in my soul that Beck loves me. It's a realization that settles through my entire body, my heart, my entire being. I regret ever doubting him or doubting us. Our love is too beautiful to have ever been what Carter accused it of being. I should've trusted Beck. He lied to me, and I can be angry at him for that, but he still never faltered in showing the lengths he'd take for love. For *me*.

I stare at the picture I'd drawn of him, at my own drawing come to life staring back at me. I look at it with fresh eyes. Beck stares back at me. My mind catapults back to that night, as I replay his recounts of how he felt that night.

It all makes sense.

I'm brought back to his heated gaze. His lingering touch. He'd given me signals that night, I just hadn't looked into them deeply.

Beck found a very unconventional way of bringing us together, but every lie and scheme he made led to us falling in love. My eyes move from the picture hanging on the wall back to the desk in the corner. Taking a step closer, I run my fingers over a familiar coffee cup that holds some sketching utensils.

I smile, tracing over the looping font of the words *Greetings From The Hamptons*. Tucked into a drawer at my apartment, I still have the sketch of this very mug. I can't believe Beck has kept these things all this time.

I can't believe he's loved me all this time.

He's loved me far longer than I've loved him, but it doesn't change the fact that now, my heart is forever his. I can't imagine it ever belonging to anyone else. I don't want it to. For the rest of my life, I want him and only him. I don't care how we started, all I care about is how we end. Or how we *never* end.

Now I just have to wait until he's back to tell him.

And I know exactly how I want to do it.

He's gone to great, elaborate lengths to have me. Now, it's my turn.

57

Beck

'Ve been in boardrooms with some of the most intimidating people in the world, and I've never felt the kind of pressure I do right now. Stepping into the penthouse, knowing Margo is somewhere in here ready to either crush my heart or help heal it, has me riddled with anxiety.

I'm ready to lay it all out on the line for her, but I can admit to myself that I'm terrified none of it will be enough. What if she can't get past the lies I told her to get her here? I thought I was telling small white lies that wouldn't make a difference, but white lie after white lie has piled up. What if that isn't something she'll get past?

"Margo?" I yell into the silent space. There's no sign of her anywhere. The place has been immaculately kept. I can't help the fear that bubbles in my chest that wonders if she's left. Ezra had told me she'd been here in my absence, but what if she snuck past him to get away?

My throat feels itchy as I take the stairs to her room two at a time. I wasn't supposed to be back until tomorrow, but I couldn't waste another second. When she texted me that we needed to talk as soon as I got back, there was no way I could stay in San Jose another second longer.

Plus, I had company business to attend there—*and* personal business. Both were done. I made the deal, and I made sure that Carter won't ever be bothering Margo or me ever again.

Now I just have to make sure Margo wants to even stay with me, or if she wants to say fuck you to me and our entire family and leave for good.

I'm worried that's exactly what she's done when I find her room empty. I race into her closet, some tension leaving my body when I find her belongings all still tucked neatly inside.

Searching the rest of the upstairs, I retreat back downstairs. I hadn't checked the bedroom we shared because I figured she wasn't sleeping there. But maybe in my absence she decided she liked it better.

If that's the case and she does end up leaving me, I hope the sheets still smell like her. That I can pretend that her warm body is nestled into mine as I mourn what she and I could've been if I hadn't told her lies.

I'm about to walk into the bedroom when I hear music wafting out from my former office. I stop, wondering if that's where she's been hiding. My heart picks up pace at the thought. Because if Margo is in there, it means she's found the last secret I'd been keeping from her.

It wasn't always supposed to stay a secret. I'd intended it to be a surprise one day, but not until I knew she was mine. Not for fake, but for real.

If I've been taught anything the last few days, it's that even the most carefully laid plans can backfire. I hesitantly open the door, my suspicions confirmed when my eyes land on Margo working intently on something at a desk in front of the windows.

Even as I step into the room and close the door behind me, she doesn't look up. The music is too loud. She's too entranced with whatever she's working on to notice me. I'd give anything to close the distance between our bodies and bring her into my arms. I want to know what she's working on, what's got her so inspired that she hasn't answered any of my phone calls.

I use her being distracted to my advantage. I lean against one of the pillars, watching her in awe as she works hard at the task in front of her. She shades and erases at the project in front of her. The canvas she works on is massive, far larger than the sketchbook I normally see her work in.

It must be over ten minutes by the time she looks up, the few songs that have skipped by telling me I've been watching her for a while. She jumps, almost falling out of her seat when she notices me.

She picks up the speaker system's remote, turning off the music in the room. In the silence, her whispered, "Beck," comes out loud and clear.

I'm disarmed by how beautiful she looks. Margo wears one of my dress shirts, the fabric falling to her mid-thigh. She's got her hair piled on top of her head in a messy bun, tendrils of hair spilling out of it. She's tied a scarf around the top of her head, attempting to keep the flyaways at bay. It doesn't quite work the way she's expected. Her hair still looks a mess, but she's never looked more beautiful.

"I thought you got home tomorrow." The pencil she was holding drops onto the table. When I take a few steps closer to her, she stands up, blocking my view from whatever she's been working on.

My heart hammers in my chest, threatening to beat right out of me from nerves. I'm hopeful. Maybe too much at the sight of seeing her still here. Seeing her wear my clothes, I can't help but let myself hope this is her actually staying. Maybe this is her forgiving me.

There's nothing I want more in the world than her forgiveness—than to be deserving of her love.

But I want this so bad that if her wants don't align with mine, she will crush me. I've been desperate for her for over a year. Because of that intense need for her, I always held onto the hope of us ending up together one day. That hope will be lost if she leaves me today.

I don't know how I'd keep going after that. It's not a thought I even want to entertain.

"I got your text," I begin, "and made arrangements to fly back immediately after. I couldn't wait to hear what you had to say. The anticipation of wondering if you're going to leave me...if I can't fix this, it's been eating me up inside."

She doesn't relieve me from my stress. If anything, she makes it worse by hesitantly looking around my old office, the one I had converted into a studio in hopes that she'd really become mine forever.

"I don't want to just assume things, Beck, but did you do this for me?"

"Of course," I answer immediately.

She moves a piece of hair from her face. She doesn't give me any indication of where this is going to go, making me even more anxious for what's to come. "When?"

"After Colorado. After it occurred to me that you may actually one day feel for me what I feel for you." I think back to the plane ride home where the idea first popped into my head. I'd been determined to make this place feel more like a home to her. I knew she was deserving of a space where she could create art. She's so fucking talented, I just wanted to give her somewhere deserving of her creative outlet. Her tiny little desk in her LA apartment was terrible. I wanted to do better for her. "I came home and put this into place, most of the work being done while we were at the office. I just wanted you to have a space to call your own here. One where you can work on your art. Did I do okay?"

Her eyes gloss over as she watches me carefully. I'm fighting the urge to close the distance and crash my lips against hers. She's so fucking perfect that she takes my breath away. I swallow, trying to suck in air as I wait with bated breath for her answer.

She looks away from me, her narrow shoulders rising and falling with a deep inhale and exhale. "It's absolutely perfect. I can't believe you did all this." Her eyes scan over the room, landing on one of my most prized possessions.

The sketch she'd drawn of me from the night that kept me up many nights as I recalled every moment. For the longest time, I kept the picture in the drawer of my desk, pulling it out when I was alone to look at how she'd seen me through her eyes.

I obsessed over the drawing. I traced over every single one of her pencil strokes, wondering if she noticed the way I looked at her that night. As my eyes memorized every line and shading she'd made night after lonely night, I wondered what she was feeling while sketching it.

Surely she felt what I felt. I felt so strongly for her so quickly, that I couldn't imagine her not feeling anything.

It'd been devastating when she left me alone on that beach. I had to steal the picture as proof it happened. To remind myself that while she straddled me, her bare knees in the sand on either side of me, we had a moment. It was more than a moment—it was insight into everything we could be. Everything we *should* be.

Hopefully today is the start of that, and not the ending.

She walks over to the picture, stopping in front of it. The tender way she stares at it only fuels the hope brewing in my chest. If she was going to leave me instead of loving me, I don't see why she'd gaze at the thing that first brought us together with so much adoration. "You had it all this time."

"I snuck into your room and took it the morning I left. I couldn't leave without it. I needed something to remember the moment on the beach, in case it was the only moment you and I would ever share."

"Beck..."

"I've stared at that picture for countless hours. Wondering how you saw me that night, obsessing over all the things I could've done differently. If you'd let me kiss you, would you have climbed back in Carter's bed? If I'd told you that he didn't deserve you, that he wasn't faithful, would you have believed me? There are so many things that have gone through my head while staring at the talent of your pencil strokes on that paper. But one thought was always the most present. The desire to watch you draw for the rest of our lives. It was so intense, that the moment I thought maybe the tables were turning after that night at that stupid inn, I knew I had to create a space for you to do it."

Margo looks away from the picture. There's still hurt in her eyes when they focus on me. I hate myself for being the reason behind that hurt, for not coming clean to her sooner. I'll spend every dollar to my name, use every second of the rest of my life to try and win her back if that's what it takes.

Her lips tremble as she tries to fight back tears. My fingers twitch in my pockets as I do everything in my power to try and comfort her.

The problem here is the person she needs comfort from is *me*.

"What happens if I can't forgive you?" she whispers, her attention returning to the drawing.

Her question feels like a stab to the heart. A slow stab with a twist of a knife to really secure the hurt. I don't even want to go down that road. It's something I've tried not to think about since the moment she learned of the things I'd done to make her mine.

I come to a stop next to her, the both of us staring at the picture in front of us. "Then I will never step foot in this room again. Fuck, if you leave me Margo, I think I'd have to sell this place and find a new city to live in. I can't look at New York without thinking of you. My heart can't live here if it's not living here with you."

"You were here first," she states.

I shake my head in denial. "It doesn't matter. It's *you* who loves this city. I just love you. I can't stay here if you're not here. It'd never be the same. I'd never be the same."

She turns to face me. When her hand reaches to hold mine, my heart lets out the smallest glimmer of hope.

"Do you want to see what I've been working on?"

"Yes. Forever."

Margo pulls me toward the desk in the corner of the room. Abruptly, she spins to face me, placing her small hands against my chest. "Wait."

"What?"

"Close your eyes."

I look at her confused, trying to keep a reign on the mix of feelings coursing through my veins. I'm so fucking nervous—but I'm also hopeful. *Maybe* I haven't lost her yet. Maybe I'll find a way to keep my girl and the city she loves forever. I push a strand of hair from her face, relishing in how it feels to touch her again, even if it's only the smallest caress. "Why do I have to close my eyes?"

Her bottom juts out slightly. "Please. Just do it. I need to do something first. I don't want you to see."

I sigh, doing what she's asked. My eyes seal shut even though all I want to do is watch her every move. I'd open them if I wasn't terrified of her changing her mind if she caught me peeking. When I hear her small footsteps get further from me, I almost risk peeking, just to see what she's doing.

"Don't look until I tell you!" she yells from farther away, almost like she was reading my mind.

I groan. "I don't see the point in this."

"Just trust me, okay?"

I'll always trust her. Blindly and without any reason. I just need to get us to a point where she'll trust *me*.

There's a loud rustling sound, and a few other noises I can't pinpoint until I feel her stop in front of me. Her hands find mine. Her cold fingers squeeze mine as she speaks. "Okay, open your eyes."

I open them right away, taking a relieved breath when I find her smiling at me. Surely if she's about to obliterate my heart, she wouldn't be smiling at me. That'd be a little cruel. *Right*?

"I've been working on this piece from the moment I found this room." Her cheeks are slightly pinker than they were before she made me close my eyes. The skin around the corners of her eyes slightly crinkles as she stares up at me with excitement—and maybe even some nerves. "I've been making it for *you*."

When her teeth dig into her lip anxiously, I wonder if I'd ever survive a life without her. If this goes south, if she ends up telling me she can't love me anymore, I don't think even leaving this city she loves will be enough to cure my broken heart.

"For me?" I ask hoarsely.

Margo reaches up to cup my cheek. I lean into it immediately, reveling in having her touch me. My heart constricts at the tender look in her eyes. "Yes," she says. "For *you*."

She tugs on my hands, walking backward toward the desk. She's lowered it so it now sits flat. A large canvas, one larger than the tabletop sits on top of it. I can't see what she's worked on at first, only seeing white canvas hanging off the side.

My steps come to a halt when what she's drawn comes into view. It's the most beautiful piece of work I've ever seen. My hand comes to my chest, my breath taken away from the sheer talent of the piece of art in front of me.

Her answer to if she'll ever forgive me—if she loves me—is written all over it.

One side of the picture is a perfectly sketched out photo of her and I back in LA in that terrible, dingy conference room. It's almost come to perfect life, me sitting on the edge of the table as I spoke to her. I even hold the ugly as fuck balls pen in my hand. Her attention to detail is stunning. I knew she was talented, but this is unfuckingreal.

As breathtaking as that side of the photo is, it's what's on the other side that has pulled the air from my lungs. In the picture Margo has drawn herself in a white dress—a wedding dress. It looks like I'm pulling her from a chair onto the dance floor. There's a wedding band on my hand that's outstretched toward her. The picture is drawn in such detail, the colors distinct, that it seems real. I could imagine the exact scenario happening.

It looks more like a photograph than a sketch.

I tear my gaze from the picture to look at her.

She smiles. "I may have lied just a little. I drew the picture for you, but I hope you don't mind if it goes on display somewhere."

"What?"

"It's going to be the focal point of the exhibition show I'm having—at Camden's gallery."

"You—"

She nods up and down, tears misting her eyes. "I spoke to him. I hope you aren't mad at me, but I needed to talk to him and know that he wasn't speaking to me because I'm your fiancée. I put on a dumb disguise and showed him my work. He loved it and was shocked when I came clean on who I was. Actually, I think he was upset at first that I didn't tell him who I was. But it doesn't matter. I got in, Beck! We're going to start with one photo. But once I get enough for an entire showcase, he said he'd fit me in for one. And I want *this* to be the focal point of the entire thing."

"I'm so fucking proud of you," I answer. Reaching across, I grab the collar of the shirt on her body and bring her into me. "I knew you'd get it, Margo. You're so god damn talented. I knew he'd see it."

"I still can't believe it," she whispers between us.

"What you drew...the wedding...does this mean?"

She nods confidently at me, tears coming down her cheeks. "I love you, Beck. Nothing is going to stop me from it. I can't believe you've gone all this time hiding how you felt. I'm sorry I didn't see it before. That you weren't the one I spoke to at that bar, but I want to spend forever making it up to you. It should've only ever been you, Beckham Sinclair."

I waste no time pulling her mouth to mine. When our lips collide, I don't know if the salt I taste is from her tears or mine. All I know is I'm never risking losing her again.

58

Margo

"I've been waiting so god damn long for you to say that." Beck pulls away only far enough to get the words out. They're said against my lips as his deep indigo eyes stare at me with so much love, I have no idea how I never noticed it before. It's something I'll never miss, or take advantage of, ever again.

"So, you like the piece?" I wrap my arms around his neck, needing to pull him closer to my body. It's only been a few days that we've been apart, but they drug on miserably without me being able to touch him like this. If I didn't have the distraction of getting the job with Camden and finding this studio, I don't know how I would've spent the miserable minutes without him.

Never again. I promise myself. I know there are times when we're bound to be apart. He owns a jet for a reason. He has to travel a lot, but I'll make sure he calls me any chance he has. Or at least that I'll still get dirty emails from his company email while he's away.

I just know I never want to go days without speaking to him again. It allowed me the clarity I needed to know how deeply I was in love with him, but I never need that space again.

Beck continues to pepper kisses over my jaw, my neck, my throat. He slides his work shirt off my shoulder, biting down on the tender flesh of my shoulder. I laugh, my fingers clutching the fabric of the shirt he wears. "Beck," I scold. "You didn't answer me if you liked it."

His fingers are quick at unbuttoning the shirt of his I wear. "I love you baby, but the question is a little unnecessary."

I frown, my back arching on its own accord as his hands push open the button-up and run down the bare skin of my side. "How so?"

He takes a step back, leaving me to stand in front of the desk alone. It feels cold without his touch. "Because of course I fucking love it. In fact, if I wasn't so fucking proud of you for getting into the best gallery in New York, I'd say fuck Camden and selfishly keep the art for myself."

My eyes narrow at him as he smirks back at me. "What?" he asks, feigning innocence. "I'm selfish, Violet. You know this."

"It's going on display." I take a step backward, propping my hip against the desk.

He takes a step toward me. And then another, all while keeping that cocky grin I'm so damn in love with on his perfect lips. "Yes it is. And I'll be the first damn person in line to see it."

Beck closes the distance between us. He reaches up to open the button-up, revealing my bare breasts.

"If I learn that Ezra saw you wearing this, I might fucking kill him," he notes. He traces his knuckle up my ribcage with the lightest of touches, causing my skin to prickle with desire.

"I haven't seen another human in a day," I answer honestly. "I don't even know what time it is. I locked myself away in here, only coming out to take care of my basic needs."

His hot breath hits my neck as his hands find my hips. He lifts me effortlessly, setting me on the corner of the desk. He picks up the canvas and sets it carefully to the side, all while keeping his lust-filled eyes pinned on me.

Beck pushes my thighs open, focusing on my center. He runs his fingertip over the fabric of my panties. "Speaking of *needs.*" His voice is like gravel, it is muddled with passion. "Did you take care of yourself, baby? Or do you need me?"

My hips buck to try and get friction from his featherlight touch. "I didn't. I didn't want to, knowing things weren't settled between us. I just wanted *you.*"

He stares at me hungrily. His tongue comes out to wet his lips. "Looks like I have some making up to do."

I nod enthusiastically. "True. You've got some apologizing to do…"

Beck keeps eye contact with me. Slowly, he lowers to one knee and then the other. With me on the desk and him on the ground, he's now perfectly lined up with the part of me that's aching for him. "I know just how to say I'm sorry, baby. I'm down on my knees for you. Ready to apologize the best way I know how."

"Maybe I should make you beg for it." My head falls backward when he presses his thumb against my clit. Even with the layer of fabric between us, it feels amazing. He knows exactly where to touch me to have my eyes close in pleasure.

"Can I please eat that sweet little pussy of yours, baby?"

I moan—loudly. His fingertips hook in the sides of my panties. He pulls them down my legs agonizingly slow. By the time he's throwing them off to the side, I'm already wet and panting in need for him.

I muster my last bit of wits, loving having him grovel on his knees for me too much to stop just yet.

"Fuck, you're so turned on I can smell you," he notes. His fingertips press into my inner thighs as he keeps my legs wide open for him.

"Can I make you feel good now? Tell me yes. Tell me I can apologize by making you come all over my face. I'm fucking starved for you."

My resolve breaks. My head nods up and down eagerly as I push my legs open even wider. In the process, my knee knocks into a half-eaten package of Twizzlers, the package falling to the ground with a loud *smack*.

To my dismay, his focus goes from between my legs to the package of Twizzlers on the ground. I'm irrationally pissed off at a package of candy, mad that it's taken his attention from me.

"When you said you've been taking care of your *needs,* please tell me it meant eating food with actual nutritional value and not these terrible things." He picks up one of the red swirled candies, the piece hanging limply in his hand as he shakes it in the air.

I roll my lips together, trying to hide the smile on my face. "I *think* I ate a sandwich at one point."

An aggravated growl passes through his lips. He sits back on his haunches, pinning me with a disapproving stare. "Margo, you can't live on *Twizzlers*. Plus, they're disgusting. I don't know how you love those things."

Shrugging, I run my hand over the inside of my thigh to bring his attention back to what he started. I need to feel him desperately. I'm close to promising him I'd never have the candy again if he'd just seal his mouth to my clit and ensure I see stars.

"They're delicious," I argue. "Maybe you should try them."

He shakes his head, looking down at the candy in his hand. "Nev—" His words break off randomly. Slowly, a smirk spreads over his lips. "Well, maybe I *do* know how to make them more enjoyable."

My eyebrows knit together on my forehead as I try to figure out what the hell he's saying.

"Can we maybe *stop* talking and hating on my favorite candy and you know get back to what we started?"

His lack of a response has me opening my mouth to keep talking. "Less talking, more licking," I demand.

"Whatever you say," he drawls. Thank god he rises once again, his hot breath hitting my inner thigh.

My eyes flutter shut in eager anticipation of finally feeling his mouth against me.

The lightest of pressure around my knee has my eyes widening. I open them to find his mouth lined up perfectly with me, all while he traces the fucking Twizzler against my sensitive flesh.

"What are you doing?" I ask.

He focuses on watching the path he traces with the candy. "You told me I should try it. So I'm going to try it."

Before I can ask him what his words mean, he circles my swollen clit with the end of the candy.

"I didn't mean—" My words get cut off when he rubs it through my wetness, coating it in me. I watch him, way more turned on than I should be, when he sticks the Twizzler in his mouth. His teeth dig into it, tearing a piece of the vine—the part that he just coated in *me*—and begins to chew.

"You're right. It's *delicious*." He throws the piece of the candy to the side, apparently done with it. "But still not as delicious as my girl."

Finally, his tongue licks me up and down. He holds me to his mouth despite my squirming. And then Beck takes his time apologizing to me, pulling two orgasms from me before coming up for air.

"Beck," I pant, moving my hips against the table. My body

already feels spent, but I don't care. I need to feel him inside of me. "I need you. Now."

I'm done with his apologies. Now I want him to get rough with me and make up for it by making love to me.

He pulls away, kissing the inside of my thigh tenderly before he stands up. His hands are quick at pulling off the different layers of his clothing that shield his perfect body from me.

Buttons fly to the ground as he rips his shirt open a little too gruffly. They make little *tings* as they all fall to the floor. "I've missed you so much," he confesses, pulling his arms from his sleeves and discarding it.

I'm not shy about looking at his taut, perfect muscles. Everything about him is *mine*. I still can't believe it.

"I missed you too," I tell him as he steps between my legs, his body completely naked. My hand snakes between us, not wasting time by teasing him and going straight to wrapping around his heavy length.

He only allows my hand to pump up and down his length a few times before he's pushing my hands away. Before I can even protest, he leans close to my ear and nips at my tender skin. "As much as I want to draw this out, I fucking can't. I need to be inside you—immediately."

I nod against him, bucking my hips in an attempt to line his cock up with me. His shirt slips down my shoulders. If I wanted to waste time, I'd pull my arms from the holes and shed the shirt completely, but I don't want to waste another second without him being inside me. "We have the rest of our lives to take it slow, Beck. Fuck me," I plead. "Remind me how I am yours and you are mine."

"Gladly," he says through clenched teeth. Without warning, he shoves himself inside me, a pained sigh falling from his lips as he sheaths as much of himself in me as he can fit.

The expensive drawing materials rattle as his hips move faster. I moan, my nails digging into his skin.

Beck grabs me by the throat, his fingers wrapping underneath my chin as he reminds me that there's no way I could ever be anyone else's. His lips crash against mine. My tongue eagerly meets his as we can't get enough of each other.

My hands scratch and scrape at him, trying to pull him closer to me even though it's impossible. We're as close as we can get. He possessively squeezes my throat while his lips work tenderly against mine. It takes no time for an orgasm to build all over again. His grip on me loosens by a bit, my head falling back in ecstasy as the pressure begins to build even more.

A loud clatter rings out next to us. I briefly glance over, noticing a paint bottle knocked over, its contents spilling out over the table. "Beck, my supplies…" I say before a moan overtakes my body.

It's as if he knows how close I am. He pushes even deeper inside me, knowing how much I love it when he pushes so deeply it hurts. "I don't give a fuck," he says against the hollow. "I'll buy fucking new ones. Scream my name for me, baby."

I do *exactly* as I'm told. His name echoes off the walls as the both of us finish. He slows his hips, pumping in and out of me until he stops moving. My head falls to his shoulder as I catch my breath.

I love how Beck can fuck me and make love to me at the same time. My legs tremble from the orgasm as I still ride out the aftershock of it.

Beck's hand reaches up to push the hair that'd fallen into my face. He looks at me with so much love and adoration. His eyes say so much without saying a thing at all.

I can't wait to spend the rest of my life being looked at the way Beckham looks at me.

His thumb brushes over my cheek. "Have I ever told you I loved you?"

I smile, resting my forehead against his. "Maybe. But you could say it again."

"I love you, Margo Moretti. I love you so fucking much that you drive me absolutely wild."

"I wouldn't have it any other way," I admit.

"Good. Because I don't plan on stopping."

My eyes flick to the canvas to the side of us. "Hey Beck?"

"Yes?"

"I love you so much my entire future looks like *you*."

His sigh of relief hurts my heart a little. I hate that he's spent so long wondering if I'd ever love him, or if I'd ever feel *anything* for him. I'm going to spend every day for the rest of my life proving my love for him. It's what he deserves, and I can't wait to do it.

"Does that mean you're still going to be Mrs. Sinclair one day?"

I smile, pressing a kiss to his lips. I'm ready to wear his ring on my finger again—for the world to know that my heart will never belong to anybody else. "I better fucking be."

EPILOGUE

Beck

3 Months Later

I look at the crowd of people waiting outside in awe. There's a line outside of the building, and the doors don't even open for another hour.

I hold the bouquet of flowers to my chest as I walk toward the back entrance of the gallery. It's been hours since I've seen Margo—longer than I preferred. She's been caught up preparing for the event happening tonight, and I let her have her moment. But once this show is over and she's no longer preoccupied, I'm going to keep her locked in our bedroom for days so I can make up for lost time.

The security guard waves me in, my face familiar from the many times I've stopped by since Margo and Camden came to an agreement for showcasing her work.

At first, it started with one piece of art. It didn't take long until Camden was fielding calls on when there'd be more pieces by this new-to-the scene artist. He called in the friend card, begging me to ask Margo if she'd complete pieces sooner so they could get an entire showcase on the books.

She didn't take it well at first. Probably because I fired her.

I smile at the people on the first floor of the gallery, all of them setting up a welcome area for the party tonight. The event was supposed to be exclusive to the VIP members, but Margo kept pushing Camden to somehow make it available to the public.

He eventually agreed. My girl is persistent like that. VIP members will be able to look for an hour before waves of people from the line outside will be let in. Margo's been a nervous wreck for days, terrified no one will want to buy her art.

She doesn't know she's already had her first buyer—me.

When I make it to the second floor, I stop in my tracks when I spot her.

Margo Moretti.

The woman who has been the object of my desire for years.

She hasn't noticed me yet, giving me the perfect opportunity to watch the woman I'm completely in love with. I knew the moment she came back into my life at the Hamptons house that I'd do whatever it took to make her mine. While my methods were rather unconventional, I can't regret a single one of my choices. Who knew what would've happened if she actually did pick up my phone calls. If I didn't have to resort to leaking information about my dating history and forcing myself into her life as her boss, I don't know if we'd be where we are now. And I'm more than fucking thrilled how everything turned out.

Margo has her dark hair slicked back. Her normal curls are nowhere to be seen, instead she's styled her hair perfectly straight. It's not a hairstyle I see her do often, but it doesn't matter to me what she does to it. She's breathtakingly beautiful no matter what.

My phone vibrates in my pocket. I look down, seeing Ruby's name pop onto the screen. I sigh, backing into the stairwell for a moment before Margo spots me.

I swipe to answer. "Is it done?" There's no hint of emotion in my voice. I don't want there to be. Not with her.

"That story has been killed," Ruby answers. "Although, I thought the title *Black Ties and White Lies* was pretty fucking epic for the name."

I grunt. I wouldn't hate the title if the article on the center of the website tomorrow wasn't originally planned to out everything that's transpired between Margo and me. All the lies included. I'd be fine with the world knowing the lies I told to get her, but I don't want Margo's name anywhere near it. Especially with how big tonight is for her. I don't want anything clouding it tomorrow.

"You've got to admit," Ruby speaks up, not caring that I didn't give her a response. "It was kind of catchy."

"You'll think of a better one for the article I've paid you to write instead."

"The new one isn't so bad either," she says reluctantly.

I smile. I cut a large check to Ruby to have her change course on the article running tomorrow. It no longer focuses on the past between Margo and me. Instead, I gave Ruby a VIP ticket to the event tonight and made her promise to write about the newest up-and-coming artist in the Manhattan scene. "Send it to me to read first," I demand.

Even though she's a reporter, she isn't as terrible as I first believed her to be. She's just out for herself, I can't really blame her on the fact. She worked with me to change course on the article. I'll always appreciate her for it.

"Your brother keeps calling." Her tone comes out annoyed. I feel her sentiment. I'd be annoyed too if he was still bothering

Margo and me. My little trip to San Jose a few months ago halted all threats and calls from him.

It's been nice.

"Sucks for you," I answer. "Look, Ruby. I've got to go. I'll see you in a bit."

"Goodbye, Mr. Sinclair. Nice working with you. See you."

When I return to my spot from earlier, I find Margo looking right at me. She smiles brightly, rushing across the clean, white space to wrap me in a hug. "You're here," she says with enthusiasm.

I kiss the top of her head, pulling her into my body. I instantly relax after being able to touch her. I've been at work all day and she's been here since early this morning. I'm relieved to have her in my arms once again. I already look forward to everything that's in store for us after this event.

"There's nowhere else I'd rather be."

"Okay don't be mad, but Camden told me that the centerpiece...the one of you and me...it's already sold."

I feign surprise. My eyebrows raise. "Did it now?"

She bites her lip anxiously, rocking back and forth on the same pair of heels she wore to our engagement party months ago. Ones I fully expect to see her in tonight—with nothing else on. "I'm sorry. I told Camden we didn't have to put it up for sale, but he told me it was too late. It was already purchased. I can always make anoth—"

I cut her off by kissing her lips. "I think it'll make a great centerpiece in a bedroom. Don't you?"

She looks at me confused. Her puffy lips, lined in a delectable red that I want to ruin so bad, turn down in a frown. "Maybe? I don't know. Are you not hearing me? Someone else bought it. I don't know where they'll put it, but it sold—for a lot of money I hear—but it won't be ours."

I press a kiss to her temple before reaching down and grabbing her hand. I lead her through the different pieces of art she's been working hard day and night on for the past three months. All of them follow the same concepts.

Her showcase is called "What If." The focus of it is on her concept of taking people or scenarios she's seen and reimagining what their life is—or what their life could be.

I stop us in front of the one deepest into the gallery. My personal favorite—the one that solidified our past, present and future.

The one of us in the conference room joined with us on an imagined wedding day.

"Are you mad? Why did we have to come to this one?" Margo questions, looking at me skeptically.

"Because I'm the one who bought it, Violet. There was no fucking way anyone else was owning it but *me*. Or us."

Her mouth hangs open. She looks from the canvas to me and back again. "No you didn't."

"Yes I did."

She rolls her eyes at me. "I don't think I've been this mad at you since you fired me."

I smirk, my eyes roaming every single one of the pieces she put her heart and soul into for this showcase.

Fuck. I'm so god damn proud of her. So painstakingly in awe of her talent—her beauty. Essentially everything about her.

"You can be mad, baby. I *love* how you take out your frustrations on me." A flush creeps up her neck as she no doubt remembers the mind-blowing sex we had the night I fired her. It was the weekend after I'd come back from San Jose. She complained she was sore from it for days.

"Beck," Camden says, looping around a canvas to stop next to Margo and me. "I knew you'd sneak in early."

I scoff at him, shaking hands with one of my closest friends. "Did you expect anything else? Had to see my girl before she's busy warding off buyers all night."

Camden whistles, tucking his hands into the pockets of his custom suit. "I've already had so many of them up my ass, asking if they could see the pieces ahead of time." He looks toward my future wife at my side, giving her a tight smile. "I might beg your girl here to do a long-term residency on one of the floors."

Her eyes go wide in shock. "No," she says in disbelief.

I laugh. "About fucking time, Hunter," I chide.

Before we can have any more of a conversation, one of Camden's employees comes up and sweeps both of them away from me.

I barely get to speak with Margo the entire duration of the show. I don't mind. Watching her do what she loves and talk about her art is the perfect way for me to spend my time. Plus, it gives me the chance to talk with her friends and family that we'd flown out for the occasion.

Every single one of her pieces sells—for a *lot* of money for an artist that isn't well known.

It's after midnight when we finally walk out of the gallery hand in hand. I'm exhausted, and I know she probably is as well, but I'm hoping that she'll allow me one stop before we go home.

Margo looks up and down the sidewalk, her eyebrows drawn in together. "Where's Ezra?"

I turn to her, grabbing onto both of our hands. "I was wondering if we could make one more stop?"

She cocks her head suspiciously. "To where?"

I smile, running my thumbs over the top of her hand. "Well, baby, it's a surprise. So it'd defeat the purpose if I told you where..."

Her teeth dig into her lip as she smiles eagerly at me. Her eyes twinkle with excitement. "I *do* love a surprise."

I wrap my arm around her, turning her body in the direction of our next destination. "Perfect. We'll walk."

It's a short walk, something I'd done on purpose. We walk until I stop in front of a row of brownstones. On one side there are the brownstones, on the other there's an entrance to Central Park.

"What are we doing?" Margo questions hesitantly.

"What do you think of these?" I ask, turning her to the large, stone buildings in front of us. The row of houses in front of us are some of the most expensive in the city. Their proximity to everything in Manhattan something that is coveted by many.

"I think they're beautiful, but why?"

I take advantage of her focus on the houses in front of me. Behind her, I lower to one knee as I reach into the pocket of my suit, my fingers connecting with a velvet box.

"Beck?" She turns around, a gasp falling from her mouth when she finds me on one knee behind her.

"Because I want to buy one for us. I know you love being high above the city, but one day I'd love to settle down in something like this with you, Margo Moretti. I want to raise kids here with you. Fuck, I want to do all the normal things with you in a house like this."

"I'd love that," she chokes, her hands finding her cheeks in shock. "But why are you on one—"

I pull out the ring box, holding it up between us and opening it.

"Not too long ago I told you I don't want to propose to you the way you deserved because I didn't want to ruin the moment for you. I hated the thought of any other man ever being on his knee for you like I am right now, but I didn't want to propose to you if things were still supposed to be fake between us. So, I waited. And I didn't. But all along I knew one day, I'd love to get down on one fucking knee for you. To ask for forever with you."

"Oh my god." Tears well in her eyes, threatening to spill from her eyes as she looks at the contents of the box.

"I'm proposing to you with what I want to be your wedding band because while you may have been wearing your engagement ring thinking it was fake, it *never* was fake to me. I always wanted you for real—never for pretend. I bought this ring for you in hopes that one day it'd be real. I've loved you from the moment I met you, Margo Moretti. When I slipped that engagement ring on your finger—my grandmother's ring—I hadn't told you how much you meant to me at the time. I didn't want to scare you away with how raw and real my feelings were. It's all been laid out on the table now. You know *exactly* how I feel. So if you say yes, when I slip this band on your finger next to my grandmother's ring, I want you to know it's because I plan to marry you and make you mine forever. And if you want a different ring, we'll buy it. I'll buy you a million rings until you find the perfect one if it means you're mine to love forever."

I have to pry her hand from over her mouth. Both of our hands shake as I run my finger over the ring that used to belong to one of the women I loved most in the world. It's incredibly sentimental to see it now, resting on the finger of the woman who stole my heart from the moment I laid eyes on her.

My heart hammers in my chest. The look of love in her eyes tells me everything I need to know. She's been proving to me from the moment I got back from California that she loves me, that she wants this. But I'm so nervous to make this proposal everything she's ever dreamed of—and hopefully maybe even more. "So, Margo Moretti. Will you marry me? For real this time? For forever?"

Her bottom lip trembles as she loses control of her emotions, her body overtaken with joy. "Yes," she croaks. "Absolutely. Over and over again, I'll always say yes." She flies into me, wrapping her arms around me and cradling my head to her chest.

I don't know how long we stay in that position, but eventually she pulls away. I hold the box up again, offering it up to her. My fingers still tremble with nerves as I pull the band from the box. It slides down her finger effortlessly, the band creating a crown of diamonds around the top of the ring. It makes the classic ring more artistic. It's not an ordinary band—it's why I thought she'd love it. The style is a mix between vintage and modern.

"It's beautiful," Margo marvels, staring down at the ring and band combination.

"Do you like it?"

"I love it," she confirms. She looks up at me with tear-stained cheeks. "I love *you*. I can't wait to be your wife, Beck."

I stand up to kiss her, sealing our mouths together. Our first kiss felt like a promise of the possibility of more. This kiss is a promise of *forever*.

My hands slide underneath her coat, needing to feel even closer to her. "How does a wedding tomorrow sound?"

She shakes her head at me, looking up at me with a mischievous gleam in her eyes. "Absolutely not, Beckham Sinclair. I want a big-ass wedding with *all* the cheesy things."

"You just want to spend my money," I tease.

Her lips rub together before breaking out in a wide smile. "No," she answers innocently. "I just want everyone to see that you're off the market. That you're mine."

"I think anyone could see the way I look at you and know that I'm hopelessly, madly, desperately in love with you."

"A big show of it still wouldn't be too bad."

"Anything you want, baby. It's yours. We'll invite all of New York if that's your wish."

She angles her body to look at the houses behind her. I never envisioned myself wanting to move out of my highrise penthouse suite. But I don't see us staying there forever. Eventually, I'd love to move out here. To have an actual *home*—one where we can raise the basketball team of children I want to have with her.

"Which one is for sale?"

I point to the corner one—the biggest one with the best view.

"That one."

Her fingers find mine, her cold hand sliding into mine. The air isn't as frigid as it typically is in February, but there's still a bite to it. Both our cheeks are undoubtedly going to be rubbed raw from the cold and bitter air by the time Ezra picks us up.

"I should've guessed. That's the biggest one."

"You know me so well," I joke.

"It's kind of a shame. I liked the sex above the city."

"You can visit me at my office *any* time and we can make that happen."

"Promise?"

"Hell yeah, Violet."

I pull my phone out, telling Ezra that he can head our way. I look back at her to find her watching me. "Plus, we don't have to move *yet*. I just wanted to plan for the future."

Her nose crinkles with her smile. "I like planning a future with you, Beckham Sinclair."

"Let's do it for the rest of our lives, Margo Moretti."

We walk hand in hand down the quiet Upper West Side sidewalk, the two of us discussing the future. She wants to get started on wedding planning right away as she takes a break from creating new pieces for Camden. I let her ramble on for as long as she wants. Even as we get into the back of the car, Ezra takes us through the city back to the place we call home for now, she doesn't stop talking.

I'll let her talk about our future all night if she wants to. The excitement is like a caress to my heart because there was a time I wondered if I'd ever have a present with her. I tried not to be too hopeful for a future.

But now, that's exactly what we have.

I'll spend the rest of my life loving Margo Moretti.

I can't fucking wait.

Exclusive

Bonus

Content

Beck

"You girls are going to behave tonight, right?" I ask, fixing the bow on top of my youngest daughter's head.

Harper rubs her lips together before giving me a wide grin.

I groan, knowing exactly what that smile means. Harper isn't going to listen at all tonight. She's probably going to try and wreak havoc, and we'll just laugh because, as our last and our youngest, she can get away with just about anything.

I crouch down, smiling at Harper. She just turned three, and everything they say about the terrible twos is wrong. It's the three-year-olds that you should be terrified of. Especially the youngest sister of three girls.

I've sat across from some of the most powerful men in business, and my three-year-old daughter scares me far more than anyone else.

"Mommy says she'll give me ice cream if I listen to you," Harper announces, her blonde eyebrows lifted a little. She stares at me as if she's deciding if the ice cream is worth listening or not.

I can't help but laugh. The problem is, she doesn't listen, and I find it hilarious, even when I shouldn't.

"Did Mommy *really* say that?" I ask, looking over at Celeste, the oldest of our three girls.

Celeste gives me a look that tells me she wants nothing to do with me right now. She's almost twelve, and I actually don't know what age I'm more terrified of—the three-year-old or the preteen.

"Mom *did* try to bribe her with ice cream," Celeste confirms. She snorts and rolls her eyes before focusing on the book in her lap. "Like that would actually work. Harper never listens."

Harper lets out a disgruntled whine. "Hey! Be nice, Celeste," she cries.

"You listen," Amelia pipes up as she descends the stairs into the entryway of our brownstone home in Manhattan.

I let out a sigh of relief now that Amelia is here. At seven years old, she's the peacekeeper between her toddler sister and her preteen one. People still ask me and Margo if we're going to have a fourth and try for a boy, but I smile as I look at my three daughters picking up a conversation about how long Margo is taking to get ready. The truth is, I love having three girls. Sometimes they terrify me, and I have no idea how to handle certain situations, but I wouldn't trade it for the world.

Plus, after having a rough pregnancy with Harper, Margo made the appointment for me to get snipped. We're done having babies. We're enjoying the three girls we have and loving how different their personalities are.

I look at my watch before glancing up the stairs. We have about thirty minutes until we need to be out the door. Ezra, my longtime driver, should be here in ten.

And my wife is still getting ready.

I glance at my phone again, wondering if I should go upstairs and check on her. I know she's nervous. Tonight is a big night for her.

Tonight's event showcases the last ten years of her artwork. She was nominated by an art committee as one of the most prominent artists of the last decade. It's a huge honor for her to have received it. The exhibition is at the Metropolitan Museum of Art.

My baby—my Violet—is having an exhibition at the Met.

I'm so fucking proud of her.

I look at my daughters, all three of them in dresses they picked out themselves. Margo wanted them to feel included in the event, so each one got to design their own dress for the night.

"Will you keep an eye on your sisters for me while I go check on Mom?" I ask, my eyes focusing on Celeste.

She sighs, but there's a crack in her preteen attitude for a moment as she gives me a soft smile. "Yes."

I smile, reaching out to run my hand over her loosely curled hair. "Thanks, sweetheart."

Celeste rolls her eyes at me, but her smile grows at the gesture. "*Go*," she says, pointing to the stairs. "Make sure Mom's okay. You know how she gets about events."

I laugh. It's been over a decade since she first started taking the art world by storm, and yet she still gets so many jitters. It's something Camden Hunter—a good friend and the first gallery owner to showcase her work—and I always laugh about. She has all the talent in the world, but she's always so nervous to be recognized for it.

I take the stairs two at a time until I finally reach the landing. I walk slowly to our room, hearing her voice echo down the hallway. She must be on the phone with someone.

My guess is it's a group phone call with all of her friends. I don't think she goes a day without talking to her group of girlfriends, and I love that for her. I love even more that they all made it a priority to attend the event celebrating her tonight.

"You look hot as hell," I hear coming from Margo's phone as I walk into our primary bathroom.

"Emma," my wife scolds with a small laugh. "I'm not trying to look hot. I'm trying to look sophisticated."

I slowly walk into the entryway of our bathroom. I tap my knuckles against the wood framing the opening to warn her of my presence.

Margo's eyes find mine at the same moment Emma speaks again from the phone sitting on the counter.

"Being sophisticated is hot! You look amazing, Mar. Now, get going so you're not late to your own event."

Margo gives me a smile before turning her attention to the phone screen. "Beck just came up here to probably give me a sweet nudge that we need to go. I'll see you guys there."

A symphony of goodbyes rings out from her phone. Margo picks it up and slides it into a small purse, her eyes still trained on me.

"Are we late?" she asks, her attention moving to her reflection in the mirror.

"We still have a few minutes until we need to leave. I just wanted to come check on you."

I close the distance between us and wrap my arms around her middle. Her body melts into mine, and for a few seconds, we're both quiet. We've been together for well over a decade, and still, just the simple press of her body against mine makes my heart race.

"Are the girls ready?" Margo asks, her voice soft. Her eyes find mine through the mirror, and we just stare at each other. I soak in the moment with her, knowing the rest of the evening will be busy and crazy in the best possible way.

I nod, leaning down to softly kiss her exposed shoulder.

I let out an appreciative growl as my eyes rake across her body through the mirror. I hadn't seen her dress until now. She'd shown me sketches of what she envisioned for the night, but seeing it in person is tempting me to make my wife late for her event.

The material is violet. I fucking love it.

"You're beautiful," I announce, my hands drifting over her hips. The material is soft against my palms. It clings to the curves of her body perfectly.

"I'm nervous," she admits, her stomach muscles tightening as my fingers drift lower. I wish I had the time to lift the skirt of the dress and bury my face between her thighs. I know an orgasm would help ease her nerves, but I don't think we have the time.

In one quick motion, I grab her by the waist and spin her. Her hands immediately fall to my chest from the sudden movement.

I gently cup her cheek and tilt her face up to meet my gaze. "There's nothing to be nervous about. Every single person in attendance tonight is there to support—and celebrate—you, baby. You're the star of the show."

She laughs, her breath tickling the palm of my hand. "That's exactly why I'm nervous. Of all the artists they could honor, it doesn't feel right for me to be the one picked."

I scoff. She's one of the most talented artists in the world. She's done so much for the art industry in the last ten years, and no one deserves the honor more than her. "You deserve all the recognition in the world, Violet. Your talent…" My words fall off for a moment as I try to put her years and years of hard work and talent into words. "Your talent…the work you've created… it's remarkable, baby. I can't wait to celebrate you tonight."

Her cheeks flush at the same moment a wide smile dances on her lips. She tucks her face into my chest, her arms wrapping around me. "Why do you have to be so perfect all the time?"

Her words come out a little muffled against the fabric of my suit jacket. "You know exactly what to say to calm my nerves."

I press a soft kiss to her cheek. All I want to do is lift her onto the counter, press my lips against hers, and make her come against my fingers—or tongue—before attending the event. I don't because I don't want to ruin her makeup. I also don't want to make us late, so the most I do is trail my lips against her jaw and playfully nibble at her ear before pulling away.

"I love you," I tell her, putting conviction in my words. She doesn't know this, but there are a few people giving speeches tonight to honor everything she's accomplished, and I'm one of them. I'm not always the biggest fan of public speaking, but for her, I'd do anything. I've pored over my speech for weeks, making everyone I've come in contact with listen to it to make sure it's perfect. I can't wait to give it tonight. It takes everything in me not to say it all right now. I remind myself to be patient, knowing that it'll be more special for her to hear it at the event, surrounded by her loved ones and peers.

Margo's hands find my cheeks, her eyes raking over my face. "I love you, too," she tells me, her lips twitching with a smile as she lets her fingers dance along my skin.

I close my eyes for a moment, relishing in the feeling of even the smallest touch from her. I know we're seconds away from Ezra showing up or one of our daughters running upstairs and asking for a snack or asking if it's time to leave yet, so I soak in the last few quiet seconds we have together.

My mind flashes back to years and years ago, to the moment she and I sat on the beach in the Hamptons in the middle of the night. I remember the concentration in her eyes as she paid close attention to drawing me. She was still dating my brother at the time, but it hadn't mattered to me. I knew one day she'd be mine.

I also knew that night that she had incredible talent. I was confident that one day the world would be in awe of the art she creates.

I was right—of course I was.

Over the years, I've sat next to her as she created pieces that took my breath away. I've woken up in the middle of the night to the sound of her pencil working against her drawing pad. I've seen her work hung in galleries around the world and have been with her when her art sold for incredible amounts. Her career has changed and grown so much over the last decade, and I'm so honored to have been by her side for all of it.

"Mom!" Celeste yells from downstairs. "We're going to be late, and I want to see my friends!"

Margo and I both laugh at the sassy tone in Celeste's voice. It's nice she's excited to see her friends. It was always a dream of mine for my kids to be friends with my friends' kids, and we got that. I'll take her excitement to see them—even if it comes with a side of sass.

"Coming!" Margo yells back, shaking her head. She doesn't move from the embrace, even though we both know we're on borrowed time before one—or all—of our kids come searching for us.

"I could have *you* coming," I drawl, my lips turning up in a cocky smirk. I run my teeth over my lip, something I know drives my wife wild.

Her eyes go wide for a moment before she playfully swats at my chest. "You will, baby. *Tonight*. After the event."

I press one soft kiss to the corner of her mouth before letting out a deep groan. I knew she wasn't going to let me give her one quick orgasm, but I still had to try.

"I won't be giving you just one orgasm tonight, Mrs. Sinclair. You'll be getting at *least* three."

Margo lifts an eyebrow as she walks over to grab her purse from the counter. "Really? Lucky me."

"You've been a good girl, and I'm proud of you. Maybe we'll make it four."

"Four what?" Harper asks as she runs into the bathroom. She's already ripped the bow from her hair, and God only knows where she discarded it.

Celeste and Amelia come running in.

Amelia's hands find her hips as she shakes her head. "We tried keeping Harper downstairs. She wouldn't listen."

"Told you she never listens," Celeste adds.

"Four what?" Harper repeats, her eyes bouncing between me and Margo.

We look at each other with mischievous grins. I bend down and scoop Harper into my arms. "Where's your bow at, sweetheart? We've got to get going."

"Do I get four bows?" Harper asks, her small hands reaching for my face so I give her my undivided attention.

Margo wrangles our other two daughters out of the bathroom as I focus on our youngest.

"No," I answer softly. "Only one bow tonight. But it's big, and it matches your dress perfectly. It's like a princess bow," I add at the last second, knowing that'll convince her to tell me where she left the bow.

Harper's eyes light up. "My bow's in the plant!" She points down the stairs at the potted plant by the front door. "Hurry, Daddy! Get my bow."

I roll my eyes with a smile. My world is now being bossed around by four girls, and I wouldn't change a thing.

It's a mad dash of making sure no one forgot anything and rushing out the door once Ezra arrives with a limo.

The girls squeal as they look around the limo, excited to be riding in one tonight. They're preoccupied with looking out the windows and pressing all the buttons, and I use the opportunity to look over at my wife.

She watches our daughters with a serene smile. Something about the moment makes my heart constrict in my chest.

This is pure happiness.

My wife. Our daughters. Our family and friends gathering to celebrate her amazing accomplishments over the last decade.

I reach across the seat and grab Margo's hand. I squeeze, loving the way she squeezes back, her eyes still watching our girls.

I sit back, my eyes following hers.

From the very first moment I saw Margo, I knew I wanted her to be mine. I knew I'd do anything to make her mine. There was just something about her that made me know she was the love of my life. It was a journey for us to get to this very moment, but it was worth it.

I lift her hand to my lips and press a kiss to her soft skin. "I love you, Violet."

She looks over at me with a smile, and even after all these years, her radiant smile and the glimmer in her eyes make my heart skip a beat.

"I love you, too."

I smile, looking forward to a lifetime more of moments just like this.

ACKNOWLEDGMENTS

Black Ties & White Lies is a book that changed my life forever. There are so many people I need to thank who helped me and cheered me on in the two years since *Black Ties* released. It's been an incredible two years and I can't believe this book is now in bookstores! Somebody pinch me!

First, to you, the reader. Thank you for taking a chance on me and reading this book. Whether you just discovered me, or you've been with me for years now, thank you for being here. This book completely changed not only my career, but my life, and I'm forever in awe that people want to read the daydreams from my head. I know your reading time is precious, and I appreciate you spending that time reading *my* words. I love you and I'm so excited to be on this journey with you.

To Aaron, my husband, thank you for everything you do to help make my dreams come true. I couldn't have done any of this without you and appreciate you beyond words. I'm so grateful to call you my partner and teammate in life. I love you forever.

To Nina, thank you for believing in not only this book, but believing in me. I'm so incredibly lucky to call you my agent and have you championing my books. Thank you for everything you do.

To Jessica and the entire team at Entangled, thank you for taking a chance on me and making my dreams come true. Because of you, I'll be able to see my book on bookshelves everywhere and there aren't enough ways I can say thank you enough for that. Working with you has been a dream.

Kelsey and Tiara, thank you for everything you do to help keep me organized. I know it isn't easy to keep someone as chaotic as me on track, but somehow, you both manage to do it. Being able to work with my best friends is amazing and I'm incredibly lucky to have you both by my side for this journey.

To Valentine and everyone at Valentine PR, I'm so happy I found a home with VPR. Thank you for everything you've done to help further my career. Your help means the world to me and I'm so lucky to have you on this journey with me. I appreciate all of you so much.

To the amazing people on my content team, thank you for shouting about this book from the rooftops. This book was a success because of you. I'm so eternally grateful for every single one of you. I've connected with so many amazing people since I started this author adventure and it means the world to me to have all of you to connect with. I'm appreciative of the fact that you take the time to talk about my stories on your platform. I notice every single one of your posts, videos, pictures, etc. It means the world to me that you share about my characters and stories. You make this community such a special place. Thank you for everything you do.

I have the privilege of having a growing group of people I can run to on Facebook for anything—Kat Singleton's Sweethearts. The members there are always there for me, and I'm so fortunate to have them in my corner. I owe all of them so much gratitude for being there on the hard days and on the good days. Sweethearts, y'all are my people. Thank you. I love you.

Don't miss the exciting new books Entangled has to offer.

Follow us!

f @EntangledPublishing

○ @Entangled_Publishing

♪ @EntangledPub

♥ Join the Entangled Insiders for early ♥
access to ARCs, exclusive content, and insider
news! Scan the QR code to become part of
the ultimate reader community.